Thief in Law

Other Works by Michael Dirubio:

Unity - 2013

System 112 - 2014

T*he Journal of Daniel Alfredson* - 2014 *Empire Man* - 2015

Quinru California - *

* forthcoming

Thief in Law

Dedication: *This book is dedicated to my wife Judi. Thank you sweetheart for listening to all my complaints.*

Authors forward:

I don't normally do these, but I would be remiss in not thanking some people who took time out of their busy schedules to read and help with this project. Specifically, I would like to thank the San Leandro Writers Group for help and inspiration: Sandra, Joe, Steve, Bill, and Diane. Also, I would like to thank the team at Ravynheart for taking a chance.

Chapter One

Snow, as a general rule, is not known as a lifesaver. Huge snow storms usually get a bad rap, as in, 'Church van crashes on snow packed road- 10 killed'. However, in this instance, the large low pressure system that coalesced over the Carolinas and slowly churned northeast on October 27th, 2012 had a silver lining. Davidson didn't know it, but that killer snowstorm, "Snowmaggeden" as it came to be called by the media, saved his life.

The morning of the 28th dawned bleak, cold, and overcast in the New York City area. The 5:00 am news was full of ominous warnings and the whole station was in full on Storm Watch coverage. In a sparse office on Jones Street in Brooklyn, three people were engaged in fielding phone calls, eyeing the news, and worrying. The scrawl on the TV screen showed static and school closures which added to their consternation.

"As long as the flight goes out we are still a go," the tall man said with a frown. He'd said much the same, three other times this morning, to various people. United Airlines flight UA 276 was due in from Antwerp, Belgium at 15:45 today at JFK. The plane was already at Luckthaven Airport waiting for its 11:15 am local takeoff. 387 passengers, 13 crew and thousands of pounds of luggage and cargo sat while those in charge anxiously watched the radar, praying for that takeoff.

***

The air ops boss at Kennedy was also looking at the radar screen. The man who held that title, John Massimino, was under enormous pressure. Fifty-three, balding, with a large gut and clogged arteries, he didn't need this storm. Shoe- horned into the cramped cubby hole that was his office, he took calls, trying to deal with the crisis. The FAA, the other two airports, the Mayor, a Congressman, the airlines, everyone wanted to know what he would do. Could he shut down the airport before a flake of snow even fell?

He weighed two options: One, let the planes come in until the snow got ahead of the plows, leaving thousands of planes out of position and people hunkered down on cots in the terminals, or stop everything in its place and let the people clear out of the airport to allow for quicker recovery when the storm passed. It was a billion-dollar decision. One last check of the radar and he made the call. JFK would shut down at noon. That would give the airlines a chance to divert flights and not have equipment stuck in place. The howls of protest could be heard all over the world. The other two major New York area airports soon followed suit and announced shutdowns. *Chicken shits!* Massimino thought, *where were they when the heat was on?*

The press conference later, announcing the closures, was huge. CNN, Fox, and the majors were all covering the event occurring in their own backyard.

"With an abundance of caution...." John announced the preemptive closure of the airport. In no way would that phrase cover his large ass if the storm swept past and only spat a few flakes on the city. He was willing to bet that only he and school kids were praying that the storm walloped them.

***

At 12:10 P.M Davidson rose from the couch in the office as the burner cell phone rang. Feydor calling for the fourth time that day.

"It depends on the type of closure. International flights get special treatment. United hasn't canceled the flight yet," he told the man and rubbed his eyes.

Feydor asked Davidson more questions about the operation.

"I don't know," Davidson said, sharply. "The plan still works as long as the package moves. The company won't load it until twenty minutes before the flight. Graeme is there now, watching."

One final query came from the man and Davidson reached a limit. He exploded, "Feydor, you'll know as soon as I know!" He clicked off the phone without waiting for a response.

"Fuck's his problem?" Ira, the other male in the office, asked.

Smiling wanly, Davidson shrugged. "He acts like he needs the money."

Ira grunted at the small joke. No, Feydor did not need the money. Not at

all.

So why the pressure to get this job done? Davidson could not figure that. And he didn't like not knowing things. Unknowns tended to upset him and he was tense enough right now. The third person in the top floor office, Gretchen Gonsolvo, clicked off from her own phone.

"That was Graeme. No word. The package is still at the customs holding cage," she told the air and the two men simultaneously.

Davidson folded back onto the couch. *This could still work*, he thought. The basic plan was flexible enough. Thieves needed to be flexible. You never knew about things. Shit happens, as they said. But not to Davidson, not to his crew. They planned for shit, anticipated it, and worked around it. That's what they got paid to do, and why they were the best.

The three thieves watched Jim Cantore, the Weather Channel stud on the TV. He was broadcasting a report from DC. The capitol was on the leading edge of the storm, and would take the initial hit. Cantore was on the National Mall as heavy snow in small, serious flakes fell from the sky and whipped around in the wind. "Heavy snow! Blowing snow!

Drifts in the six-foot range!"

Reagan International went the opposite direction from Kennedy. They tried to stay open. By midnight they would be dealing with twenty inches of snow and people stacked up like cord wood in the terminal. That was a bad scene.

***

United finally figured out things were bad about 1 pm. Flight 276 was one of 2,633 flights cancelled over the next two days at the Northeast's major airports. Plans were disrupted all over the place. Hundreds of disgruntled passengers in Antwerp scrambled to make alternate arrangements. The company quickly shifted the package to Air Canada flight 3734 to Montreal leaving at 5:30 am the next morning. Graeme was given word his much smaller package would go on the same flight.

"Probably go 'round from Montreal to New York after that," the De Beers logistics agent told the thief.

Tired, grey eyes looked at his informant and told him, "Your envelope is at the house. Thanks, friend." *Not his fault the weather was bad.*

He called Michael Davidson and broke the bad news. The leader of the gang was sanguine about the situation.

"Wrap up everything there please," he asked his friend. "A cold trail, Graeme."

The gregarious Irishman did not need to be told this, as he was a professional, but the emotional letdown as the gang ramped up to pull a big job was playing hell on Davidson's nerves. A clipped, "Got it," came from the man as Graeme hung up the phone.

***

Fuck him, he didn't have to deal with Feydor and Roybokov, Michael thought.

"That's it," he told Ira and Gretchen in the office. "Scrubbed. Ira, call Ricky and tell him to ditch the van per plan. He lays low, and I mean flat, until Tuesday."

The short, thin, fastidious Brooklyn-born Ira Levinson simply mumbled, "okay," and went about his business.

Gretchen caught Davidson's eye. *You don't have to be a dick*, the look said. Davidson grimaced in return. He did not have to be hard on his people, but he was dealing with some shit here.

"Just scour the office and break down everything," he told the woman. The gang did not normally have to worry about job tools and evidence in their office. But this job was different; it was going to be on home turf. JFK was less than thirty minutes from his house on Greene Park. A rare luxury; steal $100 million in diamonds that day, and sleep in your own bed that night. Maybe it was the proximity to his own place, or the weather, but something had his nerves on edge. Antsy was the only way to describe it. He tamped down the feeling. His gang was professional and seasoned. They did not make mistakes. The core four had been together since 2001. He and Graeme longer than that even.

Michael recalled the Fortezza job and how they met Gretchen and Ira. *Good times*. Even Ricky had been with them over four years now.

Davidson moved towards the pair, who were smashing USB drives and phones, and then bagging up the debris. He slid past the triangle of desks, and the sitting area in the open room, before going into his private office with the last burner phone.

The office occupied the top floor of the seven-story Slattery Building on Jones Street in Brooklyn. The 1920's era building was unsuited for any type of modern corporate work. The parking sucked, the neighborhood was a slum, and the view was exceptional.

Exceptional in that yes, you could see across the East River towards Manhattan, but the real view was of the massive electrical works situated across the street. The enormous substation brought all the power into this side of the borough. It also smelled like PCB's and hummed incessantly. The result was that cell reception sucked and internet service was spotty at best. What really sold the place to Davison was that the enormous transmitted voltage made listening devices worthless. Old fashioned tape recorders got demagnetized and did not work. Forget about electronic bugs. Even credit cards tended to get screwed up. The mag strips always got fried. That was fine, the gang paid cash for everything anyway.

Ignoring the hum, Davidson closed the door and sat behind his desk. As the leader, he rated some privacy and so got the office while the rest shared the outer area. He punched the buttons for the phone number from memory.

"Yes." The heavily accented voice said.

"It's me. That package we wanted won't be arriving today. Or even tomorrow." His voice was steady.

"Ty che, blyad?" Basically, 'what the fuck?' in Russian. Feydor Slutskaya barked out the question displaying his own nerves.

Michael knew enough of the language to translate that and he kept calm. "Can't be helped."

"What happened?" the fence asked, in a less strident voice.

Davidson snorted. "What do you mean? Look outside the window!" Snowflakes were just beginning to fall in the late afternoon sky. "Snowmaggeden happened, that's what happened. The shipment is going to Montreal and then via armored van to New York." He relayed the full extent of the bad news."It's..."

Feydor interrupted him. "Fucking move the operation to Montreal then, or just hit the van on the way!"

Two calming breaths didn't help- Michael still exploded, "The fuck you say! We can't just shift to Montreal. I can't plan it or get the resources there in twenty-two hours." Davidson took another breath and went on in a bit softer tone. "And forget about the van. I don't know which company, or the route, or the specs on the vehicle. This is not the wild west, or the 1920's, you know that!" The man just got on his last nerve.

Feydor Slutskaya breathed heavily on the other end of the phone. As the main fence for the Bratva, he did know that.

Davidson flashed on something while he waited for the man to speak. Only one person in the world would dare tease Feydor about his last name. One man could call him slut and get away with it.

"He's going to be pissed," Feydor said referencing that same man.

"I get that, man, but I don't control the fucking weather!"

"Call him," the fence directed. "You tell him."

Davidson cursed and hung up the phone. He rose and paced around the small office. Shit! Feydor creeped him out, but Demetry Roybokov scared him. Davidson remembered numerous incidents over the past fifteen years where enemies and even friends had disappeared after pissing off the mob boss.

Davidson agreed whole-heartedly with the sentiment among his men, that Demetry was a whole other level of crazy. And a whole other level of scary. And vengeful. Not a good combination to have angry at you. He steeled himself and worked the phone.

The old man picked up the phone himself after the third ring with a deeply accented, "Da."

"Mr. Roybokov, it's Michael," he said, trying to be cool and professional.

Roybokov said nothing, not showing his hand or his temperament.

"Sir, I'm calling with bad news. I scrubbed the job."

"*You* scrubbed the job, Michael?" the head of the Brotherhood asked quietly.

"Yes, Sir, I did... I...."

"And why did you do that?" he interrupted.

Davidson hated the quiet version of the man. That meant he was mad. Very mad. But why?

"I did it because snow canceled the flight and De Beers made other arrangements for the package." Davidson detested giving out this much information over the phone about his activities. *No getting around this in court*, he thought. Too much was in the open.

"You did not plan for this? I thought you figured all the contingencies," the old man asked.

He winced and controlled his anger. No shouting now, not with this man. "No, Sir, not an event of this magnitude. Acts of God are beyond my control." He was breathing heavily.

"Acts of God or loss of nerves, son?"

"Mr. Roybokov, you know I still have the nerves..."

"You have been quiet since 2009, Michael. Too quiet," Roybokov said, interrupting again.

"Sir," Davidson pointed out, "nine figure jobs are hard to come by. With Toronto earlier this year and now the snow, we..."

"Unlucky!" The word had a definite edge to it.

"I wouldn't say that, Sir. I think our partnership has been very lucky. Lucky to the tune of $1.5 billion for you," Michael countered.

"You have walked away with $400 million for yourself, my friend," Roybokov pointed out to him.

"I have to split that and I have expenses." He sounded a bit whiny to his own ears with that line.

"We all have expenses and we all have bosses, Michael," Demetry told him, half explaining his anger.

"I'm sorry, Sir, I don't know the kind of sharks you swim with," Davidson said, honestly.

The gangster actually laughed. "Pray you never get in water with them,

son!"

"Maybe if Kat quit buying half of LA your money woes would be okay," Davidson tried to be funny.

"Kat is acting on my orders and succeeding, where as you are not," he shot back.

So much for funny, Davidson thought quickly. Ekaterina Roybokov was a socialite. Daddy swam in filth so she could walk red carpets. Davidson remembered an incident from seven years ago. The tall blonde beauty was just sixteen when he had come home to find her in his bed. The thief didn't hesitate. He wrapped her up and took her home untouched. She was responsible for two floaters in the East River that he knew about and Davidson was not going for a swim, if he could help it.

"Sir, give me another two or three months. It will be dead over Christmas, but something will pop up," he promised. "If not, we will knock over a Zales."

"Zad Chec!" (Damn you!) Roybokov swore and laughed.

"Am I still your thief-in-law?" Davidson asked sincerely.

"Yes, yes, of course," The Russian assured him. "You might not be part of Bratva (Brotherhood), but you are my thief-in-law." The old man used the expression for the most successful thief in the Russian mob organization.

Davidson thanked his boss.

"It is a shame. I was so looking forward to watching the world's greatest thief work." Roybokov clicked off the phone.

Davidson sat wearily. *That was harder than stealing*, he thought. The old man was running out of patience, for sure. Problem was, Davidson wasn't lying when he'd told him jobs were hard to come by. The big jobs were few and far between, and even this job was a repeat of the KLM job they'd pulled off a few years back. Taking diamonds from a commercial flight was tricky.

He was hoping time and distance from the other job in Antwerp had dulled the airlines and the shipping companies into complacency.

Okay! He still had work to do. Rising he went back into the main office space and handed Ira his phone, IDs, and badges. Levinson smashed and worked over his items. The wreckage went into the rapidly filling garbage bags.

"Ricky texted. He is good. We will see him Tuesday," Gretchen reported.

Davidson nodded to that report.

"Graeme is due in from the continent on Sunday," the small Brazilian woman went on.

"I'll pick him up," he said, absolving the couple of the responsibility. The woman gave him the flight information and the boss committed it to memory per normal.

"Let's hope the storm swings through quickly," Ira noted, as they wrapped up operations.

Lastly, the three put the extra cash they had on hand back into the safe. The big office stand-up held about $100,000 and several clean guns, among other things. The majority of their IDs were in another unit, but the office still had an emergency supply. The gang could travel quickly and securely from this place, if needed.

Trash bags went into the Dumpster beside the outer door, and then the three faced each other in the garage on the ground level of the building.

"You two hole up," he directed the couple. "I'm not going anywhere. Be back here on Tuesday."

The pair were at odds, now that the job had fallen through, so they agreed. Three separate cars left the Jones Street office into the growing storm.

All over the city, around 3:45 pm, people dropped what they were doing and headed for safe harbor. Included in that exodus were two teams of gunmen in unmarked white vans just off Dixon Road near JFK. The target was not coming; they'd just gotten word. The heavily tattooed men packed up and went home. Snow as a lifesaver rarely gets its due.

Michael Davidson joined the fleeing New Yorkers as he navigated the streets back to his house. The Fort Greene Park area of Brooklyn was just 'adjacent' enough to qualify as gentrified. Turning left onto Washington Park Avenue, he drove the Audi A8 slowly down the block. Many large turn of the century Edwardians stood sentinel along the east side of the street. The west side was given over to the park itself; leafless trees looming in the rapidly blowing snow and gloom. He touched the button on the visor as he got to 187 and the garage door cranked up.

Davison loved the subterfuge of this house, as it appealed to his hidden larcenous nature. The garage door was neatly cut into the foundation wall and painted gray and mottled. It blended into the rock until most people forgot it was there. The headlights from the car illuminated the cavernous rough-walled space. The floor was shiny Terrazzo epoxy and spacious enough for his car and the truck he kept in there, as well. The right side wall was given over to the utilities for the building and the backup generator he'd bought for emergencies. The left side wall held his rack of security cameras and a monitor along with the short flight of stairs that led to the interior main hallway. Crap was piled everywhere else, like everyone's garage. Clicking on the huge overhead fluorescent lights, Michael stopped to review the security cameras as he always did. *Force of habit*. He quickly scrolled through the two exterior scenes and the three interior shots. There even was a remote shot of his office, now dark and secure. No problems awaited him, but two items of interest did. He committed them to memory as usual. Home. The place always said home to him and it was secure.

He'd purchased the 110 year-old building in 2003. Flush with cash from a recent job, he needed someplace to launder his money. The house provided him with an opportunity to do just that. The subdivided unit was a true forty-five, as they said in real estate parlance. The Realtor walked him through the width of the house which was forty-five feet wide.

"Some of those row houses are only twelve feet wide," she told him, flirting just ever the right amount. "This unit is almost four times as wide, so you don't get those long, narrow rooms."

Yeah. I don't want long, narrow rooms, he thought watching her move.

Six thousand square feet overall, the blue and grey painted house held a large upper home with a smaller downstairs renter's unit.

"The lady will have to move," was the agent's sad pronouncement to Michaels question about the situation.

Well, shit! *Now I feel bad,* he'd thought. He toured the top floor with its three large bedrooms, hidden office, and workout room. Eventually, they made it to the roof deck and back stairs that led down to the renter's unit. "You'll want to block these off," the pretty brunette said, looking back and up at him from the lower stair. His imagination went wild, thinking about that look. $1.9 million consummated the deal, and the agent, in short order. He had some extensive work and upgrading to do, which took some time, but the place was home.

His mind returned to the present as Davidson opened the door to the interior hallway and waited for the inevitable. Down the hall a few feet, the tenant's door flew open to his movements and a querulous voice said, "Is that you, Mikey?"

She must have been waiting by the door for him to come in. "Yes, Mrs. Spack, it's me." He walked down the hall to see her. "How are you?"

"Oh, I'm glad you are home, Mikey. It's gonna be a bad one! A bad one!" The old woman opened the door so Davidson could come in, which he did. He could never get away with just a quick hello with her. "Did the snow change your travel plans, Mike?" Mary Spack asked in her heavily-accented Jewish New York voice.

"Sure did, Mary. I'm trapped here for the next few days," he told her truthfully. "You are all set, right? We got your supplies two days ago."

Even at eighty-three, the woman was still sharp mentally and she could look after herself, mostly. It was just...

"We did, we did," she admitted and looked back towards the kitchen in her unit. Her spotless, nicely decorated living room sat at the front of the house where the snow could be seen out the window.

"Gonna be a bad one," she said under her breath. She looked back at Davidson. "I got dinner cooking. So, since the snow changed your plans, Michael, you'll eat with me."

Davidson always loved the way she phrased those kinds of things: "So, you'll come, you'll eat." Like it was already *fait accompli*. It would just be rude to refuse her simple request. *You got to eat anyway, right?*

"What are we havin'?" Michael asked.

"Brisket and latkes," she told him.

"What time we eatin'?"

"6 pm sharp," she replied with a smile now that her mission to get a dinner partner was accomplished.

Michael eased himself out on the pretext that he had to get dressed and he went back up the hall to the main stairwell. The main outside front door was to his left as he rounded the landing and went up the long flight of creaky wooden stair treads. It was actually three- stories-plus worth of stairs. Mary got eleven-foot ceilings in her place, while he had the full fourteen-foot-high treatment. The other eight feet? That was a secret. His front door was a solid, period mahogany job. The deadbolt and lock were state of the old-fashioned art. The door opened onto a small vestibule which brightened considerably when he turned on the Tiffany chandelier. The travertine marble gleamed dully as he retrieved the pile of junk mail from the basket set atop the small antique table aligned under the wall mail slot. He paced off the three steps to the real front door to his place. Solid wood, metal clad, the door had an electronic lock which was fingerprint activated. His right thumb on the pad clicked back the bolt.

Michael went in and dropped his leather messenger bag on his dining room table. The living room was the right side of the space and ran half the width of the house, which made the room about twenty by twenty-five feet. Oak hardwood floors shone under Persian rugs while the walls were a rich cream color. A butter leather, Italian-made, tan-colored couch and kings chair sat opposite of the entertainment center. The flat screen TV sat on top, and a full rack of very button-y stereo gear, along with cable and TiVo boxes gleaming with black electronic sophistication, lay riding underneath. The maple dining room table was on his left, with seating for ten, and sat near a nice spread of windows providing a view out to the back of the house.

Opposite to the living room was the kitchen opening; a half wall with a marble counter top serving as a breakfast nook with four chairs. The doorway arch to the kitchen proper was wide and welcoming as he went in to grab a bottle of water. Gleaming polished cherry wood cabinets and stainless steel appliances dominated the cook's kitchen. Unlike a lot of bachelors, Michael could cook and liked to do so. He kept rolling through the kitchen past the butler's pantry and out the hallway entrance. A left turn and he went down the darkened hallway. Bathroom on his left, followed by the laundry room ticked by as he continued on. The spare bedroom had its door closed on the right. The end door off the hallway was his goal.

Michael opened the door to his master bedroom suite. As part of the remodel, he'd knocked down a wall here to combine two bedrooms into one really large space. His huge bed was opposite the door off to the left between a series of windows. A desk also sat on that wall, gleaming oak. A four-piece bathroom with a sauna attached was along the right side of the space. The closet was on the left. The windows in his room looked across the side yard to the darkened neighbor house. That was item of interest number one on the security tape.

A 'sold' plaque hung on the 'for sale' sign in front of that house. Stan and Debbie, his neighbors, had sold out due to the rising cost of living in Brooklyn. Davidson tried to buy the place so he could attach the two houses and make a super house like the gay lawyers down the street had done- but no such luck. A full price plus bid at $2.975 million snapped up the place right out from under him. Dammit.

Swigging the water, he went into the bathroom and peed for what seemed like an eternity. A quick piss shiver and he was done.

The light from the bedroom gave his face an eerie, shadowy look as he washed his hands at the bathroom sink. He was tall, at six feet two-and-a-half inches. He kept himself in great shape by running and doing exercises several times a week. At forty-three, the man was fighting the battle over weight every day. A hundred seventy-three pounds today. Light brown hair topped his head which he kept parted, short and off his ears. No gray yet, thank God. Well, maybe a few stray strands intruded at his temples. But that just made him look distinguished, right? A square jaw and brown eyes, which he could squint up in a good death stare, made him attractive enough. Women came around, but weren't a fixture in his life. His profession was his undoing with the ladies. He tried to tell the truth as often as possible, but of course he had to lie over that little item. He'd invented a fine cover story, and told it with conviction, but somehow, over time, the few women he got involved with sensed *something* off.

Sighing softly, he went into the walk-in closet to hang up his leather coat that he'd thrown on the bed when he'd come in. The closet was the envy of every woman he had ever shown it to. Racks for his suits, and cubbies for his shoes, and drawers for his drawers. The real gem in the closet was the hidden staircase that led down to the blind middle level to the house. That was the secret about his staircase. Again this appealed to his nature. His real office was in here with his home gym and another bathroom.

Exiting, he moved back into the bedroom and sat behind the huge oak desk. The last four days' mail piled up on the right hand side. Mostly junk from his home delivery, as Davidson got his real mail from a post office box. That pile was large as well. Bills, statements, letters from the lawyers and CPA's, and a direct deposit slip from Anderson

Consulting LLC to his account. The final piece was from Excelsior Holdings. A form letter informing the residents at 187 Washington Park Lane that the five-year repainting for the house was scheduled during the Spring. A smile quirked his lips, because he knew that juicy bit would be a part of the dinner conversation with Mary. He knew all about the painting, however. After all, he WAS Excelsior Holdings. And Anderson Consulting. Both the holding company and the shell LLC were part of the ways he laundered his money. It was how he'd bought the house. His name did not appear on any document associated with anything. Well, his real name didn't appear anyway. That was how rich people all over did it; shell companies to buy real estate to keep their anonymity.

He opened the direct deposit slip. *How much was he paying himself now a days?* $47,000 a month? Grossly overpaid. He would just have to muddle through. 9/11, and its aftermath, had made his life hell.

The drudgery part of stealing was trying to figure out what to do with the loot. You can't eat diamonds, and Con Edison will not take a gold bar as payment for electricity. Michael excelled at the details of shifting money around so it showed up in his account as actual, spendable, untraceable money, but 9/11 threw a serious monkey wrench in his schemes.

He worked down the pile and dealt with the details of running a criminal enterprise. Accounts committed to memory and details handled with the mail, he shredded everything in the machine next to the desk. The desk clock said 5:28, red colon blinking away unconcerned with his crime. Time to get ready for dinner. He trudged back across the room, showered quickly, and changed into his best casual jeans and a chambray work shirt. Leather moccasins accented his feet. He cringed at the fact that this comfortable, casual, cool look cost him over $1,700 at the stores in New York. *That was true thievery!*

Slipping through the kitchen on his way to the back stairs,

Michael grabbed a bottle of Australian Shiraz to go with dinner. The peppery taste of the wine would go nicely with the meat and potatoes. The small door off the kitchen led down to its twin in Mary's unit. These stairs saw much more use than Michael would have thought in the beginning. It quickly became apparent after he moved in that A) Mary would outlive him, and B) bother him. A quick knock and he opened the door to the smell of fried onions and the oil for the latkes.

"Mikey!"

"Hi, Mary," he said handing her the wine.

"Oh, good, thank you." The old woman had no clue the bottle cost $195.

"Can I help?"

"Be a good boy and light a fire for me, please?"

Michael moved into the parlor to comply. He rued the day he decided to fix the fireplaces back to their original glory. Amazing what a million-dollar renovation budget bought you. He figured with the extra work and the permits and such, each fire cost around $5,000. But...

The crackle and pop provided the perfect background noise to combat the wind and the snow piling up outside. Since caveman times, the human psyche needed fire to dispel the cold and they needed the extra protection tonight.

Dinner came out and onto the dining room table. Mary and Michael were alike in that both were closeted perfectionists. A white lace cloth lined the table. Water and wine glasses, competed with the silver tableware for sparkle power. Candles and warm challah were in place with everything situated just so. Mary sat the last of the food out: Egyptian carrot's and a salad went down next to the platter of brisket and the potato pancakes.

"Open the wine please, Michael." Mary directed, as she blessed the candles. The Havdalah and the HaMotzi followed quickly.

The pair sat now that the Sabbath had officially begun. Even though this was a Thursday, that didn't seem to matter to Mary. Raised a lapsed Catholic, Michael liked the flexibility in the Jewish religion. Bacon? Sure! Pork? Never! Sabbath on a Thursday? Meh!

You had to love a religion that did not even require the belief in God as a prerequisite to joining.

"Smells good," Michael commented as he helped himself.

"I'm practicing for Passover," she smiled at him, handing over applesauce for the latke.

The pair ate and talked. He felt very comfortable around Mary. She was old school and had lived in the area for her whole life.

"I was a youngster for the hurricane of '38, boychik, but that was a storm! We had to spend a week on the heights with Uncle Saul," she said, eyes back in time.

The Spring painting note came up as Mike knew it would. Mary did not miss a trick. "They just have to protect the investment, Mary. They aren't raising your rent are they?"

"No, No. Those people have been pretty good to me actually," she admitted.

Those people. He laughed on the inside.

Michael remembered meeting her for the first time. The Realtor had put in the bid and the offer was accepted, but Mary was being forced out. He heard her story and melted. Mary and her Henry lived in the unit starting in 1965. Henry was in business as a CPA. He'd died in 1994 and left his wife a fairly comfortable nest egg, but he didn't count on the rent explosion in the boroughs. The tech heavy portfolio took a huge hit in the dot com burst and 9/11. The upstairs couple finally left in 2002 and Mary simply did not have the money to remain in the area, or buy the unit when

the owners decided to sell. Michael had her down to the office on Jones Street under the guise of a new city program to allow seniors to maintain their homes. Mary got the place for $850 a month and of course that included utilities. The other new tenant- i.e. Michael, would be in charge of the renovations and any problems Mary had.

He looked like a nice boy. But, he was from Colorado. The WEST. They had horses out there. Mary quickly became his Jewish grandmother. He watched out for her and she showed him old Brooklyn.

Dessert was a crisp lemon sorbet. Tart and sweet in a perfect combination. "My sister Ilene sends me her Meyer lemons from California." She pronounced every syllable: Cal-i for- Ni-A. Michael just smacked his lips in appreciation.

Dinner was pretty quick, with just the two of them, and the dishes piled in the sink for later. The odd pair sat on the couch, sipping coffee and watching TV like an old married couple.

Brian Kelly, the WGN weatherman, reported the carnage going on outside from the box. Davidson began to worry about Graeme coming back on Sunday, but he thought it would be okay. The news reported the problems at Reagan in DC, and the better shape for the local New York airports.

Jeopardy came on and Michael was feeling full and relatively good, despite his work problems. And Alex was just asking such easy answers; all he had to do was supply the question.

"Who was Marie Antoinette?"

"What are the Green Bay Packers?"

"What is Deuteronomy?"

He rolled through the first round without a miss. Mary clapped as he finished up. "You could be a contestant!"

"Not with my schedule," he answered back.

"I'm sure that fancy consulting company would give you some time off."

"Nope," he squashed that idea. "We just had a job fall through and now we have to hustle for another contract."

She knew about hustling.

The second round provided no more problems than the first and Mary was delighted at his abilities at the game show. Final Jeopardy came and he was pleased to supply the question for this answer: "This Army Officer has his name on the fourth highest peak in the United States."

"Who was Zebulon T. Pike?" he said with satisfaction.

"How could you know that?" Mary scoffed.

"Mary, Pike's Peak is in Colorado Springs. I saw it every day when I was a kid growing up. No self-respecting Coloradan would miss that question."

"Uh huh. Were there Indians around you then?" Manhattan was as far west as she travelled anymore, and the Hamptons as far east, an occasional visit to her sister's notwithstanding. Alex confirmed his knowledge about mountains in Colorado.

Michael laughed at the Indian comment, and told her no, while rising. "I'm going to bank the fire, you close the flue tomorrow, okay?"

She agreed, bid him goodnight, and he left her as he travelled back upstairs to his place. The fire downstairs left a subtle smoke tang to the air and he closed up his kitchen and living room for the night. Jumping on the bed, he flipped on Sports Center and watched the highlights and stories. He was going to be home all weekend and he could watch a bit of the games. And low and behold there was a game on tonight. Muting the sound allowed one to just watch the good part: the violence. He picked up the new Stephen King novel and sat back to read, glancing at the TV occasionally. A rare pleasure for him. When was the last time he'd watched a football game and read a book after a nice dinner? Too long. The down time also gave the man a bit of time to roll things over in his head. It was pretty full: Demetry, the job, Mary, his family.

He took no real pleasure in the Jeopardy thing, as he was just showing off for Mary. Hell, he could go weeks without missing a question. *Brain is just wired that way*, he thought.

With an IQ that topped 164 he should have been a prodigy. A good home and good parents, he had gotten every advantage. Love, clothes, and college, he could have become anything. Yet he stole for a living. Davidson often justified to himself that it wasn't pickpocketing or armed robbery; but that might be putting lipstick on a pig. Stealing was stealing.

Strangely, he did not have real moral qualms about stealing. Was that a defect in his personality? He was not sure. He boiled it down to one small fig leaf: He didn't steal from people. Not any more, anyway. He had at one time robbed a few houses, but it was a complicated thing.

Complicated. That was a very interesting word and one that described his love-hate relationship with crime. Some thieves stole for the thrill, and Michael was not above feeling that aspect. Some stole for the money and that played a part for him, no denying it. But what he really loved was the puzzle box aspect of the whole thing. The challenge of looking at a locked safe, or vault, or store and figuring out how to defeat the various alarms and measures the companies used to keep guys like him out, always thrilled him. It drove him, really. And the security changed all the time! Every time a thief was successful the puzzle box changed its faces. That's why he stole. Of course, he was willing to admit that that all might be bullshit and he was just a klepto.

The other aspect to his personality that he would admit to was one of compartmentalization. He could wall off parts of his mind, when he needed to, in order to accomplish goals. Stray facts and feelings got shunted over when he needed to put them in the corner and deal with shit. It was almost like being an actor, he knew. He could put on different faces or *personalities* when it was required.

It wasn't lying, exactly. He still felt the emotions and the guilt and all of it, just later when he could process and deal with it, not during the heat of the moment. Davidson had no idea if that was good or bad. It just *was* with him.

Outside the snow piled up as the game wound down. A few chapters of Mr. King got him ready to sleep. One small problem: The final item of interest from the security tape kept intruding into his brain: Why would a piece-of-shit, brown Crown Victoria be parked outside of his house for three hours on Thursday? His security tape showed them clearly. Two cops on a stake out on his street. The thief-in-law drifted off to sleep worrying about those cops.

Chapter Two

Friday and Saturday were cabin fever, cake days for Michael. Other than two brisk workouts in his exercise room, he barely budged or sweated. The snow ended Friday at noon, after dropping twenty-six inches, but the damage was done, and New York was on its knees. The subway stopped, the roads were impassable, and the airports closed. Da Mayor came on TV and asked the citizens for patience. John Massimino was being hailed as a very smart man.

The whole thing reminded Davidson of the stories he'd heard about the '83 blizzard in Denver. Twenty-eight inches dumped in twenty-four hours on that much smaller city. At the big press conference the next day the first question was: "Mr. Mayor have you instituted the cities snow removal plan?" William McNichols, the long-time Mayor of Denver, looked into the camera and went, "Uhhh..." He was voted out the next year.

So, it was Da Mayor's turn in the spotlight and he did have a snow removal plan. It might not have been the plan most people would have used, given the choice. The plowing went in this order: Rich peoples' streets first. Then the major arteries. Then the poor sections of town. Da Mayor was an asshole.

The airports reopened on Saturday, but no one could get to them. Michael began to wonder if he could get to Graeme. *That's going to piss him off even more*, Michael thought. He and Graeme were having discussions about things. Not fights- just discussions. Shoveling the walks and the stoop, and brushing off the backyard trees, earned him a brisket care package from Mary on Saturday evening. She was enduring the storm just fine. The tiny woman told him while passing over the food, "I'm in my bathrobe early. Bluebloods is on. I want to see if Tom

Selleck takes his shirt off!"

"T.M.I, Mary, T.M.I!"

Sunday dawned bright and warm and blue skied. Everything turned into a slushy mess. The plow crews, after fifty-five straight hours, had most of the city cleared. What they would admit to anyway. Harlem might have been an exception. The grumbling about that was just beginning. An IM was waiting from Graeme in their favorite chat room that just said: "On my way!" Michael confirmed the 2:11 pm landing time. Antwerp to JFK on Delta. He had time.

He moved downstairs to the gym for his workout. His exercise room was large and filled with some basic gear and mats. No weird lunkhead weights or mirrors for him. A pull-up bar was bolted into the floor and ceiling and a top-of-the-line treadmill was in the main section. Normally, he would run outdoors, usually in the park. The feel of the path made the running much more enjoyable for him. He reserved the treadmill for days just like today, too slushy or cold or rainy.

He did a series of windmill stretches for his arms and a slow jog to warm up a bit. His blue sweats and tank top went nicely with his Asics running shoes. When had he become such a fashion snob? The whir of the rolling mat started in slow, and then it started to grow. He beeped buttons until the incline was set at one degree up and the speed hit a six minutes per mile pace. Stepping up his stride, Davidson began to run. His long legs stretched out, and soon were lulled into the rhythm of the run. His breathing became even and deep, trying to relax.

He was not looking forward to his ride home today with his best friend. Things had become strained between them over the last five years. And it had become really bad the last two. The friction between them was exacerbated during their professional dry spell. Add to that Graeme was drinking more, and getting wilder with his money. Normally, he wasn't the best at either of those two activities, sobriety and saving, and his friction with Michael was making it worse. Kind of like a shame spiral.

It was not like it was in the beginning. All things change, especially relationships. Simpler? Maybe. Things were simple in the beginning, and he, personally, had certainly been less complicated. Same could be said for Graeme. Both had picked up baggage along the years.

He'd met Graeme Donniger, lately of New York City, via Belfast, Northern Ireland, and Las Vegas. Davidson had been in the city after a very momentous six months of his life. Months that saw him commit his first robbery, graduate from college, and move to Brooklyn. Why commit the robbery? Why Brooklyn? The challenge for the former, and the fact that everyone was moving west and south, causing him to go north and east, for the latter. Zigging when everyone else zagged was a favorite theme for him. That's why he had been in Vegas, with a fake ID and $15,000 in cash. One book read on gambling, and half an eye on taking down a casino, he had been a powder keg waiting to go off.

Three days of playing cards had taught him a few things; no one could rob a casino and no one consistently beat the house, even if your card-counting system was augmented with a fabulous memory. The Caesar's pit boss had realized Michael was counting cards after fifty hours. Donniger had figured it out in twenty minutes.

"You need to lose on a big bet occasionally, friend." The voice had been a lilting Irish brogue.

Head down and speaking out the side of his mouth, the voice had been pitched for Michael's ears only. Davidson had looked sideways at the man in the next seat at the twenty-five dollar table.

Young, thin, a shade under six feet, and pale; the man had been handsome, flashing those full lips and crooked teeth. Curley brown hair topped his head. Graeme had introduced himself, and nodded agreeably when Michael upped his bet on a minus six scored on the system. Both men busted. The dealer shuffled and they'd placed larger bets as the cards flew. The cards came 20 for Michael, blackjack for Graeme, and 17 for the dealer.

"There's the luck o' the Irish!" Graeme had shouted.

The pair had gone on to embark on an epic Vegas night together. Michael had achieved a near impossibility; he'd maintained a pleasant buzz from 10:00 am at Caesars until passing out at 4:30 am with a secretary named Sally from Wichita, in a comped suite.

Oh boy! At 10:15 the next morning he'd wondered out of the bedroom to find Graeme, Sally, and another woman named Wendy, indulging in a room service breakfast. Michael had sheepishly joined them.

"You're right, he is a baby," Wendy had said to Sally, matter-of-factly.

The twenty-nine year-old woman had smiled, and said, "I taught him a few tricks."

He'd choked on his O.J while the other three laughed at him. The ladies soon left to rejoin their bachelorette group, allowing Graeme to set into Michael.

"Where you living, friend?" he'd asked, mildly to start.

"I just moved to Brooklyn," he admitted, not willing to give away much.

"That's great! I live in the city meself. You know you can figure every angle, but you would need a crew of fifty to rob a casino." He'd said it straight out, just to gauge his new friend.

Silence was his only reply and Graeme grinned back to that. "Photographic memory, right?"

More silence and then Davidson said, "The term is eidetic, not photographic."

"You remembered their names after the night we had," Graeme commented pulling out a small card on which he'd written: Wendy, tall thin brunette. Sally- Blonde, short. Stacked.

He showed the card to Michael. "I needed a little help."

"I didn't have that much to drink." It came out a bit defensively from Davidson.

"Five rum and cokes with six waters in between, starting at the bar in the Flamingo," Graeme recounted.

"You had seven whisky sours."

"I'm Irish, I'm supposed to!" the man retorted. He stretched and looked out the locked window at the view of the strip.

Michael watched him and relaxed a bit. He liked the guy okay and was willing to see where this led.

"All the while winning $4,275 and tipping a whopping $1,405," he went on detailing Graeme's activities to his back. The Irishman shrugged.

"I'm generous, what can I say?" The men matched eyes as Graeme turned and went on softly. "And I watched as you card counted, observed me, cased Caesar's, and picked up two ladies, all the while winning over $10,000."

"$11,395."

"What do you do for a living, Mr...?"

"Davidson," Michael supplied.

"I might have a job that could use a man of your skills," Graeme had said with gusto and that was it.

Michael did not miss a step on the treadmill as he sweated and remembered the beginnings with his friend. Now? There was the rub. The situation had fundamentally changed from that equal beginning. Michael called the shots now. He picked the targets and worked out the details on their jobs. It got complicated because Graeme wanted to be the leader. Problem was he was not as good at the whole business of stealing. He could not keep track of the specifics as Michael could. He didn't have the attention to detail necessary to deal with the problems that inevitably came up.

As Davidson rose and became the thief-in-law in the organization, Graeme became just another gang member. And that rankled the Irishman. It caused him to drink more and be crazier with his money. Crazier with women, too. And now? Something was going to have to change. He felt bad about that, but it was what had to happen.

Michael felt the metronome in his head clicking away. He looked down at the display unit to see: 54:45 time elapsed and 9.1 miles run. He slowed and lowered the base unit. Some time at a comfortable walking pace allowed him to recover. Water bottle and towel were liberally used to wipe down his body and slow his breathing. He felt good after the run, but was not finished with the workout. After recovering he went to the pull-up bar.

Jumping to grasp the bar he levered his legs up into an "L" position.

Davidson began doing pull-ups. A set of ten was cranked out in two minutes. He dropped and allowed a three-minute recovery period. A second set followed, with legs still held in the horizontal position. A third set and his arms began to ache. His ab muscles felt tight and began to burn. Breathing heavily once more, and sweating all over again, the fourth set saw his arms quiver and chest heave as he worked to finish the set of ten.

Arms behind his head trying to allow the oxygen to replenish his tired muscles as he regretted the day he'd gone to this regime. 'Core' was all the rage a few years ago. Fuck core!

The fifth and final set started well, but by the sixth pull-up he was barely cresting the bar. Seven struggled, but he got it up there. Eight.... nope. He collapsed onto the mat and lay there a few moments gasping for air, waiting to see if he could walk without his abs cramping up. He tried to do this work out once a week. He did one or the other part all the time, but the pull-up thing right after the run was double tough. Davidson could also count on one hand the number of times he'd failed to complete that fifth set.

The trudge up the stairs and the shower felt like defeat, even though he knew in his head not many men could have done that routine. Age was taking its toll on him. He could not stop that from happening-try as he might. The eyes in the mirror staring back at him were still clear, but a few wrinkles had appeared and now he could not finish his pull-ups. Fuck. He supposed everyone struggled with the inevitable decline. His larger problem was that a huge decline for him could lead directly to his death. Declining thieves made mistakes and the Bratva did not like mistakes.

Dressing in blue jeans and a sea- green cashmere sweater and loafers, Michael went back down to his office to bang out some more work before he had to go. A steady hour produced four to-do lists. Those lists were his genius on display. A detailed list of what each gang member needed to accomplish in order to find a new target, maintain their covers, or finish off old loose ends. The list for him was contained in his head as always. Paperwork, forms, and contingencies. Those items separated Michael from every smash and grab thief out there. The attention to detail got things accomplished that other thieves could not get done. The four lists went into his leather messenger bag. He was ready for Tuesday and its challenges.

A check of the flight status for the plane (on time) and slipping on his favorite black leather jacket, Michael eased the truck out of the garage. The Audi would handle fine in the snow, but the four-wheel drive of the F-150 was preferable. A left out of the garage and he cruised over the hard packed snow that was Washington Park. He guessed they didn't rate with the city crews. A left onto Dekalb and the traffic slowed to a crawl.

The day remained sunny and about 50-ish, with the winter smog hanging low in the air. The blocks ticked off as he drove: Clermont, Vanderbilt, and Clinton. A dodge left and he was on Washington proper. Since this was a major thruway, the plows had scraped this one clean, except for a few ice spots which the truck pushed through. A few blocks more and onto Atlantic Avenue. This was the real test of how his trip would be. Atlantic was the major east-west artery in the city. Locals might prefer Fulton, but Davidson hated dealing with the Muni busses so he took Atlantic.

Besides, he loved this road. Especially the area he was passing now, the new Barclays Center. The giant complex would house the basketball team and a retail center. It was almost opened, but was behind schedule on financing and construction delays. A typical New York building project; plan, plan, plan, and then hope for the best as problems arose. Light after light ticked green as he went through. Nice timing. The turn onto East New York Avenue was not impossible; it just required a near suicidal left across traffic that did not want to ease. Horn blaring, he made it. East New York became Jamaica Avenue, which led to the almost pastoral setting of the Jackie. The Jackie Robinson Parkway went past several cemeteries in this part of the city. Since nobody visited graves in the snow, it was clear and Mike picked up speed as the truck engine growled. The sign said, 'Van Wyck Expressway 4 miles'. A check of his watch: Perfect. On schedule.

This was exactly the kind of problem solving he did in his head all the time. Graeme had landed twenty-eight minutes ago at 2:15 pm. Four minutes late. Seven minutes to taxi off the runway and into the international terminal gate. Only six needed for his mate to deplane, as he was in first class after all. No bathroom breaks for the Irishman either, since he had a penis. A six-minute walk to the passport control area. Seventeen more in the resident alien line. Bags coming down the carousel now. Eight spent collecting the bags and run them past the drug sniffing beagles. Michael crossed the airport belt road at this point. He was on the JFK grounds moving past cargo road where the van would have carried them onto the tarmac last week had things gone better. Too late now. Fourteen minutes more for Graeme to walk to the passenger pick up area and then to the smoke cubical for one (no- two cigarettes) and...

Michael navigated the maze that was Terminal One Passenger Pickup, and yanked the wheel hard to the curb as he saw Graeme walk out of the door of the smoking cube. The man hoisted his bags into the bed of the truck and hopped in. The whole exchange took forty-two seconds and no phone calls.

Graeme Donniger was forty-four now and feeling his age, the same as Davidson. Brown curly hair thinning now and receding a bit, he also had some gray sprinkled in. Because he was an inch or two shorter than the American, Graeme had a bit of a paunch. In no way did he exercise or watch what he ate like his friend did. His Irish brogue had also retreated over the years as New York City imprinted new rhythms on his tongue.

"Get any sleep?" Michael asked as he retraced his route and hit the 678 towards Manhattan.

"Bah- A bit. I'm a little knackered."

Michael was sure a few whisky sours had helped get him that sleep. "Okay- Take the rest of today and tomorrow and get your legs under you. We will hit it again on Tuesday. OK?" Mike asked out of the coming argument.

"My legs are under me now, shammer," Graeme said emphatically. "I didn't do anythin' more dangerous than sit in a car. All week!"

Accepting the reality of what was going to happen, Michael sighed. "Good. That's how it was supposed to go."

"But it didn't go, did it?" The man steamed. "It got all bolloxed up just like the Toronto job!"

"Fuck man, I'll tell you the same thing I told Demetry, 'I don't control the weather!' Neither did De Beers. They had to scramble to get the shipment changed and we just can't turn with them like that!" He stopped speaking and took a calming breath.

"What did Demetry say to that?" Graeme asked after a moment.

Davidson steered the Ford around a slower driver paying attention to the road before he answered. "What do you think? He was pissed. Sorry, angry," he corrected. "Demetry is under a lot of pressure."

"He's under pressure? The fuck he know about pressure?"

"The man is moving with people you do NOT want to know about, Graeme."

His passenger mumbled something that to Michael sounded like "...take his side" and then slammed the dashboard. "That job was worth $15 million easy!"

Deep in his guts, Michael quailed. "You need money, Graeme?" The question was soft, but the ramifications were not.

"Christ," his friend muttered, rather than answer the awkward question.

"How much?"

No answer from the Irish.

"Dammit- how much?" Michael was becoming angry now himself.

"A hundred fifty large," was finally admitted to.

Davidson said nothing to that admission. There was not much he could say about that, short of an out and out fistfight. His friend was a polar opposite in many ways. The old saying about crime not paying set aside, both men had been well compensated for their efforts over the years. Through his offshore accounts and the holding company investment portfolio, Michael could lay his hands on nine figures in a few months, if he had too. Investments and hiding money were not Graeme's specialties. Water through his fingers was the operative expression. He knew at least $60 million had gone into those

fingers. And now he owed a lot of money to people Mike figured would not be too happy about not being paid.

"You'll have the check on Tuesday."

"I'm not a basket case!"

"I'm the one trying to help you here!" Michael shouted back.

"I need to work, not take charity," Graeme countered.

He had no way to answer that. They'd covered the ground before.

The silence between them stretched, and then Graeme said, "Mikey, I'm telling you Dubai would be..."

"The biggest cluster fuck in the world!" He interrupted.

Irish fumed in the passenger seat, watching the cars go outbound on the Jackie, while they went inbound to the city.

Continuing in a calm and reasonable voice Michael said, "Graeme, Dubai would require a huge crew- at least sixteen, and more like twenty extra guys."

"We've worked with stand-ins before."

"Yeah, four at the most, and those jobs sucked didn't they?"

He steered the car back onto Atlantic Avenue as the men debated the merits of the job. Mike made the turn onto Flatbush from Atlantic.

"You're going to..." Graeme started, and then stopped. He was going to ask if Michael thought going on the Manhattan Bridge was better than using the Brooklyn Bridge, or even the Williamsburg. But that was like asking Picasso if he thought that blue was an appropriate color. Michael Davidson knew what he was doing, and that rankled Graeme. Irritated him to no end, sometimes. Somewhere along the line, Michael had become the leader. Even as far back as the Kings Bay job Michael didn't doubt that Graeme remembered the Vegas trip and his proposal to Mike that, 'I could use a guy with your skills.' Or what happened next.

***

December, 1998

Michael and Graeme had driven down from the City to the booming metropolis of Jacksonville, Florida after Vegas. The Extended Stay America had a two-bedroom place for the bargain price of $1250 for the month. They paid for it on a Sutton Industries credit card; the first time they ever setup a fake company to hide their activities. It was Mike's idea and execution. The place was basic in that it had a small living room, kitchenette, and each bedroom had an en-suite. Situated at the 295/95 beltway north of Jacksonville, it was perfect for their needs.

Graeme's job turned out to be Petty Officer Third Class, Submarines, Allen Rossum. He was married to Graeme's second cousin. Rossum knew a few things: Graeme had a reputation in the family as a thief, a Third Class Petty Officer in the US Navy made less than $19,000 a year in pay, and the Compass Point Bank on the upper base was ripe to be robbed.

The three men had held several meetings at the inn while they planned the robbery. Rossum was assigned to the USS Pennsylvania SSBN 736 Gold Crew as a Sonar Technician. The ballistic missile carrying submarine was home- ported at the gigantic Kings Bay Naval Base north of Jacksonville, just over the Georgia state line about ten miles away from their hotel. The base was home to four of the huge submarines, their crews and families, with another five due in to the place after they were finished being constructed in Connecticut. The base itself was over 30,000 acres, divided into an upper section and lower section. The lower section was where the submarines were outfitted and loaded with the missiles, while the upper part contained the support areas that made the place a small city. Commissary, gym, housing, training facilities, and offices. And, most importantly, a bank.

Significantly, the upper base was also where a whole detachment of Marines were housed. 350 strong, the Marines were on hand to protect the nuclear weapons from terrorists. Neither Mike nor Graeme were keen to take on U.S. Marines.

"In any scenario, the Marines are directed to SWFLANT to protect the warheads," Rossum told them.

"SWFLANT?" Michael asked.

"Strategic Weapons Facility Atlantic," the young Navy man told them. "That is the place they store the warheads until they get loaded onto the subs."

"Please! No more acronyms."

"And the Marines are not on the gates?" Donniger asked.

"Nope. Private security. Wackenhut, the same guys as at the airport," Rossum said, kind of smugly.

The men exchanged looks. That was key.

"What about the bank?" Michael asked next.

"Only one guard inside," Rossum explained. "The best part is that the alarm only goes to the local St. Mary's police department, not anywhere on base!"

"How do you know that?" Davidson demanded.

"Because a shipmate's wife is a teller. We were at a ship function and she told us they'd had a false alarm and it took the cops like ten minutes to get onto the base."

The thieves processed this. Another very critical piece. And Michael took charge saying, "Get to her. Confirm that piece of information."

"How?"

"Tell her you went in the other day and the guard was asleep on his feet. You are worried something is going to happen," Michael directed and Graeme nodded along.

The minutia and logistics took several days of planning. Both men went onto the base many times with Rossum or his wife to note procedures. They also cased the bank and found it an easy target. Potentially.

"What are we going to wear," Graeme wanted to know.

"Uniforms, of course," Davidson told him. "We will blend in perfectly if we get this right."

Rossum helped, and it reminded Mike of his first robbery. Of course, on that job he'd looked like any other college student because he WAS a college student.

Graeme wanted to wear the one-piece coverall he sometimes

watched Allen wear. Michael put that idea down.

"It helps us with tools, but we can't technically wear that off base, right Allan?"

Rossum went into detail on Navy uniforms and the rules for wearing things on and off of the base. "We have six different types of uniforms. The coverall is called a poopie suit and..." He spent twenty minutes lecturing the men.

"Is there a book that goes over the uniforms?" Davidson asked.

Rossum brightened. "Sure! At the uniform shop."

The book was procured and Michael took a crash course in Navy regulations and haberdashery. The details were fascinating to him.

"As much as our IDs and badges that get us on base, the uniforms have to be right," Davidson told Graeme, after the man complained. "If we get it right we blend in and become anonymous. Since it's Winter, the white uniforms are out. We can wear the dungaree uniforms on or off base, but not to a store or gas station so... Working blues it is!"

Graeme allowed Michael to dictate what they would wear and how they handled certain situations until that became the pattern with the two men. It was his idea to rob the place, but Michael made the details flow.

Haircuts? US Navy perfect at a cost of five dollars at the Commissary barber shop. A car was purchased for fifteen hundred cash from a sailor who was transferring. Of course, they would scrape the base sticker off and get a new one! Uniforms were obtained, tailored, and pressed.

Davidson very, very carefully attached the ribbons and warfare pins. He liked Allen's nickname for the devices: chest candy.

"Don't you get it, Graeme? A sailor's uniform has his whole career in code right on it. The chevron tells the rank; one strip for a Third Class, like Allan, up to three for a First Class. The higher ups -Chiefs and Officers- wear the beige-colored uniforms. Even the insignia on the chevron tells what kind of job you have: Sonar tech, Electronics, or even a Mechanic."

His partner was not impressed. Michael laid out the ties and the name tags they'd stolen: ET 3 Hill and ET3 Andrews would never miss them. "Just salute when I do and look bored."

Graeme grumbled, but practiced the hand salute. Details.

The final meeting took place on the 29th of December. Rossum was getting ready to deploy. That meant he would go to sea on a submarine, isolated from everyone for three plus months. Perfect.

"The base is on Christmas stand down right now. About half of the base personnel are on leave and off base entirely, so traffic and people are not around." The man went over his knowledge of what was going on. "Liberty (off time) was pretty liberal for all commands. We have to check in at the off crew offices every Tuesday and Thursday."

Allan went over how each submarine had two full sets of crews: a Blue and Gold version. "When we have the sub, we live and work on it and take it to sea. When the Goldies have it, our jobs are just like a civilian office job. Well, mostly like a civilian office job. We work 7 am to 4 pm, usually in a huge building, and go to short training schools, and other things."

Davidson had one more serious question. "What about guns?"

"What about them?" Rossum came back. "Funny thing about a Naval base is that no one is allowed to have guns. We have them on the subs, but you aren't going anywhere near there. Guns are allowed in base housing as long as they are unloaded and locked up." He grinned. "Even the Marines keep their guns in an armory. Only the security guard at the bank will have a gun. And he's much more Barney Fife than Dirty Harry."

That was fantastic news.

"So when do we hit it?" Graeme asked.

"When is this stand down thing over with?" Michael asked their accomplice.

"Monday, the sixth."

"We go Friday, the third," Davidson answered immediately. "That is perfect for us. The bank will get in money for the upcoming weekend, and the upcoming week when they are going to be hella busy with sailors coming back from vacation."

"Leave," Rossum corrected.

"Whatever."

Thursday, the 2nd of January, they checked out of the Extended Stay Inn, after packing carefully and wiping down the place. They had all the equipment and clothes they would need for the next day. A shit bag Motel Six, on the highway 40 exit from I-95, was a huge step down in terms of comfort, but it was anonymous and had easy access to the base. They drove the operational car and the car they'd driven down to Jacksonville with over to the new motel. Backpacks held the things they would need for the actual robbery. Taser, gun, zip ties, spray paint, latex gloves, and collapsible duffel bags.

On Friday, two impeccably dressed young sailors checked out of the motel. At 9:32 they started towards the base in the new used car, backpacks beside them. A quick cell call to Rossum announced they were moving and he was in position at the main pass and ID office. That was not the access point for the two robbers, however.

They were going to a smaller checkpoint commonly called the St. Mary's gate. The ten-mile drive took no time as the traffic was light and the roads were new and wide with dark blacktop. Graeme had never seen such nice roads before. He remarked on them to Michael. "Focus!"

The gate was a non-event. A standard ID check of the sticker on the car and their badges. The bored private security man barely glanced at them or the faked badges. The pair drove onto USS Benjamin Franklin drive. Every street was USS something on this place. There seemed to be zero traffic around. "Everyone is on vacation." Michael reassured him. Nerves and tension ratcheting up as they drove.

A left onto USS James Madison as the men went past the gigantic red brick training building they'd seen on numerous visits. Mike always thought the base looked like a cross between a college campus and a prison complex.

Keeping strictly to the speed limit, the men put on latex gloves and the black combination caps that would hide their faces along with the sunglasses. Luckily, the weather was bright enough to justify the eyewear. Neither spoke as they pulled into the bank parking lot. Only five other cars in the large lot. Good, not many customers at the 10:00 am opening besides the four workers they knew to be inside. Into the trunk to gather their gear. Packs held low and ready.

The pair hit the door hard. Graeme immediately pulled the taser he held low at his side and shoved the black box, cracking and snapping, into the guard's side. The man arched, gave a strangled cry and went down like a lead weight.

Michael, trusting his partner, continued into the bank proper and had eyes only for the manager. He put aside his feelings for a second to allow himself the space to work.

Shoving the gun forward, he shouted, "Stop!" at the woman. The heavy set fifty-five yearold woman with a very, very out of date hairstyle froze with her hand near the alarm button.

"Uh Uh. Move over here. Come out from behind there!" His command now took the other two tellers into account.

All three women joined the one elderly male customer and the young female account holder on the patron side

of the divide. All of the people, whether customer or employee were wide-eyed and ashen with shock. A glance back at Graeme showed the guard down and zip tied and that he'd locked the door with the closed sign out facing. Good. Graeme next pulled the spray paint out of the pack and blocked the camera lens at the entrance.

Michael was busy zip-tying the hands of everyone and getting them set down out of sight of the door. The whole process took four minutes. Getting the patrons and guards secured without incident eased a giant knot in Davidson's stomach.

A shot of black paint got the back- angled camera. The men opened the back packs again and started pulling out the lightweight duffle bags.

Graeme took the teller windows while Davidson broke for the vault. Per procedure the door was wide open at this point. The money was still in the bulky satchel bags from the armored car company delivery. That was kind of them. Bundled wads of cash started going into the duffels. Satchels went in next.

It was easy to spot the dye packs as he went through the cash. Michael actually hated to grab the fifties and hundreds in the bundles. Twenties were untraceable, but hunddy's? Serial numbers were all accounted for on those.

It became problematic to spend large stacks of hundreds right after a robbery, but he took them as greed overcame reluctance. Graeme joined him in the vault. "Time?"

"Eleven minutes total," Graeme told him checking his watch. The vault camera showed their profiles as they zipped up the duffels and checked for anything left behind. Neither said a word to the frightened people as they walked past them on the way out. Graeme locked the door behind him. Both men walked -*walked* to the car and put their duffels and packs into the trunk. Gloves stripped off and shoved into pockets as they drove off fourteen minutes after pulling into the lot.

Despite every nerve and instinct yelling at him to 'RUN', Michael Davidson calmly turned left at the light onto USS Stimson Avenue. He cruised past the auto garage and the gas station and up to the main gate guard shack. There was no check going out of the base. Graeme always said that the left across traffic and into the main pass and ID parking lot took the most balls that he had ever seen. The lot was half full of sailors, contractors, and other visitors completing the hoops the Navy wanted everyone to go through in order to get onto their secure facility. Lots of sailors exchanged cars here, so what they did was not even strange at all.

Michael pulled in next to Rossum sitting in his car. The man was pale behind the wheel.

"Easy sham," Graeme told him. "No problems and no one got hurt."

A huge breath escaped the man. Mike was back at the trunk shoving tens and twenties into a back pack. Allan was getting a flat $40,000 for the job. He was actually lucky. $40,000 in tens and twenties was automatically spendable cash. He would not have to launder the money at all.

Setting the pack onto the back seat of Allan's car, Michael said, "Go to sea as planned, man. Use that to pay cash for everything for a while. Slowly, SLOWLY, put that into the bank over the next year and boom, you have a nice nest egg."

"And shammer," Graeme warned, "don't call us for money in six months."

The pair watched as Rossum went onto the base with no issues. Back into the car and off the base property, the men started the clean-up process. The cars were wiped down. Uniforms, tasers, and guns went into plastic bags, and then into an Arby's Dumpster off the highway. Graeme and Michael split the remaining $244,000. The men drove straight through seventeen hours to New York City in the two cars and dropped them off at a chop shop around 5 am. The pair stopped for breakfast while Graeme read the newspapers and ate. Michael settled for juice and worked on his nerves.

"Thirty-two minutes those people lay there before they worked their way free." The grin on the Irishman's face was ear to ear as he read the short article on the robbery.

The police suspected deploying sailors had robbed the bank, but they had zero leads about the money and no good description beyond young, white sailors. But the robbers still had one problem.

The money, what were they going to do with the money?

"I've got some ideas about that," Mike told his partner.

Davidson had some ideas about what to do with the money and Graeme knew a guy. The two discussed which way to go.

The Irishman had to admit that when he won out over Mike's plan to establish a false company to move the money through, the results were less than perfect.

Feydor Slutskaya did indeed take the money off their hands- at a price. Both walked away with $80,000, which was actually pretty good for fenced money. What's more, it came in the form of cash with receipts that made it look like they'd pawned something to get the cash, so the cops or the banks could not squawk.

Michael managed to hold back a few bundles of the $100s. "Just some emergency money, in case we need to run."

The shit side of the whole deal was Feydor. The fence was bad news, and connected to even worse people, if that could be believed. And Graeme had connected the two thieves to him. It wasn't long before they were pulling jobs at Feydor's behest, and then directly for Demetry.

The upshot? Michael just seemed to take over like he had in Georgia. He figured out things and it worked. Worked well! Michael became the thief-in-law, not Graeme.

***

Present Day

The car plodded along Atlantic Avenue, back towards the Barclays Center, while Graeme mused on his status with Mike. He remembered. Remembered the nerves and the tension on that first job together. Now, Mike was floating through life, while Graeme could not catch a break. Money, looks, and leadership. Sometimes it just boiled down to a man wanting to be respected. Even just listened to. He knew they could pull off Dubai. He just *knew it*. After a long silent period, Graeme started, "Mikey, let me take Dubai to Demetry."

He was horrified. "No! God, no! Graeme don't you understand, Roybokov is in some kind of trouble. Big trouble. I think he owes huge scratch to some global money guys. Not the crap you owe the leg breakers, more like $300 or even $500 million. I'm not sure about that yet." Michael concluded as the truck started across the Manhattan Bridge. The one-way bridge was perfect for getting into this part of the main borough. "If he does owe that much, then he will grasp at anything to get him out of trouble."

"Then that makes Dubai perfect," Graeme crowed. "This is the answer to his prayers! With him to back us we are covered..."

"Man, you are not listening," Michael said coldly. "We can't pull off Dubai! Hell, we can't rob Fort Knox, either. You tell that man we can do it- If you get his hopes up, and then something goes wrong- He will kill us all."

Graeme did not want to hear that, so he shook his head.

Davidson overrode him. "You, me, Ira, Gretchen, and our families. Anyone he can get to." Michael went on coldly. He had to make the man see he was playing with fire.

Graeme finally looked his friend in the eye.

He returned the stare. "You know me, man. Eighteen years we been doing this. Have I ever played you? Lied to you?"

The answer was a grudging, "No."

"I've worked it a billion times in my head. Your plan isbrilliant. Simply brilliant. No one could come up with better- but the Ministry and the mercenaries.... They add a dimension we've never seen before, man. Without a serious breach in the Ministry, or something else happening, we can't do it. We can't get close to the gold."

Maybe the flattery about his plan got him, but Graeme finally came one atom's worth over to the other side. He remained silent, however. Michael mistook that silence from his partner.

He played his only remaining card with his long-time friend.

"If you want to do this, if I can't talk you out of it, then go to

Roybokov and put it to him. You can put your own crew together and try it. We would end our partnership, though," he concluded, sadly.

Head whipping around, Graeme snapped, "You'd do that buck!?"

"To save my life, I would," Michael said, dead serious, no pun intended.

"You keep saying that, but Demetry wouldn't... not you!"

"Your first task on Tuesday is to find out why a shitty brown Crown Vic was sitting outside my house for three hours last Thursday."

Irish stared at him like the man had grown a second head.

"I'm not paranoid, I have the video tape to prove it."

"Shyte!" Graeme breathed.

"Indeed." Davidson steered the truck off the bridge onto Eldridge while Graeme worked through the ramifications of Michael's revelation. He didn't like anything that car represented. He was silent while working it over. Nothing immediately sprang to mind as to why that car was their however.

This section of streets in Manhattan was a maze of one way roads. Michael hated it. He kept turning left to get around towards 2nd street. At least this area was plowed.

Finally, he pulled up in front of the Brownstone set in front of the New York Marble Cemetery which was across the street from Graeme's house. The penthouse was Graeme's only smart purchase. $6 million three years ago after the Paris job put the man into a stable housing situation. Mike was willing to bet the amount of mold in the refrigerator would be frightening. He hadn't been in the place in two years.

Graeme pulled his bags out of the bed and stuck his head into the window.

"Thanks, Mikey." He had the grace to acknowledge that, at least.

"Rest. We will come at it fresh on Tuesday."

Michael started on the drive home as Graeme went on up. Neither of them saw the two other men watching them from the white Olds parked down the street.

Chapter Three

Tuesday, November 3rd, 2012 was cold, cold, and more cold. The wind was the main problem. It bit and cut through a person without regard for anything. Michael heard a woman on the sidewalk waiting to get into the coffee shop tell her friend, "This wind is disrespectin' my jacket!" He fucking agreed with that. He headed for the office on Jones Street. Arriving at the offices of Anderson Consulting around 9:50 to find Ira already in and a box of bagels on the table, Michael realized he was hungry. A nice lox schmear slathered on and a yummy good bagel fixed that problem. Ricky came in at 10:00 with Gretchen hard on his heels. Graeme finally strolled in at 10:20. The group was quiet and subdued as Davidson sat in his office.

Seeing the final member come in, the boss gave him some time to get a cup of coffee and a bite, and then he came out to address his troops.

Everyone called this the living room area because the couch was placed here. Cable TV was on and was showing the usual digital static. Michael hated it when the picture suddenly pixilated and scrambled up. The problem was the substation, he knew, but he had no idea on how to fix it. No matter the amount of shielding they put on the cable, the EMI seeped into the bones of the TV, like the cold wind did to them today. The others looked at him expectantly.

"Morning. How was everyone's time off?"

It was anything but an innocuous question. Both for the fact some cops were watching him, and he wanted to see if the others had noticed something, but also for an incident from more than eight years ago. A long weekend was followed by a session in the office when Ira casually forgot to mention he'd been arrested for shoplifting. The court summons was the first Mike heard about it much later. A lousy pendant was all the man had stolen.

"Jesus! What the fuck Ira?" he'd asked at the time.

"It was just sittin' there, Mikey- I thought Gretchen might like it."

This was before the two were a couple. At the mention of her, Gretchen had blushed and said yes, she might like a pendant. Graeme had snickered while Michael fumed. Lawyers, money and time got Ira into a diversion program. Other than the occasional speeding ticket, it remained the group's lone brush with the law.

Today, the gang members just shrugged and said nothing of consequence.

"Ricky? What did you do this weekend?"

The Oregon born and surfer blond pretty boy gave his cheekiest grin. "Spent some time with a girl I know. Nothin' much, really."

Michael was satisfied and pleased with the youngest member of his band. Ricky used to work at the local Dunkin' Donuts, where Mike got his coffee. He hated Starbucks coffee-too burnt-tasting and it gave him bad heartburn. The two struck up a friendship based on nothing.

Rick Sanderson was a barista from the west who took a quick liking to Michael. He was in junior college trying to figure things out.

His stepfather had moved them to Brooklyn after an Army career and Rick couldn't seem to find his direction. Some long conversations with the kid told Mike that Rick was very smart, but unfocused. In 2008, they'd needed an extra hand for the Paris job and Rick came along. He was a natural. Now twenty-six and headed for what seemed like a life of crime, Michael had some minor parental twinges over that. He just nodded to the young man at his description of his weekend's activities.

"Ira? Gretch?"

Both people on the couch smiled. "We got to AC just before the roads shut down and spent the weekend at the Trump." Gretchen popped up with this answer. Her accent trilling the rolled R in 'Trump'.

"How'd you do?" Graeme, the other main gambler in the group, wanted to know.

"Down two," Ira admitted.

Which meant probably seven or eight thousand down, Davidson knew. He also knew that having grown up poor in Rio, Gretchen would not let Ira lose a lot of money. She acted as a break on his wilder impulses and he served as a faithful presence for her.

She had abandonment issues, Michael knew. Well whatever, it seemed to work for the pair. He didn't know their current marital state. He figured they would tell him if it became an issue. They weren't going to step out on each other based on the number of times the dark-skinned woman casually stroked Ira's arm. And every time she did the man smiled back at her, so they were good.

"Since I know Graeme just got back, and I was home all weekend, I'm going to call that a win for us despite the setback from the weather. Graeme, where do we stand in Antwerp?" Michael asked.

Graeme stretched a bit, still working through the jetlag. "I wiped down and sterilized the flat, and returned the car to the storage unit. I paid off Andersjack," he announced. That was their contact in the Antwerp customs shipping area. "Not his fault the weather turned."

The contact was a very valuable commodity for the gang. No one begrudged the man his money.

"What ID did you travel home under?" Gretchen wanted to know.

"Same as I went out on- Peter McNichol. UK resident with a work visa. The passport and visa still have nine months on them, I'd like to keep this one- ya?"

The Brazilian smiled, and said, "Certainly." She ran their papers, and she was the best Michael had ever seen. Far be it for him to get in the way here; they were pros.

"The van- Rick?"

"I dropped it with Carmine. He took care of it. Uniforms and everything else went into bags and the Dumpster." A toothy grin accompanied the statement.

"The guns?" Michael probed just a bit. He would never do this to Ira or Graeme, but with Rick...

The grin slipped. "Just like you told me- Filed down, and wiped down, and tossed into the river."

They'd bought illegal guns from a source of Demetry's. Davidson did not trust the men. Both the boss and the supplier.

"Good, thank you." Rick seemed mollified. "The three of us," he made a gesture to encompass the couple on the couch, "took care of the office so we are pretty far along on the wind down from the failed job. I know we missed a golden opportunity last week. We can't just grasp at the first thing to come along to try and make up - but -we need to be on the lookout for another score." A quick glance at Graeme who just stared at the TV, bored. Good, he wasn't going to bring up Dubai. "To that end- I have to- do lists." Papers made their way to each person.

Gretchen took one quick look and groaned. "Not again!"

"Your turn," Michael told the woman. She'd drawn box duty.

"This is going to take two, maybe three weeks!"

"It takes what it takes."

The storage units were another of Michael's operational ideas. The gang maintained storage boxes courtesy of the holding company in most major US and European cities. The units contained a car, IDs, clothes, a little money, and guns where they could get away with it (the US and South America mostly). The gang used the storage units whenever they had business in a city. One memorable situation had Ricky and Michael spinning away from Interpol in Paris by simply switching cars at the facility.

Gretchen would get the Boston, London, Zurich, and Rio units ready for use. Guns had to be cleaned, plus the bills for the units were on auto-pay, but they got suspicious if no one ever showed up. She would ensure the leased cars were licensed correctly, clean, ran, and then gas them up. Also, she would see to the maintenance, if any was required. Burner cell phones had to be updated. All in all the job was easy but time consuming. Michael handed her a list and a full packet of paperwork from many different countries, detailing her duties and requirements. Gretchen would also take some replacement fake passports and her disguise kits for each unit, so they could do simple things like dye hair and put on a fake beard, if they needed to change a look in a hurry. It was necessary, but boring work.

"Anderson Consulting will pick up the tickets, just input the route as you go, and don't forget the keys!" Michael told her.

"Yes, boss." Gretchen looked good even when pouting. Ira bent over to speak to her and she soon left to get started.

The boss turned his attention to Ricky. He usually got the shit jobs, but this time Michael had something of substance. "I want you to do the New York box."

He handed over a detailed list for the man to work from. Sanderson went over the list, and said, "I got this. If I have any questions I will come to you."

The work would take the kid three or four long days. The plates needed renewing, and the gang kept more tools and some operational cash on the storage unit, as well as a grab box for when they went overseas. The grab box was something they could take on the plane or even mail over if they had to. They stored guard uniforms in here, workman vests, and even hardhats. The place was kind of a mess which was why Mike wanted it organized again. The facility was off the Van Wyck, near the airport.

Entrusting Rick with this job was a step up and a test for the man. Davidson wanted to see how he responded.

Graeme and Michael watched Sanderson step out of the office with a purpose to his walk. The Irishman soon brought up something much more urgent. "Cops outside my door this morning. I lost them coming in."

"Fuck! Get on this please. We need to know who is running them."

The man went into the corner desk area to make some phone calls.

The only people left in the living room area were Ira and Mike.

"Cops?" Ira quirked an eyebrow with the question.

"Uh, hum. Saw two by my place, too. Be on the lookout, okay?" Michael wanted to downplay the thing until he knew what was going on. He didn't want to hide anything, just minimize it. His friend was willing to go along.

"How was Sunday?" Ira wanted to know. He felt the problem between Mike and Graeme was a much more serious problem than some police who may or may not be watching them.

Sighing, Davidson just shrugged. "Okay." No sense hiding his frustrations. The situation with Graeme affected them all.

"Take South America," he directed. "I'll take Europe. Which half of the US do you want?"

"East," Ira said promptly, Brooklyn roots showing.

"Okay. We'll circle back to Asia and the Middle East as we can."

Crime was a global entity now that money flowed so inter-connectedly. They were forced, and lucky, to be able to go around the world for targets. But, that meant they had to go around the world for targets. The gang leader shuffled into his office to get a little distance and allow his people to work. The gang went about its business in a professional manner, and he was a hands-off boss for the most part.

One time, he'd put Gretchen on box duty and she was gone six weeks.

"Trouble?" Michael had asked when she came back in.

"Handled," was the only answer he'd ever gotten. If it was really bad, they had a 'flee' text signal they all knew.

On his way to the office, Michael discreetly put an envelope on Graeme's desk while the man was on the phone. The two men locked eyes and Graeme nodded and mouthed, "Thanks. Today."

Good. He would pay off the loan sharks. He could easily do that while trying to track down their watchers. It took time for the contact to get back to you sometimes. Everyone took some vacation time and had other things to do. It might take four or five days for Donniger to hear anything and report back.

In his office, Davidson got down to the drudgery of crime. Pulling off daring heists while beautiful women hung on you was a cool fantasy, but the reality was very different. This is where it started. A barrage of discreet phone calls and IMs in chat rooms to a hard won series of contacts began. Almost every job ever pulled off had a large percentage of inside information involved. Thieves simply could not pull off jobs without that proprietary knowledge. And sometimes even if they had it, it was not possible. He'd told Graeme they could not rob Fort Knox. No one could, short of a full scale military takeover. Same with casinos, or the vaults at De Beers. Dubai fit into that same category.

Large, fixed positions of diamonds and gold were very heavily guarded and as such, unassailable. The gang preferred much softer targets like art museums. And it was even better if the art was newly installed or traveling. Much better. So the vital piece of information could be a very minor bit. What day the exhibit moved, which flight it would be on, or the name of the company doing the moving. That kind of thing had proven valuable in the past and it was exactly the sort of info he needed now. So he crafted a very specific message to the shipping agents and customs clerks and security people that he knew in Europe. The IM was very innocuous, "Hey- we are vacationing in your area soon, any must see attractions?"

The people on the other end of that IM would respond with something like: "It's very crowded here in the early Spring- try back in the Fall." About half of the inquiries he sent got this negative response.

The other half sent this kind of reply: "The weather is perfect in early spring, you must see the D'Orsay!"

That did not mean the gang was going to rob the D'Orsay museum, just that a job in or near Paris was a possibility.

Those types of replies required a follow up e-mail or even a personal visit. Based on what was out there, Michael would sit down and evaluate the targets and see to feasibility. A round of contacts usually got three or four decent possibilities but it took months sometimes to flesh them out. One of the reasons they'd had a long dry spell was the cruise ship... fiasco? Mess? Cluster Fuck? Mike had trouble pinpointing the exact wording.

Two and a half years ago Michael Davidson saw a news story on the booming cruise ship industry. New, ever bigger cruise ships were coming on line, with some of them holding 6,000 passengers. And all of the ships held multiple bars and casinos to cater to those thousands.

Quick math went like this: 2500 rooms times fifteen dollars per day for the housekeepers tips times a ten-day cruise meant $375,000 in cash usually. The crew members would turn that money over to the cruise line for deposit into their accounts. The bars would generate another $125,000 in cash as tips. A few Miami cruises showed Michael that most people added the tips electronically so that might not be a revenue stream. However, the casino was the bigger score. About 2,000 dedicated gamblers all losing an average of $500 for the cruise and boom: a cool million.

The $1.5 million potential for the single cruise liner was not what interested the gang. The cruise terminal at Port Everglades did, however. Saturday and Sunday could see six cruise liners pull in and out of the huge facility.

People and money flowed in and out on a huge scale.

Ira and Gretchen took three cruises as a happy couple while researching the job. Graeme, Ricky, and Michael all watched the terminal building, watching money flow in and out all the time and noting procedures. A full month in Coco Beach, Florida had fully tanned everyone and caused some serious weight gain in Ira, but they could not seem to justify the job. The main money was in the casino, but it held problems as well. The ships held almost $2 million, in case people got lucky, and for the ATM's stashed onboard. But most of that money *stayed onboard.* All five of them spent a full week in the Bahamas trying to figure out how to steal that money off the ship. Yeah, you could steal it, but what then? Pitch it overboard? Too risky.

A chance comment in a dive bar on the docks perked up Michael's ears: Two of the huge ships were going for repositioning and would be undergoing a full week of refit before they moved. *The money would have to come off the boat!*

Based on a burst of activity in the schedule, Michael figured there might be $10 million moving out on Sunday, the fifth of May, at the cruise facility. Both the repo ships would be offloading all of the cash onboard as well as the regular moves. $10 million was a tempting target. They planned it like the KLM job: duplicate armored car guard uniforms and paperwork. Walk in early and snatch the cash and go. And a week before the magic date the company changed up its practices. The money started going off by helicopter, landed right on the upper deck of the building, instead of armored car.

Davidson knew the shock on his face mirrored Ira's as the two men watched the money fly off. A few discrete inquiries showed them the cruise lines changed up operations every few months. That ended that idea.

"I got a good tan and Ricky learned how to snorkel," Ira had summed up. Good thieves...check that, live thieves knew when to pass on a job.

Hours later, stretching behind his desk, Michael noticed a few replies in the chat rooms. One of them was from Trevor. He was another one of their De Beers contacts.

The diamond monopoly held site's every month so he was always a favorable reply to these requests. Michael Davidson loved stealing from De Beers. He'd done it twice. Once on the retail end and once on the uncut side. His most fevered fantasy called for the gang to attack the London vaults where the untold diamond riches were held. His mind always conjured a Scrooge McDuck vault with piles of diamonds while he swam through them with a naked Angelina Jolie somewhere in the background. But he just couldn't do it, could not figure out that puzzle box. So again, they hit where the consortium was vulnerable. The sites were not normally one of those times.

De Beers site holdings were legendary. Another fantasy job involved the meetings. Site holdings were how the company disbursed the diamonds to its customers. Every month, a select group of retailers and wholesalers of diamonds got invites to the meeting. They showed up in London and the company gave them two items: An envelope with a bill, sometimes as much as 50 million pounds, payable in full before they got the second item: A box with diamonds in it. The customers *never* got to see what was in the box beforehand. They had no say in the quality or quantity of the stones. What was more important; they never got to complain. Bitch and the monopoly cut you out completely. How are you going to sell wedding rings with no stones?

The fantasy involved somehow swapping out those boxes with empty ones. Since no one would complain, and De Beers had stiffed people before, it seemed like the perfect crime. No one would say boo. But there was that tiny, tiny problem of how to get in there and swap out the boxes.

At least the holders never used to complain, Davidson knew. At one time the monopoly held ninety percent of the diamond market. New sources from Australia and Russia were putting a serious crimp in the business. De Beers had been forced to change up their ways. Those new sources were why the gang could hit them in the uncut area. And now Trevor had a clear message: London on the first of April is gorgeous. And the museums are free!

Fuck me, thought Michael. He made a mental note to call Trevor directly.

A cup of coffee helped start the Internet search for targets. Google was proving to be a very valuable tool for the search. He just input, '2013 traveling art show- 1 Jan to 1 July', and the results came up in a half second. News article after news article detailed the world's art as it traveled the circuit. Not that he was interested in stealing Tut's mask or the Mona Lisa, however, lesser known works were sometimes very, very valuable. A personal favorite was Fredrick Russell sculptures. Cowboys on bucking broncs brought in $2 million each. And in transit they were obtainable. Vulnerable.

He could not help turning over Dubai in his mind one more time.

In transit, that's where Graeme wanted to hit the gold. The Sultan was trying to diversify the small emirates economy by setting up the largest gold exchange in the world. Dubai was already famous for having gold vending machines, but now they wanted to catch up on the trade and jewelry aspect. A cool billion in gold was coming into the country, mostly from Switzerland. The exchange would be open in July of 2013, so the timing was right. But, the logistics! And the military style troops guarding that shipment was horrendous to deal with. He put it out of his head. Too big.

Art, on the other hand, was small and portable, just like diamonds. A quick correlation to movement of pieces and the cities and he matched up some of his friends in those places and the firms likely to be called upon to work security. More messages flew.

When a noise caused him to look up, Michael realized it was 4:00 pm. Alone in the office, a quick check of the big calendar in the main area showed red pins for Graeme and Ira on Thursday.

Ricky hadn't been back today so he might be done by the time everyone rolled in later in the week. A pin followed the trend for the boss. No sense in killing himself working.

The drive home was uneventful. No Crown Victoria waited for him outside his apartment nor any other car. Lights on in 184 as he got near the house; the new owner looking around. He hoped like hell it wasn't a Wall Street hedge fund asshole who'd bought the place.

He nestled the car into the garage. A check of the video showed Mary sitting on the couch, watching TV and snoozing. Good. He didn't feel like socializing tonight.

Upstairs he culled the junk mail, changed clothes, and started a quick dinner. Just a soup and salad. He ate it man style; in sweats and an old t-shirt with fuzzy moccasins on his feet. Straight out of the pot for the soup and straight from the box for the salad. A tad sloppy, but all he could muster tonight.

"Drink it in, ladies," he said to his reflection in the refrigerator shine. A sigh. Single, and likely to stay that way.

"So what do you do?"

That fucking question always got him. He could lie, but it just seemed like, what was the point? Starting a relationship with a lie was kind of an oxymoron. It seemed self-defeating.

He'd done it years ago, right after he'd moved in. Victoria. Pretty, smart, and a lawyer. She worked on some stuff for Anderson Consulting and sent some signals. He picked up on those signals and they dated for a good six months. Until that fucking question came up. Davidson admitted to cheating on her just to avoid the real question of, "What are you hiding?"

That sucked. But what also sucked was the stream of prostitutes he saw for a while. Then he discovered Tinder.

Holy shit! Michael met a ton of bored, divorced professional women around thirty-five years old on the 'dating app'. However, the basic problem with them was still the same as the professionals. What was the old complaint about hookers? "I just didn't feel the love!"

A soft snort escaped. Graeme did not have this problem. He could say anything to any girl. Michael had seen him do it. Ricky? He hated that kid- his youthful good looks and nature- right then. Ira and Gretchen had each other. Well, that was nice for them, he had to deal with his own reality. He went through the bedroom and into the closet to access his personal office. Something had to be found to keep Roybokov off their backs.

Logging onto the same chat rooms and websites as before, he waited to see if Europe had changed status now that it had woken up.

A small news item caught his eye. KLM was selling off the 747 involved with the 2005 Diamond heist. A small smile played on his lips.

The KLM job was his second favorite burglary. It was the gang at its best: just the four of them (Ricky not yet a part) and sheer balls. *Balls!* A tip led them to know that a large package of diamonds was running into Antwerp. His crew was perfect! Perfect! Schiphol Airport in Antwerp provided the stage. Antwerp was, still is, will always be, the diamond cutting and polishing capitol of the world.

Roughly eighty percent of the market in uncut stones ended up in the Belgian capitol for cutting. The legitimate trade was worth $20 billion a year. The blood trade worth another five. The critical tip came from another anonymous customs clerk. The monopoly was engaged in a huge price war with the Russians and the Australians. D flawless stones went from thirty thousand dollars per carat down to six thousand as the company flooded the market hoping to crush the new competitors.

However- in doing that they had to give up some of their famous control. De Beers cut and polished in London when they distributed out cut stones. Most of the carat weight from the sites would be in rough stones, but some would be cut if the stones were particularly fine. Those retailers and wholesalers would then move the uncut stones to Antwerp for work before getting them back for setting and sales. In 2005, what the customs person told them was De Beers had to move a huge stash of stones out to Antwerp for cutting due to a higher volume level beyond the capacity in London.

Vulnerable.

Davidson and Donniger found out who was transporting the stones and what flight they would be coming in on. A duplicate van, uniforms, and paperwork, plus endless hours of drilling readied the crew. The job went off like clockwork. The four of them (even Gretchen disguised as a man) pulled the armored transport van up to the gate. IDs and badges were perfect and the paperwork was all in order. Michael spoke to the cargo master and customs agents on the tarmac. Stamps and signatures and receipts were exchanged. Lot 245779 was dutifully signed for and transferred. The other two men hauled the seventy-nine pound crate into the van without issue, while the little one drove.

Fourteen minutes after passing the gate, the van exited the tarmac secured area and flowed into traffic off the grounds.

The cargo master knew he was screwed the instant he saw the second van turn onto the tarmac from the gate area. That van was held up on Konigsberg Road by an accident, sorry they were late.

The smile on his lips broadened as he remembered the real fun of the job: The aftermath.

The police reported $160 million in diamonds stolen. The real total was more like $271 million. And no diamonds were ever officially recovered. Michael knew ten of the best stones were taken out and cut and turned into a stunning necklace that he'd seen both on Mrs. Roybokov and on Demetry's mistress. The rest of the stones? That was a good story...

***

Summer, 2005

Davidson sat at a beach-side table near a regulation thatched hut tourist bar on Grand Cayman Island. The sun beat down on him and he sweated in his suit, with his underclothes also heating him up. Maybe it was the eighty-two degree, tropical heat or the number of sniper rifles trained on him. The earpiece squawked telling him about the helicopter. And the snipers. He was confident, but cautious about this part. Compartmentalized.

Two months after the KLM job, it was time to get paid. You can't eat diamonds and they had to get money. The bar was almost deserted at this time, but the beach was strangely busy and allocated with people. A large swath of open beach was directly behind Mike, with two groups of sunbathers on either side. There also seemed to be twenty Jet Skis at the water's edge. Clicks in his ears indicated his people were in position. He looked up to see a man in a dark suit coming towards him. Davidson carefully reached into his jacket pocket and started laying out pictures on the tabletop.

The man neared the table. Geoff Pedersen- De Beers head of security and an Afrikaner. Michael picked up two pictures.

"Good morning, Geoff. One- Tell those guns not to get itchy and two- that helicopter has to go." Michael spoke with a German accent with a faint speech impediment. It was his favorite voice impression. Just a hint of Colonel Klink from Hogan's Heroes.

Pedersen noticed the picture the thief was holding. He spoke while watching that picture, "I'll kill you myself if you threaten my kids- Ya?" The South African was accent thick.

Davidson shook his head. "Geoff, you need to listen to me. I don't want to kill your children. And I won't as long as things go like they are supposed to. Any problems and they will pay the price. And what's worse- you don't get the diamonds." His acting abilities were never better.

Pedersen scowled and said nothing. Mike could see the wheels in the man's head measuring and figuring.

"I know one of those guys could get me right now," he said, voice low, meaning the gunmen. "You think, 'I could do it and move the kids to my sister's in Lion's Head.'" Michael named the area of Cape Town where the sister lived. He showed Geoff a picture of the villa and the woman.

"Or maybe even Aunt Tarla's place in Rissington." Again the photo accompanied. "Hell, worse comes to worse, the mistress in London." Another picture of the stunningly pretty woman.

Pedersen locked eyes with Michael who gave him back the best death stare ever.

"Problem for you is- we know about them. And we know about the kids of every security person who works for you." Michael gestured at the table, at the smiling, happy, little faces. "We work for exactly the same kind of people, you and I. My boss would think nothing of killing every one of these people. You- and your boss -need to wrap your heads around this: You've lost. You really want to go to the mattresses with us?"

Pedersen was white under his dark tan. Shock visible, he could say nothing.

"Say it, Geoff- 'lost. I've lost.'" Nerves and fear walled off, his voice was hard and emotionless.

"I lost."

"Good. Now get those gunmen off me and move that fucking chopper!"

The security head spoke into his cufflink. Corresponding clicks reached Michael's ear a few tense seconds later. Davidson breathed easier, but kept sweating. He did not want to kill children, and was sure he could not really do it, but he could damn well act like it.

"The transfer," his voice, high and soft, was somehow scarier to Pedersen. The agent reached into his jacket and pulled out a phablet. He sat the device on the table and in the chair opposite. Michael gave him a bunch of numbers to accounts. He watched as $100 million went into numbered Cayman Island accounts.

"You got the bearer bonds?"

Another hard stare from the Afrikaner.

"You guys get these things for pennies! Just think of this as the cost of doing business."

An envelope was produced and sat on the table. It was thick.

Michael took the envelope and ran a small device over it that he'd pulled from his pants pocket. A small beep.

Davidson stiffened. He opened the envelope and found the tracker- a wafer thin device glued onto one corner of the bonds. "You fuck! You were told to come alone. You were told no guns, no helos, and no tricks!" Davidson pinned the man opposite with a stare. "Pick which child dies." His voice was utter calm and held disdain.

"Wait!"

"Pick, you lousy fuck!" Rage made him stand. This was the hard part: the man had to *believe*.

Pedersen grabbed at his sleeve, standing as well. "No!"

Michael shoved him off and calmed down. A voice in his ear fed him some info.

"Back that tracker van off two hundred yards."

Pedersen gave the order and sat back down and Michael was mollified. The corner was nipped off the offending bond and the packet went into a foil pack which was in turn wrapped in a

waterproof bag. "That stunt is going to cost you, Geoff." Michael watched him for a second. "Give me your watch!"

The De Beers agent balked. He wanted to get out his gun and shoot him, Davidson knew. But: Davidson held the upper hand and he wanted those diamonds.

"You want to unleash this carnage? We have the $100 million. My boss will not think that is enough- he wants the full $175 million. You want the deaths of every offspring in your division on your head? The mob is vindictive like that."

The man unlatched the Rolex from his wrist and handed it over. Michael slipped it into the bag.

"Now stand." A little more work and he was clear.

He did so, as Michael walked back a few steps. Steady on his feet, Davidson was proud and continued his hard line stance. "Hands at your sides, arms out," Michael directed.

The man complied. "Where are the stones?"

"Move four paces to your left and two forward."

Michael moved further back towards the surf as he began stripping off clothes. Clicks sounding in his ears as he tore out the ear piece which told him what he needed to know.

"Where!" Pedersen was frantic, almost reaching for the gun in his leg holster.

"Another pace forward."

Twenty yards now separated the men and growing as he moved back. Beach goers started to move, converging, swirling around Davidson. Ira and Gretchen mixed in with the two groups of sunbathers as men and women flooded the area.

"Perfect," Michael called. "Buried about two feet down right under your feet!"

Pedersen dove for the ground to start digging frantically, calling into his cuff. Greed for the gems overriding his vengeance for threatening his children.

Sprinting the last ten yards into the surf, Davidson yanked off his trousers and shoes. The bathing suit was revealed as the jet skiers all converged, Graeme among them as they swarmed the water side. A minute later the pair was running parallel to the beach out of range, while the helo swooped in to crisscross the area. Davidson whooped in joy. Both that he'd gotten away with it, and that no one had gotten hurt.

The great thing about Cayman banks and bearer bonds is that you can conduct business shirtless in a bathing suit and with no ID other than account codes. $75 million went into his accounts.

***

In his home office on Washington Avenue, Mike opened the drawer to find his favorite watch: A gold Rolex. He loved stealing from De Beers!

He went back to his search, warmed by the memory. It was getting colder and he needed to find a score.

Chapter Four

Thursday morning was chilly at forty-one degrees in Brooklyn. Davidson woke early at 6:45 to see the clear, but still dark skies. Dawn was taking its sweet time and he had to get moving. Deciding to run in the park was an easy call. Ft. Greene Park was the revolutionary home of Nathaniel Greene, so the name came naturally. He loved the park. Not just for its nice trees, but also for the large wide running and biking paths that crisscrossed the area. A few other early rising runners were milling about as the light got bright enough to see by. Most were doing stretching exercises getting ready to work out. Eschewing the ballet moves, a series of twenty-five jumping jacks served as a warm up and he started off running.

Down Washington, he crossed by his house for the first time. He ran a vague figure eight pattern and then a perimeter run to finish off. His pace was fast, and Michael liked to run alone. It served to free his mind and allowed for his best thinking to come naturally. One small part of that mind set the 5:54 mile pace and set his feet and breathing on its rhythms. His compartments showing again.

The rest of his brain got to roam free and deal with his problems and concerns. Often his mind would make connections while running that he never would have in a conscious state. Who was following him, staking him out? Cops, he knew, but who? And why?

The more important question might be; what was he going to do about them when the answers to the other questions appeared? Kill them? Not a viable solution. The cops were also following Graeme, which meant they knew some of his gang. He made a mental note to check with Ira to see if the man had noted someone following him after their previous conversation. Same with Ricky, he supposed.

Arms swinging fore to aft, he breathed deeply and noted a runner ahead of him a ways. You can't kill cops. Bad for business. No- not just bad, but stupid. Some cops were crooked as the day was long, but you still couldn't kill them. All 18,000 of their New York City brethren would take it badly, if you did. Funny, it didn't matter what shit the dirty cop had pulled, if he wore the blue, in a cop's world it was Us vs. Them. Any hint of a criticism put you into the 'Them' category, let alone kill one of them.

The gang had one tenuous contact in the FBI and a few better ones on the city police force. The best contact they had with law enforcement was the Interpol agent in Paris. Rarely did they reach out to these men and women and this did not rise to that level yet. Yet.

"She runs well."

The thought bubbled up and burst on his forebrain. He was slowly gaining on the runner ahead of him, who was a female. Strange, in that he usually passed other runners without a hitch, but this woman was running along nicely. White Asics (expensive ones, he noted), black Lycra tights, a white runner's coat with a burnt orange Long Horn logo.

Great, a Texas fan. White knit headband and mittens. Those tights were gracing a pair of long, long legs with an ass to die for perched on top.

That part kept getting nicer as he overtook her. Davidson put on a burst of speed. Just upped the pace to 5:45 per mile for a few hundred yards. He pointedly did not look at her. Her fluid strides fell in behind him, arms pumping along while she breathed evenly. Part of the 'not looking at her' was fear. Michael did NOT want to look at a sixty year-old face attached to that ass. Selfish, but there it was.

They both settled back into the normal pace as his mind wondered free again. Experience taught that he would soon be alone on the path as he wound down the miles. Three in with six more to go. Let's see in thirty minutes where she was.

Roybokov was his real worry. Davidson had a small clue why the Bratva head was so insistent on a job from the gang. Money was needed, that was obvious. Why?

The Russian mob was still a powerful moneymaking organization. Drugs, loan sharking, and prostitution were all still on the table. Thieving still brought in money, as items tended to fall off trucks on a regular basis. However, the US Attorney in Manhattan was on another organized crime kick. Every US Attorney wanted to make a name for him (or her) self as a defeater of the mob.

Terrorism consumed everything in law enforcement for a few years after 9/11, but the cycle came back round to the mob in the last few years. The other leg of that problem was also the fault of the Jihadists. Opium was dirt cheap as a result of the Afghan War. And now that Craigslist and Backpage were running escort ads, ordering a girl was like ordering a pizza. The third side of the triangle squeezing Roybokov was also 9/11 related: Money laundering. If anyone felt like banks were protecting their clients from the feds, watching money flow in and out, they were sadly mistaken. Even the Swiss now allowed accounts to be monitored. Tax havens still existed, but the supply of ways to move money around without the IRS or the Justice Department knowing about it was running dry. And both Michael Davidson and Demetry Roybokov were scared shitless of the IRS. Money- it boiled down to money.

Suddenly he became conscious of breathing from behind him.

"Whoo, whoo, huuuhhhh! Whooose."

Two shallow breaths followed by a deep exhale, forcing a deep inhale. It was the same pattern he used, only a feminine version. A quick glance back showed the woman behind him still, breathing regularly and another check of the fit- pro showed them seven and a half miles in. The sun was just over the trees, with the US Prison Ship Martyrs Monument visible on his right in the middle of the park. The pair was in the left hand corner of the park at Myrtle and Edward, running on the wide bike and jogging path which was clear of snow. There were still some stubborn drifts under the bushes and trees, but the park was mostly clear. Trying to regain his train of thought, he found he could only concentrate on that breathing sound from her. Who was she? He knew every wheeze and hack in the park, so she must be new. What did she look like? The temptation to turn and look at her was great. *Did she breathe like that when she fucked?* That thought slipped in. *Dammit!*

He faltered a step, thinking he could make her orgasm if he just kept up the rhythm of the run and the breathing. Another false step. His moves made her change step and breathing as well. Davidson tried very hard to put one foot in front of another for a time. Christ, he hadn't been this self-conscious on a run in ages. He managed to not trip for a time.

The runner's high kicked in around the eight mile point for him. A nice high to lead him back to the Washington Avenue corner, near the cross-training equipment. A beep from the Fit-pro showed 53:52 and 9.01 miles ran. Pulse 135 and respirations 74. Whew!

He angled off the track towards the pull-up bar and started walking with arms held behind his head as he recovered.

"Hey!"

Turning at the voice he looked right at the woman from the run.

"Thanks for the run! Your pace is fantastic! Like a metronome." She took a deep breath. "Helped me out a bunch."

Dumbstruck, he managed to get out a, "You are welcome," as he took in the sight of her.

She smiled and the oval face, blond hair, creamy skin with red cheeks and lips assaulted his vision. Thirty-two? Thirty-five at most! Gorgeous, fucking gorgeous.

The two walked and breathed and Michael struggled to get an intelligent sentence out of his mouth.

"Do you live around here?" Why couldn't he get the damn question to come out? Instead, he stared at her ass. Deciding that he wasn't going to be able to say anything intelligent to this woman, Davidson went over to the pull- up bar to begin his core routine while she turned to keep going out of the park. He thought her done when she half-turned and pitched her voice at him. "See you around and thanks for the nice view!"

Oh my fucking god!

He almost missed the bar. He cranked out the full ten pull-ups as she watched him while walking away on Washington Avenue, leaving the area before the trees blocked her from view. No way was he failing on all five sets today, even with the slight boner he was sporting.

Buoyed into a good mood by the meeting, an hour later Davidson eased the Audi out of the garage. Dressed in his corporate outfit, which consisted of pressed khaki's, blue button down shirt, and Italian made loafers and belt, he felt ready for the mail run.

The Brooklyn Central Post Office was housed in an old, Romanesque building on Cadmon and Johnson Streets. The unsubtle edifice was converted to a US District Courthouse after extensive renovations, and the Postal Service moved into the back half of the building where the trash couldn't be seen. Davidson was forced to park across the street and take a death defying trip dodging cars on Cadmon, while they sped past, to get to his destination.

Long lines greeted the regular mail customers, but the business window was less busy, as were the post office boxes. Congress was still talking about shutting down several branches of the USPS, as they were concerned that the mail service had lost $3 billion last year. Except that $2.93 billion of those losses were due to the fact that that same Congress was making the USPS prepay for the retirement of former military members who now served as letter carriers and sorters and such, regardless of the fact that no other federal agency had to do that same thing. And regardless of the fact that Congress had to okay the raise in the price of stamps, which no other federal agency had to do. And to top it all off, those assholes in Congress got free franking privileges. He thought the Constitution erred when it granted free mailing of fundraising letters or Franking to Congress. In Davidson's mind, it was a wonder more postal workers weren't running over congressmen in DC every day with those little jeeps.

A wire buggy held all the accumulated mail for Anderson Consulting LLC and for Excelsior.

Davidson wheeled the dolly over to the post office boxes to get his personal mail. His real personal mail, not Michael Davidson's. He had parents to protect as well as a sister and nephews. Michael wondered how many businesses would be ruined if the DC boys managed to shut down the post office system. Every home business in the country relied on a post office box to do its work. Just like he did, even if it was illegal. He also knew a very interesting fact that no one seemed to want to talk about: The US government sent tons of classified documents and data through the USPS. Up to Secret level classification was just fine through registered mail and the postal service. It would cost more billions to setup the various delivery companies as certified classified level carriers if everyone was forced to switch. Those idiots in DC had no clue about how things really worked when they started railing against the post office. In his mind it was a modern miracle: paste less than fifty cents to an envelope and it got across the country in three days, correctly delivered 99.99999% of the time. Let's see Fed Ex manage that with 2 billion pieces of mail a day.

Four packages were dropped off for various mail drops around the country and the world. The one urgent one was to the UK mail drop. It had US I-9 visa forms and UK work visas inside. Nine thousand GBP, and a similar amount in Euros in various denominations, were also included. It was all perfectly legal as long as the green return address card was affixed to the package and the proper stamps applied. Gretchen would gather the paperwork and the money at her end, and put it with what she had hand carried into the country to plus up the storage box in London.

The mail went into a paper bag and Davidson exited the building to start the dance against the cars again when a shitty brown Crown Victoria caught his eye, two men inside watching him like vultures. A pivot on his heel, like he'd forgotten something, and he went back inside. Stalling while he thought, Mike shuffled through his mail, dumping the junk. Should he lose them? Maybe. No, that might alert them that he was on to them. Maybe he...

Again, he exited from the building. This time the rush against traffic was completed easily and he fired up the car. Straight home, he drove with a casual pace.

Inside the garage, he watched the video until the car with the two men was parked on the park side of the street and down three doors. Another flip of the security CCTV showed Mary in her place just going about her day. *Here goes.*

Into the hallway, Michael went down the hall to Mrs. Spack's door and knocked rapidly.

"Mary? It's Michael."

"Mikey? Wait a minute, Bubbeleh."

The door opened and the tiny woman looked up at Mike. "Nu- What's with you?" she said with a twinkle in her eye.

"Just checking to see if you were alright. I saw two guys in a car outside and I wondered..."

"Hoodlums!" Mary used the strongest word she knew to describe undesirables.

"Probably not. It is nothing, I'm sure. I just wanted to see if you were okay and you are. Anyway you are too tough for any hoodlums around here." He laid it on thick. "Forget about it."

Mary Spack preened under the praise. "Shabbat dinner tomorrow night, boychik. You'll come, you'll eat. Nu?"

A real laugh over her assumptive phrasing of a question escaped from him. "Chicken and potatoes?"

"Of course!" "See you at six sharp!"

Mission accomplished.

Having dinner with the old woman was a small price to pay if his plan worked. He stood in the living room back away from the windows, watching the street, and sure enough, twenty-eight minutes later- a squad car pulled up alongside the just visible Crown Vic. Four minutes later the black and white pulled away followed by the unmarked car. Mary had done it. Michael knew the cops watching in the car would have to come up with a plausible explanation of why they were parked on the street. Because they had moved right away, he didn't think they were officially on a stakeout. If they were, the spot would have been registered with every precinct and Mary's call would not have elicited a response. That did not mean they couldn't have come up with a bullshit ploy for them to be at this address, but the regular cops would have noted the presence of the other vehicle in a report. Since they hightailed it out of the area, it told him the watchers were not on an official mission. At least that he knew of. He put up the fundraising letter from his nephews basketball team and got back into his car. He needed to see if Graeme had found anything.

***

Three members of his crew were sitting in the living room area of the office when he arrived. Ricky was going over the New York box list with Ira and Graeme. Excellent.

"Glad you could join us," Graeme said acidly.

Sweeping Ira and Ricky into his look, Michael related his morning with the car watchers.

"White Olds?" Ira asked surprised.

"Dammit, Ira! How long have they been watching you?"

"Hey, I just noticed them yesterday, Mikey, I swear."

"Rick?"

"Haven't seen a thing, honest, Mike."

His gaze settled on Graeme. The other men swung heads to look at the Irishman.

"Well?"

"Yeah- They are cops. Hattenfeld and Temescal out of the 74th in Brooklyn. My guy says they have been showing times on E 2nd."

Donniger told them.

Sour faces from Michael and Ira, while Ricky just seemed confused.

"Here's the rub, shammer- those two are vice cops, not burglary or even RICO boys."

That set off some synapses firing in his head. Davidson thought for a few minutes, pacing through the living room area. Ira and Graeme caught Rick up on the ramifications of cops tailing three members of the gang. The physical description was basic: Older, heavier, white guys.

"It means they know who we are!"

"It means they have a reason to watch us," Ira added, a bitter grimace twisting his lips.

The pacing stopped from Davidson. "Maybe not. What if this is connected to Semilov from six months ago?"

Alexi Semilov was the man in charge of running girls for the Bratva. Roybokov liked to have people in charge of smaller kingdoms. The Semi ran the girls, Michael was his main thief, Sergei Tikanov ran another crew for loan sharking. Drugs were handled by Viktor and his boys, Anton ran his gambling clubs, while Feydor fenced all the loot.

These units were autonomous and the structure added several layers between Demetry and the illegal acts. Six months ago, Semilov was arrested for human trafficking. Several associates (pimps) were picked up as part of a crackdown and sixteen eastern European and Asian girls were freed. The feds seemed to have a very detailed case about Alexi and his activities. The Semi wasn't talking and Demetry was strangely quiet about the loss of income.

"What if the feds are looking at Demetry's whole organization?" Michael let the thought thud out there, while he sat on the couch next to

Rick. The other three now had a turn at thinking it through. Graeme was the quickest.

"Fuckin' hell."

"Yeah," Ira agreed a few seconds later.

"What?" asked Rick.

"What Graeme and Ira are worried about, and what I suspect, is that the FBI and the US attorney might have opened an investigation into Demetry Roybokov's activities. All of them." Mike told the young man. "Roybokov is dirty six ways to Sunday: Drugs, girls, gambling, loan sharking, you name it. Semilov might have been the first shoe to drop, meaning the cops might be looking at us next."

The four men talked it out until the innocent kid asked the critical question. "How did they know to look at us?"

How indeed? Michael turned that over for a while. He wasn't sure, and not knowing was a splinter in his mind. "I don't know. We need to find out more about who these cops are and why they are keying on us."

"I can reach out to Rachel," Graeme said, looking at least a little guilty.

Yeah, reach out to your one-time fling who works for the FBI, Michael thought. He didn't say anything negative, just, "If you can do it without getting her suspicious."

It was probably the wrong thing to say, because Graeme went red-faced and his lips compressed.

Oh Jesus, he's pissed! Michael knew he'd blown it. "I'm just saying that if the FBI is focusing on us, then even making contact with her after three years is going to look bad."

That sentence took forever to penetrate the haze of the man's anger. The blinking was Davidson's indicator that Graeme was actually considering the problem and that seemed to make Graeme even angrier. The kind that did a slow burn.

"You might have no choice but to talk to her," Mike went on reasonably. "But you might need to kiss some ass while you are doing it."

His friend nodded not bothering to speak. The other two men watched the byplay uneasily.

"We can use our police contacts and you can make some inquiries right, Mike?" Ira asked, trying to derail the feud between the two men.

"Good thought. I have a person inside the Bratva I can ask a few things." Michael told them, not wanting to name names.

Rick kept his mouth shut, and let the others deal with the situation, which suited Mike fine.

Davidson went into his office and sorted through his mail, while he made some calls. Graeme finally came in to the small space and told him his debt to the loan sharks was square.

"Thanks for the help."

"No problem." The silence built for a time. "Look, why don't you look at this thing from Trevor while you are waiting for Rachel, or even the local cops, to get back to you?" he finally asked.

Head down, the man grunted an assent and left. Davidson blew out a breath. He did not know how he would survive a serious rift in his relationship with his oldest friend and business partner.

The mail absorbed him as he dealt with the problem with Graeme. Anderson and Excelsior were the two most recent versions of how he'd been laundering money for years. His consulting shell was on a yearly contract with Royal Dutch Shell for Oil Field Operational Services and

Consulting Services. $2 million a year seemed to come from RDS to Anderson, but in reality it came from the Cayman account to the States.

That allowed Michael to do a million legal things with the money. He could then use Anderson to provide himself a legitimate salary. FICA and state withholdings were all tax table perfect. His money came back clean, and ready to be spent. The IRS loved him! And the fake accounting let him do a bunch of very necessary housekeeping items. Things like lease a car and take it off his taxes, expense his flights, and the cost of dry cleaning. All legitimate business expenses. He combined his personal and LLC taxes into one entity, and that led him to a 401 (K), a deferred compensation package, and other investments. On the outside, it might look like he was paying thirty percent to the feds to launder his money, but in reality he was only paying around fifteen. That was almost $300,000 worth of 'expenses' that he got to take to allow himself to live well. The game was rigged for the wealthy and Davidson was taking full advantage.

The only real problem to all of it? He had the paperwork to go with the advantages, and it was a mountain of work. A team of shady Indian brothers who were lawyers set up everything for him. Another group of CPA's handled the government. He was constantly getting bills and statements and letters from people wanting something. If Michael had to look at one more company offering to 'help' him with his firm's health care needs, he was going to scream.

Most of everything was handled with a power of attorney and some extra fees, but occasionally he had to sign something. He enjoyed the endorsing of checks quite a lot. Since 1999 he'd been investing in US based mutual funds and stocks. His portfolio was extensive and growing. Davidson was a big believer in the power of compounding.

The last stack of mail was personal. Some from his family, but mostly it was newsletters and magazines from the oil field services genre. He wanted to be able to talk the talk if someone questioned him about the field.

Sometime during all this paperwork, Davidson reached a conclusion without realizing it. The first he consciously knew was when he placed a quick call to his mom. To anyone in the office listening, the conversation went like this: "Fine, just going out of town next week unexpectedly. Yeah that job fell through and RDS is sending me to the Norths: Dakota and Sea! Yes, mom! Actually Scotland. Yes. No! I'll be home soon and then a visit for Christmas probably. Bye!"

A change of scenery would do the gang some good. Plus, they could avoid the watchers. Next week, London.

He called the other three into his office. "Pack up! We move to London next week. Tuesday, Wednesday, and Thursday." He pointed, indicating Ira on Tuesday, himself on Wednesday, and Graeme on Thursday. "Draw 8K each from the safe. Make sure you have the right phones!" He directed the members. "Graeme under Peter McNichol again, right?" A nod from the man.

"Ira?"

"Todd Morganstern."

"Got it. I'll be under Michael Davidoff. Can you text Gretchen and get her to the regular hotel on Wednesday, Ira?"

"Sure, Mike."

"Okay- Go!" He pulled aside the younger man as he went to pack. "Rick, stay with me."

The man sat back in the chair watching his mentor.

"You ready?"

An enthusiastic nod met that simple question. "Yeah!"

"Okay- You are coming with me to London. We leave early, *early* on Tuesday to Dulles, and then overnight in DC before heading over on

Wednesday, finally arriving on Thursday. Graeme and Ira will take more direct routes, but Graeme will be the last to arrive." He detailed the flight routes for the other two. "You getting all this down?"

Rick started writing things down. "You got a good ID?"

"Roger Patton," the man answered, without hesitation.

Michael took the driver's license from Rick when he offered it. "Let's see: Address?"

"122 Daphne lane, apt. E210, Queens, New York, 01295"

"Date of Birth?"

"25 April 1988." That was Ricky's own birthday.

"Social Security Number?"

A series of numbers rattled off from Rick, which were his own SSN with the last four reversed. The key to a good fake ID is to use information very close to your own so you can remember it quickly. That, and to study the data closely.

"Good. Pack carefully. Passport, money, cell phone, and clothes. We pose as business men. We travel together, but not with each other okay?"

"I understand, Mike." More writing on his now crowded paper.

'We have a lot of work to do in London if this pans out, plus it will take a bit of the heat off of us."

"I'm not worried."

Rick left and Michael could only think that the kid should be worried. Would be worried if he had any idea of how bad Demetry Roybokov was. A person did not become head of the Bratva without stepping on people. Even his friends.

Davidson pushed some numbers on his cell phone.

"Feydor? Davidson. The crew and I are heading over to London." Normally, he might not even tell this to anyone, but he knew Roybokov would be upset by any break in pattern now. There was heavy breathing while Slutskaya said nothing for a time.

"Why and how long?" The accent telling the anger in the man.

"I've got a line on a job. It should only take a week, ten days at the most, to figure yes or no." He tried to sound upbeat, positive on the new job offering so quickly.

More heavy breathing. "Da. Demetry has a job for you when you return. You and the Irishman. Call him when you return."

Davidson was suddenly glad this call was not on speaker. Calling Graeme 'The Irishman', instead of his name, would have sent him into an apoplectic rage. Michael's head raced with thoughts. *What? Why?*

"Yeah, Okay. Any idea of what he wants us to do, so I can be ready?"

A short bark of a laugh. "Some sort of courier job is all I know."

Feydor would like that, he thought. The man liked to see Michael treated like a dog, fetching things. "Sure. I'll call as soon as we know on London."

The Russian stopped listening and dropped the call. Davidson was worried. Shit! Did he dodge a bullet or walk into a setup? He walked back out to the living room area as the other men were wrapping up their preparations.

"Gretchen is good, she will meet us," Ira reported.

"Excellent. We are safer apart for the next few days. Stay close to home and watch for anything. Everyone have the flee number?" The gang used a simple one -digit number text to tell everyone, "Get the hell out!"

"Seven," came the answer from all three. Good.

Everyone was out of the office by early afternoon. Michael could not detect any presence of the cops near his house when he returned.

Back in his own living room, he paced the floor. He needed more info. A discrete phone call to his source inside Demetry's organization was not returned. It would be, but it might take days or weeks. He racked his brain trying to figure out what was happening, but he could only come up with possibilities.

Dinner Friday was a very low key affair. Mary remarked on his absent- headedness when he missed a Jeopardy question. He was distracted waiting on word from Graeme or anyone.

"What's wrong Mikey? A girl got you down? A boy?"

"Mary! I'm not gay!" He said exasperated, "Have you been talking to my mother?"

Mary Spack grinned. "She would want me to worry about you."

"I appreciate that, but I just have some work problems. Speaking of which, I have to go out of town next week, so we need to go shopping on Saturday, okay?"

'Where you going, bubbeleh?"

"The North Sea via London," he said. Mary knew this was an oil hotspot.

"Chu! Doesn't sound like fun."

A smile played on his lips as he listened to her. "Tomorrow, noon sharp for shopping. We'll go to lunch first though. I don't want to food shop hungry."

"Don't I know it! That is why I bought all those cookies last time!" A pause from the old lady. "Can we go to Shelsky's for lunch?" Now Michael smiled wider. Mary loved Shelsky's Deli.

He shrugged. "What do they know from pastrami?" he said, in his best Jewish accent. "Mile End is better."

Mary waived away his expertise on delicatessens in Brooklyn. "They serve that Canadian thing!" She meant Poutine. "Old man Shelsky had a crush on me before the war."

The math came into his head. "What were you eleven? Twelve?"

"I was a looker back then."

A big laugh and he got up to leave. "Hey, you meet the new neighbor yet?" If anyone had it would be Mary.

"No- I hope he isn't a Wall Street putz!"

Another laugh and he bid her good night.

***

Saturday morning Michael hurriedly dressed and shuffled across Washington Avenue towards the gate that let him into the park. It was overcast and cold at 6:51 am.

His eyes roved along the path. Crap, she wasn't warming up at the cross fit area that kind of served as his start/ stop point. *Not* that he was looking for Ms. Texas in the small crowd of joggers. He started his run and didn't encounter her along the path. That threw him off. He could not lose himself in the run and he couldn't concentrate on his problems, so he had to worry about how his shirt was chaffing his nipples. Too much thinking about those legs and that ass.

Fifty-nine minutes later he approached the chin up bar with trepidation. *Just do as many as you can.* The first set went okay. The second, *meh*, the third set sucked ass. He had just started on the fourth when she appeared around the curve of the path. The blond hair and white coat marking her from a distance in the dull light. He was *not* going to strain on 8, 9, and 10 of the set while she ran by. And certainly he was not going to stare at her while she ran.

Abs cramping, arms quivering, he struggled to put chin over bar while his head tracked her like radar. A casual wave and a breathtaking smile as she went by was his reward. He dropped off the bar watching that ass recede into the distance.

Idiot! Normal people sleep in on Saturdays! He went back onto the bar for the last set and failed at 8. Body just quit on him. *Well, shit!*

Later that day eating pastrami with Mary he was distracted.

"Hello? Michael? You okay dear?"

"Gettin' old Mary. How do you stay so fit?" he asked the tiny 5' 1", 105 pound woman.

"Kosher wine," she said with a conspiratorial wink.

Nice. The lady could always make him laugh.

Tuesday at 9:30 am the car service picked him up to take him to JFK for the Dulles leg. Roll on garment bag, suitcase, and laptop case all matching, he was dressed in a grey pinstripe suit with a white oxford shirt and a red power tie. His purple pocket square was his one nod to fashion today. Just another business man on a trip. A text from Graeme last night was disturbing: "I have some news. Not good- will tell all at Whitehall."

Michael didn't press him. Better to tell the whole team in London rather than piecemeal it out. The banging and thumping from the house at 184 signaled the demo starting on the renovations. *That was quick. The hedge fund fucker was wasting no time.*

Hyper aware, Michael watched the cars go by and the pedestrians on the sidewalk looking for cops or strangers that watched him too closely. A quick text to Rick pinpointed him already at the airport. Good. He sat back and let his mind work on the cops. Who? Why? What to do?

The maxim about travel held true for Davidson on this trip: Leave plenty of time and you won't need it. Try to cut it close and karma would screw you by throwing a traffic delay into your path. He'd left plenty of time, so he sailed into the airport and into the boarding area in what seemed like no time.

It took him a few seconds to spot Rick. The kid looked good. Real good! Hair slicked back, he was clean shaved and in a navy blue suit. The blue and white striped shirt looked expensive with the silk tie. The blue tooth ear piece fit Roger Patton very well. Roger flirted

with the flight attendants waiting to work the flight. Roger had a fake Rolex though. Michael spotted it. *Need to remedy that for the kid.*

Head down he buried it in the laptop at the gate area seat. Kept it buried in grunt business work on the flight. Even checking into the Dulles airport Sheraton hotel, he managed to get some work done. More work during the dull evening in his room, trying to distract himself, and it wasn't working. Around 1:00 am he finally gave into the need and called the escort service.

"Tall, blond, and southern, please," he told the female voice.

"Miss Dallas will be with you within the hour. That's a thousand plus tip."

Later on he could not come. Just couldn't do it. Twenty-seven minutes of dedicated fucking with a doppelganger of the blond jogger and he could not finish. He finally admitted defeat and rolled off sweating and breathing hard.

"Ya'll want me to finish with my hand or mouth, honey?"

A deep sigh. "No, thanks. Not happening and not your fault." He paid her and she left.

Fuuucckk!

Three hours of sleep, a tepid run on the shitty hotel treadmill in the morning, and a seven hour flight to Heathrow.

Fuuucckk!

2 Whitehall Court is actually the Royal Horseguards Hotel in central London. Situated on a narrow strip of land between the Thames River and the park, the huge white building was old school and very posh. Located near the heart of British government offices in the Whitehall District, the hotel was the gang's favorite, and a regular haunt when they were in London.

Every traveler to London had a favorite district. Oneneighborhood or district that just fit them out of the giant crazy whole quilt that was London. Mayfair, Piccadilly, Hyde Park, and the Palace were all nice, but Whitehall delivered just what the gang wanted: Quiet, excellent tube access, safe, secluded, secure, nice rooms, and a hotel that served a good breakfast. Never underestimate the value of a good breakfast for thieves. Thieves did not keep regular hours and breakfast was the most important meal of the day.

Roger Patton checked in right before Mr. Davidoff. "Welcome back, Sir!" the staff said, as he stepped up for his turn.

Michael dropped his bags and went to Ira's room after the man texted the number. Ira and Gretchen rated a full suite when the gang travelled. They needed one room that was a central meeting place and the couple usually got that room. Ira opened the door to 367 when he knocked. Ricky and Gretchen were already seated on the couch in the living room area. Rain could be seen outside the windows over the river while low scudding clouds added to the gloom.

The mood in the room matched. "Hey- How's the tour going?" Michael asked Gretchen as she stood and hugged him hello.

"Fine, until the texts came in."

"Graeme has some news, but he will share it when he arrives in a few hours."

The three men brought Gretchen up to speed on the cops and the watching of Ira and Michael. She was calm. Being tailed by the cops was serious, but was not like getting shot at in her book.

Meantime, they took advantage of the free time to school Ricky on the finer aspects of blending in. Gretchen especially fussed like a mother hen with the young man.

"You look so good in this suit. You should wear them more often."

Davidson steered them back to more practical matters. He handed the man a stack of papers. "These are some tube routes. They have some mistakes. I want you to ride the underground and get used to it and fix them. Remember Paris?"

Rick nodded. He'd spent *hours* on the Metro learning the lines and the stations.

"Same thing here. And after that, I want you to spend some time in the train stations."

The hidden gem of European travel was the trains. Cheap, efficient, and direct in most cases, a train was often the best way to get from one capitol in Europe to another. "Pay attention to the procedures. If we have time, I want you on the Chunnel train to Paris at least once. Watch how the passport control is handled and watch the agents. They tell you how to act."

Ricky's head was spinning. Gretchen smiled at him when Michael mentioned that he wanted her to take the man driving in central London.

"Wrong side of the street, wrong side of the car, and a standard drive!" Ira crowed at him, listing the problems he had to overcome.

"You have to get good at it," was all Davidson told him.

Changing gears, he demanded of the man, "Let's see your wallet!"

Rick pulled his black tri-fold out of his back pocket.

"First mistake!"

"What?"

"Businessmen in Europe keep bi-fold wallets in suit jacket pockets." Gretchen informed him as Mike demonstrated with his. The contents of the offending wallet were similarly revealing of Rick's lack of experience. Other than his driver's license and an Anderson Consulting Company corporate AMEX card, he only had $200 in US currency. Two hundreds, and nothing else in the calfskin wallet.

Michael opened his as an example. "The problem is that any cursory inspection of your wallet will show that there is something wrong."

Davidson had 250 in US currency, but also 300 in GBP, along with another 400 euros all tucked into sections of the bi-fold. No denominations over a twenty. He jingled his pockets to reveal the two pound and one pound coins that Britons used in vending machines all over the place.

"Pret a Manger does not take hundreds, Rick," Ira informed him.

"Nothing over a twenty. That is euros and sterling." Gretchen had to explain what the fast, casual food place was to the man.

The other contents of Michael's wallet now made their appearance. The same Amex card and driver's license, but also a library card from the Queens area near where the address listed his fake home. An Oyster card for the tube came out. Pictures, business cards, lotto tickets, and scraps of paper fluttered out of the folds.

"Who are these people?" Rick asked.

"Doesn't matter," the boss told him. "They fill out my wallet, because that is what's in everyone's wallet."

"Blending in is the key! Clothes, especially. Nothing says American like blue jeans and white sneakers." Michael lectured, "I want you to look at what the other young, male professionals are wearing on the tube tomorrow. Ask someone where they bought it."

"I'm willing to bet Marks and Spencer, but not Harrods," Gretchen wagered.

"Look at it all kid; shoes, belt, briefcase or messenger bag. What phone everyone has, or what computer?" Ira advised.

"Don't forget overcoats and umbrellas," Davidson warned watching the skies open up outside.

Rick nodded along to all the suggestions.

"All this stuff has a purpose, Rick. The ticket seller at the station should not be able to identify you, because you used an oyster card like everyone else. The hotel staff should not be able to pick you out of a line up, because you looked and acted like every other one of the three thousand businessmen who came through here last year."

"That's why you ask for receipts on things, like laundry or meals." Another smile accompanied the advice from Gretchen.

"What if they ask why?" He wanted to know.

"My boss is an asshole, he won't let me expense this stuff unless I have a receipt." Ira put in.

"Best line I've ever used," Michael related, "was one time I asked how much something was because my company has a limit on how much they would let me charge off for dinner and lunch." That waiter knew me for a businessman right away. Remember, Gretchen, in Fortezza?"

The dark-skinned woman grinned. She did. "Rick, that waiter served us almost every day we were down in Brazil on that job. I know for a fact the police questioned him about suspicious Americans and he never gave us up."

"This sounds like work because it is work," the boss told the man. "You can't get it in a day and you need to put in the hours."

The three older members kept schooling the youngster until Graeme arrived, looking tired. The Irishman went immediately to the mini bar and pulled out a whiskey. A twist of the cap and into a glass with one ice cube. Graeme took a healing sip. "Ahhh!"

He stood in the middle of the room and waited while Davidson and the others arranged themselves. Once they were settled, he dropped the hammer. "It's the FBI!"

"Oh, shit!" "Man, we are fucked!" "What?" Gretchen, Ira, and Rick talked over each other. Michael was silent while Graeme took another sip of his drink to calm his nerves.

The boss waited until the grumbling ran down. "No, we are not fucked." He turned to Donniger. "Tell me."

"My source inside the police tells me the two cops, Hattenfeld and Temescal are vice cops and they are dirty. It seems they were on the take from Semilov, keepin' his girls clean when they got pinched."

Michael's head whirled. That was bad.

"Mike, Rachel confirmed it: The Feds are investigatin' Roybokov." More wailing and gnashing of teeth from the more experienced members.

"Did she say that, Graeme? Did she say the FBI put the cops on us?"

Graeme shook his head. "No, she just said that the RICO unit was investigating the Bratva in New York. I took that to mean Roybokov, not anyone else."

Michael's brows met in the middle, while he put ten and ten together to come up with twenty-one.

"Shammer?"

The rest of them looked at him. "What if it's not the FBI? What if it's Demetry?"

"I don't see a bit of difference in that!" Rick exclaimed.

A nod from his boss acknowledged the problem. "I agree it might be a fine point and we are in trouble either way but... listen... "Rachel just told you the FBI is investigating the Bratva. I know Abrams people have been rolled into Demetry's organization since his unfortunate accident. Maybe the Feds are still trying to get their feet under them on this thing. Demetry is much more subtle than Abrams ever was. He has more shell companies than Amazon! Let's really look at the Semilov thing. He came in from Abrams five years ago and was pulling in what - $200 million a year?" Michael paced a little around the room while spoke.

"Prostitution is not the moneymaker it was even a decade ago. Besides, what has Demetry done since the Semi got pinched? Nothing. Just shifted the new girls to Kovelev and hired new pimps." Davidson warmed up and was spitting out the thoughts in his head.

The members all focused on what Michael was saying and now they sparked up.

"Let's look at the two cops," he went on. "The Semi got arrested and is not saying anything, but why didn't they get rolled up too? Are they that good at hiding money? Nothing ties them to the girls? Not visitor logs or friendly conversations with arresting officers? No way the FBI misses that."

"So?" Gretchen played devil's advocate.

"So what if the new cops are working for the RICO unit? What if they squealed and told the feds, we can get to Roybokov if you immune us."

The possibility was good for that- everyone could see that angle.

"So now if the feds can't track the money and tie it to Roybokov, they are basically screwed. They can't tie anything else to him, so they tell the two vice guys- run to Demetry and tell him the Semi's paychecks have stopped; we need to earn. What else can we do for you?" Michael explained to the group.

"No way Demetry would miss that for a fuckin' setup," Graeme said, enthused.

"Yeah, so Roybokov sees the hammer coming and feeds us to the vice cops: watch my thieves, I think they are going to steal from me or someone else." They in turn hand us over to the Feds." Davidson finished up on the sour note.

The mood dampened quickly. "That's a devil's choice, Mikey." Graeme said dully, "Roybokov or the Feds. Neither one is going to let us live."

"Not necessarily." Heads whipped to look at the leader of the gang.

"Cards on the table- Who is ready to cut and run? Ricky?"

The man shook his head. "I just got in the game, but what can we do? I'm sure as shit not ready to retire."

"Ira? Gretchen?"

"Dammit Mike, we aren't ready quite yet. If you have a plan, we are all in with you."

"Graeme?"

The Irishman suddenly looked old, his skin a grey color, the knowledge of what they faced was understood by him best of all. "You know the answer to the question, shammer, if you have an answer to the problem."

A small grin hit Davidson's lips. "I think I do. We have six to eight months before the feds are going to move. Demetry may be another matter, but I think he is getting squeezed two ways here: FBI and his partners. That is going to give us some wiggle room." He laid out some high points for the gang and gave some directions: "Lets freeze our identities right where we are, no sense in confusing the FBI. We should all have clean new ID's ready for our retirement life."

"Gretchen, I need you to make an open JAWS purchase on the majors, use Anderson or Excelsior for that," he said, referencing the open airline ticket purchasing option that allowed some users to write time of departure tickets whenever they needed to. "Also, get to fractional. I want us to have private transport as an option if we need it."

Ira grinned. He loved fractional jet travel. It was like being a rock star: private plane, private terminal, private screening.

"You might as well finish the Rio box- you two might need it after..." Michael finished with Gretchen's duties.

"Meanwhile- I come up with the plan and we go about our normal business." The man stopped and looked at his friends. "I won't leave you in trouble. We been doing this too long and no man gets left behind! Right?"

Such was their trust in him that he got smiles and nods from them all. Michael would fix everything. That's what he did after all.

A discrete signal to Graeme and the two men excused themselves and went downstairs to the bar.

The bar in the Royal Horseguards' is a suitably wood paneled, warm fireplace, large leather chair- type of place- fit for any good Englishman. An American and an Irishman walked into the bar and ordered up two large pints of Boddingtons and sat in those chairs warming themselves by the fire.

"Do you have anything?" Graeme asked his friend, meaning an idea about their problem.

"An idea, but it needs a lot of work." Michael admitted.

"Not helpin' me confidence," Graeme offered a real grin.

Michael Davidson laughed at that face. It was good to see his old friend

back.

"I don't know if this helps, but I did look into the Trevor thing, and shammer- he has an idea. It's sound and the news is huge!"

Michael had to control the surge in his gut. "Really? What?"

"Trev wants to tell you his own self."

Holy shit- a job? That may change some things considerably. If, IF it worked out, it usually took three to four months to put things into place. That might work for them, help them with disappearing.

"When do we meet him?" Davidson asked holding down his enthusiasm.

"I told him tomorrow, half seven at the Wolseley." Michael risked the old joke, "what's half seven? Three and a half o'clock?"

"Fuck off, you wanker!"

Both men shared a laugh. Half seven meant half past seven o'clock. Still smiling Davidson said, "Let's take the kid."

"Sure."

Wonders of wonders. Graeme wasn't fighting him on every detail today. No complaining and he was sober. He thought maybe Demetry or the FBI had put the fear of God in Donniger.

In a serious voice, he said, "Graeme, after...if this works out. Are you going to be okay? We might not see each other again."

Silence hung in the air for a good long while. A sip of his beer wet his lips. Head down, Donniger started his confession. "I've been angry with you for a while. Always been jealous of ya- ever since Kings Bay. It just seemed like you were floating through life. Looks, brains, money- and you were the thief- in-law!" Another sip. "When we got Ira, and Gretchen, and even Ricky, and they just seemed to follow wherever you led, because you had all the answers."

An objection rose from Davidson, but Graeme cut that off. "No! Hear me! It was just you bein' you. And I'm not like that."

Those words were raw and ripped out of the man.

"You know what I thought when Rachel told me the Febbies were looking at us? I thought, '*Get the hell out!*'"

More silence.

"But you didn't," Michael finally said.

A snort greeted that. "Not for any noble reason, believe me. I came here because you would know what to do. That's the hell of it, you know what to do. Always have, always will."

"I don't 'always know what to do'," he started, but the Irish cut him off.

"Not helpin' me confidence, shammer."

More gentle laughter. The men fell silent as Rick stopped by on his way out to tell them he was going shopping.

"See there? The kid is going shopping because you said 'no man gets left behind!'"

"Bloody hell, I could get us all killed!" Davidson strangled out.

"Yeah- but you'll be right there next to us. If I was in charge, I would get everyone killed while I buggered off, and then got caught later. My first instinct was to run."

A shake of his head and Davidson said, "You have always been a brilliant thief, running might be the smart play."

"I might be brilliant, but I am not the thief-in-law."

"You can have it!"

"Not after you fucked it up so badly!" The man managed to laugh.

Davidson could see the weight lift off his friend. Maybe he just needed to be listened to. "Oh hey- We got another little job we need to do for Demetry when we get back."

Donniger shot him a look.

A quick shake of the head back from Mike. "Don't know. Don't think it's a setup. Feydor says it's some kind of courier thing."

The two men ordered another round and drank and talked until Rick came back carrying bags.

"Kid's good. Dedicated."

"Yeah, no way he will be satisfied with the one job and whatever happens here. I just hope he picks up enough to keep from getting caught."

Graeme stood. "Let's break pattern! Let's go out- the five of us! The Grosvenor Casino has put in craps tables."

Michael considered. "Why not? Get cleaned up and I'll tell the others. A night on the town might do us well!"

A toned-down epic night followed. Epic, in that Graeme did not drink more than one whiskey and won 1200 quid. Gretchen and Ira both broke even, which was good for them, and Rick only lost a hundred. Michael won a quick five hundred, and then met a Chinese woman, kind of the total opposite from a blond southerner a little chitchat and a lot of beautiful release.

Chapter Five

Saturday night continued the run of rainy cool weather in London. Early November was about as dead a time the city ever saw for tourists, so the tube was only very crowded with commuters heading back home and not hordes of visitors wearing cameras. Rick was fresh from his tour of the train stations and the underground, so he led the other two through the Piccadilly Square Station and up to the street. The Wolseley was a grand European brasserie just off Piccadilly Street where the outrageous prices were matched by the fantastic service. Every waiter in the place seemed to have that narrow split between a sneer and a smile. The youngest gang member was so intimidated that he forgot to flirt with the young female hostess as she showed them into the bowels of the tastefully decorated place. Large booths and tables in the lowlight held people comfortably and in some privacy. As they passed, the bar held 'Trevor Covington' standing alongside, waiting for his acquaintances, drink in hand. The trio became a foursome as the men were moved to a semi-private room.

Graeme pulled Rick aside and told him, "Just keep your mouth shut and watch Mike."

Introductions were short, as the three were old acquaintances, and then they were seated.

The waiter joined the group as the brunette hostess sashayed away. A minion quietly served water all around while his superior began the standard spiel, "Good evening, gentlemen. My name is Edward and I will be your waiter this evening."

Davidson immediately took charge. *If you let the waiter talk, nothing got accomplished.*

"Edward, good evening. How are you this day?" he asked sincerely.

"Very well, Sir, and yourself and all?"

"We are all fine and looking to conclude some delicate negotiations this evening."

Edward proffered a drink menu and wine list. Michael declined.
"Since Mr. C. has started with a libation, we'd like a round of whatever he is having, if you please."

Edward nodded.

"How are the scallops today?" Michael asked.

Smiling, the waiter informed him that the day boat scallops were the best in the city.

"Very well. We will need four appetizers of the scallops. Also, we need a chardonnay to go with that, something creamy?"

"A Montrachet," Edward asked testing the budget.

"Nice- which vintage?"

"We have a '90 that is just reaching its peak drinkability."

"That sounds excellent. We will all have the filet de boeuf with asparagus and hollandaise- medium rare all around." Mike looked at his companions for confirmations which he got. More nodding from Edward.

"For the wine- we'd like a Shiraz- The Penfolds Grange."

A look of consternation replaced the smile. "Monsieur would, of course, prefer the Hermitage."

A definite shake 'no' told a different story. "Monsieur would not. The Penfolds."

The waiter wanted to say no, and what's more, he wanted to argue. Davidson was having none of that. "Edward, the bottles don't lie, as we say in the colonies. Now- serve us the drinks, wait eighteen minutes to let us get some things off our chests, and bring in the scallops, with the chardonnay." Davidson brooked no nonsense and overrode the objections. "Wait another twenty-four minutes and bring us a cheese course with whatever wine you want, and then wait ten more minutes to bring out the filets, with the Shiraz, s'il vous plait. Another thirty-five minutes to let us wrap up our talks, and then we'll see about dessert and cigars- Oui?"

The man's jaw dropped. "Oui... Monsieur???"

"Davidoff."

A head whip to see what the face looked like in detail, was this man the...?

"I've been living in The States."

"Of course, Sir. Very good, Sir." The man left and Trevor and Graeme, who'd seen Michael's parlor trick performed before, chuckled. Rick was fazed.

His Irish friend leaned in and told the young man, "If we are gonna pay 2200 quid for dinner we should at least get what we want."

The alcohol went down nicely in the beautiful surroundings. Especially when that room was as historic as the Wolseley.

"A toast. To good health, fine looking women, and easy money!"

The four drank deep and relaxed into their chairs.

"Trev? You have something to share?" Graeme prompted.

"De Beers is leaving London!"

Davidson rocked back on his seat, stunned. "What? I haven't even heard a whisper!"

"Oh, very hush-hush, my lad," Covington told them all. "We just got the word last few days officially."

"Wow. Where are they going?"

"Gaborone!" the Shipping and Logistics agent for the consortium told the men at the table.

Graeme saved Rick the embarrassment of being the ignorant one. "I'm not really sure where Gaborone is located," he admitted.

"Botswana, Africa." Both Trevor and Michael answered together.

Trev went on alone, "Botswana has the company's biggest mines producing right now. The board succumbed to the government pressure to move the sites to the local city. They want the jobs." His voice was soft and serious.

Being the head of transport for the stones as they came in and out of the company, Trevor had thirty-five years of experience in the business. He was coming up to the end of his career.

"Are you making the shift?" Michael asked the man.

"I'm just setting up the initial staff and facilities. I pack up operations and move them out, and then the locals take over." A shake of his head held the wonder of the monopoly giving in to an African government.

"Cecil Rhodes must be turning over in his grave," Michael told their contact.

Rick didn't understand that reference either.

Again, Graeme leaned over to catch him up. "Old Cecil founded De Beers over a century ago. They killed a lot of South Africans pulling their glittering rocks out of the ground. Then they put in Apartheid as the system of government when the locals had the nerve to complain about it."

"You mean like Mandela, that Apartheid?"

"Yep."

"Holy shit!"

"When is the last site?" Mike asked, getting back on track.

"April 6, 2013. And that's the bigger news for you gabbers. The last site is going to have to be big enough to cover the two months while we do the shift."

Three sets of eyes bore in on the older man. White hair fringing his balding head, Trevor leaned in. "And the best part? A little birdie at

Lloyd's told me that several large dollar policies have been written to Indian and US diamond firms for the Hatton Garden Safety Deposit Box Company."

That old feeling hit Michael's groin. He tamped it down while seeing the twin look come onto Graeme's face.

"Why would they store them?" Davidson asked.

"It's Easter Sunday weekend. Most places are closed on Good Friday and the firms are going to have to wait until the following week to get the stones out to Antwerp."

The scallops arrived and the men ceased talking and tucked in with a will. With one bite Rick knew he was eating well this evening.

"We'll need to confirm all of this info," Davidson said after the staff left the area and it was safe to talk again.

"Sure, sure. I know it may not pan out, but the opportunity is sitting out there!"

The meal proceeded at a more leisurely pace while the talk went small after the initial bombshell. The chef accompanied the beef and the wine out to the table when that course made its appearance. Michael opened the offending bottle and allowed it to breathe. He poured the Frenchman a small glass. A swirl, a sniff, a slurp and a drink. The man's face gave away nothing. Another small pour and the chef sliced a fifth small plate with the steak cooked to medium rare perfection. A bite of the beef and then the same sniff, slurp, drink on the wine.

Slowly, a grudging look came onto his face. "What did you say to Edward? The bottles do not lie?"

"It's not exactly *better*," Michael allowed. "It's just different. Excellent, but different. Maybe for the younger, less traditional crowd?"

He gave the chef an out.

"Oui Monsieur!"

"Chef, my friends and I will always remember this meal, I can assure

you!"

Gustatory pride restored, the staff left, leaving the men to eat a pleasant dinner. The leader of the gang took in Rick and Graeme with a nod and theorized, "Maybe it's just a new way of looking at things."

The dessert was a treacle tart and some port followed by brandy and cigars.

"Jesus, I'm half drunk," Rick admitted.

"Trev, this is going to be our swansong if we pull this job off," Mike told him.

Covington waived that away. "I might have an escape plan setup for myself, as well. Got a fake job, sitting, watching a fancy house. Thing is, I own the place! Sunny spot mind you. Some place where rain falls on plains, if you follow." He chuckled at his own witticism.

The others laughed with him. "How do you want to get paid?"

"Cash deposit, like always. Same account."

"One more thing, man. The squad maybe involved," Davidson warned his agent.

A raised and very bushy eyebrow met this warning. "I thought you gobbers were ghosts."

"Yeah. We are usually. But it seems we may be on the FBI radar and, if we are, it won't be long until the squad is involved." Michael liked the nickname for the Metropolitan Police, Robbery unit, The Flying Squad.

Maybe his crew needed a cool nickname. *The Brew Crew?* No. *The stealing bunch?* No. *Assholes who take things?* Better. He'd have to work on that.

"I'll be more careful then."

"Your part is done. We'll just need a series of confirming texts in the usual code as the date gets closer," Graeme assured the man.

The dinner broke up as Michael paid the check. The restaurant comped the treacle tart. 3058 GBP. He added a bit to the tip. Trevor Covington shook hands all around and tottered off into the night. He had to get home to the missus.

The other three walked east a few blocks on Piccadilly. The rain had ceased and the cool night air helped Rick recover a bit. The men stopped across the street from a large, nine-story building that occupied the whole of the block to the corner. The Edwardian marble facade was a bit grimy from the soot, but the whole place radiated a steady calm dependability. The older two gang members gazed at the building with fascination. Sanderson noticed. "What's that place?"

"De Beers London headquarters," Michael explained.

"Oh."

"About eighty feet down, encased in a huge vault, and surrounded by concrete, with every conceivable alarm known to man... is about fifty percent of the world's diamonds."

Even Rick gawped at that. Davidson and Donniger ogled the building like peep show patrons. Greed makes beggars of everyone.

"What do you think Graeme? Ten billion? Fifteen?"

"Easily, sham. Mebbe twenty."

"We hit the uncut stones going into Antwerp. Now I'd like to get to the site holders before they can get the gems out of the country," Michael told Rick.

"We had dinner a block from the stones we are going to steal?" Rick asked. "May steal, may steal. But I like your positive energy," the boss told him.

"Lad, guess what else is a few blocks from our hotel?" Graeme added on.

"What?"

"New Scotland Yard, of course."

"Why do you guys tell me these things?!"

***

Monday rolled around and the real scouting began in earnest. Now that the gang had a potential target, plenty of things needed to be taken care of. Ira and Graeme went on a search through the city's building and planning commission files. Every building had to be up to code and it was easy to pose as contractors who had to work on the building to gather detailed architectural plans. Meanwhile the other three went into the Hatton Garden Safe Deposit Box Company itself, to see the layout first hand. The easiest cover was as customers looking to rent a box. The men dressed in suits while Gretchen favored a smart female business look. She had the broad shoulders and skinny frame to make it look sexy.

She needed some curves, Rick risked saying. Michael wisely shut the hell up on that topic.

The Hatton Garden District of Holborn was north of the river and served as London's diamond shopping district.

Hatton Garden Street itself was lined with several high-end jewelry shops and the cross street of Greville ass famous for the quality of the stones available in still more shops. The safety deposit company sat in a large multi-unit building at the corner of Greville and Hatton Garden; ground zero for diamond retailing. The building was divided into two wings, facing either the Hatton side or the Greville face. The entrance was right at the corner, with a large, clean vestibule serving as a common lobby shared by the tenants. A British Passport Services office was on one side and a management company took offices on the other.

Two retailers faced the Hatton street outer ring and the Safety Deposit Box Company sat on the second floor of the internal set of office rooms. There were no windows available for the customers, but since the safety boxes were all down stairs, below ground in the vault, windows were not a problem. The elevator which was at the back end of the lobby was out of service, so the three took the stairs up to the target company.

Michael, Rick, and Gretchen all went over the layout with a fine eye, as they waited for the early crowd to thin out a bit. Armed with several documents for a fictitious company, the trio waited outside the assistant manager's office until 10:22 am.

"Yes, some boxes are available for rent, depending on the size," the woman, Helen Buxton, told them when they entered and explained their desires.

"What do you have in the way of sizes," Michael asked in his best business voice, confident and clear.

"Full, half, quarter, and eighth cube sizes," she said.

The thieves were a bit flummoxed, as the normal safety deposit box size was 'document and large' in the US.

Gretchen asked politely for the explanation. Ms. Buxton gave a half smile and related that the sizes were expressed in cubic meters: A full cubic meter, a half cubic meter, and so on done the line.

Conversion math suddenly made an appearance as the three debated the 3.2 feet height, width, and depth of the boxes, and whether that would be enough for their needs.

"I actually think the half cubic meter size would be big enough, if we could see it?" Michael asked the manager.

"Of course, Sir."

The four played follow the leader down the four stories on the back, internal staircase into the connecting hallway and the vault room. Ms. Buxton walked briskly down the corridor and through the enormous door into the secure portion of the vault. A sign-in desk and a small gate led to the interior space. A company person signed them in and Buxton jangled some keys while the thieves noted the guards, the layout, and the wall construction. The outer space held a series of doors to small cubicles that provided users some privacy while they raided their own secure boxes. The box rooms themselves were down and to the left and right, and were surprisingly large.

The letter-size and one-eighth meter cube up to the quarter sized boxes were arrayed in the left room. Ms. Buxton gave the three a few minutes to look this over, and then said, "The other room has the full cube and half cube sized boxes separately. Most of our larger business customers need the room to access their items on a consistent basis."

Davidson allowed that they would need to be accessing the box frequently at first, and then with less regularity.

She nodded and showed the customers the half cube box in the other room. The boxes were arrayed in a floor to ceiling stack with about an inch in between the units. The heavy brass doors all held the two key locks and the outer edge was covered by a layer of thin steel plate.

All three were making mental notes of everything and Gretchen even managed to get some quiet pictures inside. They continued talking to themselves in their guise as a business as Ms. Buxton opened a half cube unit for them to see.

"I think this will work. What are the package dimensions again Roger?" Michael asked Rick.

"Ten by ten by three inches, Mr. Davidoff."

The discussion gave them ample opportunity to open the box door and look over the locks and finger the outside cladding. Michael's spatial sense was also tingling at the route they'd taken into the vault.

"I believe this will work nicely," he said with a smile to the assistant manager. "Uhh, I hate to be prickly, but what about security in here?"

Ms. Buxton did not take any offense. "We have the finest security in the world. We have never had a problem, ever! You saw the two armed guards by the vault door? We also have temperature, pressure, sonic, and motion alarms installed. The whole room is protected by sixty centimeters of re- enforced concrete capable of surviving a missile blast, so your items will be quite protected."

Michael smiled at the woman and did the math in his head. Just under two feet. "That's fantastic! Let's finish off the paper work."

The trip back to the office was in silence and Gretchen provided the application forms and documents.

"Seven to ten business days for your papers to clear, and then you get the letter approving the rental. At that time a list of key personnel will be required to have access to the vault." Ms. Buxton went over the particulars.

Gretchen took the stack of signature forms and the other receipts and asked about keys. "It is very difficult in the States to get three keys," she explained.

The woman nodded. "We have a locksmith who changes the box every time a new tenet comes in. It is easy to get three keys made right off the lurch, but more difficult afterwards." She made the notation on the forms for the keys.

The thieves nodded in sympathy. Handshakes all around as they left.

***

Outside, Michael walked down Greville Street with the others and looked at the shops while progressing towards the tube stop. Safe in the anonymous crowds, he turned and asked, "What did you think?" to Rick.

The younger member turned to the two. "I thought we had one! But that vault looks too tough. Guards and a missile blast?"

Michael smiled, but didn't answer. He asked Gretchen the same question.

Her answer was accompanied by a matching grin, "I'm not as good spatially as you, but I think..." She stopped and looked at Mike.

"Yep. The back wall is the elevator shaft. We're in!"

Rick watched the exchange and was puzzled.

Gretchen shook her head at the young man. "Rick, some of it seems obvious, but what did she say? 'We've never had problems in here before.' That means they are not looking for vulnerabilities." The vault has always been safe, so why should tomorrow be any different."

Michael took over. "She mentioned guards. That is just for show during the day. I'd be willing to bet they aren't there during the night. As for the missile blast, we won't be using a missile."

"But the alarms?" the man asked.

"That's going to be a problem," he acknowledged.

The gang boarded the tube and went back to the hotel. A quick change of clothes and Michael told Gretchen, "Wait here for Ira and Graeme. We need to get back to New York. Before we go, I want you to be on the lookout for an apartment big enough for all of us during the stay here."

"Rick, let's go site seeing." He motioned the younger man outside for some training.

The men hopped on the ever present tube with its crowd's thinner at lunch time. On a random Friday in November, the weather sucked as the pair rode from Embankment to Tower Hill Stations. A good many people got off with them as they started down the slope towards the river.

Davidson pointed out the wall which marked the Roman part of Londinium, the ancient city which Julius Caesar made his provincial capital.

The two men walked by the Tower's execution block where many famous, and not so famous, people met their fates. Rick was impressed by it all.

The moat surrounding the Tower of London had been dry for a century, as the Tower now served as mainly as a tourist attraction. Michael explained the Water gate and its significance in British history to the younger man as they went into the place. Rick was impressed by that as well. Past the White Tower with its ravens, he led Rick into younger palace rooms just like any tourist. The film was at least interesting as the men watched. Queen Elizabeth looked pretty good during her coronation.

The exhibits kept getting more fascinating as they went deeper in. The Royal Cape with its ermine trim and pearls. The golden orb and Scepter of State with its huge diamond. And finally the jewel room. The

Crown Jewels of England were laid out in a small room with a 24-hour guard detail circling around the exhibit cases. A moving walkway allowed bunches of tourists to go past the crowns and other stones. The guards were nice to the tourists, as the room wasn't too crowded, and they let the men skirt around and ride three times.

The Star of Africa was a huge, chicken egg sized diamond that was almost flawless and sat up front in the crown. The Star of India was likewise huge and a symbol of former colonial might. The Black Prince Ruby, an unpolished ruby of enormous size had been fought over for six centuries. All of these were contained in the crown jewels, in addition to more gems cut from the Cullinan Diamond. The latter being the largest diamond on earth. The last exhibit was an elaborate golden punch bowl. 440 kilos of gold in 1400 separate pieces to make up the fanciful set. Rick was stunned by the display of wealth.

The two men sat on a bench outside the exhibit room after staring at the booty and drooling.

"Oh man, that crown," Rick breathed.

"Yeah, that thing is amazing. Think we could steal it?" Michael asked, watching his protégé.

Sanderson stopped breathing for a second. *Could we? No. Yes.* "I don't know," he finally admitted.

"Good. Let's review some plans shall we. We could smuggle in some guns and take out the guards, then smash the glass and run out, to what?" He gestured around the tower grounds. Beefeater guards in their distinctive uniforms roamed freely. "A hundred dedicated war veterans just itching to shoot someone? How bout we get them to move it. Make it vulnerable," he went on. "Elizabeth is not going to last forever. They have to coronate Charles and when they do, we grab it. But, what then?"

Ricks face fell. "We can't sell it. Not even broken up. The individual stones are too famous."

"Yep. Too famous to sell does not interest me. We could grab it and sell it back to the authorities, but that is really dicey." Michael spoke from experience. "Can't steal the Mona Lisa, either. At least not to sell. Too tough to fence doesn't generally interest me."

Silence held while Rick absorbed this lesson.

"Lots of things have just vanished over the years," he told him. "Ever hear of the Florentine Diamond?"

Rick shook his head.

"Huge yellow diamond. One hundred and fifty carats. Right after WW I someone stole it and it has never been seen since. Sitting in a box somewhere. Same with the Amber Room and those Faberge Eggs. Look those up," he said to the unasked question.

"Point is, sometimes things could be sittin' on the sidewalk and they are not worth stealing." He waited a beat. "And the opposite is true: Sometimes a place has seemingly impenetrable security and it's just waiting to be taken down."

Rick looked up sharply. "Trick is to know the difference. Sometimes the answer is to walk away."

Sanderson got it. "What are we going to do about 'after' on this job?"

"That's a good question. Normally, we would wait a long time to fence the stones, however Demetry is in a bind right now. This job gives him some leeway and we need that to give us some room to maneuver. I figure we have 3-4 months before we have to have him dealt with." Michael paused, blowing out a breath. "Plus, we have a problem of the diamonds hitting the open market right after a robbery. That is going to be bad. But I think we can figure a way around it." An evil grin came onto his face. "Hey, how big is your head?"

Rick stared at his boss. "What?"

Michael used two hands to span Ricks head while talking. "Seems like ten inches or so. How thick are you?"

"What the fuck are you doing?"

Laughing, Davidson told his young friend, "You need to lose fifteen pounds. You have to go on a diet."

***

Over the next few days the team departed London back to New York. Per their normal travel arrangements, they went back in ones and twos, using different airports to get home. Gretchen made a quick two-day visit to Rio on the way back to finish off the storage unit there.

Thursday, November 15th saw a two-inch snowfall in the city. Not a lot of snow but it sent people scurrying for shovels. Michael was dealing with a crap-load of jetlag as he was awakened on that morning to the sound of banging and saws from next door.

8:35 am. Great.

He gave up after a few moments of trying to get back to sleep. *Might as well get up.*

After a quick shower and dressing in his standard work outfit of dark slacks and a dress shirt with a jacket, he spent some time on the mail run. Thankfully, there was no sign of the cops who'd been tailing them. Mike wondered if the pair had been tipped off that they were leaving the area and hadn't bothered to come around.

The accumulated mail was dealt with. The biggest piece was a series of drawings and plans from the UK. These documents were the results of Ira and Graeme's search through the public records involving the buildings around the Hatton Gardens Safety Deposit Company. Remodeling plans, work permits, and insurance details were all parts of public records in the UK. The States had much the same, if not more, information available. The details on the alarms and the vault were not available, but some vital info would lead them where to search next.

In this case, it looked like Lloyds held the main structural policy while Swiss Re had part of the reinsurance.

Many people held only a fuzzy idea of what reinsurance was and what it did. A huge company like Lloyds will take policies on large and somewhat risky businesses. The Safety Deposit Box Company was a prime example. Lloyds was spreading the risk of a robbery amongst all of its policyholders. But a company like Hatton Gardens could have the potential for a billion-dollar loss. That was too much risk for Lloyds, or any single insurance company. A reinsurance outfit like Swiss Re would underwrite the Lloyds policy and help spread the risk out for more millions of policyholders and investors. Michael, himself, had some Swiss Re in his investment portfolio. It was an excellent company, after all. But... The insurance companies and the reinsurance people all liked to know the details of the security operations in a risky venture.

Bottom line: Swiss Re or Lloyds held the vault construction plans and the alarm details in its files somewhere.

Trick was getting at them.

Michael went through the drawings and zeroed in on the notations Ira and Graeme had left. "Talk to Linda, here."

Linda was their go between when dealing with the insurance people. She made inquiries on their behalf, posing as a construction outfit doing work on an adjacent system or building. In this case, since the elevator in the building was being remodeled, they had most of the structural plans already and they just needed the alarm specs.

That was nice work on the drawings, Davidson noted. It was a little before noon and he made the call he'd been dreading for a while.

"Mr. Roybokov, it's Michael," he said, trying to be light. "You have something for me?"

"Da. I need you and the Irish."

He closed his eyes to concentrate. "'Irish' is out of the area until tomorrow. Can we make it Saturday?"

"Da. Come to the house. 3:00 pm." The gruff man clicked off the phone.

That went okay, he thought. The three o'clock time was significant. If it was 5:00, that meant, "come to meet, stay for dinner." Three meant, "I can find out what I need to know, kill you, and still make dinner at six."

However, he thought they were safe at the house. If the meeting had been set for the office in the strip club or Feydor's pawn shop then that would be some serious red flags. A text to Graeme to relay the meeting time and place took him no time. He had more work to do.

Moving downstairs on his way out to his meetings, he took the opportunity for a quick knock on Mary's door to check on her.

"Mikey, is that you?" she asked.

"It is me, Mary. I'm just back from overseas."

The old woman opened the door and took stock. "You look tired, boychik."

"Couldn't sleep in with the banging going on next door."

"Pish, I don't even notice," she waived it away. "Come to Shabbat dinner, on Friday. Rabbi Manhof and a guest will be coming. Dress nice," she commanded.

"What are we having?"

"Spaghetti," she said.

"Spaghetti? For Shabbat?" he asked.

"Same god, different approach," Mary said wisely. "It's Mrs. Scanzani's yahrzeit and her recipe. She was a good friend when my Henry died and afterward."

Michael knew the yahrzeit was the anniversary of someone's death. He was picking up a lot of Jewish customs. "I'll bring Chianti."

A quick peck on the cheek for being a nice boy and the admonition that he be on time at 6:00, sent him on his way.

The meetings went well. He wanted the Dogra brothers and the Weinstiens involved on this shell company setup. The gang used other people sometimes, but in this instance he wanted professional discretion from people he trusted.

The Dogras were a team of Indian- American brothers who cooked his books and did his taxes. The Weinstien Corporation was a group of shady lawyers who helped incorporate his shell companies and did most of his money laundering. In all things, forms had to be filled out and banks informed. Sutton Geology, LLC came into being that day with some effort on his part. That, and $10 million drawn from the Caymans.

Steve Hoban, the tall lawyer who helped him, explained the process. "We execute a fake contract with Royal Dutch Shell for the $10 million, which pays the company. Then we pay you."

"Fake contract? Won't RDS twig on to that?"

Steve shook his head. "Mike, these giant multis are doing ten thousand contracts a year. We mail the contract into their offices with a Mod 1 notation attached and marked as paid, and boom, someone assigns a number to it. Once we get that number, the IRS and the banks consider it good. Anyone does a sanity check and you show up as real. Since RDS hasn't paid out any money, they can't find it in a quick look.

All we have to do is close out the contract every year and we are good."

That part was what Michael didn't like. "Why don't we go on a two or three year contract and I won't have to pay you so often!"

Steve was horrified. "God, no! If it goes over a fiscal year the big boys will audit the contracts and find the outlier. That's why we do it now and have it wrapped up by June 1st."

The leader of the gang grimaced. He was paying these guys serious money to do this. He expected the best results. Same with his taxes. The Dogras charged upwards of $5,000 per return. His corporate returns for Excelsior and Anderson Consulting cost in the $10,000 range and took the CPAs weeks to finesse. Now he was adding another corporate return, plus he needed another holding company in the near future. Things were getting complicated. He had a lot of things to keep track of.

Chapter Six

Friday dawned cold and gloomy at the house. More banging from next door started in early, but he was already up. A short run on the treadmill didn't improve his mood, or make him feel much better. The shower still felt nice as the hot water cascaded on him, bringing life back into his blood. Davidson went casual khaki pants and button-down shirt with a sports jacket. The jacket was more for warmth as he went on errands all over the city. Food shopping, the dry cleaners, a trip to the wine shop, and the pharmacy, all added to the mail run, so it looked like a regular day for any thief. A good four hours down in his office saw him make contact with Linda and detail what he wanted in the alarm drawings for Hatton Garden.

That's a tall order, she'd told him via text.

Might be our last job, he relayed.

The best information incoming was Gretchen's text that detailed a large flat for rent available near the job site in London. A huge six-bedroom unit, with full kitchen and living room. 8667 PCM. Eight thousand, six hundred, sixty-seven pounds per calendar month. $13,700 a month? London real estate rivaled Manhattan for expense. The new Sutton Geology account was going to have to write a large check for the place. He contacted the estate agent to get the application process rolling, giving the usual fake information. The rental firm was used to dealing with agents for international businessmen trying to get places in central London via some unusual accounts and transaction magic. It made the transaction easier and it gave the gang a layer of anonymity that Michael loved.

The maudlin thoughts kept coming and intruding on his progress. How was he going to get out from under the Fed's and the Bratva thumb? Could they really pull off Hatton? If he had to vanish, could he leave this place behind? The compartments in his brain struggled with keeping all of the stray thoughts from sloshing up and over their respective dams.

A shrug to ward off the gloom from both his mood and the day raised his shoulders. He went up to shave and the normalcy of the motions helped soothe him. From his bedroom window he had a decent view into the adjoining house. He could see workman scurrying around and hear the banging and thumping coming from inside. Muffled. *Someone is putting large dollars into that place.* The thought threatened his upturned mood. The stab of jealousy was short. *Wall Street assholes have too much money*, he figured. *And don't get me started on carried interest. Time for dinner.*

A stop in the kitchen and he grabbed a bottle of Chianti for dinner and a port for dessert. Chianti Classico from Abruzzi and a Spanish Madeira. Mrs. Scanzani's sauce was a classic red, he knew.

Michael decided to go through the front hall door, rather than the back kitchen stairs, to avoid shocking the Rabbi.

Prepared for an older Jewish man, the sight of the beautiful woman who opened the door pole-axed him. Time froze for a beat while he took her in.

Tall, at least 5' 9", with huge blond hair piled up to give her the illusion of even more height. Bright smile, with full red lips, showed the perfect teeth and high cheek bones. Broad shoulders tapering to a smaller waist and those perfect rounds tits pushed up magnificently. Filled out but not more than 125 pounds, he thought. Dressed in jeans and a sweater he saw those legs and knew instinctively it was the runner from the park. 32? No more than 35.

Time flowed back in as she said, "Hello." And then recognition went further as she said, "Hey, you're the runner!"

The smile widened on her generous mouth and it stuck his feet to the floor and put his brain in mush.

"Yeeaee," Michael could not make the words come out properly.

She noticed her effect on him. "Articulate devil. Are you the neighbor? Come in."

He managed to walk in unaided into Mary's apartment. *This was his turf! How did she...?*

"Yes, hello. I am the upstairs neighbor, Michael Davidson." A sentence finally came out of his mouth correctly.

The pair stood awkwardly in the small entranceway until Mary bustled in from the kitchen. "Mikey! Oh, you met Sydney. I wanted to introduce you!"

"Not formally, Mrs. Spack. Hi, again Michael, I'm Sydney Devereaux." The melodic voice dripped southern honey. She stuck out a hand in greeting.

He took it and was struck by how warm and soft it was. He held on. "Uhhh."

Sydney awkwardly pulled back her hand and went, "Uhh."

Mary watched the two of them. "Bubbe, you okay?" she asked Michael.

Davidson willed his head to get back into the game. "Yeah, sorry, Mary. Jetlag is killing me. Hi, Mary." He gave her a quick peck on the cheek. He turned to the young woman. "Sorry, yes, I am the neighbor and I just got back from London, yesterday. Still on European time." He was setting a record! Two sentences that didn't make him sound like an idiot.

"Mikey, is that for me?"

He'd forgotten the wine. "Yes, some Chianti, here you go!" He handed over the bottles to Mary as they walked a ways into the living room and dining area.

Sydney caught a glimpse of the bottle. "The Abruzzi Reserve... uhh,

that's..." She hesitated while Mary looked at the bottle. The thing making her stop speaking was a discrete hand on her arm from Michael. A slight shake of his head at Mary and she caught on quickly.

"That's a nice area, I've heard," she masked, adroitly.

Mary hustled the pair into the kitchen and set down the wine on the counter. Dinner was not ready, which was strange to Mike.

"I'm so sorry, but I was trying to track down Rabbi Manhof. He is not here yet and I can't seem to get a hold of him."

Michael could organize and help. "Okay, what can I do?" Besides, it might help him cover his nerves.

Mary smiled a thanks at him. "Could you finish the meatballs and make a salad while I figure out what is going on?"

"I can help, too." Sydney said, ready to go.

"Sure, Mary. Go- we can get things ready." Michael hustled her off.

She went into the back bedroom to continue the phone investigation while Michael went to the kitchen sink and washed his hands. Sydney did a thorough scrub next to him. She smelled like lavender and he tried not to sniff. "Can you open the wine, while I check meatballs and get stuff for salad?" He asked.

"Sure."

He turned for the stove while she went for the drawers to rummage through for the tool and the pair ended up face to face and body to body.

They stared at each other for a full second. Her beauty was an almost overpowering thing. Blue eyes, and the scent of her, put crazy thoughts in his head. *Kiss her! Fuck her!*

The moment stretched, and then eyes dropped on both sides, embarrassed.

Michael staggered back. "'Sorry, sorry. The corkscrew is in the top drawer." He pointed.

"No, no, my fault," Sydney seemed a bit flustered as well.

He covered by checking the meat balls and slipped them into the sauce, bubbling away on the stove.

The popping sound of the cork brought his head around. "The glasses are in the dining room side cabinet." She sat the bottle down, and then after returning with three glasses she looked at the label.

She obviously knew something about wine. A questioning look asked him what was up.

"Mary would be upset if she knew the wine was expensive. My little treat," he explained.

"That's nice," she told him. She leaned back against the counter to watch him work. He retrieved lettuce and the fixings for salad.

"Where is the bowl for that?" she asked. With her accent the word contained some new syllables: 'Bow-ell'

He grinned. "Where in the South?" Not answering the question directly, just wanting her to talk more.

"Dallas, born and raised. How 'bout ya'll?" The voice dipped up and down. Accent thicker and thinner. It was honey- dipped onto that smooth skin so he could lick off the...

Suddenly he realized she was expecting some sort of answer. "Uh, sorry. What was that again?"

"I asked where you were from."

"Denver, I'm from Denver."

"Broncos fan?"

"I am," he said surprised. "I don't have to ask about you though..."

"Only Cowboys fan in New York," she sparkled.

"Not the only one, but you are outnumbered. I'll bet you are an

Aikman girl, huh?" he asked, just to stay on a safe topic.

"And you are all bout that John Elway, I'd bet."

"Since I was six."

The two started arguing good naturally about who was the better quarterback while Michael made salad and put on a pot for pasta. He started feeling better, a little surer of himself. Dishes went on the table as they became ready. Sydney poured out some wine and helped.

"Look, I see it this way: Montana, Elway, Brady, Favre, and Aikman, with Manning and Marino as the best regular season quarterbacks."

Sydney drew a breath to point out the obvious flaws in his case when Mary breezed into the kitchen.

"Otto Graham. Nine NFL championships and movie star good looks. Rabbi Manhof can't make it. Mrs. Lapinski's hip isn't feeling well." She plowed into the conversation without a break.

Both of them got a kick out of Mary's football knowledge. The three quickly finished meal prep and brought dinner to the table, all the while chatting about Mrs. Lapinski's hip and Mrs. Scanzani's sauce.

The blessings went quickly while Sydney looked on respectfully. Challah went really well with a tomato sauce.

Michael helped himself to a big plate of pasta and salad."Suddenly, I'm starving," he told the ladies.

"Mikey is from Colorado, did he tell you, Sydney? They have horses out there, just like in Texas."

"He did, but I didn't catch what you do for a living...and do you prefer Mike or Michael."

"Whichever is fine. I'm an oil field services rep and a consultant."

He told her this warily.

"Really? My parents have some wells on our land in west Texas," she told him, eating a meatball.

"The Yates Field in the Permian Basin?" he asked immediately.

She sat back, the surprise at his knowledge on her face. "We own 160 acres north of Ft. Stockton," she admitted.

"Right along the Pecos, huh?" He was playing the part and might as well go for broke on it. "Who does your folks' service work? Wait, don't tell me. Steven Aucone, right? I'll bet money on that," the last part coming out bitter.

"Who's Steven Aucone?" Mary asked.

"His family is big in the oil business in Texas," Michael explained. "He knows everyone, and is honest as the day is long." Both women watched him. "He is the reason I have to travel to Bismarck and Scotland and Georgia- the Soviet state, not the one with Atlanta," he told Mary. "He just beat the pants off me when I came out of college."

Michael used his knowledge of articles he'd read from the tech magazines to establish his bona fides with Sydney. He risked looking at her.

Sydney admitted sheepishly, "Steven's daughter Meghan is my best friend."

Mary told them, "If I ever get an oil well, I'll use him."

Michael looked askance at Mary while Sydney laughed. "Mary, you wouldn't use me?"

"Nu- You'd want me to use the best, right? You just said he's better than you."

"I did not say that!"

Both women were laughing at his expense. "How did you two meet?" he asked, to get back on a better topic.

"This sweet girl brought me cookies!"

"My renovation is going to be loud and I didn't want to alienate the neighbors so quickly," she explained.

Silence reigned for a period while everyone ate. More wine was poured around to refill glasses. Michael kept staring and catching himself. Finally, he couldn't help it. "Which hedge fund does your husband run Sydney?"

The colder look she gave him was for the sexist remark and she said, "None. I'm not married."

Mary broke in. "Mikey, Sydney is a doctor!"

Doctor being one of the five approved professions for Jewish grandmothers. Doctor, lawyer, teacher, accountant, and rabbi comprise the holy five. Musician was acceptable, as long as it was classical. Thief was not anywhere close to the list.

"Wow. What's your specialty?" he asked.

"Pediatric Oncology," she said.

The thought of sick kids with cancer depressed him and it must have shown on his face because she went on. "I'm not seeing patients, just lab work. It's a great job. I get to set my own hours and it's so close."

"Where?"

"Brooklyn Hospital Center," she told him.

"The place across the park? I didn't know they did research."

"It's a new program in conjunction with Sloan Kettering."

She told them of her med school days at Baylor, and how she was in practice down in Houston for a while, and then she wasn't. "So I called a colleague at Sloan and here I am."

Mike read between the lines and figured a boyfriend situation moved her from Houston. The three talked of Brooklyn and the old days and what was new and fun to do now. Dinner wound down and more of Sydney's cookies made an appearance as dessert. The port went well with the almond treats.

"Sorry, I missed my plate," Michael said, crunching on a bite.

"I hope my workmen aren't too loud."

He let her off the hook. "Not too bad. What are you doing to the place?"

Mary cleared the table and sent the two into the living room to talk while she cleaned. They both ignored her and helped with a few dishes as Sydney told him of the full gut job and the bathroom and kitchen remodel. "I'm living out of the one bedroom and the locker room at work."

"Who is your general contractor?"

"Gary Mastrangelo," she said. The concern on his face came through. "Don't worry. I talked to Rod and Jim and copied their rider on the contract to keep him on schedule."

She'd done her homework. Rod and Jim were the gay lawyers down the street.

Parts of Michael were standing at near attention as the two sipped coffee and spoke. Mary joined them and they had a marvelous time watching Jeopardy and Mike couldn't help but show off. Sydney was impressed by his trick.

Every answer was correct and final Jeopardy was tailor-made for him: This man said about bank robbery, "I rob them because that's where they keep all the money."

"Who was Willie Sutton?"

Both women debated if he was the most successful thief of all time while Alex confirmed Mike's professional knowledge.

"Nope. Most successful bank robber was Uday Hussein. Saddam's son."

"What?" she doubted his assertion.

"In 2003, the week before the American army moved into Bagdad, Uday drove into the National Bank of Iraq and gave the manager a note. It said, "Give this man all of the US Reserve currency, signed Saddam." Five hours later the boy drove off with 2 billion in US currency in the truck." Michael related the story while the ladies gaped.

"Fear doesn't count as a robbery," Sydney objected.

"Okay, no fear based thieving, huh. He thought a moment. "Use the Google on a guy named Stephane Breitwieser. Waiter by trade, from France. Stole 257 valuable objects from museums and other places worth about a billion dollars."

The blue eyes watched him, fascinated while he told the story. "The cops couldn't figure it out because he wasn't selling the items. He was an art lover, so he kept the stuff at his mother's house." "The police finally figured out it was him and they arrested him in 2003. They found the mother throwing statues into the canal that ran behind their house when they came to get him."

Mary and Sydney had a very uncomfortable discussion on what makes a person steal something, while Mike sat trying to figure out how to get Sydney alone and upstairs.

It was Mary who sealed the deal for him. The women were talking about the crown moldings in her apartment when Mary said, "If you think these are nice, Mikey's place has some really nice details."

And just like that he was taking her up the stairs and into his place to look at plaster medallions and moldings. The internal debate raged on inside him: Make the move, or not? She seemed interested, but the standard problem of his real profession came into play. He was torn about the problem. Confused.

Sydney made some casual inquiries about his status with regards to how "his girlfriend must love how clean the place is kept."

The answer-"I'm not involved right now," got the spark he was looking for.

The nickel tour showed off his living room and kitchen. He advised her against the fireplaces. She watched him while sipping her water and agreed, wondering where this was going.

"Let me get you my plaster guy's card." Michael walked back down the main hall into the master bedroom. He left the light on in the hall way but didn't bother to click on the desk lamp or room light. He could have rattled off the phone number from memory, but he wanted to use the card as an excuse to ask her out. As he rummaged in the desk the available light in the room dimmed.

He turned to see her framed in the doorway.

"How come this room wasn't included on the tour?" she asked lightly, but with an intensity that caught his attention.

The way the light backlit her was artistic and it left her face in shadows. She looked so fucking good...

Michael crossed the room with determination. With his mind made up, he moved to her and took her in his arms. A brief hesitation gave her the chance to say 'no', but she turned her face towards him and they kissed. She wanted this as well, it seemed to him. The slow kiss turned deep and passionate. His hands moved to her face, and then down her back. He broke off the kiss to look at her. Eyes half closed and a slight smile showed. She was enjoying this. His mouth moved back to possess her lips once again.

She snaked her arms over his shoulders and around his neck while Michael let his hands roam over her body. She felt toned and her flesh sent electricity through his fingertips. His hands dropped down to the ass that had taunted him for a week now. He pulled her in close and let her feel his need. A low moan escaped her.

Michael responded by picking her up and moving over to the bed. She cradled easily in his arms.

Laying her down gently, he kneeled down to kiss her lips, neck, and nibble her ears, which sent his nerves tingling. *This was better than stealing!*

Sydney was working the buttons on his shirt. Finally popping the last one, she unwrapped his torso and kissed his chest, her mouth tracing fire along his ribs and nipples.

He felt the play of her lips on his body for a time and then tugged her sweater up and over her head; not wanting to interrupt, but he had a new goal in mind: freeing those breasts. She was kneeling on the bed with him as he worked the lace bra's front catch. Eyes mesmerized as he unhooked the black fabric, her breasts came free with pink nipples erect.

He took a mental snap shot. Sydney groaned as he sucked and kissed her breasts. She thrust back and pushed him to lay flat on the bed. Working hard, she was breathing heavily, too, as pants and shoes came off in the wrong order, until both were naked. She grasped his warm and rigid cock in one hand, working rhythmically, and then followed with her mouth.

"Oh, God," became "oh, God, not yet," as he pulled her up to allow himself time to delay and better access to her pussy. His tongue worked her soft mound and she bucked and writhed under him. Sydney surprised both of them when she orgasmed.

Michael barely gave her time to recover from the shaking and quivering when he levered down and plunged inside of her. It was like dipping his penis into a heated vat of oil.

"Oh, God!"

She's going to think I'm religious if I keep calling on the Lord so much.

He rocked slowly, trying to build the intensity, lost in the immediacy of the whole experience.

She responded by grasping his ass hard and grinding her pelvis into him.

"Deeper!" she commanded.

He complied by thrusting his full length.

"Yes!"

Five minutes later, Michael could feel his orgasm coalesce somewhere near his toes. She was close again, too, he could tell.

The rhythm picked up. The couple raced to see who could cross the finish line first and Sydney won by a stroke or two.

Michael had never before experienced an orgasm like that one. His head exploded into a million pleasure points, wiping away all of his fears and doubts.

He might have passed out, he didn't know. A while later he came to his senses with his back arched and moaning between breaths.

He eased out of her and rolled off to his right still gasping. "Holy shit!" Sydney snuggled into his side, grinning in the half light. He looked at her and said, "I did not know it was possible for one human being to give another that much pleasure."

She laughed throatily, "I might know some tricks."

"Tricks! You should teach a class."

More laughter and she shivered a bit in the growing cold.

"Sorry, maybe we should get under the covers?"

The pair scrambled into the bed with various naked parts flashing in the half light.

"There is a giant stain on your duvet."

He waived that off. "I'll buy a new one." The pair talked quietly for a while, trying to come to grips with what they'd done together. Not recriminations, really, more like amazement it had happened for both.

Michael recognized that the doctor's part of Sydney's brain matched his in some ways. She needed to be able to compartmentalize, as well. He just hoped he would be a regular partition.

As he settled into bed, with Sydney in his arms, the whole last few weeks came down on him. Bone-weary, he yawned.

"Sydney, I'm suddenly knackered, as the English say." He searched her face.

"I'm glad you are here. I wanted this to happen, but I didn't know..."

"So am I..."

And somewhere after the "I", Michael Davidson fell asleep.

Chapter Seven

His eyes snapped open at 8:37 am with the sun desperately trying to overcome the clouds outside his bedroom window. He turned his head.

Gone.

Fuck!

He had her! Had her right there and then he'd fallen asleep. Idiot!

As he rolled out of bed, he noticed the note.

"Michael- I have to go into the hospital today. Be at the park 8:00 am sharp on Sunday for our run. You can take me to breakfast afterwards to apologize for FALLING ALSEEP ON ME!"

He winced. He was going to pay for that fuck up.

During the shower and dressing for his meeting with Demetry, among his other work items today, Michael reviewed his evening with Sydney. Fantastic. Nothing short of fantastic. He felt great! Wonderful, in fact. Eyes open, head clear, heart full; ready to start the day. He hoped she wasn't having post one-night stand issues. The note suggested otherwise. She wouldn't have wanted to run and have breakfast if she was really upset with him. At least, that's what he thought. She might have other ideas. The heart of a woman is a mysterious place. Or something like that.

Shaving, he wondered if she'd done any snooping around his house. He figured on some light bathroom cabinet monitoring and maybe a browser history look on his computer. He had a little porn on the history, which was okay, since he was a guy and she would expect that. Again, the note suggested her look (if she'd done one) hadn't raised any flags.

Of course, if she discovered what he really did for a living it was all over, but he pushed that thought into its hole and buried it.

A text to Graeme directing him to meet him at the diner at 12:30 got a prompt, "K" response.

The rest of the morning was consumed with working. Ira, Rick, and Gretchen all had updates for him. He set a Monday work day in the office.

The timeline for things kept running in his head. April 6th site. Job on that weekend. Then what? He lost an hour theorizing about Demetry and the FBI; nothing good coming from that. He still hadn't heard from his 'contact' in the Bratva. That was another delicate thread he was tugging.

Leaving the house, he drove slowly to the post office and the dry cleaners. The Crown Vic tailing his every move. *Jesus! Didn't those cops think anyone would ever notice the same car watching them day after day?*

The tail infuriated him. Down Atlantic Avenue he drove, breathing heavily to get over the anger. Some thoughts of Sydney put his mind right as he jogged the car left and then right on Tomlinson.

Paul's diner was on the left. It was an old-fashioned, 1950's-style, low-slung building, which had a small parking lot attached. He was swift and got a spot near Graeme's black Mercedes. Two spots open at Paul's? Lucky!

He zipped the leather jacket down as he entered the warm restaurant and the smell of fried onions and oil hit him. The place wasn't crowded; as a family of four was in the front booth and the counter held three other patrons. Graeme looked up at him from a small table in the back.

Michael slid in opposite his friend and partner. A small smile played on his lips as he said, "Hi."

"You got laid last night, huh?" The Irishman said it without seeming to look up from his menu.

"How in the fuck do you know that?"

"The stick is gone from your ass. Even with Demetry's goons tailing you."

He was observant, Michael knew for a fact on that. A grunt was the only answer he gave to the jibe though.

A waitress approached the men. She sat down two waters and a cup of coffee for Graeme and took out a pad.

"You want something to drink, hon." The flat Brooklyn accent marked her as a native.

"Pat," Michael said, noting her name tag, "I'll have a cup of coffee as well and I think we are ready to order." He looked the question at Graeme who nodded back.

"I'll have two eggs sunny side up, bacon, hash browns and wheat toast with a glass of OJ," Mike ordered.

"So a Number Two with coffee and an OJ?"

"Yes."

Pat swung her gaze to the Irishman. "Veal parmesan, please, and a salad," he ordered.

"Spaghetti, vegetables, or raviolis for the side?"

"How are the rav's?"

"Homemade," she confirmed.

"I'll have those." Pat left the men to put in the paperwork with the cook. "Who's the bird?"

"A doctor. She lives next door and she's fucking beautiful!" he said, letting a little enthusiasm show.

"Really?" The arched eyebrow accused him.

The man wasn't biting on that.

Graeme went on casually, "Love to meet her."

"No fucking way! You aren't coming close to her to mess this up for me."

"I'm hurt, shammer."

"Fuck that. You'd sell your mother to the Arabs for this woman."

"Well, well, fancy that."

"Fuck you." The men relaxed and ate as the food arrived. They spent a solid hour going over Hatton Gardens and Dubai.

"We pitch both jobs to Roybokov today," Michael told Graeme again. That had been his other job in London. Graeme was to fully work up the Dubai idea as an actual pitch for the mob head.

"We have to provide some light at the end of his tunnel otherwise we won't have any time or space to get out," Michael said this while his partner nodded along. They both knew the truth about playing against the Bratva. A healthy dose of fear and respect kept people upright when playing against the mob.

"I'd love to know who is squeezing Roybokov."

Davidson agreed. "I have feelers out, but so far nothing. I'm going to try something after our meal, so I will meet you at the house."

No matter the urging, Michael would not divulge what he was doing, so Graeme stopped asking. "I have a session with Ira, Gretchen, and Rick tomorrow to go over logistics for Dubai. "You coming?", He asked Davidson while Graeme looked at his friend.

The hesitation was all the answer Michael had to provide.

"You made plans with the bird!" A chuckle escaped the man. "Thinking with your dick already."

"My dick thinks better than your head!"

The insult rolled off Graeme. "Don't worry. Anything comes up

Sunday and I'll text you." He got up to leave. "See ya." He dropped thirty on the table top.

"You're picking up a check? Am I dying?"

The Irishman answered with the bird and he started walking away.

"Watch yourself," Michael warned. All he got back was a wave.

With an hour to kill, Michael wanted to get some snooping in. He needed to understand who and what was working on his boss and figure out how to work the problem.

The drive down to Brighton Beach was uneventful even with the tail following him. Street parking for the Audi was available at Brighton and 10th and he took it, even though he feared for the car. The Hard Pawn storefront was shabby and fronted Brighton, while the alleyway behind it was litter strewn and easily missed.

Davidson did not like this place or its owner and the feeling was entirely mutual.

The games started early as Feydor kept him waiting on the street for three minutes before buzzing him in. *Dickhead.*

The place was empty, except for one of Fey's burly 'cousins' behind the main display case. *A dollar got you ten there was shotgun behind that case*, Michael thought. Feydor Slutskaya looked up from a plate of chicken he was eating, grease covering his mouth and fingers as he sat opposite the cousin. "Da?"

He sized up the fence. "Feydor, we need to speak. Alone."

A twitch at his man from the boss and he lumbered into the back office through the door. The fence wiped his face with a soiled napkin. "Talk."

"How's business?" Davidson asked neutrally.

144

"You aren't providing any merchandise, so it's lousy."

"And yet the street is so busy I couldn't park." He pointedly looked at the two shadows in their car watching the store.

The fence grunted, looking all the scummier with his dead eyes and thinning hair. Michael hoped that message was received: *We've marked the tails. Pull them off.* The man finally shrugged and asked, "What the fuck do you want?"

"I'm on my way to see Demetry, and I'd like to know how long this job of his is going to take."

"It is a courier thing, like you've done before. Take two... three days tops." Feydor actually smiled a little, which did nothing for his looks.

"Good. Because I have a line on a job and I may need to move some stones and the settings through you. Take us three or four months to put together." Mike tried to keep it casual and semi- factual.

The man suddenly looked interested and greedy. "How much?"

Shrugging, Michael got interested in the fake Rolex watches on display. Some people went for flash.

"Depends, but I think a $100 million, maybe a $150 million, in stones. Could be some watches. High end, not this crap," he gestured to the case. "We'd move it just like Harry's."

The Heist at Harry's was the job the gang had pulled in Paris at Harry Winston's store on the Avenue La Montaigne. The four of them (with Rick outside) had walked in the front door at closing time dressed as women. The vault door was open as was the normal routine for the shop. The security guards never knew what hit them when the tasers came out of purses. $180 million in diamonds and watches went into three large felt- lined boxes in sixteen minutes. Ira had locked the door on his way out.

Michael moved the vast majority of the stones through his fake holding company, which was registered as a diamond wholesaler. Some small stones and the lower end watches went through Feydor. His work was only on five percent of the take. The main advantage was that the gang could move the whole batch two months after the heist without worrying about the feds swooping in. And they got more money for the merchandise. In 2008, Slutskaya was still relying on contacts within the city's gem district to move the rocks. He consequently got sixty percent on the dollar for his efforts.

In contrast, Davidson used fake receipts for made up transactions to other wholesalers and retailers and got full value for the rocks. The whole operation cemented his status as the thief-in-law and earned the antagonism of the fence.

If he was counting on a huge reaction from the Russian about the size of the haul, Davidson was disappointed. Feydor simply looked like a dead fish at him. Blood shot eyes in a round face. "You could move three times that much and it might not be enough for him."

The blood drained out of his face as Michael absorbed that. Feydor said it with a certain amount of glee and false worry. It seemed to Davidson he was gloating in Demetry's troubles. *Uh oh.*

"Who? How?"

Turning back to the office door the man spoke to the air. "Orders from the boss in Russia. Roybokov has to back the whole complex- the one at Flatbush and Atlantic."

Holy shit! The Barclays Center?

His brain smoked thinking so hard. The whole project was three billion, with a B. He knew there had been cost overruns and hints of 'issues' with financing. Some heavy-hitters involved in that center and Demetry was one of them.

"The entertainer is just a figurehead. Demetry was brought in by Putin himself. He owes $600 million as an insurance hedge against any further delays in the project. All of it. The land, the buildings, the shops..." Feydor quit speaking.

Jesus, Roybokov is on the hook for every penny! His head spun out scenarios and problems.

Feydor noticed the intense concentration. "Funny to see you worried."

Davidson stared at the man. *You do realize we are a package deal, right? I go down, you go down,* he thought but did not say.

No, Feydor did not see that.

The realization flashed along his mind. So he said, "I've setup some new shell companies to process the potential take. Make sure you send in the forms to the state offices per the lawyer's instructions."

The fence slowly thought about this, but could not see a reason not to comply. "Da."

The real reason Michael wanted this was so that Feydor's name and business would be all over the illegal movements of the stones, if they succeeded.

"This job is set?"

Michael nodded. "About eighty percent. One more major hurdle to overcome, but I wouldn't be visiting you if I didn't think we could work around it." Feydor nodded, pleased to know some money was coming his way. Mike had a million thoughts running in his head about Roybokov, and now that he sort of knew what was up, he needed some clear time to think it thought and figure his way out.

Making a lame excuse, Davidson left the pawn shop. He figured the signal for him to leave the city and Bratva behind would be Feydor's body floating in the East River.

His suspicions and fears confirmed to some extent, Mike could start figuring a way out. The Dubai job was initially a distraction to keep Roybokov focused, but now it really would be the answers to his prayers. He had to dangle the job right in order to get the mob head to pull back the cops and maybe delay the feds. *I'll let him worry about the feds.* The compartments in his head whirred to capacity when they tried to figure the ramifications to his relationship to Sydney, that Feydor's disclosure had wrought.

I'll think about that later.

He drove slowly over to the house for his meeting.

Demetry Roybokov's house sat at the corner of Pierrepont Place and Pierrepont Street in the Brooklyn Heights section of the city. Number eight was a turn of the century Italianate mansion that sat alone, surrounded by three acres with mature trees and a huge wall. The building had been through several remodels in its lifetime, but the mobster had purchased it decades ago and kicked out the eight tenants in order to recombine the units into one massive house. Michael figured $40 million in today's dollars.

What the place had, always had, was its location.

Hard on the Brooklyn Queens expressway, the house offered stunning views of lower Manhattan, the Statue of Liberty, and the waterfront.

Demetry told Davidson that on 9/11 he'd sat on his roof deck and watched the twin towers fall. No emotion showed on his face then, and none would be there now, Michael knew.

The house also afforded the man with a nice security setup, in addition to the wall. Since he was adjacent to the Brooklyn Heights Promenade, the city allowed him to use the playground as an ad hoc parking lot. This allowed him to control who gained access to the place. Two large men patrolled the lot and kept out riff-raff. The neighbors rarely complained as the goons kept their cars safe, too.

Michael parked next to Graeme's car which held the Irishman and both men exited together. A low voiced, "Really sell the Dubai job," order from Davidson got Graeme excited.

The stoop was eight steps to get to the front door, which was opened by three security men dressed in monkey suits. The marble foyer contained a chandelier much like Michael's.

Mine is better, he mused while the guard felt his crotch for weapons. His mate got a similar treatment.

The men led the pair to the little parlor, a small sitting room off the front of the house. It was the room where you were polite to guests without letting them too deep into your house.

Taking the small settee together the two men left the one comfortable chair in the room unoccupied. Michael knew this was a test: Did you take Caesar's chair in his own house?

The security squad left and Davidson knew that at least two men would be posted at the door. You did not let thieves run loose in your house.

The door unexpectedly opened and a woman entered carrying two drinks. Kat. Ekaterina Roybokov, Demetry's daughter. Michael had not seen her in a while.

Both men stared at her. Tall, blond, with a model's height and thin body. Her face was all planes and angles. Full red lips were parted in a half smile.

"Kat!" Michael said, surprised. "You look lovely." He rose and came towards her.

The now twenty-six year-old silently handed them both the vodka one after the other.

"I thought you were in LA buying up half of Malibu," Davidson tried to keep it light, but it sounded forced.

She ignored Graeme and focused on Mike. "I'm back now." The woman watched him closely for a second. Reaching her hand slowly up, she caressed his cheek and then ran her hand down his face and over his chest to his flat stomach. A soft murmur came from her.

Michael stepped back just a bit, embarrassed.

"Who is she?" Kat asked, watching him. Graeme hid his laugh in the drink glass.

Davidson didn't answer the arrow dart question, instead, he deflected. "We are just here to talk to your dad."

"Uh hum." More looking at him, with hooded eyes from the woman. He felt she wanted to say some things, but she just said. "Try not to get yourselves killed." It was her first acknowledgement of his partner.

Whatever message or mood she wanted to convey complete, Kat swayed out of the room.

Michael slugged down the vodka to steady himself.

"Shammer," Graeme warned.

Yeah- focus, I know, Mike thought.

They didn't have to wait long. The door reopened a scant minute later and Demetry Roybokov entered the room. No bodyguards came with him as Michael and Graeme stood respectfully and performed the ritual hug and kiss on the cheeks hello.

The sixty-seven year-old was still in good shape. A little thicker in the waist, but not fat and still powerfully built. Graying hair and some wrinkles lent him some age. He certainly wasn't handsome, but the blue eyes radiated power and a lack of feeling that was almost palpable. Michael figured he wore the sweater to give himself a grandfatherly air.

It wasn't working.

The Bratva head had no soft side. Truth was, he scared the shit out of Davidson, his gang, and even his two kids, Nicholas and Kat. His wife had died last year under weird circumstances and no one ever talked about that. The mistresses just came and went as necessary.

Demetry sat in the chair and the pair followed suit on the couch.

"I have a job for you both," the deep voice rumbled out, the accent still heavy after decades in this country.

Both men nodded back. Neither spoke as Demetry hated to be interrupted.

"It has come to my attention that certain advantages may be obtained by storing assets at a freeport."

Davidson sat back on the settee.

Freeport?

Donniger had no clue. "Excuse me, Sir. I'm not sure what a 'freeport' is." He asked, politely. Interruptions were bad, but questions would be allowed.

"A freeport, Irish, is a bonded warehouse and storage location where valuable assets can be placed for certain tax advantages."

Michael's mind processed the news. *Why? What was he moving? And why now?*

"I can also place, shall we say, delicate items in the freeport facilities without fear of another entity seizing, attaching, or putting a lien on them."

Ahhh. Some disparate facts clicked in his head. Michael figured he needed to really put some homework in on freeports.

"Which items will we be moving?" he asked.

"Seven paintings and four statues," Roybokov said. "I know you are familiar with them."

Both thieves knew what he was talking about. The Brechtol paintings.

That was a tight job, Michael remembered. The gangs last successful job. They'd robbed the AG Brechtol Museum in Berlin in 2009. The gang posed as the art moving company to take two crates from a bonded shipping warehouse when the works were on their way to join a traveling exhibit. The four old masters and three lesser works were simply repackaged and shipped out within an hour of being lifted. Low-level bulk freight shipments took forever to reach their destinations, but no one wanted to steal scrap electronics.

He figured the four statues as the Giacometti's he and Graeme had stolen from some homes in the Brooklyn area many years ago.

Demetry always had a good eye. The value of those skinny figures had risen dramatically in the almost two decades since the men had taken them. The shipment going to the new location represented almost a full circle: some of the earliest things they'd stolen and the last.

The three men shared a secret smile over past glories.

"What do you want us to do?" Michael asked.

"I've taken a vault at the Luxembourg Freeport. It is adjacent to the airport there, uhhh," Roybokov slipped, forgetting the name.

"Findel."

"Yes, Findel, thank you, Michael. I need you to accompany Nicholas to the vault and look over the place while the paintings go in. He has all the passwords and the paperwork, but I want you two to look it over and tell me about their security. I've heard stories of the Zurich Freeport that leads me to be a little... hesitant."

Michael wondered what that was. More homework. He nodded to the boss. "Of course, Sir. It will take us three or four days to setup the courier forms and the visit request. I'll get with Nick next week to go over everything." Michael said this, gently looking to the old man for approval.

"Da, good."

Now, the tricky part.

"Sir, while we are here, both Graeme and I have jobs we would like to pitch to you."

"Both?"

Feydor must have told Demetry about my job, but he had no idea about Graeme. "Yes, Sir, both."

Roybokov made a small gesture that said, 'get on with it'.

"The first job is at the Hatton Gardens Safety Deposit Box Company in London."

Michael went on to explain about the De Beers site brief, the change of location, and how the large transaction over the holiday weekend was going to force some of the companies to deposit the

153

stones.

"How do we know this?" The gangster was still sharp, asking good questions.

"Our contact at De Beers has told us of several large policies covering those boxes over that timeframe. It was confirmed by another at Lloyds."

"How much?"

"Maybe as much as a $150 million or more."

Demetry grunted. Michael went on to explain his thoughts on the job. He spoke for an extended period of time before falling silent.

"Do you see any problems so far?"

His thief-in-law shrugged. "There is always the unforeseen, and we have not gotten a look at the alarm situation yet, but I have been in the building and I think we can do it."

Without committing anything, the gangster turned to Graeme to hear what he had to offer.

The Irishman cleared his throat. "Sir, we have been casing the new Dubai Gold Exchange over the last six months. It is the intention of the UAE government Trade Office to establish Dubai as the leading Middle Eastern gold trading center. All forms of the enterprise are being planned: Investment, coins, and consumer goods."

Demetry stirred a bit in his chair. This was something different for him.

Donniger went on, "To facilitate this center as a trading entity, the government office has to bring in $500 million to $600 million in gold to have on deposit for the transactions and to give to the artisans."

That definitely got his attention, Michael thought.

"This job is different than anything we have ever tried before," Graeme told the man.

"Different how?"

Graeme looked him square in the eye. "This is dangerous. I fully expect to be in a gun battle with at least ten security personnel. And full on mercenaries, not Wackenhut or rent-a- cops."

The old man scowled. "Who the fuck are they?" Graeme went over the situation in great detail about the security and who the forces arrayed against them would be.

"What do you need from me?"

"I need fifteen to twenty guys who are smart, can shoot, and take orders," Graeme told him earnestly.

He could see the wheels turning in the gangster's head. Knowing this would be about half of Demetry's core people, Michael watched him calculate the pros and cons. Contrary to movie plots where the body counts got into the scores, it was difficult to find fifty loyal, decently intelligent crooks.

Too often the Bratva had to rely on fringe elements and those fringes got messy.

"When and for how long?"

Graeme shrugged. "January or February. The shipment is mid-April."

Demetry shot a glance at Michael.

"It is tight with the other job, I know. But we think we can arrange it." He spoke and gave a half look at Graeme to apologize for stepping on his toes.

"That can be arranged," Demetry said after some contemplation.

"Excellent."

Graeme laid out the plan for the boss in bold strokes. He spoke passionately for fifteen straight minutes.

Davidson could see Demetry getting excited. *Graeme has really sold him*, he thought.

"And you are sure about the flight route?"

"Since '03, Sir. The war has caused everyone to divert flights to the UAE over Saudi airspace and out over the Gulf of Oman for a straight run back in. That avoids Iraq, Syria, and Iran."

The silence in the room stretched for a long minute. The old lizard made the decision. "Da."

The boss rose and actually smiled. The men followed suit.

"I'll call Nicholas and set things up on the other thing," Michael said again.

Donniger got the big kiss and he took advantage to say, "We will setup some training and information meetings with your people after the first of the year."

The men were hustled out of the house.

Both went out gratefully and spent two minutes talking in Michael's Audi.

"That went well," Graeme breathed out.

"Yeah, tell a man you are about to put $700 million in his pocket and he will perk right up."

"That should give us some wiggle room, huh, shammer."

"Yes. We are both going to be very busy. I need you to be ready to bounce between London, Luxembourg City, and Dubai over the next two weeks. Aye?"

Graeme nodded. The men shook hands and he left the Audi and went to his Mercedes. As he drove off the Crown Vic followed closely.

Assholes.

Michael was tired. Fifty-three minutes with the devil can take it out of you. He wanted a quiet evening finding out about freeports. Besides, he had plans in the morning he was looking forward to. Plans which had nothing to do with stealing something. That whole idea was new and exciting and warmed him all the way home.

Chapter Eight

Sunday went about as well as he could have hoped for. 8 am came early, and a bit dark and cold, but not too bad. He crossed Washington into the park as nervous as he'd been in a while.

He found Sydney dressed to run in her UT coat and mittens. Once again, the sight of her caused all of the flowery things he was going to say to get bumped out of his head. "Hey," was all he managed.

"Hey yourself. You ready? Let's go." She took off running without waiting. Michael grimly followed. *Okay, maybe she is a little pissed about the other night.*

The run started well, but Sydney could not keep the same steady pace that he could achieve. She kept speeding up and slowing down, and as much as he liked the view, the changes kept throwing off his rhythm and made the run harder for him.

After a few speed changes, Davidson could take no more. At the mile point, he accelerated into the front and set the metronome in his head to its normal pace and continued running. The light kept getting brighter as he ran along the path with Sydney either right next to him or a half step behind. Neither spoke, but concentrated on breathing and placing feet in order to not think about what had happened between them.

For a wonder, he was able to put her in a compartment and work on his relationship groveling while his thoughts went through the two jobs and his plans for Demetry. The miles flipped off while he stayed in his head.

At the finish line he had all his Monday to-do lists worked out for everyone, his end game scenarios with the Bratva, and the perfect amount of begging to be accomplished with the woman.

The recovery was mostly silent, beyond some scant words as they puffed and stretched. Davidson went over to the chin-up bar and started the sets of ten. No way he was not finishing with her watching! Even if he had to take five minutes between sets.

The last set did cause him to collapse on the ground at the end.

"Impressive," she said, and helped him to his feet. She did manage to do two pull-ups herself.

"Yeah, listen. Can we start over? I mean, the other night was great, but it went a little quicker than I thought. Not that I... But I like you and I think we should... But you kind of overwhelm me and I..."

He wound down as she smiled at him. He got the hint. She wasn't that mad. Maybe even a bit overwhelmed herself.

"Hey- You hungry? I know a place." Davidson gave it his best Brooklyn wise guy accent.

She laughed and said, "See! That! That right there. I need to learn how to say, *I know a place or I know a guy*." Her voice tried the patois but it came out southern belle meets the Godfather.

He roared in laughter all the way across the street.

Sydney was hungry and he had a secret food weapon ready for her: The Promenade.

After showering and dressing for comfort, he drove out to the west end of Brooklyn. He parked a bit further north than was absolutely necessary because they were actually close to Demetry's house. He did not want her anywhere near the Bratva.

"Is it okay to park here?" She asked looking at the lot under the 278 highway.

"Not to worry."

The Brooklyn Promenade was nearly deserted in the winter

chill, but the boardwalk was still open for business. The clear, cold air gave views of Manhattan and the Statue of Liberty along the river. The iconic Brooklyn Bridge off to the right side of them.

She was impressed by the sights, and even more so by the smorgasbord. The collection of food available at Pier 6 was huge and the two took advantage.

"Why do women order a small salad on a date, but will eat 5,000 calories at a fair?" he asked. It was funnier because she was wolfing down a hotdog at the time.

"Why do men pretend to know something when they clearly need help?" She asked. It was funnier because he was struggling to use the new Square gadget to pay using his credit card.

That was the reason she intrigued Davidson. Even more than the physical, she challenged him, made him think. Her natural confidence was magnetic and he drew closer. She talked about the dispassionate things she had to do as a doctor and he could relate that. But there was intelligence and compassion, too.

She'd make a great thief.

The thought brought him up short as they walked on the pier. No, he did not want that. Davidson continued to watch her as she strolled and they chatted about nothing.

The rest of the day was spent just talking and learning about each other.

She went to UT because SMU was full of snobs, she thought.

He liked the northeast because it was the polar opposite of where he grew up.

She waxed on for a full hour about her job.

He gave her a scant thirty seconds about his.

She noticed that and let it slide.

By mutual consent the sex was off the table early so they could play catch up. The day was full for both and very comfortable. Davidson was thrilled.

The good night kiss at her house did cause him to rethink the agreement. She laughed and pushed him out the door to her torn up place. He went home happy.

The next morning, Michael parked down the street from the Jones Street office. A whole block down, which allowed him to see if his tails chose to follow. They did not. He could see that paranoia was catching as the black Mercedes of Graeme sat two spots down from his car. Entering at an early 8:22, he was the last person in the office. The other four crew members were arrayed around the table they used as a lunch spot and work table. The group was huddled over a diagram. A very large schematic spread out almost to the edges of the table.

"Hey."

Gretchen was the only person who looked up. She did a slow take on his face. "Who is she?"

Dammit!

"Shut it!" he told her as the others laughed. That asshole Graeme must have clued them in. "What's this?"

Ira took over. "We got the insurance plans on the Hatton Gardens and Greville Street businesses."

"Excellent."

"I don't see it," Rick complained. "I can't read this stuff."

"The lines here represent the data and cable lines that the alarm signals will ride with." Ira showed the youngest gang member. "See?"

The lines all merged at a tie point.

"What does that say, Ira?" Graeme asked, trying to read upside down.

"Detailed drawings on Eng detail XC117- Lloyds." Ira read back.

"Uhhh..."

"It means that the real detail on the data lines is on another drawing." Ira told the Irishman and Rick to their puzzled looks. "We are going to have to get to Linda again."

"Can't we use these?" Graeme muttered in his brogue, not to anyone in particular.

Ira shook his head. "The lines show up here, but not the specifics of the signals from the individual businesses. Without that, I can't isolate the safety deposit box company from the others."

Graeme looked worried. "Mikey, you call her again."

"She likes you," Michael said.

The Irishman acquiesced with a little grace. He left the table to place the call.

"What happens after, Ira?" Michael wanted to know about the alarm system work.

"We may have to actually go in to inspect the trunk and the lines. Maybe monitor the stuff."

"How are we going to do that?" Rick seemed perplexed.

"Easy! We turn in some forms to the Metropolitan Traffic

Authority, giving them the dates and the work and we are good to go!" Gretchen told him with a cheerful smile.

"Won't they check?"

"Yes, Rick they will," Davidson was patient, trying to teach the tricks of the trade to the young man. "But they will check with Sutton Electronics, the firm hired to do the work. And we will assure the folks that our US workmen are going to do a simple visual inspection only, without tearing up the pavement or seriously blocking traffic."

"A single manhole cover should do it," Ira confirmed. "That is if we need to go in."

Michael reached into his messenger bag on the floor. He passed out to do lists. "Ira, add the required supplies to Gretchen's shopping list."

The three gang members looked over the work lists when Graeme came back in the room. "Yeah, she'll do it as a favor to me." The sour tone was funny.

"How much?" Mike wanted to know because Linda might want to get to the Irish candy, but she was a practical person with bills to pay as well.

"Twenty-five thousand."

Ouch!

Cost of doing business, Michael supposed. He mentally added that up. Seventeen thousand a month for the flat. Transportation and special equipment in the $50,000 range. Another twenty-five thousand for miscellaneous expenses and suddenly they were looking at a hundred and twenty-five thousand to pull off this robbery.

One of the items on Rick's to-do list was to pull the required equipment from Ira, Graeme, and Gretchen and make up the fly away box.

"Let's talk time frames and travel." Michael told them all as home date planners got taken out and were prepared to be updated. He knew the gang would pick cover items to go in the burner phone calendars. He hoped like hell Rick wasn't putting in "steal $150 million from the Hatton Gardens Safety Deposit Box Company" in his date planner. His visual check said no.

'Birthday Party,' was noted on the planner. Good. He brought the others up to speed on the quickie job for Demetry and the okay to do the Dubai job. The 'okay's brought a load of talk between them about the FBI and what it would mean.

"Part of the plan," he assured them. "We need to focus!"

"Okay. We bounce to London on Thursday. Graeme and I have the courier job, I think, near the end of the week. Four or five days in jolly old England, and then over to the UAE for prelims on that job. Six days-say, starting on the 27th?"

"We miss Thanksgiving?" Rick whined.

"We don't miss it, we just celebrate where we are," Gretchen told him in a motherly tone. Even Ira looked at her strangely.

"Can't be helped, shammer," Graeme said. "I'm worried about where we are going to stay in the Middle East." Michael waited for the inevitable. "I vote for the Burj al Arab."

The boss winced. Of course, the man wanted to stay at the most expensive place in the city. The distinctive Al Arab was a six star hotel that cost twenty-five hundred a room per night, and that was just the basic accommodations. Davidson nixed that idea quickly. No way he was staying in a hotel that looked like a sailboat.

"How 'bout the Westin?" Ira chimed in.

"Too touristy. We need a business place."

"The Al Khalifa?" Gretchen tried.

"The tower?" Michael quirked a look and a question at her.

The Burj al Khalifa was the world's tallest skyscraper. Two thousand feet of graceful spires and dizzying views. It was new in the city, and the hotel not yet firmly on everyone's mind. Gretchen told him, yes, it was an option now.

"How much?"

"Expedia says six hundred a night." Ira tapped on the keys to his laptop.

He gave in. "Get four rooms, and make yours a suite," he told the couple. "We need transport and some basic equipment. Our main job is the uniforms and to find the long term housing for everyone while we do the advanced scouting. Graeme is in charge." The last added as almost an aside comment.

The others looked up at the change in protocol.

Michael stared back. "This job is his baby and he knows the area better and the whole structure like clockwork. He runs things." The members took the new info in stride while Graeme preened.

"Last thing- Get to a gun range. 9mm and full auto AK 47. Get proficient."

The gang broke up to work on their assigned tasks. Michael had a parting shot- "I am serious about the weight loss we talked about in London! 20 lbs!"

The good humor sucked out of the place. *Good they should be worried*, he thought.

He went into his office and Graeme followed him in.

"When do we meet Linda?"

"Sunday, St James Park." Graeme waited. "How's the bird?"

The grin just bloomed on his face. "Fine." The two men shared a little conspiratorial smile.

"I don't have to ask about the sex."

"We did not have sex; we are taking it slowly. We just succumbed to temptation before."

"How many times did you succumb?"

"Fuck you." Michael dialed the phone.

"Funny, now you are calling another one of Demetry's children who wants to sleep with you."

His response was the middle finger.

"Hello." The voice was rough.

"Nicholas?"

"Michael, is that you?"

"Yeah kid, I didn't recognize the voice."

"Rough night," the young man explained.

"No worries. How ya doing?" He played up the Brooklyn street because the kid liked that.

"Fine, fine. The old man said you'd be calling."

"Yeah. Can we meet at the diner tomorrow. Say noon? We need to go over the freeport stuff."

"Yeah, that will do. I got a name and number for you meantime. Phillipa Stoerman." He spelled it for Davidson and rattled off a string of numbers for the international call.

"She is Freeport Luxembourg's security liaison," Nick explained. "She says she needs forms and fingerprints if you guys are going to come with me."

"Got it- I will call her and we will talk about everything tomorrow, okay?"

"That's super, Mike. How have you been?" His voice dropped a bit and slowed down as he wanted the call to turn personal.

Michael closed his eyes. "Good kid. Been busy. Look, I need to call this lady and jump through those hoops so I can do what your dad wants."

"Yeah, okay." The disappointment dripped off his tongue.

"We'll have a long visit tomorrow, I promise."

"Okay, I'll see you, bye." Nicholas dropped the call.

Michael looked at Graeme. "That kid needs to come out of the closet, badly."

"Yeah, that's how it's gonna go alright."

But Davidson was not listening. He was beeping Luxembourg. It was 4:35 pm over there and he thought he could get a hold of the security office before they left for the day.

The two toned international ring tone sounded a few times before a pleasant voice came on the line. "Freeport Luxembourg Security. This is Helga. May I help you?"

The woman must have noticed the US number on the line and chose accented English as the language to answer with.

"Helga, this is Michael Davidoff, I am the bonded courier rep for

Prometheus Holdings. I have you on speaker with my associate Peter McNichol. We would like to speak with Phillipa Stoerman, if she is available."

"Ah, yes our Friday delivery. Certainly, Sir." She put them on hold.

Mike quirked an eyebrow at Graeme. "Efficient. 5' 10", 180 pounds Valkyrie type."

Graeme disagreed. "5'5" 125 pound librarian. A hundred bucks?"

"Done."

The phone clicked as the Freeport's head of security came on.

"Mr. Davidoff? This is Phillipa Stoerman. How may I help you?"

"Ms. Stoerman," Michael began, "my client would like us to accompany his son on the delivery. Friday, I guess is the day."

"Certainly, Sir, I will need to have the standard visit forms filled out with a copy of your papers plus the finger print cards."

"I can do that quickly if you have access to JPAS." He used the acronym for the Joint Personnel Access System. Secured facilities around the world needed a way to manage the people bringing in and out things for their vaults. The database was a way to ensure visitors were pre- screened to allow for easier access. What she didn't know was that Michael had hacked the database with help and inserted himself and Graeme as cleared persons. Now all he had to do was...

"We do, if you could provide us with your SMHIC?" She asked for the companies Special Materials Handling Identification Code.

"31778," Michael shot back quickly. He also rattled off the social security number, date of birth, and place of birth for his fake ID, as required by the database. Graeme piped up and gave her his info for the

Peter McNichol identity.

"Ah, I see both of you in the system and everything looks to be in order."

Michael was tapping away on his end putting in the visit request into the system. "Would you like us to follow this up with a fax on company letterhead, along with the ID-9 form for fingerprints?"

That pleased the woman. "Thank you, yes." She was obviously dealing with professionals.

The preliminaries out of the way, he went onto the harder stuff. "May we discuss the transfer protocols?"

"We can arrange everything; customs, handling and forms," she told them.

"Yes, but then I would be out of a job," Michael laughed easily. "So we will land sometime around noon on Friday," he started her off.

Phillipa took over. "Your plane will taxi to the north end of the airport into our facility. Ramp and customs agents will then meet you to clear personnel and cargo. The contents will be cataloged at that time."

Tricky, Michael thought. "None of those officials will be allowed to touch or photograph any of the items. Peter and myself will do all of that. All physical descriptions will be written down only. We will allow the agents to assure themselves that no other contraband is being brought into the country after our items are removed. I will personally hand over all customs forms and paperwork as provided by our legal teams."

"That is unusual. If we insist?" She tried to play hard ball.

"Then I will advise my client to use Freeport Dubai. Given some of his long term plans, that might be the best option for him."

Graeme grinned at the whole hearted truth of Michael's statement.

"Those arrangements will be acceptable," she finally relented.

He suspected that their request was not the first one she'd gotten like that.

Now the trickier part.

"Lastly, my client would like us to look around the facility to assess operations and security." He left it hanging.

"I can arrange for a tour of the other vaults if you like."

"Madame, please. I don't want to be all up in your business, as the kids say, but we need to see the layers. Outside physical, fence alarms, guard dogs- all of it. We need to see the vault alarms and the procedures for entry, plus we are worried about any Zurich issues."

His extensive Google search on similar freeport facilities had turned up an interesting story: Pablo Picasso's granddaughter was placing paintings from her personal collection into the Zurich Freeport when another client was accessing his vault. She immediately recognized some of her grandfather's stolen paintings in the enclosure. She freaked. The head of the Zurich Freeport was brought up on charges of trafficking in stolen goods.

He could hear the distaste in her silence. "I see you know your business, Mr. Davidoff."

"Michael, please. Ms. Stoerman, I don't want to see totally behind the curtain, but I need to be able to assure my client that your facility will suit his ongoing plans."

"That will be fine, Michael."

Davidson threw her the bone. "Just let us talk to the lovely Miss Helga and we will arrange everything. I also hope that you and your husband would join us for a dinner Friday at the Grand Ducal?"

He named one of the nicest restaurants in Luxembourg City.

A slight snort escaped the woman. "That's a nice bribe, Michael."

"Bribe is an ugly word. Think of it as the perks of an expense account."

She said yes and the two talked a bit on the logistics before turning them back over to Helga. Graeme took the opportunity to ask the assistant to dinner as well. "To thank you for the help."

As Davidson hung up the phone, he said, "You better hope she is not the Valkyrie type."

Graeme was already generating the visit request on Prometheus letterhead. It paid to be ready. The memo just summarized what Michael had verbally given the woman and put some dates down.

"You got all the dates set?" Mike asked.

"Yeah. Amazing what you can do with a fake birth certificate, huh?" It was indeed. Michael had three fake ID's in the system and he kept them up-to-date. "You know when the fake ID cover is really good?" he asked his friend.

"When?"

"When you get a jury summons in the mail." He pulled an envelope from the mail pile on the desk which showed an older fake identity, called for service. Graeme nodded in wonder.

"I intend to call this in. I hope he doesn't get picked."

The gang was going to be very busy. Too busy for jury duty, Mike concluded. London, Luxembourg, Dubai. Not to mention Sydney. The person, not the city. He was ready- he thought.

Graeme left after some more talk between the friends about the jobs upcoming. The Irishman was due to leave for the UK very soon. "See you tomorrow at the diner." Michael waited until the Irishman was gone before he picked up the cell phone to dial a third number. He touched the digits almost reverently.

"Hey."

"Hey yourself," Sydney said.

"You busy?"

"Marginally," she said lightly.

"How about I make you dinner tonight?" He was NOT holding his breath.

"That sounds great! My kitchen got demo'd today," She said brightly.

An exhale and a grin as he said, "Then it's a win-win. 6 o'clock, and how does steak sound?"

"Fine and yummy. Medium rare, please. Ya'll got any of that fancy Cabernet to go with it? Maybe I will pick some up, just in case."

"I'll open a Malbec for you to try. Just bring yourself."

Sydney dropped her voice to a deep whisper and said. "I might bring a toothbrush with me as well."

He felt himself go rigid. *Dammit! How does she do that? That easily?* He needed to regain some hand in this new relationship. "You can bring the toothbrush, but absolutely no moisturizers or lotions," he said, trying to sound serious.

"Really? No lotions, even if I wear my new red panties from Victoria Secret?"

His throat closed up so much he could barely get out the, "Well, maybe..."

"What do you want to do to my new red panties?"

Oh Christ!

"I'm going to run my hands up your thighs to those hips and I'm going to grab your panties in both hands and peel them down..."

A sound came from his doorway. He looked up and jerked the phone away from his ear.

Rick stood in the office door holding a piece of paper, mouth open with a shocked look on his face.

"God damn it, Ricky!" Michael roared.

"Jesus, sorry, Mike..." The kid backed out stammering an apology.

"Put a fucking bell on you!"

He could hear Syd's laughter from the receiver. When he put the phone back up to his ear she was gone.

Twenty bucks says she brings a whole case of potions and unguents with her tonight.

That twenty was right on the money.

Chapter Nine

The crack in the ceiling was new. He'd never really noticed it before. Suddenly there it was, running right over his bed. Shit. He was home, right? Yes, this was definitely his place. What day was it? That part was tougher. Tuesday, the 3rd of December. A look to his left confirmed Sydney was in bed beside him softly snoring, curled up.

He rolled onto his back and stretched. Man what a couple weeks! Busy, but productive.

He'd met with Nick Roybokov at the diner, together with Graeme, after his phone calls to go over the courier job. Nick was touchy feely, but luckily he never made a pass at Mike. Probably, because the other man was present.

The three had gone over the job in detail. It looked like everything was set: Thursday wheels up, with a stop in London to pick up Peter McNichol, who was leaving that evening for the UK. Friday for the transfer of items then back to England on Saturday.

Michael had a few warnings for the mob boss' son. "No drugs or guns on the plane. The Luxembourg customs people are going to be all over us. Even one little pill in a case leads to questions and inquiries we do not want made, right?"

The young man nodded.

"And make sure you call Graeme, Peter, right?"

Turned out the only hitch on the job was a 'friend' that Nick brought on the plane in New York to drop off in London. The boy toy pouted the whole trip over which made Nick angry. So he drank which made Mike angry.

The jet was an ultra luxurious G5 from Gulf Stream. It came equipped with 12 first class pods which held lay-flat beds and an owner's suite. The aft end of the plane contained an actual bed. The lovers took that, and argued the whole way across the pond while Michael sat in the front, trying to relax.

Friday morning early, British officials came aboard at Gatwick airport to inspect the flight log and stamp passports. Peter McNichol arrived at 8:00 am sharp, nicely dressed in a dark blue suit with red tie, Gucci shoes, and sunglasses for effect. The boy toy eyed him as they passed each other on the tarmac.

The one hour fifty one minute flight from the UK to Luxembourg was calm.

"Say as little as possible and let me answer the questions," Michael warned again to Nick. The young man was at least a bit more sober now.

Findel Airport perfectly fit the country of Luxembourg. The modern and spacious facility was vastly outsized to the number of people it served. The country was a tiny spot in Europe that wealthy individuals and corporations used as a tax haven and not much else. Hence the airport was used by a small population of wealthy clientele that relied on discretion and expected luxury.

The G5 landed and taxied to the north end of the taxiway lanes as directed. The huge white freeport buildings were arrayed in front of the plane. A few trucks were parked in loading bays, but the place was mostly devoid of people, except for the cluster waiting on them.

A crew pushed a ramp up to the door to the plane which the flight attendant opened. Nick spilled out of the doorway followed by Michael and Graeme.

Davidson took charge. He presented passports and customs forms for the three of them. He also gave Phillipa the bill of lading from

Prometheus Holdings and the cargo manifest from the insurance papers for the cargo box as she arrived at the ramp. The art was listed as paintings from various artists and the statues the same. The value was stated at $10 million. A hefty discount applied to that figure. One of the statues could be worth a $100 million by itself, if anyone knew of its existence, which they never would if the freeport operated correctly.

The efficient Ms. Stoerman and Helga were happy to help them and Graeme won the bet as the assistant turned out to be a lovely thirty year-old blonde at 5'4" with prim glasses. The Irishman attached himself to the woman and would not let go.

The Lux customs officials frowned and hemmed when they could not touch anything as Michael shifted the entire contents from the cargo box to the freeport dolly/hauler. *Handy little device*, he thought. *Not the first time they've moved art.*

The hurt feelings of the inspectors were mitigated a little when they got to tear apart the empty crate to reveal a whole lot of nothing after the goods were removed.

Job done, they left, and the small processional went with Graeme and Helga leading the way, Nick and Phillipa next followed by the dolly with two security goons toting guns while a third pushed the cart. Michael brought up the rear and tried to watch everything.

The facility was very impressive. At three stories the huge warehouse was easily 100,000 square feet. The group approached from the back end loading area and walked around towards the

front side. Specially designed walkways allowed the group to enter a huge sliding door, easily six feet wide. *Bulletproof glass*, Davidson noted as he went in.

The movement of the train stopped as Nick and Phillipa went through the ID formalities in the spacious lobby receiving area. Fingerprint pad, retinal scan, and a password were all required before they were allowed access into the secured areas of the facilities. Nick completed the tasks with a minimum of fuss, even with his hangover.

The vaults were as impressive as the rest of the place. Huge steel and tungsten doors swung on smooth hinges to gape wide after more combinations were inputted. The lock was touchy and it took Nick two tries to get it right.

Michael interrogated Phillipa about the alarm systems as Nick went through the tumblers. Again the vaults were state of the art: Pressure, temperature, movement, and sonic alarms all were explained.

"Sixty five centimeters of re- enforced concrete with a full seven more of plate steel cladding the whole structure," the woman told him.

Graeme and Michael carefully placed the paintings on the walls on specially designed hangers. The vault was big enough to hold thirty more paintings; some higher and some lower on the hooks. The whole interior was climate controlled and had special UV lights that would not destroy the delicate paintings. Recessed wall niches took the statues with ease. Another ten empty slots dotted the walls and each had museum-quality spotlights encased and ready. Phillipa gasped slightly as the Giacometti went into its niche. The light hit the slender bronze figure beautifully, showing it to effect. It was a museum- quality display for a quality piece.

Too bad, no one can see it, Michael thought. The last thing Davidson noted was the heavy steel racks along the interior of the space in rows. Big enough to hold several hundred pounds of gold ingots, he supposed.

What is Demetry planning?

The last bit of business before their tour was very interesting for Davidson. Nick took possession of a letter from the freeport security woman. Nick let him read it while Phillipa got them out of the vault and back into the reception area.

Jesus!

The letter was from Jean Claude Juncker, the Minister of Finance for Luxembourg. It said that Prometheus Holdings had paid the taxes on the assessed value of the objects at three percent. And Luxembourg would receive another three when the cargo reached its 'final destination', whenever and where ever that might be.

This was true thievery! Michael was impressed. Tax dodging with the consent of the government. And both men knew that US corporations were using the same kind of dodge when they sold overseas companies. Both partners would setup a shell holding company in Luxembourg and the sale would actually go thru the new shells along with a nice letter from the minister that avoided any taxes. Trouble was, all the money had to remain offshore.

"Shammer, I bet the corporations and the fat curs will be howling for a tax holiday to allow them to repatriate all of those overseas funds." Graeme said sotto voce while on their tour. The men were discussing the letter at length, along with other tax doges.

How much does Apple have stashed overseas? A hundred billion? He wondered, thinking about the money. Always follow the money. Wasn't that the mantra from Watergate? From his own dealings, Michael understood that moving funds from off shore accounts into the US was very, very tough.

"The game is rigged," he confirmed to Donniger. This move was saving Demetry at least $200 million and was putting his valuables out of reach of anyone. Smart.

Helga led them around the facilities and the place turned out to be a smaller, less well known version of Ft. Knox.

There is no way to rob this place, he thought. Not that he wouldn't like to try. They did soak Demetry for an expensive dinner that night at the hotel on the expense account. Phillipa and her husband joined them with the lovely Helga at Graeme's side. Nick begged off, looking for some sleep. The five of them ate well and talked of inconsequential things. Michael missed Sydney something fierce. He was the fifth wheel at the dinner, after all.

The plane ride back to London on Saturday was somber. Only Graeme was smiling, as Helga had seen to that portion. Nick was bummed the entire flight, after reporting back to his father that they had accomplished the mission and received a terse, "Da," in reply.

"I'm getting away from him so I can be myself," Nick said, after announcing he was staying in London. Davidson wished him well, but he had some serious reservations.

The plane went back to New York empty, as the pair of thieves went to the new flat to work on Hatton Gardens. The rest of the gang was already in place and Ira was intent on the alarms systems as they all reconvened in the living room that evening.

"This is the key for all of it! We got to get that Lloyd's stuff, Mikey," Ira whined.

Linda did indeed come through with their drawing. The Sunday midday meet had a whole drug deal feel to it in the dim overcast of St. James Park and Michael gladly paid out the money for the drawing. The Lloyds woman only had eyes for Graeme as the three concluded business. *How does that fucker do it?* He wondered. Helga, Linda, Rachel? The man had no conscience and Michael was a bit jealous.

"We gotta go in," Ira announced later that night after a look at the detail on the plan. The table at the apartment had added a leaf to accommodate the huge sheet of paper.

"Gretchen, what date do we have?" Michael asked her.

"Technically Tuesday, early morning, at 0100," she told him, looking

at the forms they'd sent to the British authorities.

That settled when they were moving and the gang prepared for the inspection visit after hashing thru the job.

The foray into the utility tunnels was very eye opening for Rick. Suddenly on Monday evening, the gang was donning work vests, tool belts, and hard hats going to work. A white panel van holding traffic cones and barricades was taking them along the deserted street near the Hatton Gardens tube stop and Rick was impressed that no one was tense or nervous. Gretchen parked the van and the gang proceeded to block off the manhole cover about three hundred yards down from their target. Graeme took the topside watch with Gretchen, as Rick, Michael, and Ira went down. Traffic was very light at that hour so they went into the forbidding hole without disturbing things too much.

Flashlights illuminated the damp, cramped space. Pipes and brackets made the tunnel crowded, but a raised platform and deck way allowed for the men to work their way over to the alarm line cable run. They had to duck walk in sections, but it was doable. Water and trash and two rat bodies lined the bottom of the tunnel as they crawled to the spot.

Ira was amazed at the alarm lines. Individual cables and lines ran through the protecting cover pipe, not to a single line to a multiplexer, like he expected.

He and Michael discussed the issue for a while.

"Bottom line; can we isolate the line from the safety deposit box company?" the boss asked his man.

"I don't know yet."

The men came up with a plan. It was more work, but that was what they did; work around problems. The puzzle box always fought you.

Ira detailed the plan to Michael, Rick and Gretchen. The boss was satisfied that they could get the info they needed. Since they'd installed no gear and only had looked on this trip the clean up would be easy.

"Wrap it up!"

The police barely stopped by in the two hours they were in play at the tunnel. Just a perfunctory check of their permit and that was it. The gang stowed gear and swapped out work clothes for civvies. Rick got the job of returning the van to their storage unit. He reported no issues to Michael when he returned towards dawn.

Tuesday, through Friday was spent out of the Cambridge Gate flat working. The huge six bedroom place was nicely decorated and very efficient for them. Close to the tube and the target, they could comfortably work there. Gretchen got her kudos for her work.

A decent breakfast place was also available and the gang took to having a quick meal before casing the diamond district and the target building.

On Thursday, Michael watched a group of workers pull up to the back area of the Hatton Gardens building and proceed to crawl all over the place. A few discrete questions and a new fact entered the equation: The elevator needed extensive repairs. Six months at least, maybe a year for the work.

"We can use that!"

The gang got dressed in work clothes and spent most of Friday evening wondering around the building, taking measurements and noting patterns right on the inside of the place. Perfect!

The next stop for the gang was the UAE. The United Arab

Emirates are a group of city states on the Saudi Arabian peninsula. Oil ran the area, as was usual in the Middle East. Abu Dhabi and Dubai

got the lion's share of the money and the publicity, while Bahrain settled for its usefulness to the US as a military staging area to get by. The rest of the emirates were of no concern. The city sat on the Persian Gulf, near the Straits of Hormuz. Long and thin the emirate was no bigger in area than London at around fifteen hundred square kilometers. The English city held 7 million, while Dubai's population was trickier to pin down. 1.5 million permanent residents with perhaps another million foreign workers and ex pats all mixing together. A strange mix of crowded city and open desert.

Want to turn a patch of desert sand into the cultural, financial, and shopping hub of the Middle East? Dubai can show you the way. First, find a ten billion barrel oil deposit. Then pump 500 billion into wild construction projects to diversify your economy before the oil runs out.

Sheikh Mohammad bin Rashid Al Maktoum wanted to make his mark on the world like the old Roman Emperors had done before him. The Palm Jumeirah, Palm Jebel Ali, and the World Islands were a set of artificial islands built to increase the amount of Dubai's useable coastline. Rocks, sand, and palm trees all combined to add 520 kilometers of beaches to the city and attract the likes of David Beckham to buy a mansion for his pleasure. Fifteen of the world's tallest skyscrapers dominated the landscape. The opulent Al Arab Hotel, and the shopping malls together with the freeport and the new Gold Exchange offered the world a place to buy and store all of their fondest desires.

The infrastructure needs were enormous. Twenty-five percent of all the world's steel went into Dubai between 2007 and 2011. Foreign workers, tourists, and old-world Muslim ways collided on a massive scale. It was not uncommon to see a woman wearing a hijab and another wearing Vera Wang walking side by side. Tourism became the new oil rush as the city opened itself to cruise ships, sun seekers, and businessmen. Drinking, prostitution, and crime sprang up very quickly. Twenty miles outside the city center might be desert dunes, but the unimaginable wealth concentrated here ensured a well heeled few had everything they could desire within its confines.

The 747 landed at Dubai International Airport at 2:15 pm from the UK, with the temperature at twenty-three degrees Celsius. Hot and dry after the wet drab of London. The heat was much more pronounced than the gang realized as it felt like an oven even though it was under eighty Fahrenheit.

The short drive from the airport to the Burj Khalifa Tower Hotel was on the modern Al Zakar Highway. The road was famous for traffic jams of Ferraris and Jaguars, as the ultra wealthy tried to get around in a booming city.

"The transit rail line is new and very clean," Graeme told the others as they checked into the hotel. "It's better than the highway." He'd spent the most time in the city, doing the grunt work research for the job.

The gang met in Rick's room as they realized that he had the best view.

"How do you rate?" Ira asked.

"I might have played up the small town American overwhelmed by the strange city," the young man said.

His accent was barely noticeable. Kid's coming along, Mike thought.

"Uniforms, uniforms, uniforms." Michael focused them back. "These guys are full on mercenary killers- we need to be extra careful about this."

Again the uniqueness of the UAE went into the planning for the heist. An autocratic ruler, western business model with Muslim religious beliefs all made for a very different feel than any other country in the world. It resulted in the first warlord seen in the Middle East since 1927.

The Sheikh hired Erik Noble, he of Whitewater fame, to provide 'security services' to the royal person. Fresh from having Whitewater run out of Iraq due to the killing of nineteen unarmed civilians, Noble found himself persona non grata in the US. The offer from the sheikh gave him a home, a purpose, and the freedom to prosper. Noble changed Whitewater to Xi Security and soon he had a sprawling base outside of Abu Dhabi. His six thousand men did odd jobs for the other sheikhs when they weren't guarding the main man and established his reputation as a warlord.

The Dubai gold shipment job would require fifty of the standard uniforms that the Xi people ran around wearing.

Donniger was sure anyone caught wearing one of those outfits undeserving would not fare well. Of course, no one wanted to think about what would happen to anyone caught stealing tons of gold from an autocratic despot.

The gang discussed options at the hotel. Luckily, Gretchen could move about fairly innocuously due to her dark skin and a traditional dress. She blended in and could learn a surprising amount from the other women in the area.

She and Rick would concentrate on the clothes and their procurement.

Meanwhile, Ira, Graeme, and Michael spent hours driving around the city to the main sites as per the Irishman's plan. The border crossing into Oman at Al Ain on route E44. The town of Fujairah. The lonely square of land between the E66, the E44, and the E77.

The south side of that square was an ill defined camel track out in the empty quarter. Sunburns abounded as they visited the key spots. Ira took copious GPS coordinates and spent a long time fiddling with his gear.

"It looks perfect," Graeme kept saying to them. "I told you, perfect." His excitement was palpable.

"Twenty-two to forty-two minutes, depending on reaction times and some other factors," the Brooklyn-born thief told the others after he was done calculating.

Graeme whooped his answer. "Yeaaah!"

Michael said nothing as he thought it over. Twenty-two minutes? A shit ton of work for twenty-two minutes. All he said out loud to the rest was, "God, the variables!"

The two men waited on his pronouncement. Michael nodded his blessing and grinned. "We got a lot of work to do, looks like to me." Graeme and Ira matched his grin.

The trio packed up and drove back into the city to meet Gretchen and Rick. The duo had had some success as they had two huge boxes for the storage facility. Ten officer and forty enlisted uniforms with basic gear lay in the boxes. Mike shuddered to think what it cost. Graeme was vibrating just seeing the uniforms. He knew the plan was taking shape.

The rest of them felt it, too. Michael gave orders to the rest of them to stay in the city for a day or two more and get basic equipment to go into the storage area as they didn't have most of what they needed here.

Davidson left Dubai on a Monday morning with a great sunburn and more work to complete. The plane ride back to The States allowed him to keep on track with Hatton, figure Dubai, and how to approach Demetry.

Plus he worked on his own escape and disappearance. And all he could really think about was Sydney, which was why he'd abandoned his gang in Dubai to come home early. *Being the boss ought to have some perks,* he rationalized.

Back in Brooklyn, he got out of bed and went into the bathroom. Her lotions and toothpaste and hairbrushes had pushed his things towards one corner of the vanity. She had two drawers in the dresser and some of the closet for her clothes. And the shoes! Lord God, the shoes.

He returned from the shower, clean and ready to argue about when exactly he had agreed that she could move in with him. As he reentered the bedroom and inhaled, ready to start arguing, Syd spied him and threw back the covers.

Naked. Gloriously naked. Every thought fled. Later he groused about her tactics. "I use my gifts," was all she said.

Dressed in scrubs, she was ready for work, grabbing a quick bite of toast in the kitchen.

And she was perfectly ready for his complaint about the lotions. "Does the aloe help with your sunburn?"

"A little, yes."

"That will teach you to go running in the Middle East with no shirt on or sunscreen," the doctor admonished.

Yeah, Yeah.

"What is your schedule like at work?" he asked her, trying to be casual.

"Mellow," she said, coming to his side. "We go into a stand down split schedule on the 17th to the 4th."

"You gonna go home for the holidays?" Oh so innocently he asked the question.

She waited him out, then relented and kissed him. "Not this year. Thought I would see what New York had to offer."

He grinned. "How 'bout a little surf and turf?"

An eyebrow quirked at him.

"I was thinking we could head to Hawaii for a few days. Soak up the sun, and then come back and I will show you Rockefeller Center and Macy's and all that."

He'd been gone on short notice for Thanksgiving, so he figured he owed her some dedicated time.

"That sounds fantastic. I'll pay for half," she told him, trying to be fair.

A snort blew up that idea. "Nah. I'll cash in some frequent flyer miles. I know a spot with a good swim up bar on Kauai. It'll be reasonable."

Michael sort of relented after another protest and told her she could buy a dinner at the hotel. That would not be cheap. Dr. Devereaux went to work happy and he was very pleased with himself for making her happy.

He finished dressing and hustled downstairs. A knock on Mary Spack's door brought her answer: "Is that you boychik?"

"Yes Ma'am."

She unlatched the door and gave him a perfunctory kiss on the cheek. The sense that she was unhappy permeated the doorway. "What's wrong?"

"I heard Sydney whistling down the stairs this morning." The accusation was just in her voice.

"Mary, she's happy. So am I... You wouldn't begrudge us a bit of happiness?"

Mary shrugged as they sat in the parlor, her place tidy as always. "No- just you two be careful. You don't have the best record when it comes to commitment. Remember Victoria? Eh?"

A wince. She was right about that. "Are you talking to my mother?"

But Mary was not listening. "Of course, not that I blame you with Sydney giving the goods away for free."

"Mary! That's not nice."

The little old lady felt bad. "No, No. You are right. I shouldn't have said

that."

"I like her, Mary. I like her a lot," he said, trying to get his friend to approve and give her blessing.

"Of course, you do. What's not to like?" She paused and then said, "I'm sure she was Jewish in a previous life." Wow, the ultimate compliment from the woman.

"With all that blonde hair?" he teased. The old woman had to laugh.

"Hey. When is Chanukah this year?" he asked, trying to change the subject.

"Late in December. But Mikey, I'm going to Ilene's next week. She wants me to come to California. I won't be here for Chanukah."

"That's great Mary! You'll have fun."

"They have earthquakes out there, you know." She said it in the conspiratorial voice.

He grinned at her. "Yeah, and it is sixty-five degrees and sunny every day, not ten degrees and snow, like we have here. Go and have fun."

"How long are you staying?" he asked as she nodded agreement.

"Long time. Six weeks, maybe more if I can stand it. It depends on the bagels."

A nod and a quick calculation on his part. "I'll watch over your place and water the plants. Do we need to go shopping? Sydney and I are heading to Hawaii for a week soon, too." He dumped that on her after her announcement.

"No, no. Mrs. Lipinski and I rode the fogey wagon last week." She called the senior transit van that took her shopping and to some appointments, 'the fogey wagon'.

"Okay. The three of us should have dinner before we each jet off."

"You are the one always jetting off. Look at that sunburn, you should be more careful and use sunscreen..."

He escaped as quickly as he could.

The drive to the post office and some other errands allowed him to pick up a few things. Among them was a Crown Victoria tail. *Assholes.*

Driving slowly and carefully to the office he navigated the falling snow. He was the only person in the office today. Michael would meet with the gang individually to go over assignments and tasks, but basically the thieves were taking December off. It was one of the perks of being your own boss. To a limited degree- your own boss.

Laptop fired up and mail sorted, he started on the details; bills, statements, transfers, legal paperwork. It all had to be dealt with. He wished he had a Juncker letter to allow legal stealing like Demetry. Another transfer in from the Caymans to Anderson Consulting. The new Holding company was in place, ready for the diamonds. Sutton Geology was going to be doing some business, so they had to have a grub stake.

Wrapping up the Prometheus stuff took a few minutes of his time. It was best to be ready for contingencies. The bill from the storage box in Dubai was in the mail. He paid it gladly.

The knock interrupted his thought process and put him on edge.

Feydor. The fence was dressed warmly and came into the place with a slight smile. He had the payment for the Lux courier job. "Demetry was pleased."

"The place has amazing security," Davidson told him truthfully. "Couple that with the tax advantages and I can see why he is moving assets there."

The creepy looking man shrugged. He set a large mailing envelope on the desk. "Remind Demetry we will need those men for Dubai right after the first of the year. I'd like to use your place to do the recruiting, if that's okay?" He did not want to assume anything and thought it best to be polite.

The man said, "Okay," which came out as "hokaay."

Michael wanted to warn the guy. He obviously didn't see anything coming with regards towards Demetry's operations. Davidson thought again about his key to leaving would be when they found Slutskaya's body. *Or when he disappears.* He said nothing out loud to the man however.

Pushing aside those thoughts as the fence took off, Davidson was very happy when he peaked in the mailer. Ten bundles of twenties nestled inside. Fifty to each bundle. A cool $100,000. The money was literally cold from the weather. He put five bundles back into the envelope and marked it, 'Graeme'. A quick text to the man to tell him it was in the safe waiting on him. The other bundles went into the safe as well. The gang would have money available at need. He did peel off five thousand and stuck it in his wallet. Saved himself a trip to the bank. Davidson was not too worried about pickpockets.

The laptop showed his vacation plans with Sydney. He needed to figure a way around the watchers, but he knew he needed some down time, so he worked the plan.

But even the best plans can go awry.

Chapter Ten

The annoying alarm buzzer went off at 0510. That was early, even for him. Michael shut it off and tried to shake the dream he'd been having.

It was a recently recurring one; him running through his house. He knew it was his house the way you just *knew* things in dreams. The house itself was a weird dream version: hallways and doors. Some locked and some unlocked. The doors would reveal people behind them when he opened them. His mother, Graeme, Demetry, Sydney, and others. Sometimes the people could get one or two words out to him before they vanished. Sydney said, "Hurry." Demetry said, "Don't." His mother said, "Call."

Christ, I need some time off. And he was going to get just that, starting today. Syd started her stand down from work today, the 17th of December. And they were going to Hawaii!

He went around to her side of the bed to wake the warm lump.

"Up and at 'em, Adam Ant," he tried the same saying his mom used when he was a kid, while rubbing her back.

Syd raised her head off the pillow, glared at him and said, "No!"

"Whoa. I do not deserve the stink eye."

Head slammed back down on the pillow, she muffled out, "Too early!"

"Yes."

"Arrrghh." But she moved.

They proceeded to shower and do the thousand and one little things you needed to do before going on a trip.

Forty-five minutes later, Michael's phone chirped. "Honey! The driver's here!" He called back from the kitchen.

"Almost ready!"

"Almost as in, *I need two more minutes*, or almost as in, *I need thirty more minutes*?"

No answer to that. Uh oh.

He went back to find her scurrying around the bedroom. She was mostly packed, but things kept going into baggies, which in turn got placed into the luggage in some mysterious order that eluded him. Clothes, lotions, shoes, electric toothbrush; all found a home in the bag. Wow.

"This is ready," she said, huffing and zipping the bag.

He schlepped the bags downstairs to the car. Rick nodded to him and helped load the limo while both men looked sideways at the two cops watching from the white Olds this time. He wanted to ditch the cops so a bit of subterfuge was in order. He went back in and checked Mary's place. Locked tight. She was in California and doing fine. Sydney was ready in the kitchen grabbing a to-go coffee mug.

"Purse, carry-on, ID, money, book?" He listed her things.

"Got 'em!"

Downstairs, Rick got a full ten second stare at the blonde doctor.

"Can you help us with these carry-on bags," Michael coughed.

Rick picked up his cue perfectly. "Sir, madam, we are having a slight problem with the car. It's overheating even in this weather."

Sydney looked worried.

"No, no! No reason to worry. I've already called the garage and they've arranged another car. The stop is on the way to JFK."

Now Michael put on a worried look for Sydney's benefit.

"I promise, Sir, not more than five minutes lost," Rick apologized.

Soon enough the limo and the tail turned onto Flatbush Avenue and pushed through the slush, ice, and flurries. There was scant traffic this early on such a morning.

The car service garage was set back off of Flatbush near Clarence. A covered two story structure held the cars as they got washed and processed in and out. A low office building held the reception area. Rick and his passengers never got near the building. They went into the parking structure through an opening.

True to his word, the second car was sitting right there waiting for the trio. The bags got shifted and the couple barely had time to look around before they were back inside and ready to go.

Michael did not need to look around. He knew the other limos were ready to go. The other gang members were driving, with a man and woman already in the cars as passengers. A friend drove the fifth car as all of them made for the exit portal. A sudden traffic jam was created as all the cars spilled out one after another.

From the watcher's point of view, five similar cars all drove out of the place and headed off in different directions: Atlantic City. Newark Airport, and LaGuardia, even Teterboro in Jersey. Not that they would all go very far. Just far enough to cause confusion.

He kept checking his phone. Soon enough, Gretchen texted saying the cops were on her as she went towards AC.

More tapping on his phone.

"Flight's on time and it looks like smooth sailing," he told Sydney as they got onto the 278 headed for their holiday.

The code signal made Rick relax as Mike finally eased back into the seat. He did not want Demetry to know where he was going. He supposed the man could find out, but that would require pulling flight manifests or checking hotels. He figured the mobster needed to keep all of his markers to fend off Putin and his boys.

He looked forward to six days of sun and Syd. Period. No gang, no Demetry, no jobs.

Ninety minutes later, Sydney sipped her mimosa in the first class cabin and watched Michael. *Uh oh*, he thought. *Here it comes.*

The two had almost eight hours in the air to talk. And he thought she was going take advantage of it.

She knows something is off. The conversation poked around the edges to start. Old girl friends, family, his job.

He wasn't a liar, she knew. If he said he'd been in London, his passport said London. If he had to work, he had to work. But...

He owned his own company, but never seemed to obsess over the work like everyone else. It was not cheating, she said she knew that much about him at any rate. She'd had experience in that area. It came down to what he didn't say and do that rankled her. So the couple talked across the country and the Pacific.

"It's just that there are some unconventional things about you," Sydney told him. He had no good response to that.

The relentless beauty of Kauai' s north shore showed in the drive from Nawiliwili to Hanalei Bay. Green trees followed by white sands followed by blue water.

The Princeville grounds and the hotel certainly made him less of an asshole, he hoped. The lush tropical green shone in the late afternoon sun. Perched high on a cliff overlooking the half circle bay, the waves, winds and rain had sculpted the lava rock into jagged

ridges plunging into the water. The hotel just blended in and let Mother Nature do the rest.

Princeville was the kind of place where you don't sign anything or touch your luggage on checking in. While you have a drink and take a tour of the grounds your bags just magically get to your room. Of course, the people who make that magic happen would like a decent tip, and Davidson took care of his end.

The room was large and faced the bay. The balcony doors were opened to let the sea breeze in to cool the room. The bed was large and inviting. The bathroom was marble with an interesting feature: The clear glass shower wall was open to the room, but went opaque at the flick of a switch.

"You could leave that clear, that would be okay," Michael told her as she prepared to wash off the plane grime.

"Perv."

"Man, you are tough!"

She sighed and told him, "This is beautiful."

Finally!

The lovemaking after the shower was fantastic. Except for the furrows she cut into his back. The "Ahhh!" was part pleasure, part pain.

"What's with the Fifty Shades of Grey act?"

"Just letting those bitches know you are off the market."

"A hickey works fine. Don't you trust me?"

"I do, but..."

He rolled on his side to look at her. "He must have been a jerk."

"He was. Lied and cheated on me." She sounded somber.

"Hey, I'm not him. I don't cheat, ever. And I rarely lie."

She took that in. 'You have some secrets though."

Michael struggled internally. "Everyone has secrets, even me."

He'd heard a saying one time, 'Everyone has their public life, their private life, and their secret life.' He had all three.

The thought occurred that he might come clean to her right now.

It would ruin the vacation. Wait.

He just could not bring himself to do that yet. Determined to gut it out, he pushed all those feelings and ideas down. Not healthy, but it did allow him to get her feeling better and to relax. They fell asleep to the sound of the pounding surf.

The couple woke the next day early. The six-hour time difference was killer on the body clocks.

They'd made a pact while still in Brooklyn: No crazy exercising. Just normal fun. The early swim was invigorating.

"Ten degrees in New York today," he told her.

"Sucks to be them," she said back, emerging from the eighty degree water.

Swim, drink, lounge. Repeat as necessary. Eat whenever food was offered. Poke and vodka. Fruit and rum. Ahi tuna and beer. The pool had it all.

Later, Michael woke from a nap to find Syd talking to another couple at the bar. He went over.

"Honey, this is Mike and Judi, they were just telling me about a zip line adventure."

Davidson said hello and the woman told him about the fun.

"Some easy trips on the zip line, but the best is lunch in a secluded waterfall swimming hole," she related.

"That sounds great! Thanks for the heads up."

It was the other couple's last day, so they gathered a bit of intelligence about the activities available from them and said aloha.

The place had loads to offer.

Dinner that night was at the Blue Dolphin in the small town. Fresh seafood was featured. Michael had ono. That was the name of the fish. Ono. It was a type of wahoo. The word also meant 'delicious' in the Hawaiian language.

"They named the fish, 'delicious'?" he asked the waiter upon being told the story. The local just grinned at him.

The beer was cold and the fish lived up to its name. A slack key guitarist played old school songs deep into the night. They went back and made love on the king-sized bed.

The password is thread count, Davidson thought, as he rubbed his feet on the sheets.

"These are nicer than at my house," Syd said, as if agreeing to his unspoken thought.

The island soon lulled them into the state that Hawaii was famous for: lazy. Relaxed and happy, the days flew by. The plane home did not take off until 11:30 pm, so they had plenty of time to get to Honolulu for the main flight. Sydney was awash in booze and sun and sex so she rolled with all the minor inconveniences.

Later, Michael would struggle to remember which had been the bigger slap in the face: the cold weather getting off the plane in New York two days before Christmas, or the police cards stuck in his front door that he spied when the cab dropped them off.

The business cards, three of them, were in the door jam in the early evening fading light. Dead tired and unprepared Michael opened the door while catching the cards.

Sydney Devereaux gasped when she saw the crime scene tape on Mary's door.

Not good.

"Maybe a break in?" she asked in a tone that wanted him to make this better.

"I don't know, honey."

The pair trudged up the stairs to find more cards in the vestibule door crack. He knew no one cared about a B and E. Not enough to leave multiple cards.

Entering and setting the bags in the bedroom, Mike went to his desk and called Detective James P. O'Rourke. No precinct or specialty. Maybe that was an encouraging sign?

No answer after a few rings and the message machine did its business, Michael left this number and a brief message, "Detective O'Rourke, this is Michael Davidson. I live a 187 Washington park in FT. Greene. I came home from vacation to find police tape on my neighbor's door and your cards. I'm very worried about Mary. Mrs. Spack. Can you call me back?" He gave the number.

Syd was right behind him, looking very small and frightened. "Are you going to try the others?"

He did so and the response scared him even more. "O'Rourke caught that case. You are going to have to talk to him." Davidson winced.

She noticed and said, "What?" as his cell phone rang, saving him.

"Hello?"

"Mr. Davidson?" the voice asked.

"Yes, is this Detective. O'Rourke?"

"It is. Sir, where are you now?" The man was all business.

"I'm...we are in my bedroom. We just got home from Hawaii."

The cop broke in. "I know you must be tired or put out, but could I have you meet us outside. Both of you? In say... twenty minutes?" He rushed to put in, "Please don't touch anything upstairs, any more than necessary, that is, we didn't tape off your place because we were not sure of the living arrangements."

"Of course."

Syd rushed to gather coats and hats and the couple went back out into the evening cold. He tried to stay positive, but his heart was not in it.

Twenty-four minutes later three squad cars pulled up on the street and added to the apprehension they were feeling.

"All this?" Sydney was coming to grips.

"Not for us, honey," he assured her.

A large rumpled man in a large rumpled suit got out of the first car and approached the pair. "Davidson?" No hand proffered and very gruff from the man.

"That's right detective. This is Sydney Devereaux. She lives a house down and was with me in Hawaii. She is another friend of Mrs. Spack."

He saw the slight tightening of the man's brown eyes. *Son of a bitch.*

Davidson grabbed Sydney's hand. More crime scene techs were coming out of the cars and hauling equipment out of the trunks. A second detective, this time a female, joined the three at the stoop.

"Where is Mary?" Mike asked them straight out.

"How long were you in Hawaii and where did you stay?" O'Rourke countered. Typical cop. They controlled the questions and they doled out the information on a need-to-know basis. His pad was out, ready to write.

"Detective, we just came off the overnight from Honolulu to JFK." He pulled out the two boarding passes he'd stuck into his jeans pocket when they'd gotten on the plane. We stayed on Kauai at the Princeville Resort. Is Mary alive?" Point blank.

O'Rourke scowled and the other cop, the woman, matched him. "Mary Spack was killed in her apartment two nights ago. We think she surprised some burglars."

Mike tamped down hard on the pain that lanced through him. He'd suspected, but a part of him held out hope as people do. Syd gasped and buried her head into his shoulder, tears starting to flow.

He tried to think rationally and help. "I have security camera's setup. One is in her place. The main hallway is covered too."

The heavyset cop tiredly nodded. "We found the system in the garage. The tapes were missing. Any chance of an auto cloud backup?"

Michael reassessed the man. Stereotypical cop he might look, but the man had asked a sharp question. "No- just the DAT." he used the acronym for digital auto tape. "If you don't have the tapes then the killers do."

Syd was still sobbing and Michael wanted to get out of the public eye. The crime scene techs looked ready to go in, so he asked it. "Can we go inside?"

O'Rourke nudged and his partner, the female cop, perked up. Shorter and Latino, the woman looked to be fifteen years younger than the fifty-ish male.

"Rodriguez is going to take you upstairs," he nodded to the partner and to Mike, "while I take Ms. Devereaux through the Spack place and see what's been taken."

He hugged Syd tighter. "Detective, if I may? Sydney has only been in Mary's place a few times. Mary was my neighbor for ten years. Maybe I should go with you?"

The two detectives communicated telepathically. The woman said, "I'll take Ms. Devereaux upstairs, Jimmy."

Order restored, the senior man agreed and the four made their way into the building, trailing techs and past the now, gawking neighbors.

A quick squeeze of Syd's hand and then she went upstairs with Rodriguez and the men continued down the hall to Mary's door. O'Rourke slit the seal and unlocked the door. As the cop let them in, Mike watched the door to see if the lock had been picked. Maybe. He could not get a look at it. "How did they get in?" he asked.

"Not sure. The locks may or may not have been picked. Did you have any workmen over anytime recently?"

"No," Mike said.

"Would she have left the garage door opened?"

"No. She had a remote, but she did not drive. Not for years."

The men went into the living room. The place had been tossed with items thrown around. Expertly, it seemed to his eye. Several items were missing. The TV, some candlestick holders, and a few more small things. A tech took pictures where Mike pointed out the items.

"How long did you know Mrs. Spack?"

"Ten years plus. Ever since I bought the building." Davidson gauged the man's reaction. "Detective O'Rourke, you might know this, but I own the building. Anderson Consulting is my company. I am the sole proprietor and employee."

Suspicion confirmed, O'Rourke flipped a few pages back in his pad and wrote some things down.

"What type of work do you do, Mr. Davidson?"

"I'm an oil field services tech."

"What does that involve?"

"You name it and I do it. Royal Dutch Shell has me as an independent contractor working in the Middle East and the North Sea usually." He glanced at the cop. "I arrange to hire more crew if they want production increased, or fire them if they want it shut down. I buy and sell equipment in a ton of circumstances. I have even bribed local officials to allow us to explore in certain areas of the country when we are not supposed to be."

O'Rourke looked at him with narrowed eyes. "Not kidding, Detective. The oil game can get wild and wholly at times. RDS pays me a lot of money to fix things and they don't care how it gets done."

The men locked eyes for a brief instant.

"Any chance someone came in looking for you and got her instead?"

Michael internally cringed again. The thought had crossed his mind. Strongly, crossed his mind. The detective saw the internal struggle and said, "Who? Was anyone after you?"

Davidson controlled himself. This line of questioning was right, in that someone was after him, but not for his fake job. His real line of work had gotten Mary killed.

"No, Sir. I'm just not that important."

O'Rourke was willing to buy that, for now, but his radar was up. The pair went back towards the bedrooms. He casually mentioned that the local precinct had gotten a few suspicious car calls from this street over the last weeks. Then a call from this location two nights ago about a noise and the responding cops had found Mary.

Michael churned through it. Either the two cops or Demetry's goons. Another internal cringe. He looked over the items thrown around her bedroom. She would be appalled, he knew.

The men went quickly thru the house. It was the items not taken that said low-level thieves. Tiffany lamps left. Some Chagall prints still on the walls. Missing jewelry, TV's, and computers, seemed to confirm the petty nature of the burglary.

The homicide man led Davidson into the kitchen.

He was unprepared for the blood. It covered the floor. The sight galvanized him. "We think they started in the living room and she surprised them in here." The kitchen was a testament to how hard she had struggled.

"Son of a bitch!"

Oh Mary! Why didn't you wait for the cops? Too brave by half.

O'Rourke asked some questions about the house, particularly about the back stairs that led off the kitchen. Michael answered truthfully.

The men went up the narrow stairway.

"You own both units and Mary Spack rented from you?" the cop asked him. Subtle. He wanted an explanation for the stairs and the situation.

"Yeah. These turn-of-the-century places all have them. I never blocked them off. And yes, Mary rented from me. I charged her eight hundred a month." He forestalled the questions. "What am I gonna do? Throw my grandma out on the streets? An old lady got to live in the home she'd been in for fifty years and I got about a thousand home cooked meals." He shrugged and O'Rourke wrote more in his pad. The men were near the top of the stairs. A small scuff mark marred the lower part of the interior wall. It was inconspicuous and looked old.

But Davidson knew it was fresh. He also knew the police had the sequence wrong. Mary had heard the thieves upstairs and went up to investigate.

Too brave by half.

"Mary was old school tough and a great lady, Detective."

The man had the decency to let Davidson grieve.

They backtracked and went up the main staircase to Davidson's unit. The men found Rodriguez and Sydney talking on the couch. Michael and Syd embraced as she cried some fresh tears.

"Honey, lets help these guys so they can find out who did this, okay."

The female cop told him that the only items up here that looked like they were missing were his TV and two computers.

He went through the place again with Syd by his side, and with O'Rourke and Rodriguez following.

The detectives were particularly interested in his closet safe. The marks around the wall board said the killers had tried to wrench it out.

Mike worked the dial. "Nope. All here. Insurance papers, birth certificate, passport, car titles." He stopped. "They did get a home toolkit I had in here."

Both policemen were very interested in the hidden staircase and the office gym downstairs. He explained it away as a 'funky' quirk that he liked. His computer was missing from his desk and a data stick that he never bothered to tell the two cops about. He was also silent about his real safe concealed under the floor. He'd have been arrested on the spot if he'd opened that one.

The couple answered questions about Mary and themselves for anther thirty minutes. They were separated again, this time to provide hair, DNA, and fingerprints to the CSI boys swarming around.

He felt drained as the techs finished up. "The hell of it is, Detective, Mary was supposed to be in California at her sister's. Shit, have you notified her?"

O'Rourke said that they had done so this morning. "I think she is flying in to make arrangements."

Davidson sighed.

"How long have you and Ms. Devereaux been seeing each other?"

"About a month," he answered, doing the mental math.

"And you took her to Hawaii?"

"Have you gotten a good look at Doctor Sydney Devereaux, man. She must get five offers a week."

O'Rourke could see that truth in that. Rodriguez was not all that optimistic about what they had to go on to find the killers.

Davidson tried one last gambit: "But if you find who pawned the computers and TV's won't that tell you who killed Mary?" He went with 'ignorant civilian' to ask the question, but he wanted them focused on the items stolen and how they should turn up if it was true thieves.

The Latino female was noncommittal. "We will try our best."

The silence after everyone left was deafening to the couple. Michael got Syd to agree to take her bag back to her place. "You don't want to sleep here until I get the place cleaned up." The cops had told him it would be okay to get crime scene cleaning people out to go over Mary's apartment.

She agreed and hauled her bags back to her place, as torn up as it was.

Davidson went into survival/auto mode. He went around scrubbing his house with vigor. Clothes were unpacked and shifted into new bags. His real safe was emptied and stashed in another bag. He called a cleaning crew to go over Mary's. *"Yes, Sir, we can be there within an hour!"*

Amazing what you can accomplish on Christmas Eve with money.

His mind raced with the ramifications and moves he could make. But it was not just him to consider. Sydney and his gang had to be accounted for.

It took an hour for the others to call him back and conference them in. Ira, Gretchen, Rick, and Graeme all expressed shock and sadness. Thank God all of them were okay.

"We take down the office early tomorrow," he told them, receiving groans. "6:00 am. If anyone sees the watchers we bolt!"

"Are we leaving town?" Rick wanted to know.

He considered. "Not yet. I want to work out of a hotel for the next days at least. Gretchen, can you find us something?"

"Can do, Mike."

"Graeme, you and Rick empty the safe and move the van to the storage unit. Ira and I will handle the computers and the paper," he handed out assignments.

The Irishman wanted more. "Mikey, shammer, what does this mean!"

More consideration before he spoke. "I don't think Demetry or the FBI is coming after us. I might have made a mistake by ditching the cops on my trip. I think they went into my place to figure out where I was or to get some idea of what we were working on." He breathed heavily for a few seconds- anger overwhelming him. "Mary surprised them and they killed her for it."

"This is not your fault, Mike." Rick tried to absolve him. But he knew it was.

"Did they get anything on us?" pragmatic Ira asked.

"My computer and the data stick," he told them. "That, combined with the possibility they could hit the office, means we have to clean up and work rough for a bit."

"If they have your computer won't they know all of it?" Rick asked.

"Not very soon," he explained to the younger man. "They have my computer, but it's going to take them a few weeks to crack my password and go through the crypto files on the drive. It is not like the cop shows." He smiled at the phone speaker. "There ain't some woman sitting in the backroom cracking computers and feeding them instant information."

The others relaxed just a bit, which helped Michael. "We also have my last ditch security camera." He told them about the killers taking his DAT tapes, "But they did not know I have a still camera in my office which takes a once per second shot. I have a cloud back up on that time lapse data."

So they had pictures, if he could get to a computer and the internet.

But it was not all good news. "However," he cautioned, "eventually the perps will break the data and look at my chat room stuff, which will then get fed to the FBI."

That put them all squarely in the crosshairs. And since it involved overseas things, Interpol and the Flying Squad would now get interested. Davidson and the gang spent a whole bunch of time trying not to be interesting to those organizations.

He told his people that he was tired and needed to finish at his place and he would see them tomorrow very early. He cleaned and organized with a tinge of sadness. He got very little sleep that night at Sydney's. The pair held each other and took turns crying. Davidson boiled inside.

Christmas Eve morning was dark, but clear and cold when Davidson arrived at the office space. Parking right inside the garage area was quick, as there was no need for hiding now.

The others arrived and parked similarly. Michael had stopped at a 24-hour packing store and got the last of the Christmas shipping boxes and tape available. He taped and assembled several and passed them to each desk for his people.

"Rick, you and Graeme take the safe please. The van and equipment inside as well." The two men nodded, despite the fact that he was repeating himself.

"Ira and I will do the computers and paper. Gretchen?"

"I need the phone for a bit, but I'll get the IDs and phones arranged, plus our accommodations."

The threat of jail put a certain urgency to everyone as they worked. They setup a shredder under a trash can and soon everyone was doing their best Fawn Hall impression. Mike had to explain the reference to Rick when he asked.

As the work went on, each gang member dropped into his office to report or to get reassurance.

"How long do you think until the cops break the encryption?"

"Two weeks to a month."

"How are they going to get the info to the feds?"

"Easy, just generate a fake tip and boom, they have the stuff."

"What about the local homicide cops?"

He had no good answer to that. "I'll check in with them and try to figure out where they are on the investigation." He did not think they could use their contacts to spy on O'Rourke. That would guarantee more scrutiny.

Two hours in, he got them all together to discuss timelines. Two weeks was the top and ten days more like the real amount of time he would give it before they had to leave New York.

Dammit!

They'd been so careful to stay off the FBI and Scotland Yard radar. Fall guys were provided in most of their jobs. Hell, the Brits still thought the Great Northern job was done by the IRA. Same with Harry's and Lufthansa. Even the Brazilian Fortezza job was unsolved, but blamed on four 'experienced criminals' currently in custody. De Beers knew his face, but it was a disguise, thank God. Now, all that might be ruined.

Michael spent a few uncomfortable minutes texting their network. The agents knew the score, but he wanted them forewarned. Guys like Trevor knew he would occupy the cell next to them if the gang got pinched.

Noon saw them about finished with the work. Davidson was dead tired, but persevered. Forward. The only way out was forward.

His last act at the office was to connect to his account and download the security time-lapse pictures. Fuzzy, grainy light-enhanced images flashed on the screen with the thieves huddled around the laptop.

Temescal and Hattenfeld. The two police watchers were visible in the picture he printed out. Three copies fell out and the gear was packed and readied for movement.

They discussed the ramifications. "I'm sure now they were looking for my whereabouts and Mary got in the way. They killed her for it." Sadness tinged his voice. The anger would come, he knew. Revenge was going to be had, but not now. He had to work his way out of the trap. The jobs, Demetry, the cops, disappear. That had to be the sequence and the way. The only way.

Unfortunately, that left no room for anything else. "The timeline we talked about is still good. Gretch?"

The woman stepped forward and said. "Extended Stay America on Atlantic. Roger Patton, Michael Davidoff, Peter

McNichol," she said, making sure they knew the cover IDs the men were under. "Ira is still, Todd Morgenstern and I am Rosario Dawson." Gretchen liked to arrange cover identities where she was a famous movie star.

They checked in without any problems. The rooms were drab, standard hotel rooms with small kitchenettes and a 'living room' work area.

"Drive back home and scrub down as best you can," he told them. "Cabs back here. Be ready to shift to London after the first of the year."

The gang dispersed, ready to get on with it. Graeme lingered for a second.

"Shammer, you need to focus on the jobs and Demetry, not on revenge for the old lady." That was brutal, but Michael agreed.

The Irishman's last line was way more painful and something he knew, but was dreading.

"About the bird...you know what you have to do."

Chapter Eleven

He did. A two-hour nap restored some of his brain function. And then a text to Sydney to set up a date at her house. "Work is interfering. Your place 7 pm."

Her "K" reply was quick.

He hoped a run would clear his fog. He kept it simple. Right out of the hotel and another right onto New York Avenue. He kept going until the road unceremoniously ended at a 24-hour Fitness. Every step pounded into his head: had to, had to, had to. He ran back, winded but feeling sharper.

The hours before returning home were a blur of lawyers and accountants trying to prepare for the future. And dreading the future.

Michael Davidson pulled the Audi into his garage and did not go in the house. He had everything he would need. The dark and cold was forbidding on the eve of the most joyous holiday on the Christian calendar. He walked next door steeling himself for the confrontation.

She opened the door with puffy eyes. The house was a chaotic mess from the remodel. The hug was tight and she clung to him.

"Hey."

"Hey yourself. Did you talk to work?"

"Yeah, it's quiet, no problems? What's going on?" She sensed his unease.

"Sydney, let's sit and talk."

They moved over to the couch which puffed dust as they sat. Rubble dominated the sitting room.

"What's wrong?" Concern now shifted to him instead of Mary.

He took a deep breath and looked at her. Well, not at her. He looked at a point past her ear. Looking directly at her deep blue eyes was tough and more than he could do right now.

"Honey, I haven't been honest with you." He blew out the rest of the breath and flicked his eyes to see the puzzlement on her face.

"I'm not in the oil and gas industry. I'm involved with something illegal."

Another glance and her eyes showed worry with a hint of anger and a hint of 'I knew it!'

"And I think that is what got Mary killed." He got that out before she could interrupt. His statement stopped her in her tracks and she needed a second to process. The transformation on her face went from puzzlement and confusion to revulsion and horror.

"What? How?!?" came out in a shocked strangle.

He shifted on the couch and tried to look past her again, to get past it, but his gaze settled on her face. Another mental snap shot. Not that he wanted to, but he could not help himself. He needed to remember this to help him the next time he wanted to get involved with a civilian.

"I think some guys were looking to get information about my activities and she interrupted them. They killed her for it."

She recoiled and sobbed a bit. "None of it was true?" she asked disjointedly.

His turn to recoil. "The feeling was true, just everything else was..." He willed himself to continue. Had to. "Sydney, I'm sorry. But you need to understand this: you could be in danger."

The slap came out of nowhere and it was out of character for her. "You bastard!"

Mike grabbed both her wrists and she struggled to get free and whack him again. "Let me go!"

He did that, but said sharply, "Listen! Mary's killers are still out there and you could be in danger!"

Her eyes watered again, but no tears came now as she took some breaths and calmed a little. His face burned where she'd struck him and he matched her breathing, similarly to when they ran together. Davidson did not miss the irony in that.

"I could call the police," she started.

"O'Rourke could never catch me," he started with a touch of arrogance. "Besides which, Mary's killers might be cops." he said it directly so it penetrated. "Don't trust the police."

Maybe the wrong tactic to mention trust to her at this particular time.

"I should trust you? What are you involved in?"

He started to lie. Started to give her the rehearsed speech about white- collar embezzlement when he looked into those eyes again. Those beauties became truth agents as he admitted, "I'm a thief. And a good one."

The damn burst and the story poured out. All of it. College, Graeme and Las Vegas. Kings Bay. The early jobs. The high end stuff. He emphasized Demetry and the Russian Brotherhood.

"This is the FBI versus the Russian mob and the people in the middle are going to get killed. Syd you have to be careful." He finished, voice a little raw after ten cathartic minutes talking. It felt strangely good to have it out in the open.

For her part, Sydney admitted to being alternately fascinated and horrified with what he was telling her.

In a calmer voice, she told Michael she was glad to have her nagging suspicion confirmed, but could not process the magnitude of the situation. Davidson nodded.

"I mean, I suspected an old marriage or maybe even kids somewhere, but not a *thief.*"

"What you need to be aware of is that I work for some very dangerous people," he said.

The horror aspect lit up her face another time.

"I should go to the police," she said again, sounding tired and defeated.

"Please don't."

The *honesty* in that short request brought her back and up short. She looked at him on the couch. Searched his face for hints of lies.

He scratched his nose peeling from his Hawaii burn. From Two days ago when life made sense. She remained silent, because she had no response for him. At least one that would help in this situation.

"Please don't look at me. I can't think when you do that," he complained. Michael almost leaned in for a kiss. *That won't go well*, he thought.

To cover, he said, "Syd, I need some time. Time to work out my business and to get Mary's killers."

"Michael, you can't beat the FBI and the Russian mob. You'll end up in jail or dead."

"No, I won't. Not yet. Demetry needs me for the money and the cops are just on to me. Now that I'm in the database, my career is over. Please Syd. I need just a little time to do what I need," he asked again. Not quite pleading. "I need to know you are safe while I do what I have to do make this right."

He had realized a bit ago that she was in some danger. He also knew the two cops trailing him, Tweedle Dee and Tweedle Dum, could not afford to be near the vicinity of a second killing. The Feds might be dense, but not *that* dense. Even the FBI would notice that there was a killing in a house belonging to a person they were watching. Two killings?

"Just don't tell on me and watch yourself."

He pulled an envelope out of his jacket. "Watch the news. April," he told her, thrusting the envelope in her hands. "You'll know when I make my move. Then take this to O'Rourke. Tell him everything."

He watched her stare at the envelope in her hands knowing she felt thrown, hurt and angry. Her face took on a leaden cast.

"Sydney, I'm so sorry..." he said yet again.

"Is Michael Davidson your real name?" She asked pointblank.

His heart froze. "No," he admitted.

"Get the fuck out." She said it softly and it went right through him.

That hurt. Michael stumbled out of the brownstone and onto the porch as a few flakes of snow fell. Fuck!

Mechanically, he called a cab and walked the three long blocks to the corner of DeKalb and Vanderbilt. The Brooklyn Public House lights shone bright in the dark night. He'd been inside a few times, but not now. The cold dark wait outside a warm safe place was perfect for mood and situation.

Recriminations started in his head.

I should have known. Should never have started up in the first place.

Unfortunately, that was a rationalization for him. He could have never NOT started up with Sydney Devereaux. She drew him in like a magnet. *Or a diamond.* It wasn't his fault!

But it was. All of it. Syd and Mary.

The whole thing was his fault. Suddenly, the bile and pain rose in his throat until he leaned over and vomited against the brick building.

It was mostly stomach acid and regret that came up. Thankfully, no one was around to see him as he wiped his mouth and moved down to Roman's, the Italian joint next to the pub.

The cab ride back to the extended stay was silent which allowed him to think. Michael was never going to see Sydney again. Never set foot in his house again. Mary was gone. Buried in California today. He felt bad about that, knowing she was not in her beloved city.

Focus! He had a limited amount of time to setup Demetry before O'Rourke or the Feds started asking questions. Then it was across the pond to pull off two impossible heists and vanish. He had to compartmentalize and get out of the puzzle box.

He worked the phone. His mother. The time difference made it early afternoon there. She always picked up. Even blocked numbers. His mother was from another generation as far as the phone was concerned. And human interactions. *She still wrote Thank You cards!*

Barbara Davis was very disappointed her son Michael could not come home for the holidays. Work was making him sad, she said that she could hear it in his voice. To top it off, he was going to be very busy the next four months overseas. The Middle East and the North Sea. "Be careful and call when you can. I love you dear."

"Love you too, Mom."

The next days passed in a trudging blink. Michael and the crew stayed near their rooms exclusively. Food was delivered and the only outings were the mail runs and to a gun range.

The thieves spent at least two hours in the small gym at the hotel, daily. The exercise dulled the stress and allowed them all to lose weight. Even Ira toned up a little.

Michael ran with a purpose on the treadmill. That purpose being to exhaust himself so he could sleep. It even worked some nights.

January 3rd saw the outside agency prelims finished on both jobs. The New Year was a non-event as far as five grouchy people were concerned. They were ready to make the shift to England to continue the alarm line probing.

Forms allowing the gang another trip into the tunnels under Greville and Hatton Gardens Streets were filled out with the municipal transportation office and the police all duly notified.

Dubai preps were also going well as the players focused. Gretchen had secured the thieves a villa on the palm. A house on palm Jumeirah Island that jutted from the city into the gulf was available at need for their activities.

She still had to find some place for the extra men to stay. That was proving more difficult. Dubai was a tricky place to house twenty foreigners. Not twenty simple construction workers, that could be done no problem. But when the men involved were gangsters and used to a certain 'lifestyle' it proved problematic. Michael was very concerned that simple things were going to derail their job.

He hoped the new men realized that Dubai was not like visiting a

European city. Rules and regulations can and did trip up visitors all the time. Simple things like drinking alcohol on the beach or asking a young, unmarried woman to dance could result in a catastrophe.

He knew the event was coming where some Russian got drunk and flipped off a policeman. They put westerners in jail for that sort of thing. He also worried what the authorities would do if they knew the gang was going to rob them of $500 million in gold. Tortured and buried under the jail. If they were lucky.

The fourth was an unusually warm, clear Monday. Forty-eight whole degrees. Brooklyn bustled with everyone back at work and school from the holiday shut down. Michael knew Syd was going to the office today, but did not want to dwell. Much anyway.

No choice but to deal with the cops and Demetry.

The cops were first on his list. Toweling off from his workout, he dialed from memory. He figured 9:15 am was a good time to catch the detective.

Sitting behind the desk of the 'work area' in the hotel room, he pulled a face. He did not love this room.

Luckily for him the detective was at his desk doing paperwork. Very similar to what Mike and the gang had been doing this week. Thieves and cops hated paperwork. Funny. Each made it more complicated on the other.

"O'Rourke."

"Detective, this is Michael Davidson calling. About Mary Spack?" He phrased the question into the dead spot around his name.

"Yes, Mr. Davidson, I remember you," O'Rourke said. "What can I do for you?" The gruff voice tried to be pleasant, but it really conveyed, 'why are you bothering me?'

"Well, I was wondering how the investigation into Mary's death was proceeding? I've heard nothing in the news so..." He let it drop right there.

"Contrary to TV shows Mr. Davidson, homicide investigations take months." The man sounded weary and determined in equal measures.

"I understand, but I was wondering if any of our stolen items had turned up?" They'd discussed the route the investigation was going to take, but Davidson was on some shaky ground here. He had ulterior motives for bringing this up.

He could hear the cop frown thru the phone. *Would a civilian know this? That was the question O'Rourke had to be asking himself,* Davidson figured.

The silence stretched. Just as Michael was going to be forced to say something else, O'Rourke said, "No, so far none of your items have turned up in the pawn shops."

The opening was small. Delicately. It had to be done delicately.

"Oh. I was hoping maybe you'd found out who pawned my computer and who was responsible for Mary." Just restating it, in case the veteran homicide cop had missed something. More probing. "Is it strange that nothing has turned up yet?"

This time the frown was verbalized into a grunt as O'Rourke mulled over what he'd said.

"It is possible they dumped the items to avoid us."

"Oh! I didn't know low-level burglars were that rational about things."

The kicker had been applied- now he had to wait.

The cop made a chuffing noise in surprise. "Yeah, luckily for us-thieves tend not to think ahead."

Holding his hand over the phone, Davidson exhaled. One down, one to go.

"Uh huh. Also, I know this may be nothing, but I was talking to Rod and James, the gay lawyers from down the block? Anyway we've both noticed a strange car parked on the street near our houses. A tan Crown Victoria. James said he only got part of the plate: '77'. The investigator dutifully wrote that down. It was not unknown that witnesses would remember something incongruous, but vital after the crime.

"Are you sure this isn't a neighbor's car?"

"No, I'm not at all," Michael admitted. "I've only talked to the guys about this."

He knew it was a mistake as soon as he said it.

O'Rourke pinned him to the wall. "Has Ms. Devereaux seen the car?"

Shit!

More hand holding over the phone as he got up to pace. He'd talked to the neighbor lawyers to set this up, but not Sydney. He had to say something.

"Uhh... no. No, she hasn't. We've had a bit of a falling out, I'm afraid."

"Really? Sorry to hear that."

"Yes, Detective, my job got in the way," he said, truthfully. And Davidson saw a way to turn the negative Sydney remark into a positive. "In fact, Royal Dutch has me out of the country for a while."

The cop was instantly on alert. "How will we be able to get a hold of you?"

He was ready. "Just leave a message on my machine. I check it religiously when I'm gone. I'll call you back within twenty-four hours."

"What if we need to see you in person?"

"I'll fly back home in that case," he assured the man.

Michael had him on that. Davidson was not a suspect and the cop could not prevent him from leaving.

Time to wrap it up. "Well, thank you, Detective. I've taken up too much of your time. Please let me know if anything breaks on Mary's case."

He hung up after receiving assurances from the man. *Now we'll see.*

***

For his part, James O'Rourke hung up and instantly called Rodriguez. It took two hours for her to call him back. He sat the whole time thinking. The call bugged him. He'd been getting calls from Sydney Devereaux, but they were the normal, upset, crying 'why aren't you doing something' variety. Davidson was *different*. Oh, he would have his partner track down the Crown Vic and expand the pawn shops they were looking into. but he wanted to do something else. He wanted a look at Michael Davidson.

***

Davidson stopped pacing and sat back down. He had another call to make.

A much tougher one. But he had help on this one.

At 10:15 the cleaning crew was just finishing his room when Graeme walked in.

The Latino crew was used to these guests hanging around while they worked. The rooms and the people were starting to get a little gamey in the maids' opinion, Mike could tell. They left the men to their devices.

"How are you, shammer?" Graeme asked, with concern.

"Okay," The American allowed.

"Why is it our lives are always in opposite directions?" Graeme wondered aloud. "Whenever you are fine, I have women and gambling problems. Whenever my life is settled, yours goes to shyte?" The Irishman showed tremendous insight and caring and Davidson was touched.

"Well, Sydney is my burden to carry. Demetry we have together." Davidson worked the numbers and put the phone on speaker while both men sat together on the couch. He waited on the head of the Brotherhood.

When the old man came on the phone his voice was hard. "Michael, where have you been?"

"Hawaii for a while, Sir, and working lately," Michael answered quickly. "I don't know if you've heard, Sir, but my tenant was killed in a burglary while I was away."

"What? I did not know this!"

Demetry might have been acting. Might be. He'd made his pronouncement to gauge the man and see how he would react. He would like to know if the cops were acting on Roybokov's behalf, or the FBI. or rouge. Davidson could not tell which was the case and he needed to know. Not much escaped the gangster or his people. The news announcement should have been enough to clue him in. Michael skated out onto the thin ice to do what he had to do. "I had to talk to the cops. I had to give them my DNA and fingerprints to let them process the crime scene."

Both men in the shitty hotel room could hear the old man breathing on the line. Michael shot Graeme a look and touched his arm. *Let Demetry speak first.*

"This is terrible!" the Russian spat.

Cold. "Thank you, Sir. Mary was a special lady and I will be dealing with whoever is responsible." Davidson purposely misunderstood the reason it was terrible: Not that his crime career was over, but the tragic death of a friend.

Roybokov made a noise that could be sympathy or something else.

That was as close as the two men would get to declaring war. Both might know it, but that was all they ever spoke on the subject.

"I'm not a suspect because I was out of town when it happened, so I'm clear of the cops. But we do need to speak about London and Dubai." Davidson steered the conversation back to safe ground.

"Da," the boss agreed.

"We've done more work on the jobs and both are still feasible. I will again brief you on London and Graeme is here to talk about the UAE."

"Hello, Mr. Roybokov," Graeme perked up.

"Da," the crocodile said again.

Michael spent five minutes bringing Demetry up to speed on Hatton Gardens. Demetry was most interested in the shell corporations and how they would sell off the gems.

"Same as the Paris job. Fake invoices and bills of sale from estates and private individuals. Sutton Geology will do the shipping and Vulcan Holding is registered as a wholesaler. I suspect Anderson and Prometheus will have to get involved with Dubai as well." He paused to consider. "Sutton can ship the gold also from the Middle East."

"Do you want any of the stones for personal use?" he asked Roybokov.

"Only if they are larger matched stones. Ten to twenty carats." Demetry growled and said, "We should be talking to Feydor, as well."

"Hold on, I will conference him in." Michael knew that the Bratva head was always secretly impressed by the uses of new technology. Computers, video conferencing, shell corporations were all knew to him. The arcane workings were beyond his capabilities and the people who did it were wizards, like Michael.

The surly fence was quickly on the line and straightened up as he realized the boss was with them. The three exchanged hellos with the newcomer.

"Feydor, we intend to move most of the gold and platinum settings for any rings or necklaces through you. We will add those gems to the loose stones from the sights. That way it helps hide the fact the stones are coming from De Beers. I expect there to be coins and watches, too."

"How much?"

"Ten percent, tops. Say, $15 million." Mike told him. Slutskaya agreed with little grace. Michael had clued him in before and instead of acting like a professional, he wanted to bitch. They had all had this argument several times before over the years. Feydor got mad every time he was reminded.

Michael rattled off routing numbers and bank accounts for the holding companies. He also directed the two men to sign some forms that gave certain powers of attorney to 'officers' of other corporations. Both men grumbled about their exposure and the power that gave the thief.

"This is how money gets moved around in the post 9/11 world," he said tiredly. Tired of having this conversation- tired of it all. "We do it the same way every time. Lufthansa, Great Northern, Harry Winston, even as far back as Fortezza!" The thief-in-law listed the gang's greatest hits. It was a not so subtle reminder that they were the best in the business.

One final knife into the fence. "We do it the old way, you see $90 million in your pocket. My way- a hundred and forty or more."

The answers came on top of each other. "Fine," from the boss and "Da," from the underling.

"Dubai, on the other hand, is presenting a whole laundry list of problems," Michael shifted topics. "Graeme."

The Irishman spent twenty solid minutes on the gold heist, bringing the boss up to speed.

"We should see $500 million."

Greed radiated from the phone as Feydor and Roybokov salivated over all that gold. *$2,000 per ounce?*

Michael came back on to go over the shell companies again. More routing and more forms to fill out. None of the bitching this time as both men took the only preserver available to the drowning man. They would sign.

"That's not all we need, Mr. Roybokov," Graeme reminded him. "We have spoken about using your men."

The boss had some thoughts about the men. "Viktor is assembling them for you."

Michael took this one. "With all due respect to Viktor, he has no idea of our needs. Graeme and I want to choose them."

Demetry objected and Feydor loyally supported him. "We will tell you who to work with," the fence said, out of place. Mike ignored that and laid a hand on Graeme to let him handle it.

"Mr. Roybokov, no offense to you either, but you don't know what our requirements are. For instance- Can any of Viktor's men drive a large truck?" Silence greeted this as neither man had any idea of the answer. "If they don't- we need to train them and that takes time away from the other things we need to be working on."

The silence that greeted this spoke volumes to Davidson. "I need to start with the basics; pretty clean records, no visible tattoos, good English speakers. I can work down to any man we are forced to take."

Even Demetry saw the rightness of this line of direction. "I will gladly take the crew captains: Viktor, Anton, and Sergei, but I need smart as well as muscle on this one." Michael gave the boss an out.

The bone to take the three capos would help Roybokov maintain the illusion of control. Davidson also agreed with Graeme that the main lieutenants from the Bratva would keep Demetry's men more in line.

"Okay, Michael. When and where do you need these men?" Roybokov said.

They settled on Feydor's place in three days. "Send fifty and I'll take the top twenty. Passports or IDs with them, please," Graeme instructed.

Grumbling from Feydor. He would take shit from Davidson, *maybe*. The Irishman? *No.*

"Groups of ten starting at 8:00 am," Michael interjected before the goings got heated. "We will need Viktor and his mates on hand the whole time," he told Demetry.

He thought that completed what they needed to talk about when Roybokov threw the curve.

"Michael, I want you to make another run to Luxembourg."

Another courier job? What? Why now? What angle is he working? Michael could not find one, then glanced at Graeme and got a shrug.

"Certainly, Sir. We are going to be busy, but not too bad. Same as last time? Will Nicholas be coming along?" He got that all out quickly.

"Da. Since you will be in London together I want you both to do this."

"Do you have a timeframe?" He hoped it sounded light and also that Demetry would have them do it right away.

"I'm not sure yet myself. I have to meet Medvedev's people sometime in late February, maybe March. I will know then."

That was a slip up! Davidson was sure Roybokov was not pleased to have divulged his business.

And the objection wanted to come out. To tell the man he could not do it in the middle of both jobs. Davidson bit back the retort and said, "That is going to be rough, Sir."

The chuckle was not warm or friendly. "You will survive." The mob boss clicked off.

"Feydor?" Graeme asked into the silence over the phone.

"Da, asshole!"

"Have coffee ready for us Thursday," the Irishman added lightly, then clicked the phone off.

Both thieves sat back on the cheap couch, relieved and worried in the same amount. They talked about the call and what it meant. Most worrisome was the new courier job. Followed by Demetry. Followed by Dubai. Then London, and then everything else in the world. Both men were exhausted.

"Check in with Trevor," Mike told Graeme. "Make sure the site is still on. And get to Swiss customs. If the UAE is going to ship sixteen thousand pounds of gold out of the country they must have some idea what is going on." Graeme nodded.

Michael conferred with the rest of his people. He told them, "Four or five more days in this prison and we can get clear."

And that was how he thought of this place, a prison. The small space and limited movement confined him. He tried not to dwell on Syd, but he had no luck. He worked out to grind down his frustrations. The only good things about Extended Stay America in Brooklyn?

They did not get arrested and they all lost weight.

Chapter Twelve

Thursday's session at Feydor's was a nightmare: long and arduous.

Graeme and Michael arrived together by cab after a long expensive trip to ensure they were not being followed. If Michael had to guess, he would put even money on the cops getting on them *after* the meeting at the pawn shop. The pair was ready to text back '9' to the rest just in case.

Feydor greeted them at the front door to the closed pawn shop with a growled, "You are late!"

"Fashionably," Michael agreed.

The pale man led them thru the deserted shop past the L-shaped counter. They did not go to Feydor's office, instead the fence opened a small door set behind the counter. The door revealed a long narrow staircase leading to the basement. Michael could feel the hairs on the back of his neck stand. The creaky wooden stairs were dimly lit by a bare bulb. *Silence of the Lambs, much?* he thought.

The stairs ended and a surprisingly large room opened on both sides of the staircase. Two more 75-watt ceiling outlets provided light as the room went left and right.

The walls were roughhewn stone and lined with boxes and shelves. The right side held two supporting metal columns, and in chairs and ass-to-ass on a small couch sat ten men. All eyes looked at the three new arrivals. A curtain was hung across the back side of this portion of the room

Mike swiveled his head to the left to see more boxes and the furnace set. Ancient and industrial, it was huge. A door set into the far wall told him that the alleyway had an entrance down here. Interesting.

The men approached the group on the right. One of the men, Viktor Lubchenko, rose and silently joined them at a glance from the fence.

Without a word, the fence led them back to the curtained off wall. The pushed aside blanket reveled another door which Feydor opened and then he turned on the interior light in the new room.

This room was much smaller, as it only held three chairs and a desk. The far wall had yet another door, as did the left side wall.

Fuck! How big is this basement? Maybe they should look for Jimmy Hoffa in here, Michael thought.

The thief went to the desk and Graeme started setting up his equipment along the right side wall. A folding tripod became a white screen and the case he schlepped in, produced a video camera and still unit, both on supports. Davidson arranged the forms and papers neatly on the desk. Plenty of pens and pencils ready to be used.

The Irishman put two chairs on one side and the third as an interviewee spot and Feydor and Demetry's Lieutenant chaffed at the wait.

As Graeme took a few shots to test the camera, the capo had had enough. "What is that for?"

"Viktor, do you know the foreign worker visa requirements for the United Arab Emirates? How about what an Omani driver's license looks like? Any clue as to how long the tourist visa for the UK will last?"

The man blinked owlishly at the rapid fire series of questions for which he had no answer.

"Shut the fuck up and let me work," Mike nodded coldly.

That remark brought a reaction from Feydor; *No one talked to them that way!*

"Why are you still here?" Davidson watched him as he asked the question, voice hard. The fence spluttered.

"We can pack up and I can tell Demetry we can't go forward because you have your panties in a bunch. Okay, fence?"

The man started to say something. The men watched the Russian swallow his comeback. Such was his fear of Demetry and his knowledge that only Michael and his crew could pull this job off; it made him weak.

Viktor's eyes tracked Feydor as he left the room. He shifted back to the two gang members and nodded.

Graeme smiled at him and told him to call in his first man.

"Oleg!".

The new arrival swaggered in. Young, at twenty-four, he was blond and square-jawed. A crew cut emphasized his knobby, round head. The blue eyes and the muscles on his 6' 1" frame gave him an air of power. The neck tattoos and the sneer told of his menace.

Graeme grinned at the kid and positioned him in front of the screen. "We need to take pictures of you for your new ID."

Oleg complied, getting into position. "Smile, this is not a mug shot!"

The third generation Russian- American laughed back. Graeme sat him down after he was finished with a "That's good- thanks."

"Where you from, friend?"

"Odessa, by the sea," the young man said proudly.

Graeme and everyone laughed at the reference to the Brighton Beach Area of Brooklyn that held a lot of Russian immigrants. "Love it!" Graeme told him. "You

married?"

"Nah. No one can pin me down!" the boy bragged.

Graeme nodded along. "I bet you get a lot of tail though, huh?" A falsely modest nod and a laugh.

"Yeah, I get a bit."

"You like to party?"

Again the laugh, this time with everyone's added in. The boy responded with, "I do a little."

"A little?" Graeme scoffed. "I bet you rock it every night!"

More laughter among friends. The boy relaxed. *Hey these guys were cool. Not like Viktor said.*

"I do my share." Of course, the man did not want to deny his prowess- what was the sense? "I can drink and do blow all day and fuck all night!" He finally relented and admitted to his greatness. More laughter from the others as he bragged on. "I'm perfect for whatever job you guys want to do. Whatever you need. I'll kill anyone who gets in our way!"

The boy was amped up and rolling now. "One time, I jacked this lady...I was so high on meth, I..."

"Oleg!"

Viktor's shout cut off the boy and the laughter.

Michael and Graeme waited while the capo took the young man outside. He returned ten minutes later.

"I sent three others home. I made some calls-better candidates will be here soon. You can talk to Joey and Popper- Samuel," he told the men, "in the meantime."

Point made.

The real work candidates started showing up and the men got into the task of finding the right help.

"You have any food allergies?" Graeme asked a thirty-five year-old man.

Viktor shot a look at Mike, who sighed.

"We are going to have these guys cooped up in a house for a long time. A house or place which we will stock with food so they don't have to go out and call attention to themselves. I need to know if Samuel here is allergic to shellfish."

The mob lieutenant goggled at the detail. More detailed questions followed to the men: Can you drive a truck? Do you play video games? Any back problems?

Over the hours Viktor was joined by Anton and Sergei, the other two crew leads in Demetry's organization. The new men became wary of the gang members, unsure of positions as soon as they saw Viktor be cowed.

The group worked through lunch and then dinner. Each time Feydor was ordered to provide food. The greasy meals were his petty revenge.

By ten that night, fifty-three men had been whittled down to seventeen decent candidates. By and large, they were older, more stable members of the brotherhood. Dumb crooks, most of them, but under a veneer of control.

"All twenty of us in one house?" Sergei asked near the end.

Michael shrugged, "Depends on what we can find and arrange. Why? You think that's going to be a problem? You three will be there to keep the peace."

The compact Russian eyed the thief-in-law. "Maybe Popper-Samuel don't like Joey so well."

Groans came from the two gang members. "That would have been helpful to know three hours ago," Mike said. "Any other *things* we should know about? And I mean everything- Who's afraid of heights, whose mother is sick, all of it."

Another two hours of discussions did not change the lineup, it just set some rules: Joey and Popper were not on the same team. Leo was a kleptomaniac and Pavel and two other were vegetarians.

The men left the pawn shop after midnight in a cab. The long winding route back to the hotel was boring but safe.

"How is Rick coming with the bulldozer?" He asked in the back of car with Graeme.

"He's good. Training is complete and he needs some work in the Middle East, but he is ready," the Irishman responded.

Jesus, this was complicated!

"You don't look so good, shammer."

"Shut the fuck up, please." He needed to be miserable for a while.

***

Tuesday's American Airlines flight to London was as nervous as he'd been starting a job in long, long time. Even the first heist he'd ever pulled off, the bank in Ft. Collins, Colorado, was less panicky than this. And he was a kid when that happened.

Michael kept looking for O'Rourke or the feds to jump out of nowhere and arrest him. *Did the cops talk to Sydney? Did she squeal on him?* Obviously not. He was sitting in business class on this plane and not in a jail somewhere.

He'd spotted the three Bratva lieutenants when he boarded. Sitting in coach, Anton had even waved at him as he went on back.

Christ!

This cluster fuck was all Demetry's fault. He'd insisted that, "His men be involved in every aspect of these jobs."

Michael came close to losing his cool. "Mr. Roybokov, I cannot work this way. I'm not ready to house them in Dubai and I haven't briefed them."

"They can go to London and help you there."

The puzzle box changed a face and he had to plan on contingencies. They sent the three stooges, as the gang referred to them, on the JFK to London flight with Mike. Graeme was on the early Dulles flight, while Rick was heading out of Logan. Gretchen and Ira followed tomorrow out of Canada.

Michael had raged at the gang for a solid hour back at the extended stay over the circumstances. The rest recognized it for the stress release it was. He finally calmed and realized this might not be such a bad thing. *They needed fall guys for London, fine. These idiots looked perfect for the job.*

Davidson gave the three men as little information as he could get away with: "Bring your own passports. Here is the flight number, airline and time, and hotel reservation. I'll call you when I'm ready for you."

That evening, sitting in the Cambridge Gate flat with a glass of vodka in his hand, Davidson called Viktor's room at the Holiday Inn.
"Hey."

"You asshole! Heathrow security pulled me in for three hours!"

"Really? Why?"

"They said I looked suspicious. I couldn't answer some questions they had about why I was in England!"

"Yeah- British customs uses an Israeli-style questioning method for inbound passengers. Anyone who can't rattle off why they are here and where they are staying, gets put through the ringer."

"You could have told us, you dick!"

The thief had had about enough. "Demetry said take you, I took you. I did not have the time to brief you properly. If you are mad, he is the one you should take it up with."

Silence other than heavy breathing on the line reigned. Russian mobsters needed constant reminders of who was in charge, Michael was realizing. "If you think London was hard, wait till we get to Dubai. Any idiot can go to London for a week. For now, I want you three to take in the sights. I mean that literally. Go to the museums, the Palace, visit a pub."

"What? Why?" Viktor was confused, seemingly a permanent state for the mobster.

Sighing, Davidson patiently explained. "Because one of the exit questions is- What did you think of the British Museum and do you like the open courtyard?"

"Who gives a fuck what the courtyard looks like?" More anger from the man.

"You do, you idiot! Tourists visit the British Museum and marvel at the glass enclosed courtyard, while terrorists and thieves don't have the right answer and get searched!"

"Oh."

Fuck me!

"So you three will sit in the Holiday Inn and play tourist. And wait on my phone call Monday morning. I will have a job for you on Monday night."

"Okay."

"And Viktor? Tell the other two to not even think about getting drunk and calling in a hooker. I want you three off the radar."

"Okay, Mike." The answer was not as grudging as it could have been. The Russian hung up the phone.

Graeme looked up from the couch across from Michael. He'd arrived an hour ago. "Job?"

"Yeah, let's put them in the vests Monday night when we go into the tunnel."

Donniger grinned. "They'll fuck it up."

"I'm counting on that a little."

Monday, the 12th of January, saw England reasonably cleaned up from winter storm Ili. The huge wind and rain storm had lashed the country and poured buckets. It was really a northern hurricane as winds hit 120 mph in Scotland and Northern England. London got the rain and the headaches.

But by Monday the storm had swept onto the continent and Russia and life was returning to normal.

The gang spent the preceding days prepping for their trip into the tunnels. Paperwork was filled out, but equipment needed to be purchased and transportation arranged. The storage box bulged with new gear.

Gretchen was none too pleased to have to generate three new sets of Sutton electronics ID badges for the Russians.

"You think this is easy!" She flashed at Mike. "These are going to be pretty crude."

He soothed her, but did not tell her he wanted them to be a little suspect.

"Ira?" He called to the rest of the group looking over the detailed tunnel plans.

Levinson glanced over at Mike from the drawing. "I need at least two hours to trace the lines and install."

All five of them bent heads over the drawings. The table at GranGate held the electrical utility tunnel drawing with the Lloyds stuff next to it. The drawings were detailed and technical. They showed tie points, the main trunk, and other items for the alarm lines. What it did not show was reality.

Experience had taught the gang that any construction drawings did not always reflect the reality of a build, especially in an old utility tunnel in a major city. Things that weren't there were shown on the drawings: support posts, brackets, isolation points, clean outs. Lots of things. Conversely, things that were not on the drawings actually were physically present in the tunnel. Small things like whole pipes and systems could exist in real life and not be on the drawing.

That's why they'd gone in before and why they needed another two or three trips to complete the task. This alarm system was a critical tent pole in the job. It had to be isolated or neutralized. Period.

The goal for Monday night was to see if they could isolate the Hatton Gardens alarm signal from the maze of lines coming through the cable bundle from all the other Greville Street businesses. An old school, hard-wired line like this was harder to spoof, but not impossible.

Ira possessed the necessary gear and now he also had Graeme and Rick as workers, not just Michael. Had them, because Sergei and his friends would be topside holding the signs and exposing themselves.

Gretchen was scheduled to drive the van and shuttle tools and gear. He wanted her able to bolt if something went wrong. That made Ira feel better.

The knock on the door caused heads to whip around. Skittish- all of them.

"That's them," Rick said, and went to the door. He let the capos into the flat.

Anton Kusnetsov looked around at the living room and the kitchen of the flat and said, "What the fuck?" The short, rotund man did not like the disparity in accommodations, it seemed.

Mike needed to teach yet another lesson. "I had to get whatever was available for you because I had no idea you were coming on this trip. If you want a better hotel room, I would suggest the Four Seasons over on Park Lane. Rooms run about 1700 pounds a night."

"I've only got thirty-five pounds left!", the Russina whined.

Michael pounced. "And why is that Anton? Huh? Because Demetry sent you out here to spy on us without regard for what you'd be doing. Look at Viktor and the airport."

All three looked thoughtful which did not match them at all.

"I planned to brief all of you on the operation and the customs part of it, give you cover IDs and Dubai money while setting up everyone with a place to live." He breathed heavily to calm himself. "I will still do that for the rest, but now we are going to have to come up with a different plan for the three of you."

After exchanging glances, the three outsiders looked at the gang leader.

"I'm tired of doing this over and over. I'm the boss out here. I take care of my people!"

That seemed to penetrate for the men. Stick applied, now he wanted the carrot dangled.

"Anton, why do you only have 35 pounds left?"

"My card don't work." The man said defensively.

Mike gestured to Gretchen who came forward and handed each of the three an envelope.

"That's 2000 GBP in smaller bills," he told the men.

By the way the other two clutched the money, Michael knew they were broke as well.

Gangsters.

He'd seen it before. They ate meals at Demetry's restaurants. Clothes fell off trucks. Cars appeared. Wives took care of mundane things. *These guys can't function in the real world.*

"Your cards have to be connected to the bank system here." He detailed the 'star' symbol and how they would have to target the ATMs accordingly.

"Dubai is even worse."

Another gesture and Rick stepped forward. "Rick is going to take you to a department store to get some clothes for tonight."

"What are we doing tonight?" Sergei asked mildly.

"Standing around our work sight, holding a caution sign, looking bored." Davidson said this slowly and sincerely waiting for the challenge.

Everyone watched the capos. The five gang members waited. The Bratva guys looked at each other and then finally at Sergei. A million questions and objections wanted to come out, they all knew, but the man just smiled and said, "That sounds good."

The pecking order might need to be established a few times, but once it was set, the brotherhood fell in line.

The room in general relaxed. Michael said to Rick, "Set them up with Oyster cards, too. Fifty quid."

Still more goodies needed to be given out. Davidson gestured to Gretchen again and she brought forth the badges from Sutton Electronics and a cell phone.

By unspoken knowledge she handed it to Sergei Tikanov. The man pocketed it without a thought or a question. The thin, wiry Russian moved with controlled economical motions.

So he was in charge. Good to know, Mike thought. "That phone only had one number preprogrammed. Me. Only use it to tell me you have been hit by a bus."

Even gangsters chuckle at jokes.

"If you get a '9' text, just the number '9', go straight to the airport and go home. Tell Demetry we are arrested or dead." Michael related this to the guys.

As Rick gathered his charges for their shopping trip, the boss had one last bit for them. "Be at the Farrington tube stop in your new clothes, with badges at midnight. Sober and rested. I will brief you on the job in the van."

The four men departed and the Russians were reasonably happy now.

"Jesus," Graeme intoned.

"Yeah, tell me about it. The thing is to let them interface with the cops tonight." Michael told the others and they spent a few minutes, going over what the plan was.

***

Hours later the storm still had the pavement wet and a foot of water greeted the gang as the manhole cover was opened. "Lots of interesting things floating in there, I'll bet," Gretchen murmured, looking down. She wasn't the only one noticing that.

Sergei and pals were arrayed topside with hard hats, yellow vests, and shiny new work boots looking sharp. The entrance to the utility tunnel was an access man hole in the middle of Greville Street, near the safe deposit box company. Since both roads were major thoroughfares the police were interested in the goings on this time.

They had been since the van pulled up and parked. Paperwork was checked and 'Sutton Electronics' was vetted. At least in the form of checking with the metro utility people to ensure the form was valid. Since it was, Michael held a full brief topside.

He even had a checklist. "Don't hassle the drivers! The Metropolitan police..." he waited until the nice officer supplied his name.

"Robert."

"Robert will deal with any problems, okay?"

Down into the opening went people, tools, and strings of lights. The van had a nice power connection to run the string, British efficiency on display.

Ira immediately scurried down the tunnel towards the 'T' with Hatton Gardens. Since it was two hundred yards from the opening, the string of lights ran out after twenty yards. Headlamps and torches took over.

Michael, Graeme, and Rick ferried the equipment after the electronics wizard.

The 'T' did indeed have the access plate the drawing indicated. Gretchen stayed near the opening, in case the cops or the Russians had an issue, but the rest concentrated on the work.

The plate gave way and exposed two hundred individual wires running in the bundle. The data lines were all white in color in the headlamp glare.

Ira muttered to himself as he worked. He kept clipping a multi-meter around the individual wires and grumbling. Little colored flags got wrapped around the wires after the results were read.

"Same scheme?" Graeme asked.

"Yeah- green for alarm, red for status, black for backup, and white for ground."

Michael shifted. "I want Rick to see this."

The men jockeyed around so that the protégée could see what was going on. If anyone in this world could isolate the Hatton Garden line from this mess it was Ira.

"Have him explain it to you, he is the best in the business," he told the younger man.

Ira continued checking and marking wires with the flags. "These old school systems are tricky. They have a separate wire for the alarm and another one for the status..."

"Status?" Rick interrupted.

"Yeah. With modern alarms it is not as simple as open or shut. Alarm or not. You have to have an alarm status that tells you it really is an alarm condition."

Rick did not understand.

"Look at the vault door. You can't just have a signal that says, 'Door open, alarm.' What happens when the door is opened to allow merchandise to come in and out? So the status signal will act as a blanking pulse to tell the system it is not actually and alarm." Ira waited for the inevitable question.

"Can't we just set the status line to active to blank out the alarms?"

"Nope- companies are smarter than that. If a status line has been active too long- and the time varies- that in and of itself is an alarm condition," Ira explained.

Rick could understand that.

"It gets even better. Most of these systems have a test signal that will set the status line and then deliberately cause an alarm condition to ensure it is working properly. No test signal and no test alarm- boom- that's a different alarm." He continued clipping flags om wires.

"Okay."

"On the digital signals it is easier to tap in to a multiplexor and read the overnight alarm signals. Then all you have to do is loop it back against itself for eight or twelve hours and--"

"Boom," came from Graeme, Michael, and Ira together.

"You have access to the vault," Ira finished up with a grin.

"Where did you learn all this?" Rick asked, fascinated.

"He used to work for the alarm companies, naturally, shammer!" Donniger announced with glee.

"Not since Y2K," the 40-ish man answered.

"Y2K?

Davidson explained. "People freaked in 1999 because '999' was an emergency shutdown signal in old operating code. Nobody knew if the 1999 date was going to cause things to shut down."

"Things?"

"Yeah! ATMs, Air traffic radar systems, the power grid. People thought it was going to be Armageddon."

The millennial could not believe it.

"How could anyone be that dumb?"

Ira laughed. "Kid, never underestimate how stupid people can be. Anyway, everyone and their mother wanted their system tested. And a lot of it fell to me."

Ira paused while getting more flags. "I got tired and I finally figured out how easy some of these systems are to spoof. So I got the idea to..."

"Branch out?" Graeme helped out.

"Apply my talents in a different direction," Ira corrected.

"Oh! You mean like to take your talents to South Beach!" Rick crowed.

"Huh?"

After that, it was just drudgery. Ira isolated the groups of wires he would need to monitor and attached clips around groups of the data lines. Those fed to a meter which in turn fed a small laptop. The whole mess needed to be secured safely in the overhead. The ever

present duct tape took care of that need. "How much data will you need," Rick asked as they stowed and taped it all.

"Three weeks plus would be best. I can get by with less, but I may have to force the system in some ways if we don't get the full run."

Michael clapped Rick on the shoulder. "There are some things we can do to help."

The man looked at the boss and waited.

"We need to keep detailed records of the opening and closing times on the businesses around here to allow Ira to correlate the signals with certain establishments." Michael told him.

"Okay!"

The four men retreated back down the tunnel and reached Gretchen waiting at the bottom. "No issues," Ira reported in. She smiled.

"We are fine, too," Graeme groused.

The others smiled and all emerged into the London night to find the Bratva and the Bobbies all jovial together.

"Wrap it up!" the boss announced and the tools and vests went back into the van. Davidson had the cop sign his checklist form. "Sutton pays us eight straight hours for this, but they like to know how long the jobs actually take."

He felt it was these little touches that made them blend in so well. Robert was happy to oblige.

"We might have to go in again, depending," he told the man setting the stage.

"Not my call, Sir," the man told him and they all moved off.

The Bratva went back to the tube stop while the gang got into the van for the short ride to the storage unit. Michael left the Russians with this directive,

"Stay out of trouble. I'll call you in a couple of days to figure out how to get you over to Dubai."

***

The good thing about thieving was that it usually required a ton of concentration. And work and concentration were very helpful in getting over a bad breakup. He did not dwell on Sydney all day, every day. He didn't work at it constantly, like a tongue probing a sore tooth, unable to stop himself.

Instead, it was random, hit and run kind of a situation.

Davidson spent days, along with the rest of them, watching Hatton Gardens and the diamond shops along Greville Street. They developed a pattern. Rise early, stake out prime spots to watch the openings. Then breakfast and go into the shops to see if the vaults opened at different times.

There were exceptions. For instance, Michael was casually in this diamond shop that did the unthinkable: it opened at half eight. As such, he was wondering around the shop, dressed in his rapidly deteriorating suit and an overcoat against the chill, waiting for the safety deposit box company to open.

The lovely saleswoman would occasionally say something or do something that reminded him of Sydney and the pain and regret would come flooding back.

Never should have gone to that dinner, he thought again.

"Can I help you with anything?" The pretty blonde asked with just the right hint of 'anything'. The well-dressed American was handsome and trim.

The smile back never reached his eyes. "Just browsing, thanks."

A check of his phone for the time, and then he went outside to watch the workers rolling back gates and shutters to open the stores.

Pretending to text something was a great way to note times and places. Not that he needed to. His memory could have rattled off who did what for Ira just as well.

Job completed, he strolled with apparent ease down the block to The Oasis. The breakfast place served as the gang's meet point while data was transferred to Ira.

All eight of them commanded a large table in the corner of the place. They'd been generous tippers over the week so taking up the spot for an hour a day was no problem. Mike let everyone relay data to Ira who had it all on his tablet, ready to look at when he retrieved the laptop.

"I hope you all have enjoyed your time in England, but we need to move on." He told the assembled men and the one woman. "Dubai in two days."

The Russians all looked eager. The past days had them more tractable and now they only asked irritating questions, not challenging ones.

Graeme stepped up to layout their route to the Middle East: "London to New York, to London to Dubai."

"What? Why can't we just go straight to Dubai?" Sergei asked.

"Because Sergei, Anton, and Viktor are in England on tourist visas. We need James, Patrick, and Richard in Dubai on our related work visa." He said this, slipping envelopes to the three men which contained their new IDs for the Middle East. "You can't overstay your visit time in the UK. It is six months, but it's a zero sum game: One in and one out. You just can't fly in as one guy and fly out as someone else. It raises way, way, way too many red flags with the authorities when they see that guy 'X' is still somewhere in the country when he should not be."

"That's when they start asking questions about you, and putting notices to the airlines to track you," Gretchen added.

"Once you are back in The States, the counter is reset and you can fly right back out as these guys," Graeme said motioning to the packets.

More interesting stuff flowed to Demetry's men. Flight itineraries, hotel reservations, work authorization forms, fake driver's licenses, ATM cards from Vulcan Enterprises. twenty-thousand AED- United Arab Emirates money. And, maybe most critically, some pages of research info on customs and etiquette in an Arabian country.

As Sergei looked over the sum of things that Davidson's people had given him, and he grudged a comment. "Very thorough."

Michael knew this was another level for the capo. They just did not do things like this. Strong arming shopkeepers, running girls, gambling, drugs... those were his areas. He was no doubt thinking this was some CIA-type shit that was above his pay grade.

"Please make sure you read and understand what is in that packet," Donniger went on. "Number one item is not to drink alcohol in public. Like on a beach or in a park," he told them. This was his show, as he was in the lead position for Dubai.

Everyone took some time to familiarize themselves with the basics when Sergei said, "What if we have a problem and miss our flight to Dubai?"

"You should be good to go. It is a seven-hour layover. However, if a problem arises, think like a business man. Go to the airlines customer service counter and rebook. You have a fully changeable, refundable ticket, so that won't be a problem. Mikey and I will be on the same flight, but do NOT acknowledge us!"

The Irishman gave way to Gretchen. She was the travel agent for the group. "We have you booked into the Marriott in Dubai City. You all are taking a van into the city, so hook up at the island outside the arriving passenger lower level." She spent some time going over the procedure for the men.

Graeme took back his talking stick. "Current plan is to have you guys scout out the area where we are going to get rooms for everyone. Then we bring in the groups and start training. We will need you to stock the place with food and water and stuff for the rest of the men."

Nods answered from the Russians.

Everything looked set. The capos actually bid them goodbye and left the restaurant. Anton told the others he was going to miss beans for breakfast.

Mike paused, watching the people on the sidewalk. People bustled by, getting to work or going about their day. The stooges moved off, talking amongst themselves.

The remaining gang members finished up their own business back inside.

Mike listed to do items. "You three have to retrieve that monitoring gear. The work form should be in the post today or tomorrow. We target the twenty-fourth, Ira?" he said, pausing to confirm.

"Yeah, Mike. That should give me enough data to correlate and isolate from there." Rick, Gretchen, and Ira were going back in alone to gather the gear. No big setup, just ten to twenty minutes inside and back out.

"Good. Graeme please check in with Trev and the Swiss again vis-a-vis the site meeting and the gold shipment."

The Irishman nodded while Rick snickered. "Vis-a-vis?"

"Laugh it up, kid. You get the shit job over the next few days. I need to know every person who goes into and out of the Hatton Gardens Building. Especially, the workers in the back."

"Ahh, Mike that's gonna be so boring!"

"Yep, and we have to have that information. We know they have renovations starting on the place. That is going to be our cover and entry point, posing as workmen, so..."

"So I have to know who the lead supervisor is, when he is on site, who his subordinates are, and what is going on," Rick finished up for him.

The four others smiled at this statement, proud parents as the golden child aced the spelling bee.

"Things all set with the fractional?" Michael asked Gretchen.

"Yes, Sir!" She was a bit peeved. The men were using the private jet to buy themselves a few hours of time in New York to deal with the mountain of paperwork Michael was sure was awaiting them at the mail drop. He was sure some forms from the lawyers were in there, not to mention all the fake W-2's. Even prepping for the biggest jobs of their lives, taxes had to be paid because the universe demanded order. Davidson was deathly afraid of the IRS. *Ask Al Capone or Wesley Snipes if the IRS messes around?* That's what he always told people.

"You can use the jet next week when you guys get to the Middle East," he told the other three. That made Ira happy. Besides, they were only using it to New York. He and Graeme were catching the same outbound flight as the Russians. They wanted to avoid issues. Well, he knew there would be some, but any they could avoid now...

***

As the gang left The Oasis, none of the five saw the youngish man at the counter watching them. The bland- looking, thirty-five year-old was perfectly dressed and blended like a chameleon. The large window gave off a perfect reflection and allowed him to watch the gang without looking directly at them. He'd overheard some things. The movements of these people were very important to his superiors. He needed to report in.

Chapter Thirteen

"Arabs don't trust people in sunglasses, my friends," the van driver told the Russians in decent English.

The hotel shuttle was making its way on the crowded street from the international airport terminal to the Deira section of the city.

The capos, plus Mike and Graeme, occupied the van along with another two passengers.

Sergei and his friends took off their shades. The twenty-five degree Celsius day and cloudless sun caused them to squint in the glare. He and his pals had on respectable suits, but no ties. Michael could live with that. He and Donniger had on the 'UAE foreign worker uniform'; company polo shirts in dark blue, khaki pants with lightweight boots and a tan belt. Both had the keffiyeh around their necks. The colorful and practical scarves kept the sand out of clothes and eyes in the ever-present desert wind. It was the first thing they'd broken out after meeting up with their charges on the street.

The van moved slowly along Siddique Road under the Dubai metro green line tracks. Cars and bikes crowded the lanes all looking to exploit openings. The driver ceased his rambling attempts to educate everyone as the van pulled into the Marriott check-in area.

The hotel was a standard, nice, US-type business hotel. It was a far cry from The Khalifa Tower however.

That was okay, because Michael and the gang were not staying here, only the stooges. Hundreds of foreign workers and corporate types came through each week and the lobby area was crowded. Davidson hoped to have them blend in and pass through unnoticed. They were reasonably successful at check-in.

Each of the men got a junior king suite. Gretchen felt they might need the room to have meetings. Graeme hoped they would only be here four or five days.

That depended, of course, on the Ministry for Trade and the Foreign Worker Department.

The five men crowded into Sergei's room after check-in to rehash the plans. "Everything is a rehash with Mikey", Graeme grumbled under his breath, but Michael heard him. He was willing to admit to his own faults, so he let it slide.

"Can you lay out the job for us," Sergei asked. He meant the actual heist, not the side issues they'd been dealing with.

"Sure," Graeme told him while looking at Mike. "Let me go through the chronology again and I will add to it okay?"

The man could live with that.

"We have four or five days- maybe a week- to arrange living quarters for the team while we continue preps for the job." The now-thinner Irishman walked to the 15th floor window to survey the dusty city. He grabbed a bottle of water from the provided fridge and took a sip.

"We have to pay to register and authorize all twenty of you. Our visas are current. That has to be done before we can apply for housing. Certain numbers and types of workers can only go to certain places here. We have applied for twelve rooms all together in one of the housing units in this section of the city."

A gesture out the window to the view and the Deira units became obvious. Standard, six-story apartment units dominated the coast section north and east of the skyscraper-dominated city center.

The somewhat drab housing units provided a home for the numerous Somali construction workers, dishwashers, and oil field people that drove the city.

Graeme agreed with the look from Mike. 'Yeah, we won't get all twelve together, but we will settle for in the same building. We have to expedite the applications for visas and housing at the ministry offices." And by expedite he meant bribe. The mobsters understood this part.

Anton, his bald head going pink from the brief sun exposure, said, "What will we be doing while you are busy?"

"Just like we said, friend. Get to know the area. Find a market where you can buy food. Scout out a local bar or restaurant where groups of you can meet." He was as tired and jetlagged as the rest of them, but the guy should have remembered this part anyway.

"Ride the metro here and get used to the surroundings." He paused. Michael reached into his messenger bag and pulled out lists for the capos.

Graeme allowed them to read a bit. "You have to be the experts to help the others when they arrive. It's important."

The Irishman got quiet. All eyes watched him. "Why do Arabs hate sunglasses- Viktor?"

A shrug from the man for an answer.

"Because of who wears them," Graeme said with conviction.
"Dubai and the whole UAE is very different from The States or Europe. Power is concentrated in the hands of the few in this place. There are no guaranteed freedoms here like in America."

The Russians listened, rapt.

"That means that you can get picked up at any time, for any reason. And I do mean any! You had to surrender your passports at customs, initially, Ya? That means you can't get out of the country unless the government allows it. If you get picked up as a foreigner- you ain't gettin' a phone call, you ain't gettin' a lawyer, and you ain't going anywhere fast." He laid it on thick.

"It's kind of worse for the locals," he continued. "Basic dissent is crushed around here. There is no free movement unless the government allows it. Add to that, the security situation and the locals can get quite restive and angry." He took a breath.

"So that means the people in power need to protect themselves from the unwashed masses."

"Mercenaries."

The one word thudded out there. The capos were a little confused, because they had no experience with mercenaries.

"The government and the power players have mercenaries as body guards." Graeme tried to gauge if this was sinking in. It had to some extent.

Sergei shifted forward on the little couch and said, "So the bodyguards all wear sunglasses and it intimidates the locals. That's why they hate sunglasses."

Graeme touched his nose. "Think about it, Viktor. Local guy goes to a cafe to get something to eat. Some rich dude walks in and his goons throw everyone in the place out who he doesn't like. Or worse."

"And we look like the mercs when we wear the sunglasses," he repeated.

Graeme did not want to tell him that it was a bit more than that.

The Bratva men carried the same swagger as the security men. The Brotherhood was used to being the muscle at home. So he kept it simple.

"Uh huh. Just ditch the sunglasses and buy the keffiyeh, the scarf, and you'll blend better."

At that cue, Michael again reached into his bulging bag and took out company polo shirts for the Russians. All three of them liked the cool Vulcan "V" symbol on the left breast pocket. Mike noted that for Rick. The kid had slaved and ripped off the Star Trek logo a bit to make a fake company symbol. He wanted to tell the man his efforts were appreciated.

"How do we spot these guys?" Sergei wanted to know.

"They will be armed and they will be dicks!"

"Who are these guys?"

Both thieves spent a good ten minutes detailing the Xi Services men and its founder's history.

"But, if they are based in Abu Dhabi, we won't see them here, right? Anton asked.

"Unfortunately, the guys get loaned out for all sorts of operations," Mike said, and then quickly backed out. Graeme just nodded instead of getting mad.

"Operations like guarding huge shipments of gold coming into the country," Sergei mumbled.

"Oh, yeah," Irish agreed.

"But if they are so tough, how are we going to pull this off!?"

So Graeme Donniger told them exactly how they were going to do it.

At the end of his speech the lead Russian breathed, "That could fucking work."

"Why's everyone always say that when I tell 'em the plan," he complained to Davidson.

Michael opened his mouth as if to tell his boy that *NO ONE COULD FUCKING PULL THIS OFF*, when the look on Graeme's face stopped him.

He's right, no arguing in front of the children.

"Anyway, thanks friend. I have been working on this for a while," Graeme told Sergei.

"Where do we start?" A suddenly eager Viktor asked.

"Just like we said: get to know the area and get ready for the rest of the men to get here."

Another looked passed between the two thieves. Michael came to stand next to his friend. He had a folded sheet of paper in his hand. "We could use some help with this though," he said handing the paper to Sergei.

The crew lead read it and nodded to himself and the others. "Yeah, I know a guy."

Michael and Graeme beamed. That was exactly what they wanted, help from Demetry's men.

They passed the burner cell to the Russians before leaving. The flee text would still be '7'.

That item brought on a long discussion of how to flee... "If the government is after us and they have our passports?"

"You do get your passport back in a few days," Mike admitted. "Especially if you are at the place where you said you were going to be. Meantime, if there is trouble, get to the US Embassy. Give them your fake name and say you got robbed. Every other answer is, 'I don't know.'"

"Tell them you came on a job hunt and it turned out to be a scam," Graeme added.

Michael approved, as if thinking, *yeah that was good*. The stooges did not have a locker with fake passports and IDs ready for them to flee the country if they had to. One in and one out went by the wayside if the cops were after them.

"Hopefully we will be back in a few days to move you into the rooms."

***

The men left the hotel by taxi and went to the villa. *Dubai is, without doubt, the strangest city in the world*, Davidson thought. Sitting in a traffic jam in an Audi just like his personal car for a taxi. He counted seven Bentley's in view during the stop-and-go crush on the Al Zakar Highway. Current rumor in the city said that the airport long-term parking lot was full of abandoned Maserati's, as debt-ridden foreigners fled the country. Several cars had looked dusty when they'd entered, but that was difficult to assess with the wind.

Eventually the cab turned onto the Sheikh Zayed Highway and headed southeast, paralleling the coast. The ultramodern skyline slid past as they approached the enormous Bin Rashid Office Park near their destination. Every large US corporation had offices in the oasis setting. IBM, Microsoft, HP, DreamWorks; all of them had a presence in the commercial hub of the Middle East.

They marveled as the cab exited onto the Dubai Pearl roundabout which sat at the base of the Palm Jumeirah Complex.

"Oh shit! Math actually has a purpose beyond gambling?" Graeme laughed as the two men discussed how large the roundabout was.

"Pie R squared, idiot," Michael joked with him.

That made the circle 3.14 miles in area. The five large buildings going up, dotted the interior. Glass and steel, the units would house over twenty-five thousand people, the builders hoped. Shops and the added attractions were supposed to come later. The cab swung around and the men could see that there were no workers currently laboring to complete the project.

The collapse of 2009 had killed so many of the city's crazy construction projects, Michael wondered which of them would be finished.

As the men crossed the bridge onto the Palm artificial island they gawked again at the canyon of residence hotels lining the road as they passed.

The first and most complete of the island groups, Palm Jumeirah, was enormous. The 'trunk' held hotels, shops, a monorail, and enough bars to keep anyone's liver busy. The fronds branched out from the trunk, arcing out into the sea. Each one was wide enough to hold seventy large vacation homes on a side of the strip of land, a hundred and forty luxury homes on each frond, and the place held fourteen fronds. That's a lot of sun seekers. The whole figure was ringed by a barrier strip island that protected and enclosed the tree shape. More hotels, shops and bars, and a giant water park were located on this strip of land.

The collapse in the economy was at least partly why they were here. Gretchen had been able to get them a large villa (five bedrooms with a pool) for a relatively cheap twenty-five thousand AED a month. That was about twenty-two hundred US dollars. The Nakheel sales office lady could not have been more helpful. And of course, the villa had a garage!

Nakheel was the current owner of the perhaps sinking albatross island group.

Sucks to be them.

The men paid off the cab and entered the villa.

Gretchen had performed at her usual high level. The place was perfect. Big, comfortable, and anonymous. The ride in exposed that there were not many people actually staying on the fronds right now.

After unpacking and looking around they went to the beach, which was just out their back door.

Graeme was slightly put off by the skim of oil on the barely moving water.

"Supposed to have breaks in the barrier island circling the place," Michael told him. "The idea was to allow the current to come in and refresh the water every so often."

"Not working is it?" Irish answered, looking down.

"Yeah, you have to be careful putting things where they don't belong."

Practical matters took over as the pair drove the rented SUV, which was stored in the garage, out to a market to stock the place with food and drinks. Resort prices killed Davidson. five hundred US dollars for the food! The men unloaded bag after bag into the cabinets and the refrigerator of the fully equipped kitchen. Both men worked out in the fading sunlight to battle jetlag and fatigue. Graeme even managed to keep up with Michael for the first few miles of the beach run. He broke off as his partner kept driving forward.

Later he found his friend catching the last rays by the pool.

"Careful! You'll lose that doughy, soft body and that pale skin and no one will know you are Irish."

"Fuck you, shammer. All I have to do is sing a lovely song and the women will know where I ken from." He laid on the brogue.

"We have the Ministry, Monday."

"And we have to scout the locations and do some bulldozer work on Tuesday," Graeme answered right back.

Still work to do.

***

Monday left Michael with a skim of slime on him like the waters around the villa. A certain amount of bribery was expected, but the 'institutional level' corruption here was bad.

"I'm so sorry, Sir, I don't think you have paid for the work authorization forms, yet?"

"Then, my friend, how do you explain this receipt and this canceled check?"

Yeah, pal. Not my first rodeo.

Davidson and Donniger were at the housing offices wading through the red tape in order to get the units they needed for the muscle boys. But the ministry man wanted to play games. In the end it took two more envelopes, one for the underling and one for his supervisor, to get the forms signed and the rooms allocated.

On Friday, the 25th of January, the five men moved a ton of food and toiletries and items into a block of twelve rooms on Al Jamiah Street in the Deira section of the city.

The block and the building looked like college dorm rooms on a massive scale. The spare two-bedroom units had a kitchenette and a basic living room with bedrooms on either side. The thieves were being nice to the mobsters: they were one to a room. Davidson knew the other foreign workers were often four to a bedroom to save money.

The three Russians had put their time to good use, as all were sun burnt and proudly wore the keffiyeh with new found ease.

They met in the lowest unit, which Michael suggested they designate as a group meeting place. "Don't store anything on the ground floor, too tempting," he advised.

"Okay, we have to go back to London to find out how the monitoring went and gather my people to get back to The States. Once we are there we get your guys and we bring them over in two groups." Michael set out the plans with Graeme going along.

The capos picked Anton to stay behind and watch the rooms while the other two got to ride on more airplanes.

"I heard back from my friend about the list you gave me," Sergei told the group. Graeme perked up at the news.

"Trouble is, he only could refer me to a local. He has done business with this man before and says he is good, but..."

"Yeah." Michael was not happy. Graeme joined him in that worry. Locals. The only way to get the stuff was through locals.

However, a weapons buy of this magnitude was going to raise red flags all over the place; FBI. Interpol, XI Services, the Ministry, everyone was going to have their hackles up. It won't take much for the mercenaries to connect the dots between the guns and the gold.

He and Graeme had had this argument several times over the months as the man had been pitching the gold job. How do we arm ourselves without causing them to cancel the shipment? Or at least change it from one big move into tons of smaller, less tempting ones?

The thieves had the whole conversation again, unspoken in the

room.

"Set the meet for two weeks," Graeme directed Sergei. "All of us will go get the guns when the time comes."

It was all they could do.

Graeme smiled and Michael worried. It was all they could do.

Chapter Fourteen

Must be getting used to it, Michael thought as he stepped out of the tube stop from the Heathrow Express into the drab weather of London. The abrupt change in weather was hardly noticeable. The Holborn Circle Station was near the Cambridge flat and he and Graeme were back to pick up the rest of his crew.

The Russians were staying near the airport and out of his hair for ten minutes, which was a godsend.

Ira and Gretchen and Rick were ready for them and each had a report on the things they were working on.

Rick led off with good news. He'd gotten a detailed account of the people going in and out of the Hatton Building doing the renovations. The lead supervisor, his crew leads, and the workers all had brief write ups and even some pictures.

"Jesus, Rick this is fantastic!"

The man preened under the praise. If Rick had the good, Ira had the so-so news.

"We got the monitoring gear back, but the results are not so hot." Levinson told the men that the alarm lines were not so easily spoofed.

"It looks like some of them are ganged and some are dummies." He gave a grudging compliment, "Someone very smart came up with this system."

The gang spent an hour working through the puzzle box challenge. How can we mitigate? Can we bypass? Loop back information or false signals? They looked at everything.

More work with the Lloyds drawings and the schematics gave Ira a line on another way in: "We are going to have to test some of it though, Mike."

Levinson detailed how he wanted to work it and they incorporated that into the amount of work they had to do. Davidson thought it was a good plan.

The bad news came from the woman. Gretchen Gonsolvo flipped a photograph onto the dining room table where they were all seated while they worked. The grainy black and white headshot showed a youngish, white guy who looked harmless enough. Faces stared.

"He's been around," she told the others.

"Shyte!"

"Who is he?" Rick wondered aloud and that was the key question.

"Private security, Flying Squad, maybe another of Demetry's guys? At this point we don't know," Michael said. But he intended to rectify that situation.

The gang and their two Russian charges were scheduled to go back to The States in a couple days. That gave them precious little time to find, and perhaps deal with, this new wild card.

"Ira- Suit up and find him. Follow him."

Gretchen was the best at disguises in the gang, but Ira could hold his own though. Michael wanted the electronics man on this because the guy had been tailing Gretchen, it seemed.

Adjusting to circumstances was his specialty and Davidson made some adjustments.

"We come over on the fractional," he said to the group. I'll coordinate with Feydor and Demetry and get the helpers in two groups, like we said, but we come over on the charter planes."

"Mikey, that is going to raise our profile in Dubai. Coupled with the big buy..." Graeme was worried.

"Can't be helped." He watched everyone struggle with the complexities.

"I know it is a calculated risk, but it's one I feel we have to take. I want to break pattern here and in Dubai. It might help us with the FBI and the Ministry."

***

Two days later, Ira got lucky tailing their watcher. The wig wearing man came in, stripping off his beard and yelling, "Flying Squad!"

The long discussion that news prompted, and the even longer one on how to respond, led to a small play for the three stooges.

Waiting at the Heathrow private terminal for the jet to board, all seven of them resided in the passenger lounge. Michael drew Ira off a bit for a 'quiet discussion.' It was one he knew Sergei would overhear.

"Ira, I can't help it! If the Robbery Investigation Division of Scotland Yard is tailing us we have to move carefully!"

He let just that part slip and then he moved off with Levinson. The gang really did have a way to defeat the cop in London. Well, not defeat- more like neutralize. But he did not want the Russians to know that. And he wanted parts of the information to actually get back to Demetry.

By letting Sergei overhear that part, he knew that Demetry would know that his two tame policemen had put the gang on Interpol and the Yard's radar. That accomplished a few things he hoped. One, he hoped the cops and the FBI would concentrate on him, and two, he wanted Demetry to think he had another control rod over them.

Much more subtly, Mike rea;oized that Sergei was coming to respect him. The Russian approved of the way Mike handled business and his people. Demetry had undoubtedly order the three lieutenants to spy and report on the gang. Which they were doing. The fuzzy bit came when trying to predict where the *watching* would end and the *removing* would begin. Any feelings of goodwill Sergei had for them would be helpful.

Money. It all came down to money for the Bratva leader. Michael suspected Demetry would wait until the jobs were completed.

Sergei? Michael was hoping it was getting a little more complicated for the man. The capo knew that Alexi Semilov, the Bratva's pimp was setup by Demetry months ago, sacrificed to the feds. He also knew that Demetry was feeding the feds info, through the cops, on Michael's activities. *But! Davidson's activities were Sergei's activities!*

Where did that line exist for the capo? The man brooded all the way over the ocean. The pressure on the gang seemed to ratchet up a notch at the same time. Groundhog Day found Davidson checking into the JFK Hilton. Two scant days in NYC before he moved the groups to the Middle East. The weather in New York was blah- mid-forties and cloudy. The room matched the weather. His mood matched both. The gang was in nearby rooms with the Russians enjoying a brief stop at home.

An uber-ride to the post office brought a mountain of mail and work. Forms, paper, bills, statements. *Jesus Christ!*

He had a goal for the day: Taxes. He had to get personal and business taxes done both fake and real. He made the lawyers and CPA's come to him to work out the details and the forms.

His room looked like an explosion of paper. Twelve straight hours of work brought in the goal. Mike had the returns ready to keep his illusions going. *This one might be the last fake one ever. No, probably not. A few more to transition to reality.* His thoughts were dulled.

"Keep working on those fake receipts and invoices for the diamonds," he told the Dogra brothers as they left.

The mental process bogging down was not helped by what little sleep he got that night. His dreams had prevented a restful night. Running. He'd run from things all night. Demetry. The cops. Sydney. *Damn!*

The hot shower was restorative early the next morning. The Dogra brothers had dropped off his returns early as well. They would electronically file them, but they had the usual customer copies for him.

Per his normal routine, Mike checked his messages from his home machine. Five totally illegal robo calls and a kicker: "Mr. Davidson, this is Detective O'Rourke. It is Jan 29th at 3:17 pm. We need you to contact us and come down to the station. We have some questions for you about the Spack case."

Shit!

His mind working furiously on the problem as Davidson dialed Graeme. "It's me. The cops want to see me about Mary's case."

The Irishman's stomach drop could practically be heard through the phone.

"What are you going to do, shammer?"

What was he going to do? Run? Not ready yet. Bluff? What did the cops know and what did they suspect? He speculated.

"See what they want," he told Graeme.

Davidson figured the crooked cops had finally cracked his computer and shifted some of that info to the feds as evidenced by the Flying Squad guy watching them. The info must have gotten to O'Rourke as well. But what exactly did that info give the homicide cop? Gave him his chat rooms and some messages.

O'Rourke was no dummy. He knew those were not innocuous messages. *But, that didn't prove he'd done something illegal.*

He finally figured the chat session for a fishing expedition by the police.

Davidson called the others to have their phones ready and be able to move quickly, however it went.

A deep breath and he called the man. "Detective O'Rourke, this is

Michael Davidson."

"Yes, Mr. Davidson, thank you for calling. Are you in the city, Sir?" The cop probed immediately.

"Yes, I just got in from Dubai yesterday and checked my messages."

The cop wanted him down at the station. "To answer some questions."

"Certainly, Detective. Anything to catch Mary's killers."

The uber drive over was expensive.

The station house was on Prince Street. Davidson realized the gang's storage unit was only a few blocks away. Well, this was Brooklyn. Everything is a few blocks away from everything else.

The desk sergeant led him past the chaos of the city's battle with crime. Debris, both people and paper, competing with each other to cause more of a mess.

The large homicide detective still looked as tired and disheveled as he'd done before. The man took him back to an interrogation room. "Quieter in here."

Davidson avoided the, 'am I under arrest,' quip that wanted past his lips. *Don't give them any ideas*, he told himself.

"When did you get back in the city?" O'Rourke asked.

"Last night? No, two days ago. Sorry, jetlag is getting to me." Davidson parried.

"Uh hum. Who do you work for, again?"

Here we go. "I told you, Detective. I am the sole employee/owner of Anderson Consulting. I do oil and gas field services on a limited contract for Royal Dutch Shell. RDS," he added helpfully.

The cop took in the answer and asked several more questions about his business. Davidson knew the cop could have pulled some of his info, but banking records took time. Phone records took less. And that was a rub for him. The gang used burner phones which caused a red flag.

Davidson was sure there were NO phone records for him which was causing the cop some heartache.

"Detective, this is my cell number," he rattled off the phone he wanted to give him. It would show calls in Dubai and London, just like he'd said.

"I use a charge-as-you-go phone, because it is easier to use in

Europe and I don't want to be tied to a huge plan and bill with my travel schedule."

The answer was perfectly reasonable, and correct, and the cop clearly thought it stunk to high heaven. Davidson could read that on his face.

"Look, here is my contract number and my contact at RDS. Check them."

Michael rattled off the number and gave a business card to the man.

O'Rourke glanced at the mirror in the room and Detective Rodriguez came in and took the card and left again.

While he continued to fence with O'Rourke, Davidson knew Rodriguez would be checking.

Again his detailed preparedness saved his ass.

The Latino woman called the number and Ira answered. "RDS, Human Resources, how can I help you?"

She explained who she was and what she wanted.

Ira faked confusion. "I'm not sure if you want Human Resources, Contracts, or our Legal department. I'm going to start you with my boss, Ms. Lawrence."

Jen Lawrence, aka Gretchen, got on the line.

After the question she came with the prearranged speech. "I can verify that Michael Davidson is a contract employee on a limited, current contract and on assignment. He has committed no illegal acts as far as we are aware of and any acts he may have committed are solely his responsibility."

Large corporations are always worried about their liability and at pains to tell you they aren't responsible for anything.

The female cop returned to the interrogation room and whispered in O'Rourke's ear for two minutes.

Davidson made a mental note to buy Ira and Gretchen a gift. Their rehearsed routine had saved him again.

"Detective, what the fuck is going on? Why are you focusing on me? You know I was in Hawaii when Mary was killed. RDS didn't kill her as a way to make me work harder. What are you doing to find Mary's killers?"

The cop scowled. "That is the same question Sydney Devereaux asks me every time she calls."

A flood of relief went through Davidson. Sydney had not given him up. She was still badgering the cops about Mary, also.

"And?"

"Something about this does not add up. Robbery gone wrong and they haven't pawned the goods? It doesn't feel like a random act, too methodical," he mused aloud. More scowling and grumbling from the cop.

Gently now...

"Well, someone was there who didn't belong there. Who?" Davidson gave the man another bone besides him to chew on. O'Rourke mulled that statement over, but didn't answer him.

The cops kept him there another two hours asking about his banking and business details. Davidson briefly considered showing the cops his fake tax return. *No, let them dig. That gives us more time.*

In the end they had no firm grounds to continue questioning or holding him so he left at 3:30 pm. Davidson delighted in dropping the fake tax returns- mailers all addressed and stamped, right into the police mailbox at the station house. His messenger bag felt, and was, lighter.

A quick call to Ira to thank him and report that he was safe while he waited on the cab. The growing dark was getting colder as he made the other two 'had to' calls.

Feydor Slutskaya picked up on the second ring. "Da."

"Feydor, it's Michael Davidson."

"Da." Still a charmer.

"Have the first group at your place, tomorrow 8:00 am sharp. The second group the day after that." The fence bitched and moaned, but it was the plan and he agreed. The last call was harder still.

"Mr. Roybokov, it's Michael." He gave the Bratva head an update on Hatton Gardens and on Dubai. "We take the men out over the next days."

"Good. Michael please keep me apprised of your movements."

What? Why? Oh yeah, so Demetry knows where to have the FBI pick us up. Or to have Sergei kill us.

"Of course, Sir," the good employee told him.

"Michael, I still need you to go to Luxembourg for me," the old man reminded him.

"That is still three or four weeks away, though, right, Sir?" he asked.

"Da. Around the beginning of the month."

"Certainly, Sir."

The line clicking off was abrupt. Davidson wearily put the phone way. His movements brought a wave of his own smell out of his coat into his nostrils. Stink.

He stank. Fear of the cops, his dealings with Demetry and the brotherhood; all had soaked into his suit. The same tired, blue suit he'd been wearing for a while now.

As the cab pulled up he made a decision and a mistake.

Home. He went home. *I'm hungry and tired and need new clothes. Best place to restore and resupply is home.*

On some level, he knew it was a mistake, but the rationalization just came into his head. He *deserved* a night at home. He *deserved* new clothes. So home he went.

The cab dropped him off at 187 in the last of the daylight. The trudge up the stairs slow and the amount of junk mail in his vestibule alarming as he went into the darkened house. The musty, closed place felt fantastic as he moved around. Dropping the messenger bag on its familiar spot on the table felt just so right. Roaming the kitchen with one overhead light on was perfect.

He decided a decent meal would be first. Rummaging in the cabinets he came up with a nice idea: quick sauce.

His grandfather had taught him how to make a spaghetti sauce that was the opposite of Mrs. Scanzani's: quick and easy. He had the basic ingredients. A can of crushed tomatoes, small can of tomato paste, garlic, oregano, salt and pepper, and the final secret addition. A can of tuna fish packed in olive oil.

Dumping the whole list of ingredients into a skillet he set it to a fast simmer. A pot to boil a pound of pasta and he was done in fifteen minutes. Combining in the pot the noodles and sauce, he added in a ton of grated parmesan cheese.

Delicious.

Michael ate it man-style- out of the pot, until he was bursting.

Cleaning up from the meal also saw him throwing away some bad food in the fridge. Now he was really out of food.

He sat in the dark in the living room and battled depression and the urge to go over to Sydney's house. Most of his fantasies involved Sydney seeing him and rushing over naked.

Not gonna happen, his brain said. *Might gonna happen*, his dick replied. A car moving down the street brought him out of the reverie.

Exhausted and sore he went into the bedroom to pack two more duffels. One for London and one for Dubai. God, it would be nice to have some different underwear.

The bedroom was dark except for the closet light. He did not want to attract attention to the fact that someone was home. He moved towards the bathroom. Sydney's darkened house was visible through the windows.

Gone. Thank God for that as well.

He wanted to see her, but knew that would be a bad idea. And that made him feel like shit.

Davidson luxuriated in the shower in his own bathroom. His soap and his shampoo. He pruned up and used up most of the hot water. And that was saying something, because he had a huge hot water tank.

Shaving and brushing his teeth required a light which he clicked on. The ablutions and the normality of the tasks soothed him. He was feeling better. More settled. He intended to sleep for a while and get up early to get back to the Hilton before Feydor's and the flight to Dubai.

He toweled off his hair again and walked out into the bedroom... Oops, forgot to turn off the light.

277

He turned to do that when the sound of the phone ringing jarred him.

Startled him, because it was unexpected. Davidson jumped and whipped to look at the phone. When he did he saw some items that were just coming into his consciousness. The house next door had its bedroom light on.

Sydney's house. Sydney's bedroom. Sydney.

He could see her form outlined in the curtains and back lit. *She can see me better*, he thought. *No curtains.*

The internal debate about whether to answer the phone took three rings.

He picked up the receiver, saying nothing, not trusting his voice.

"Michael?" Her voice was raw and rough.

The small sounds coming from him were not words-justacknowledgment that he was he.

"What are you doing here?"

He took a deep breath to open his throat. "Thank you for not going to the cops," he said, instead of answering her question.

It was Sydney's turn to just make some noises.

"Listen. I got a call from O'Rourke. I went down to see him today."

She gasped on the other end of the short telephone line.

He was very pleased by that sound. Maybe too pleased.

"I...I think the cops that killed Mary finally got into my computer and sent some incriminating stuff to O'Rourke." It came out in a rush.

"Does he suspect you?" Was that concern in her voice?

"Yes and no," he managed lightly. "Nothing about this adds up. Not me, not Mary or her killing. He can't figure what's going on and it's driving him crazy." He inhaled and exhaled to think. "He said you have been calling."

"I want them to find who's responsible for this!" This whole episode could not be easy on her, Michael knew.

"You have the picture. Give it to the cops when you read about... my work."

She started to say something, but he cut her off. "Syd, you have to be careful! Those guys are still out there!"

"What are you doing here?" she asked again.

Yeah, what was he doing here?

And he could not come up with a good explanation. *He wanted new clothes?* Just buy them! *Wanted to sleep in his own bed?* Stupid! For what? Longing? Nostalgia? Stupid, stupid.

"I missed...*(you, us!)* home, I guess." It sounded lame to his own ears.

"How have you been?" he got out, but she had already hung up the phone.

She turned off the bedroom light, plunging her house into darkness.

FUUUUCCKKK!

He dressed and called an uber. Stupid and amateurish to return here he told himself on the way back to the hotel.

Mental kicking hurt just as much as physical, sometimes.

Chapter Fifteen

Feydor's pawn shop basement was still the same warren of rooms. The place was crowded that morning with the five core gang members, two lieutenants, and the twelve new found hired muscle men.

In addition, the pawn shop owner and his three henchmen all managed to get in the way, so the place stank and was hot, even at 8:30 am on a cold day.

Michael setup the smaller side room with the desk as a work space while Graeme and Gretchen got everyone in order for the main briefing in the bigger room.

The Irishman gave everyone the full briefing. The hired gold haulers got the whole kit. IDs, new passports, driver's licenses, credit and debit cards. Even company polo shirts.

Rick and Mike took advantage of the time to go through the new comers' bags. Contraband- alcohol and porn mags being the most prevalent items- was dumped. Graeme yelled at everyone for that, while Ira took bags of the stuff outside to the garbage dump.

Strangely, Gretchen did not slap Michael down for having her man perform such a menial task.

The answer resided in Ira's special project for the boss. The little man was scurrying around, dropping bags off and slipping around the basement so much that Slutskaya and his boys lost track of him. Which was just what Michael wanted.

"Flight is at 1:00 pm," Graeme told the group. "Mike and Sergei will take you over. Viktor and I will follow the day after with the second group. Anton is sitting in your apartments right now, so we have a place for you to stay. You have a couple days to get acclimated, and then we start training."

There were no questions of consequence and Gretchen took over to start in on customs procedures and a review the full info packet she'd given the capos in London.

The woman's attention to detail astonished Michael. She'd been that way since she was nineteen when the gang had met her in Fortezza, Brazil in 2004.

Mike, Graeme, and Ira were in town to rob a bank. Brazil was undergoing one of its once-per-decade currency crises. The government had decided to move all of its reserve currency to a new vault in Fortezza, a small town on the edge of the gold fields. Moving the money made it vulnerable. Just like the gang liked it.

The gang had needed fake IDs and work visas. Gretchen was pointed out to them by their inside contact as 'new, but good.' She'd come through with the paper and Mike just kept going back to her for help. First, with the rental house, and finally with the tunnel.

The plan called for them to bypass the alarm lines and the drawings they had were incomplete at best. They started the tunnel in an attempt to find the alarm line. The rental house was situated over a mile from the target vault. Every day they kept having no luck and kept extending the tunnel nearer the bank.

It was hard work and they kept at it using some workers Gretchen had hired. When they could not find the line, Michael tried to keep up everyone's spirits by saying, "Well, it has to be around here somewhere."

It became a pattern: extend the tunnel towards the bank and say "Well, it has to be around here somewhere."

Michael also remembered the outcome of that job. The tunnel did find the alarm line tie point eventually. Directly under the vault.

Ira bypassed the signals and the gang, now four strong, and the workers took two full days to bore in and unload everything.

The four laborers got 95 million Brazilian reals and four gold bars to split up. While the gang had to console itself with $251 million in US dollars and another 500 lbs of gold.

The gold was shipped directly from the rental house as geological samples, while the money went wrapped in bags shipped in a load of agriculture (bananas) to The States.

The smile slipped as he regretted what had happened to those four laborers.

He left strict instructions to their hired muscle about what to do with the money, but of course they'd gotten drunk and bragged. The cops rounded them up a week after the job. Funny, no one seemed to buy their 'three gringos and a woman story.'

Davidson caught Gretchen's eye as she briefed the men and yelled across the room to her, "Well, it has to be around here somewhere!"

The woman, Ira, and Graeme all laughed at the inside joke

The work of getting the large group of men ready to go to the Middle East soon consumed Davidson's attention, moving him back to the present.

Donniger came up to Michael's side as he smile bled away from his face. Graeme misinterpreted the expression. "Shammer, you worried about the cops?"

Michael spent a few minutes detailing his thoughts on the session with the police. "He suspects something... But he can't prove anything yet, and when we are in the wind I'm going to have Sydney give up the bad cops so we are covered."

"You saw her?" Graeme asked lightly, but seriously.

Michael said nothing to that question.

"Do not go back home, Mikey! That can totally fuck us."

When exactly did his relationship to Graeme turn upside down? Now he was the one passing out wise advice while Mike made stupid mistakes?

Again, he only trusted himself to nod at the man's words.

No matter. In seventeen hours he would be in Dubai, and then traveling so much he would not have time to worry. He hoped.

As bad as his last trip to the Middle East had been, the private flight into Dubai was a cake run.

The advantages of fractional jet travel were never more apparent. The group was whisked aboard the plane and flew directly to Dubai International. The mobsters all behaved on the plane... to an extent. And when anyone stepped out of line, Sergei squashed it.

The bored customs man pocketed his envelope with practiced ease and stamped away. He knew, "exploring for oil near al-shuwab," meant a wide variety of things, but the money eased his way.

Plus, Michael had the proper forms and all approved. When Sergei quirked a question at him, he explained. "Think of it like this: If you do business in California and then move to Nevada you have to get a Nevada business license, even though you had one in Cali right?"

Al-shuwab was in a no man's land near the Oman boarder. The Dubai emirate land and the Abu Dhabi protectorate all converged in an area of trackless desert. The only true authority out there was water and Bedouins.

Michael, Rick, and Sergei got the men settled into their rooms. Anton was next to useless, but he was at least a familiar face for the muscle.

"Relax for a while as the next group comes in tomorrow. Stick close to the rooms and ask these guys any questions, okay?" Davidson hooked a thumb at Anton and Sergei. He did not anticipate any real problems this early. Not until the men had been here a month or so and got bored.

The next evening, the 7th of February, was an ordinary Tuesday in Dubai. Frond E on Palm Jumeirah saw some rental activity as a larger party inhabited a villa on the southern side. The desert wind was giving the tourists a break as the sun slid down in a cloudless sky.

Michael and Rick had a small celebratory meal in preps for Ira, Graeme, and Gretchen as they were just now dropping off the last of the troops.

The three pulled up in the SUV Gretchen had obtained for the group. Its twin stood parked in the large garage. The garage that was rapidly filling with their gear.

Steaks cooked away on the grill with asparagus ready to go on next.

Gretchen was soon schooling Rick on how to tell if the steaks were medium rare. "Put your hand like this..." She pinched her thumb up against her index finger puffing up the flesh near her knuckle. "Poke it. That is what medium rare should feel like. That way you don't have to cut into the meat to check it and it stays moist."

Rick was impressed. "How do you know so much about grilling?"

"You ever hear of a churrascaria, Rick?" Michael asked the man who shook his head. "Point is, Brazilians know a thing or two about barbeque," he said to the no response. The woman flashed her smile at the

young man and told him all about the nice restaurants in Rio and Sao Paulo.

Michael left to find Graeme and Ira head down over maps. "We take delivery in three days," Graeme confirmed to the other two.

"Good, what about our reservations?"

Ira perked up. "The seventeenth through the nineteenth at the camp. Then the twentieth through the twenty-second at the Hilton," he told the men who both nodded. "We go again the ninth through the eleventh of April and the go-date of the twelfth." Ira finished up.

"What about another training session in March?" Graeme asked.

Michael just looked at the man. "I think we should. We left the dates open to give us flexibility, for both London and here. We should use that."

The whole gang discussed it as dinner was laid on the table.

These dinners were typical of how Michael liked to work. Eat and drill everyone on plans, contingencies, and protocols. This was a bit different as Graeme was the one drilling them for Dubai.

"The site for Hatton is still the sixth, Trev confirmed again," Michael reported. Rick was working on the specialized equipment with more work to do in London. Their electronics expert had to run a stress test on the alarm signal to help isolate the safety deposit box company and he also had a backup plan for that.

Dubai was still evolving, given the men being here and the logistics involved. Rick was working on the heavy stuff, while Gretchen was getting the transport and the radios in order. Whew!

The two leaders spent hours going over their to-do lists. The rest put up with it because Michael's obsessiveness had saved them many times. Graeme was doing his best thief-in-law impression with his work on the gold job.

Gretchen and Rick shared a look.

"Reminds me of Paris," she said to Sanderson, murmuring.

Rick agreed quietly but Michael had overheard the remark and it set off his memory of the Paris job.

***

The heist at Harry's was a simple, *ballsy*, job. After eluding Interpol, Mike spent countless hours drilling the rest. Drilling them on how to walk and talk and dress. As women. They kept at it until Gretchen was the most mannish one among them. All four of them, made up and perfectly dressed, went into the luxury jewelry shop just before closing time. Per normal, the vault was opened to put the display rings and necklaces back in.

Guns and zip ties took care of the other two customers and the guards. The staff was terrorized. The gang, especially Michael, felt bad about that. But, they kept to plan and eight minutes and forty- three seconds after securing the place they all walked out to the parked van with Rick behind the wheel and drove off with a huge haul.

***

Davidson let the good feelings wash over him before starting in to detail how the end game was liable to go for the gang. He spoke for a few minutes.

"I won't see you again after that," Michael concluded sadly.,

That statement came out and seemed to put a damper on a long, pleasant evening and night.

The gang detailed their escape plans. Donniger in Split or Dubrovnik. South America for the couple. Michael was unsure yet about his plans, but probably Paris or Monaco.

"Rick?"

"Maybe head west. LA or San Francisco. I think New York is going to be too hot."

The somber mood clamped down on everyone, until Ira spoke up. "I don't know what we are all moping about? None of us is going to survive Dubai anyway!"

"Definitely, shammer! We are all gonna get killed pulling this one off," Graeme crowed.

Laughter gripped the group as each morbidly detailed their own grisly demise.

"The hard bitten leader of the gang? I'm going to be so full of bullet holes, they won't even be able to identify the body!"

"Bonnie and Clyde ending for us, guaranteed!" Ira laughed.

"I might survive," Rick said defensively. "I'm the young, cute one."

"Fuck you!" seemed to be the consensus on that idea.

The next day Michael made an endless series of phone calls. Demetry, Nicholas Roybokov, his contacts both in London and Switzerland. Even Feydor. They all had to be kept in the loop. The last was the most important. Abdul. The local arms merchant.

"You've seen the list- can you get everything?" Mike asked.

"Very difficult, my friend," the weapons man said, subtly. And that started the negotiations. The feeling out and serious back and forth took hours over the next day.

"I've never been so insulted! I will buy from the Israelis." Mike told the Arab. He'd considered buying a shipment and trying to bring it directly to the villa by boat. The Palm had security craft all over outside the breakwater strip for just that kind of thing however.

"Hold on, my friend, hold on. These are dangerous times and a dangerous cargo. I must have assurances."

"So do I, Abdul!"

They set the swap: $2.2 million in diamonds for the guns. *You mean that necklace Gretchen has been wearing is real!* Rick was aghast. *No better way to smuggle money into a country.*

"Delivery next Thursday, the 16th." That would work perfectly with their reservations and the work they needed to do. Michael relayed the meeting point to the man and overrode the objections.

"My money, my meeting point. One truck and five workers. Unarmed. And Abdul- I'll know if you have a backup squad anywhere near the place."

The man grumbled, but acquiesced

Davidson and Donniger spent the next hours yelling at each other about the weapons buy. "No way the mercs are not going to connect the dots between the gold and the guns!"

"Give me an option? We have to have the guns!" Mike yelled back at the man. The Irish knew this was a risk!

The men came up with a small fig leaf they hoped would work. Hope was usually a poor plan in Davidson's opinion.

"We have to exercise the men over the next days," Graeme said. "It might work."

And exercise was a literal term. Graeme had the men running and working out like a military unit, which they kind of were.

Meanwhile, Rick Sanderson got to spend three days on a bulldozer in the desert. If the man thought high end thieving was going to be women and fast cars all the time he was learning quickly. Grunt work sucked. He reported his final measurement as 7,500 feet on the dot.

"I still need to know location for the pit." Rick reminded them.

"Working on it, shammer," was the answer from Graeme.

Everyone worked feverishly, caught up in the lure of gold.

***

The date for the swap arrived far too quickly. *The Russians were ready*, Michael thought. *Barely.*

The brief the night before had taken hours. Detailed maps and detailed questions came from the three capos. Even Anton. The small dorm room in Deira was hot and stuffed with people. Graeme took the lead as he was directing Dubai.

"Five vehicles, five per car," Graeme told them. "Radios set on channel 73. Ira will pass us the all clear." He pointed at the map pinned to the wall.

"Rick and his group, here." He paused while the assigned men raised their hands and nodded yes.

"Sergei, your men here." More hands. "Gretchen, here."

"Mike and I and our teams will do the actual transfer here."

The temperature in the room went up with the tension.

"We are going to be unarmed, but they might have guns?" Topper asked.

"This isn't America. There aren't 300 million guns floating around. We have to take the risk."

That did not set well with these men. They were used to doing the intimidating, not the other way around.

"If it all goes to shyte- survivors will fly home according to the evacuation plan. Got it?"

Distaste showed but Graeme had one bit of advice. "Attitude! These guys have an attitude. That alone will help carry you through this."

Chapter Sixteen

If this truck breaks down we are fucked.

The same thought, in various forms, was no doubt going through more than one person's head as the convoy made its way across the desert. The vehicles turned off the 'road' and onto a path that led deeper into the wasteland.

The early morning wind and sun beat down on the five SUVs- well four now that Rick had turned off to take up his post.

The drive on the E66 south and west of Dubai City was uneventful, and that was just as the gang had planned.

The radio piped up with Ira reporting that no movement had been detected.

Ira was in position with his Mercedes SUV a farther few miles from the team as they drove to the rendezvous spot. Levinson was no more than five miles from desert camp which was the gang's destination after this task was complete.

Desert Camp was part of the al Mahatta luxury resort north of the party. That resort was situated on the Marriquaba Oasis. And that happened to be the only reliable water for sixty miles in any direction.

Since water was a precious resource the government did the only logical thing possible. Turn the oasis into a high end resort that allowed westerners to complete their 'desert sheikh' fantasies.

Desert camp was an even more remote series of tents and plunge pools that begged for a Lawrence of Arabia themed sex session.

As luck would have it, Vulcan Electronics LLC, had corporate team- building exercises booked at the camp for the next two days. But first, Vulcan had to buy its employees some guns.

Ira was already checked into the resort and on station providing eyes on the area to ensure privacy.

And privacy they had. The one large Mercedes SUV and the other four H1 Hummer SUVs were alone in this huge chunk of sand, rock, and sky. This part of the Emirate was part of the empty quarter and it was living up to its billing. The resort and the camp were the only things out here. Except...

Except for the thieves and one other thing which the gang did not want the arms people to get a look at. They had a plan to try to mitigate the buy, but if the Arabs saw what lay seven miles from Ira, the job was blown.

Gretchen and her team deployed off the convoy, as did Sergei. Michael and Graeme drove on to the GPS coordinates he'd given Abdul as the meet point. Reaching the designated spot, the men came out of the large Hummers. Each was dressed smartly. Keffiyeh scarf with sunglasses, desert cammo tactical pants, a polo shirt with a Kevlar vest over that. Shooters knee pads wrapped around legs and the tan desert combat boots were heavy, but broken in by the amount of running Mike had had the men doing over the last few days. The men looked like what they were supposed to look like: XI services mercenaries.

"Truck coming in on the highway." Rick's report crackled with static. "Three in the cab visible, back covered on two- ton truck."

The man's voice was calm and the report was excellent. Nice point for Rick.

"Eagle?" Michael squawked

Levinson, using his code name. "All clear, recovering." Ira loved playing with his toys. The tension in the two main vehicles eased as it looked like the Arabs were playing nice and by the rules as far as being alone. They would see about the rest.

A dust cloud announced the arrival of the large truck long before it pulled to a stop twenty yards from Michael, Graeme, and the assembled, spread out Russians.

Three men came out of the cab and seven more out of the back, all sporting guns at the waist, which told of Abdul's counting abilities and his adherence to the rules.

The two groups of men stared at each other for a full minute.

"You got our merchandise?" Graeme asked, after a while.

The shorter Arab in the middle answered back, "You got our payment?"

The Irish nodded at the robe wearing man and he and a thug named Constantino went forward towards the big truck. Constantino was chosen for his huge physique and scowl. The truck was not running, but hissing and pinging in the heat.

Graeme shook a stone out of the leather bag and placed it on the hood of the truck and stepped back just a hair.

The Arab- Graeme was thinking he was Abdul, made a motion to one of his men and that man went back and took a box from the back of the cargo truck. The box was hustled to the front where two electronic leads came out and were placed on either side of the glittering stone.

The leads were in place and the device switched on. The portable electric tester beeped and a green light flashed. Diamonds conduct electricity at a constant rate different from other gem stones and, most importantly, cubic zirconium. Abdul then took a loop from his white robes and checked the stone. His grunt was audible.

Michael was impressed. *Not his first transaction and he recognizes the quality.*

As Abdul stepped away from the rock without taking it off the truck bumper, Graeme said harshly, "Let's see 'em!"

The man quickly looked around at the mercs.

Here it comes, Michael knew.

"Why do you want these guns, my friends. I thought you guys had all the guns you needed."

Graeme sighed as the rest stiffened. "Look, the man says buyuntraceable guns, I buy untraceable guns. I don't ask stupid questions."

Hands strayed to belts. He pinned Abdul with a stare.

"Our air cover says you are alone. Are we dealing here or what?"

The look of disgust at the air cover remark marred Abdul's face.

Fucking foreigners!

A second motion from the arms dealer and a large black plastic box came out of the back of the truck.

Two men humped the box to the sand at Graeme's feet. The man stooped and with practiced fingers, flipped the latch catches on either end to open the box.

Five HP5 submachine guns lay nestled in Styrofoam padding. Stubby, black gunmetal death lay exposed in the sun.

Graeme pulled one gun out while Abdul stepped forward and produced a clip from his robes like magic.

Donniger expertly loaded and racked the weapon. The foldable stock came out and he pointed the gun at Oman. More clutching at guns and jumping as he unleashed a full clip on auto. The empty slide came forward and he unloaded and safed the weapon.

"Nice!"

The tension level went down dramatically and the transfer went much smoother after that. Crates were unloaded and moved to the SUVs. Stones were tested and guns fired to ensure a full value to both sides in the deal.

Thirty minutes saw the bulk of the commotion finished and the last crates and boxes being shoved into the Hummers.

A   quick glance between Michael and Graeme started the play acting for the Arabs.

The two men walked alittle ways towards the empty desert and started a low-voiced -argument'. Finally, Davidson said, "No way I'm buying a SAM from him!" Just a little too loudly.

Abdul sensed another sale.

"Something you need that was not on the list? A man-portable missile perhaps my friends?" The man oozed charm now that more money was a possibility.

The pair frowned back and Michael settled it: "We hit them on the ground during the transfer. We don't need a missile."

Abdul had to be satisfied with his diamonds and his intel.

The last of the boxes went into the SUVs and the Arabs loaded up into their truck and drove off without further words.

"I hope that diverts them," Graeme muttered. *Let the authorities think we are going to hit the gold convoy as it moves.* They might change the route, but the gang would be ready for that.

"Assets secured. Everyone meet at site Bravo," Graeme ordered on the radio. The convoy of vehicles moved out. Six total, once they picked up Ira. The SUVs moved farther north and east from the swap point. Even *farther* into the empty quarter. Wind and sand and rocks and things seemed to dominate the landscape.

The sun went towards its zenith as the cars finally got to the destination. Everyone milled about smartly at the chain link fence entrance to the...

Why in the fuck would someone build an airbase way out here anyway? Michael wondered for the millionth time.

And 'airbase' might be a generous term. There were a series of low, corrugated tin-roofed buildings and there was a landing strip. A chain link fence surrounded the whole place. So airbase kind of fit. Here, at the 'back' gate, there was only the track to let rugged jeeps and Hummers move around. Mike knew the main entrance was miles east and north off an exit from the E44 highway. That might have been truly called a road. Dubai must have built the place in the 60's when they thought that Oman would be a problem. Research said the facility had been abandoned for two decades at least.

It showed. Sand had, until recently, covered the runway. That was until Rick took care of it with his bulldozer. Sand was still piled up near the low buildings and Graeme had been clearing out a few of them a little to allow the equipment to be stored there.

"Ira- put up the drone," Graeme ordered.

Levinson -aka Eagle- put up his bird. The drone was a four bladed craft that was top of the line. Able to operate in a 20 mph wind and a ceiling of 10,000 feet, this baby could carry a surprisingly heavy payload.

In this case, a high resolution camera with visible and infrared lenses. A burst transmitter sent the signals back to a monitor which now held a serious crowd as Ira sent the drone up.

A smooth burst of power and the monitor showed the ground falling away. The buildings became obscured and ill-defined as the sand blown on top hid them, but the newly cleared runway stood out very well. The cars off the gate showed plainly and the camera picture rotated as the drone circled back to look at the other end of the base.

The truly empty end of the base. More buildings and some sand covered roads, but no activity and no people at all.

Perfect. Just as Graeme had said many times. Perfect for their needs.

The men clipped the fence gate lock and installed their own chain and lock.

Driving the short distance to the buildings, Graeme and the capos held a conference. Two teams would practice hauling while a third would work on the guns.

Soon Michael was walking around and yelling at people while they sweated.

Sergei watched him and came up next to him while his group fired off a few rounds with the machine guns. "These Heckler & Kochs are nice guns, but I don't think they are capable of downing a C5 military transport plane."

Graeme heard him and joined the two men. "That isn't the hard part, and not what we have to practice, friend. The tricky part comes after. Let's go!"

It was a sore, tired, and sweaty group of people that returned to Dubai City on the 20th, before their journey to the Hilton. Mike wanted to stash the guns and get a change of clothes before they scouted the city of Fujairah.

The five of them lazed in the pool at the villa while the Russians were scrounging in the Deira rooms. All of them were sunburned and sore.

"Look at the sand in this pool," Gretchen remarked.

"I thought it went well," Rick said to the group in general.

Graeme agreed. The kid had done well. Taken charge of his group and gotten them all pulling in the same direction.

"It's what happens when the bullets start flying, shammer," Graeme told Sanderson. "That's what counts."

Ira and Gretchen nodded to that statement.

"You think the guards will come out shooting?" he asked seriously.

"Half a billion in gold, Rick? What do you think?" Michael remarked tiredly.

Davidson did not like guns in general. Rick did not have

experience with them like the rest did. The guns at Harry's were unloaded. No real danger. Rick was not with the gang on the Great Northern job.

Those guns had been loaded. And the threat to use them real.

***

The Great Northern Bank robbery in Belfast Northern Ireland occurred in 2006. The gang employed three extra members of the Provisional IRA as muscle during the heist.

The plan was simple and brutal. The three provos, plus Graeme and Michael, had broken into the bank manager's house the night before the robbery.

They held guns to the man's family; his wife and two children. *Get us into the vault or we kill them.*

Of course, the man had crumbled. He let them into the vault early the next morning while the three provos and Graeme stayed with the family. Mike much preferred the work in the vault. It was successful.

Successful in the fact that they got away with 75 million pounds, but he hated the guns.

It bothered him. Seeing the look on someone's face as a gun was pointed at them was very disturbing for Davidson. That terror. The realization that they could die always marked an individual during a robbery.

It marked him as well. He'd done it because the puzzle box could only be opened that way, but instinctively he knew he'd avoided the Dubai job because of the guns.

Funny, but the wrap up of the Northern job was bad as well.

The British authorities picked up hundreds of suspects in conjunction with the robbery. IRA and provos were all scooped up on whatever charge could be leveled.

The three robbers were nabbed on unrelated offenses and convicted. They never blabbed.

All three were killed in a botched escape attempt from Britain's notorious Wakefield Prison.

Using guns in a robbery did not end well usually.

***

Michael tried to focus them on the next day's trip.

"We have to work on the logistical end tomorrow at the port city right?"

His friends agreed. It was not going to be any physical work, just a lot of protocols and showing the capos and the other Russians where things were. *This is the dock, here is the storage place. The shipping office is here.*

That kind of thing.

Graeme wanted to work on other aspects of the job. "We have to tickle our Ministry contacts, Mikey, when we get back. Five days should be long enough for word of our buy to get back to them."

Davidson nodded. They had to know what the response to their actions would be. When he said as much to the rest, it seemed to unleash a flood of pent- up irritants.

"I still need to know where to dig that pit," Rick complained again.

"You will know when we know."

"I have to return that bulldozer..."

Ira broke in. "Returning a bulldozer? That's easy! Mike I need to test out that alarm system on Hatton. If we can't isolate the alarm signal, we are going to have to..."

It often happened this way on a job. Weeks out from the actual date for the work, the stress and workload seemed to weigh on his people.

He let them bitch. Most of it was blowing off steam and he knew that this was an especially stressful time for them. *This is the last time we get to do this. Besides, they always managed to tamp down on the friction.*

Donniger and Davidson rallied them and helped formulate game plans.

"Did you send that package to Downing Street?" Mike asked Gretchen.

The woman told him, "Yes. Two weeks ago. I haven't seen any kind of response."

"Send it to Fleet Street as well."

Gretchen agreed. She was handling their Flying Squad tail problem. They had more than a few problems being worked on. Michael knew they were still vulnerable and was bailing as fast as he could.

Chapter Seventeen

If this is Tuesday, this must be Paris, Michael thought.

Well, it wasn't Paris- it was Luxembourg- and it wasn't Tuesday, it was Thursday.

Thursday, the 5th of March 2013, at 11:53 am European Standard Time. The Gulfstream jet was on final approach to Findel airport and the freeport.

Michael had been gently awakened twenty minutes ago by the flight attendant. The bright smile and mass of blond hair momentarily lifted him as he came out of a troubled sleep. "Syd?"

He was disoriented and unsure of where or when he was. The flight attendant kept her hand on his chest. "Mr. Davidoff, we are landing in a few minutes. I need you to bring your seat up and buckle in. Okay?" She rubbed his chest just a little.

He came back into himself and nodded to the woman. More blinking and he complied with her instructions. "Sure, thanks."

He was exhausted, sore, and this side job for Demetry was not helping his mood, disposition, or sanity any.

The past three weeks had played hell on Michael Davidson.

The hired Russian help was going to kill him. Or the gang was. Or the feds. Either that, or he was going to take an HP5 and turn it on all of them.

Christ!

The gang had just completed their third training session at the airbase. Hauling the gold was turning out to be just as tricky as Michael feared it would be. Add to that a side trip into London to work Hatton and secure some vital equipment, and he was stretched thin.

A trip into the large bathroom when he'd boarded the plane at Heathrow, gave him a long look in the mirror under the harsh lights.

He did not like what he saw. A little more grey in his two shades lighter hair. The sun working its power on his hair and skin, he was blonder and now had a deep tan. His weight was down to 166 with a striking amount of muscle and definition on his frame.

But, it was the eyes that got him. Still brown, but now sunken and a bit *crazy*, if he had to say it.

Anyone would have the crazy eyes if they'd been dealing with the shit he was contending with, he thought.

The last training run had been decent but not what they needed. It wasn't the workers' fault, really.

It was a math problem.

A gold bar weighed 26 pounds. They came in a three bar billet box package. That meant the package weighed 80 pounds, give or take, per box. Problem was there were going to be 200 of these boxes on the plane. Over 16,000 pounds on the plane for the shipment.

The thieves had to move that gold from the plane to the SUVs. And they had to do it in a short amount of time.

Ira had figured a twenty to forty-five minute response time all those weeks ago when they'd scouted the place after the London work. It depended on the ferocity of the Ministry's response everyone knew. And as Michael and Graeme kept telling Rick and others: Expect a fairly robust response for that much money!

So more math. One lift of the billet box from the cargo hold to the slide ramp. Graeme's brilliant plan called for the gang to set up cargo hauling box slide ramps at the plane cargo door to facilitate the move. The standalone ramps were easy to setup and they had them stored in the airbase abandoned buildings.

One lift from the pallet on the plane to the ramp. A quick slide to the earth and a lift from the ramp into the SUV and its shipping container.

That was 400 separate lifts. Given the twenty minute time frame it took to get a chopper from the city to the defunct airbase, which gave them a grand total of three seconds per lift.

It could not be fucking done!

The gang had setup the slide ramp rollers for the first time after the gun buy. Gretchen and Rick had mocked up some thirty kilo weight plates as billet boxes. The teams had 16 of the dummy weights to practice with. Michael set the weights on a raised concrete foundation near the runway. The slide ramp was near the stack and led down to a parked SUV.

Go!

Topper grabbed a dummy box plate and lifted it, grunting. More grunting and an earth shaking slap set the thing down on the roller ramp. It slid alarmingly fast down to the bottom! Two men jarred shoulders as they halted the slide. The shift into the bed of the Hummer took both of them and was a struggle.

That one box took over a minute to move. The look between Michael and Graeme was epic. Never had the words, *I told you so!* been uttered so loudly and so silently.

"Okay, we have to figure this out. That's why we are here," Graeme told them all.

Adjustments were made. A bumper system was added to the bottom of the ramp. More billet boxes were mocked up. Another ramp system was procured as the suggestion by Gretchen that the plane was big enough to haul from both sides without getting in each other's way was agreed to.

At the end of the first training session they were exhausted and defeated.

But...

Progress was made. The teams did achieve a thirty-nine minute average for three full runs at the end.

Days later, after the quick stop back at Dubai, The Hilton Hotel in Fujairah had a whirlpool that saw a lot of action the days the thieves were booked in. Even Gretchen was tired and she was the toughest of them. The team cased the city for the second half of the job, which involved getting the gold out of the country. Stealing it was the perhaps the easier part of the plan. They had to get the gold to the US and Fujairah was the key.

The days after the first run became a blur of details and work for all of them. Michael took care of the first fight between the Russians.

Sergei called him when one of the guys would not be training with them on the second visit to the airbase. "Shithead hit asshole, which caused asshole to kick shithead in the balls." Tikanov relayed the news. "Shithead won't be joining us today."

"Dammit, Sergei! You are supposed to prevent this kind of thing from happening."

The capo breathed heavily on the phone. "Tough to control them sometimes," he muttered.

Michael and Graeme knew that. They decided not to send the men back to Demetry. That would be, in effect, a death sentence.

Adjustments were made.

And then the courier flight back to Luxembourg arrived. The interruption to the schedule killed Davidson. Shifting gears to fly to New York was very difficult.

The ID logistics was the toughest part. Peter McNichol and Michael Davidoff were not in Dubai. Alistair Grant and Mitchell Parnell were, however. Since the Freeport officials were familiar with Peter and Michael, they had to be them again.

That would necessitate a Dubai to New York trip as Grant/Parnell. Change IDs. A New York to London to Lux run as McNichol/Davidoff, then retrace back to the UK and New York. and then going back into Dubai as the right people.

That was a lot of flying just to make a one-day trip to the freeport.

Hence, Michael's confusion with the flight attendant as she woke him.

The Gulf Stream landed at Findel without incident. The lovely Helga and Ms. Stoerman met them at the plane with a ramp and the usual gaggle of customs and freeport personnel.

Nicholas Roybokov was drunk and maudlin as the customs people went through the six large crates they were hauling this time. More paintings and statues. Some gold. And rich people's cashier's checks: bearer bonds, along with some stones.

"Christ, is there anything left at the Brooklyn house?" Michael asked Nicholas when the two got a moment alone in the vault.

Helga, Graeme, and Phillipa were outside fussing with something and Davidson took advantage to question Nick.

"What do you mean by that?" Nick asked alarmed.

Davidson watched the kid. What did he know? What did he suspect? "Nicky, cards on the table. What's going on?"

The direct questions broke the man down. A few tears came as Nicholas confessed that his father was 'disappointed' in him and was under pressure from his 'business dealings'. "I think he's getting ready to run, Mike."

There it was. Confirmation that the Bratva head was moving assets to the Freeport for retirement. And he knew who would be left holding the bag.

The gay son of a devious gangster held onto Michael for a moment of misery when Davidson broke free. "Nicky, we have to help each other."

The two men spent a scant few minutes plotting a strategy. The whole cast of characters: Demetry, Putin, the FBI, and the gang tied into one giant game of musical chairs. Last one left without the chair would be dead.

Michael was amazed that Nick knew as much as he did. Davidson had always assumed the man was a civilian.

Turned out, he knew plenty. "Putin is getting squeezed by the sanctions."

The US had slapped severe economic sanctions on the Russian leader and his cronies when they'd attacked the Ukraine. The younger Roybokov reached into a briefcase set upon the gold racks. He pulled out a decorative piece of paper.

A stock certificate. A 100-share block of Anadarko- the state-run Russian petroleum giant.

"My father had to invest in these periodically." He slipped the stock back into the stack. "It was fine when oil was up and the share price was a hundred and twelve. Now that oil is down, and the shares are worth six, it's a different story."

Davidson grimaced. That envelope contained sheets of funny looking wallpaper now.

Jesus. Billions gone, just like that!

Demetry was getting squeezed worse than he'd imagined. "He has plenty stored in this room, Nick. He doesn't have to seek total revenge."

He gestured around the vault. At least a billion in assets were stored here. Davidson could only imagine that the incoming cash was going to be the liquid portion of his nest.

Davidson had to wrap up the talk. It would look strange if they were in the vault alone for too long.

"Nicky, I'll give you a cell phone when we get back to the plane. Use it in an emergency, of course, but also try to keep me in the loop about his moves, if you can."

The young man nodded. "Same goes for you."

The two men shook hands and exited the vault. Both watched as Phillipa sealed it.

The dinner at the castle that night was much the same. Davidson was extremely horny, but frustrated. And it did not help that he knew Graeme and Helga were knocking boots next door. *Asshole.*

As a response to all the flying and general craziness, Michael decided to stay in London during the trip back. Three days in the UK to let him decompress. Graeme continued on to Dubai per plan to lock down the help and ensure no more problems.

Ira, Rick, and Gretchen were already in London at the flat when he arrived. They were on a normally scheduled visit to work on Hatton Gardens.

The *other* major heist they had working.

Rick reported the equipment purchase and was very happy with it.

"You go to the class tomorrow, right?" Michael asked yawning.

"Yeah, Mike, no problems."

I'm tired. Really tired, he thought.

Gretchen flopped a paper on his chest. One of the London rags. The headline screamed: "Yard Official In Gay Sex Romp With Employee!"

Finally, some good news.

He grinned up at Gretchen. "That was expensive, but we only need to distract them for a bit."

Gretchen's solution to the robbery squad investigator watching them was to smear the man and his boss by faking some pictures of them in a homosexual love tiff. A contact of hers was very, very good with photos. The man had mocked up a series of photographs of the two men together in compromising positions. What's more they had time coded the shots to coincide when the investigator had been briefing his boss at home!

The whole thing stunk and would not hold up to scrutiny, but...

But they didn't need a year's worth of free time. They needed one month. Between the new boss coming in to oversee their cases and a new investigator to watch them, he figured they had six weeks. Eight- if the press continued to hound the men.

"Took them long enough," he commented to the woman. She'd first planted the pictures with the supervisor's boss at Downing Street. With typical British government efficiency, nothing had been done and the photos swept under the rug.

So she'd upped the ante by sending the pictures to the Fleet Street rags to get some traction.

And it worked!

Michael drifted off to sleep with one less worry. There might be fifty more things to keep him up, but this one was dealt with. At least his people put a blanket over him while he slept.

***

The next evening was going swimmingly for the gang. Rick was back from the class and alternately bitching and bragging, which

Davidson thought was a good sign.

They'd had a productive day with Ira figuring a way to test out the alarm line. The forms were dutifully filed with the police and the metro people when the knock at the door galvanized them all.

"Cops don't knock, they just bust it down," Ira reasoned.

Rick went to answer the door.

Ekaterina Roybokov sailed into the room, wearing a full-length mink and smelling of cigarettes and whiskey. She surveyed the room. "Leave."

The Empress of all Russia ordered the surfs from the room. All except Michael.

Davidson was gratified his gang manned up and looked at him for direction.

Kat just eyed him and waited.

"Give us a minute, would you guys?" he asked his friends.

The three left with Gretchen especially giving the young woman the evil eye.

Kat had her on youth and height, but Gretchen grew up in the slums of Rio. Michael would bet on the Brazilian, but figured Kat would get in some shots.

The young woman rounded on him the second the trio left the room. "What did you say to Nicky?" The scowl on her face came slowly.

Several answers went through his head. Both the truth and lies. His silence seemed to unnerve the girl.

"He called me saying all kinds of wild things!"

"What kind of things, Kat?"

"He said you told him daddy is getting ready to run!" Her words tumbling out and slurring just a little.

"Is he, Kat? And is he getting ready to feed me to the FBI, like Semilov?" The accusation seemed to take a physical weight and it caused her to sit heavily on the couch.

"Michael, you don't understand what he is dealing with," her tone now pleading. "He's under so much pressure!"

Michael raised his assessment of her drunkenness up a notch. She did not seem to realize he was a participant in this conversation. A snort and she said, "Nicky is so in love with you, you know that?"

He moved to sit in a chair so they would be on the same eye level. "I can't help that and I can't help that your father does not approve of his gay son!"

"No! He just wants you to be his son."

Distaste showed on his face. "You know that is not true. Your dad sees me as a milk cow, not a son. I'm hamburger once I dry up!"

The girl's mental state swayed. Davidson could see it happen. She blinked and refocused. "He wants me to bring Nicky home." She said it quietly, with tears filling her eyes. Both of them knew what would be the outcome of that.

"I don't think that would be a good idea," Michael told her.

"What choice do I have?"

"Tell him you couldn't find me or him. Tell him you need a vacation. Tahiti is lovely this time of year. Soak up the sun. In three weeks your dad will be too busy to notice."

She wasn't listening. Kat stood and went to the chair where he sat.

Leaning down, she kissed him. *Cigarettes and whiskey are never a good combination to try and seduce someone*, Michael thought, regaining sole possession of his tongue.

"That would be a bad idea, too."

Sadness came over her as he rejected her. She swayed and he had no more alternatives for her. Mike eased her out the door into the arms of her bodyguard.

He texted Nicky as the others came back into the room. "Watch yourself," was what he told Nicholas Roybokov. That was all he could do for the kid.

The other three gang members were concerned to say the least.

"Demetry is tying up loose ends," he told the others.

"Your conversation with Nicky got back to him quickly," Ira said. "What kind of bugs does he have on our operation?"

That kind of question scared the shit out of Michael. What kind of ties and reports was Roybokov getting on him? He knew the three stooges were a direct line, but the Bratva head seemed to have others. *Time to go to ground.*

"We are out of here. Pack and wipe down everything. Don't forget Graeme's stuff!" he said, as the other's scattered.

A text to Graeme in Dubai- 'Watch out. R snipping loose ends.' And then the four relied on Gretchen to find them some place to hide.

Every seasoned traveler to London had their go-to place, some district or spot where they could just land for a day or two. Davidson and the others were due back in Dubai City tomorrow. They just needed one night where they could regroup and wait on the trip to the private terminal.

The Thistle chain of hotels in Central London was a middleclass business-type place. The Marble Arch version was a good representation of the whole. Clean, comfortable rooms and, of course, breakfast was included. Ninety- eight pounds a night. Michael had her get four rooms, but they only used one. He paid cash.

"Okay- Ira you have first watch, Rick you take the couch and relieve him. Gretchen and I will snuggle in the bed," he told them as the tense group checked in.

He was gratified to hear the bitching. It meant they had recovered a

little. It was a tense night and an even tenser trip to the Middle East.

Chapter Eighteen

It was a long ride on the Al Zakar to the Palm that the gang took on that Thursday. None of them even noticed the weather anymore. Battle hardened, they knew it was coming down to the end game now. Michael had the plan and they were working it. But even a thief like him could be fooled. Had been fooled. Now? His only answer was to go over it and over it until it was rehearsed to death.

"I want everything in place by April 9th here," he told them. "London is set. We don't have to be back until the 30th. Rick has everything in place there. We just need the alarm line locked down.

Ira?"

"Yeah, Mike. We're good. Forms should be at the mail drop on the 30th when we get in.

"Your pupils here are good?" A glance at Graeme. "No problems, they are ready."

The Irishman was content to let Michael lead the checklist for both jobs. That was a wonder.

"Gretchen... the van, SUVs, and clothes for both jobs?"

"Good, Michael. And before you ask the shipping boxes are ready, as are the IDs and Fujairah."

He should not have doubted her.

Another look at Graeme. The unvoiced question was one Graeme was ready for. "Talked to her today, shammer. Set!" The grin split his face.

A wave of relief went through the group. Good news finally! Their Ministry contact had come through with some small tidbits of information.

"Okay! Rick you are ready? The bulldozer back afterwards, yes?"

"Got it, Mike. Graeme and I will plan it."

The gang had about a week of downtime before their last training runs with the Russian help at the desert camp and the airbase. Davidson knew they would do better with two additional days of training, but they were prepared. Any eventualities would just have to be dealt with.

The villa was a welcome sight after their disturbing visitor in London, and the fact that no one broke in to arrest or kill them was an added bonus.

The next two days proceeded without interruption and the thieves were fully up to speed and back on their game. The London and the Luxembourg incidents seemed to be less threatening as time passed.

Michael took a nice swim that evening and prepared to deal with paperwork. His work habits were set from a lifetime of dealing with minutia. Davidson always felt he'd have been a decent accountant or an IRS investigator.

Toweling off his hair, he checked his Washington Park machine by rote.

Three robo calls and..."Mr. Davidson, this is Detective O'Rourke. I did not receive my weekly phone call from Ms. Devereaux on Monday. I've tried calling her, but she has not called me back. Her work doesn't seem to know where she is either. That is very peculiar and I want you to call me when you get this message."

Ice gripped him.

Sydney! He dialed from memory and was put through to the homicide cop.

"O'Rourke."

"Detective, this is Michael Davidson. I have not heard from Sydney in quite some time. Have you tried her parents in Dallas?" Davidson said without stopping.

He could hear breathing on the other end. "Where are you Davidson?"

A loaded question. *This guy is a bulldog.* "I'm in the Middle East," he said, truthfully.

"I talked to the parents about an hour ago. They have not heard from her at all in over a week."

The cop left the rest unasked and just let the silence build.

"If I hear from her I will have her get in touch with you, Detective. Please let me know if you find her." His voice was calm, but he was anything but.

"What the fuck is going on, Davidson? What are you involved with?" O'Rourke barked at the phone.

Davidson clicked off the cell.

His mind rocked and his heart hammered in his chest. *Demetry has Sydney.* Loose ends. *She might be a string out to me to ensure good performance. How? How did they get her? The bad cops? His trip home? Did they have a bug on his phone?*

More random flashes went off in his head. He was suddenly certain that the envelope he'd given Syd was gone. And just as certain that the three stooges and the hired muscle would be watching the gang here in Dubai. Probably had been for a while. Watching them like fish in an aquarium. Nicky? Kat's visit made sense now. More flashes along his synapses.

And he then knew! Knew where they were keeping her. Certain of it in fact. Just like he did with a Jeopardy answer. Dead certain.

Davidson grimaced at the horrible image in his head. He had to get her back, that much was sure. How?

"Ira!"

The argument took thirty minutes. The discussion took forty-five and the planning took another ninety. In that time, a disguised Graeme Donniger ascertained that a Russian thug was standing on the corner of frond E and the main trunk road and Viktor was in a car sitting on the Dubai Pearl roundabout watching the cars come off the Palm.

"You were right, Mikey," Irish told them, stripping off the beard. "The idiot is standing on the corner watching! And Viktor is sittin' pretty as you please on the roundabout."

"How did you get out there?" Rick asked, interested.

"The monorail has a connecting tram system, friend."

The artificial island was a huge city and complex by itself. The monorail system went up the main trunk of the Palm, and then over to the barrier breakwater; a strip of land so wide it held several high end hotels and a huge water park. When a vacationing tourist (or an enterprising thief) wanted to get around the Palm, the nice people included a connecting tram bus that ran the length of the palm fronds to the monorail stations. The last main station was actually on the mainland on the eastern edge of the Dubai Pearl roundabout.

Graeme was able to board the tram, slip past the watching thug and ride the monorail to its base stop. After glassing the roundabout in the night gloom, he could spot Viktor because the man wasn't exactly hiding.

"Okay, so we have to be disguised," Michael told Gretchen, who started rummaging through her case.

And that wasn't the only problem. IDs would be a killer. And they had to account for the travel.

Mike went through the options thinking at lightning speed. "Let's give them the mirror."

Gretchen groaned. "Mike that is not going to be easy. I have to hire the people... train them. We have to contact the cruise ship people..." Ira went to the woman and took her aside. They spoke together for a few minutes and returned.

"Okay. I'm on it," she told Michael. "But you make sure nothing happens to Ira!"

"I'll be very careful with him," Davidson assured her.

What he was proposing was a nightmare in terms of timing and logistics and difficulty. Davidson was sure of two things: only his gang could do it and Sydney's life depended on it.

Thirty-six hours later, at 5:58 am, the two men and the remaining gang members were as ready as they could be.

Gretchen Gonsolvo kissed the blond-haired, shoe-lift wearing, sunglasses sporting, Robert Torkleson (Ira) goodbye.

She handed an envelope to Davidson. "We are all set. 7:00 pm

tonight- thirteen hours from now." "We can do this," Ira told everyone

in general. The now dark-haired and bearded Davidson, traveling as Mitchell O'Connell, slung his very light suitcase onto his shoulder. "Let's go."

The men walked out the back door to the beach area and out towards the tip of the frond. Just five houses down and they split back through an access path to the street. Dead calm weather with the wind taking a break this morning.

The cab was waiting for them. The foreign driver said nothing as the men tracked sand all over his floor boards.

The stupid thug at the end of the block, Samuel- Michael's head told him, was literally standing in the street watching what few cars were around. He looked right at Ira and Michael as the cab went past. Nothing.

"Thank God for stupid," Ira said from his perch, making him look taller in the seat.

Michael growled just a little. "First part is easy." *The next was harder and the last harder still*, he knew.

He had the whole flight to prepare. Six hours of sleep for both of them and two hours of intensive back and forth as they drew the layout from Mike's memory and went over the plan.

The jet was fast and fairly grimy for a private plane.

He constantly texted the gang back in at the villa as he went through the airport terminal. If Sergei or anyone else was watching the airport, he didn't see them.

The jet landed at JFK at 9:57 am local time. Time zones were a friend in this direction.

The cab to the storage unit cost sixty-seven dollars. Time was the biggest expense.

Michael opened the door to the unit with a rolling clank. *Funny, only the second time we have needed one of these units and it's in our own backyard.* He'd ponder that later.

The storage car was loaded up with tools, two guns, and some of Ira's gear. Mike drove as they exited the storage place. "11:37, Mike, about twenty-five minutes."

"Check."

He drove to the nearest 'beachy' area. Down Atlantic Avenue that happened to be the Brooklyn Promenade. Which also happened to be near Demetry's house. *Can't be helped*, Michael thought as they parked.

He remembered coming here what seemed a lifetime ago with Sydney.

March 22nd was iffy in New York weather-wise. The early spring period could be twenty-two degrees and snow or like today: decent. Temperatures in the mid-fifties and bright sunshine which got people outdoors.

And they needed that for the mirror. Ira was texting furiously and Michael jockeyed around looking for the right spot of people, seagulls, and music.

He found what would have to do and could just see the Pierrepont Mansion to his left. *Hang on Syd- I'm coming.*

At 11:53 Graeme texted them- 'Bad guys, eyes on- All set.'

It was time for the mirror.

Mike pulled his phone from the jacket and pushed buttons.

"Da."

"Mr. Roybokov, It's Michael, Sir."

"Michael," the mobster said somewhat surprised. "Where are you? Why are you calling me?"

"I'm sorry to disturb you, Sir. I'm in Dubai, actually, with my team. In fact, we are just sitting down to dinner. It's beautiful here."

"Really? Hold on a moment, I want to take this call in the den. I might be a while."

"Certainly, Sir," Michael told him.

Take the call in the den, my ass!

Davidson knew Demetry would be calling his goons in the Middle East to verify.

He gestured to Ira with his chin, hand over the phone's receiver. He did not want some stray English to go over his phone from another person. What he would not give for an Arabic speaker to start yelling right now!

"Text Graeme- Tell him 'verifying'."

8,000 miles away, Graeme, Gretchen, Rick, and two actors made up to look like Michael and Ira were sitting at a seaside restaurant on the Palm Island. Apparently, without a care in the world. 'Mike' was on his phone.

Ira leaned in and showed Davidson Graeme's answering text- 'Bad guys talking on phone, verifying.'

Davidson knew Demetry was talking directly with his men. Or perhaps Sergei was relaying the information, but either way, he was assuring himself of Davidson's whereabouts.

Three full minutes passed. Sweat made rivulets down Michael's back.

Demetry came back on the line.

"I'm sorry. I had to take care of something. Having dinner, you say?"

The crocodile gave a fake apology. Michael knew he was full of crap. "Yes, Sir. I'm calling to tell you that both the London and Dubai projects are still a solid go. They are on schedule as we have discussed. I'm taking advantage of the down time to do a little pre-job celebrating with my people."

"It does sound loud there. Is this restaurant on the water?"

Stalling to talk to his men, Davidson knew. "Yes, it is on the deck overlooking the water. I also wanted to tell you that, while we have had a few problems, Sergei, Viktor and Anton have whipped your men into shape. They are going to be a tremendous asset on this assignment." He laid it on thick.

Another gesture with his chin to Ira- Get ready.

Levinson texted furiously.

Demetry made some off the cuff comment about going into the ocean and Michael told him. "Not in my favorite business suit, Sir."

"We are probably going to go silent over the next weeks, but I will call to work out the shipping arrangements. We also have the companies in place to handle the results."

Demetry was only half listening as he was obviously talking again to Dubai.

"Da. All right. That sounds fine, Michael."

"Thank you, Sir. Enjoy your day."

At the phrase, "Thank you." Ira texted Graeme- *hang up*. Tricky with the network time lag.

In Dubai, the actor holding the phone to his ear took it away and put the phone into his nice blue suit jacket when the curly headed guy kicked him under the table. The Ira actor took a sip of his drink.

For the stand-ins, this was their craziest fucking job ever. But the two out of work cruise ship dancers did not seem to care one way or the other what they got paid for. As long as they got paid.

And now, the five people in Dubai could enjoy a leisurely meal.

Back in Brooklyn, Ira and Michael walked back to the car. Ira checked his phone.

"Graeme thinks they bought it. Demetry's men have backed off."

"Good."

A last glimpse of the mansion and they drove to Brighton Beach. Now the next hard part.

The storage car was a ubiquitous silver Toyota Camry. It was chosen for the fact it was the single bestselling car in history, not because it was comfortable for a stakeout.

The car was parked on Brighton and down the block. They had a decent view into the shop, even if they had to use binoculars.

Hard Pawn. Feydor Slutskaya's pawn shop. The shop that had a rat's nest warren of rooms in the basement. And Michael Davidson was certain that one of those rooms held Sydney Devereaux.

Peeing in bottles was difficult and gross, but they could not leave the car and attract attention to the fact that they were watching the shop. It was difficult enough. Thankfully, the depressed economy had enough men sleeping in cars that they garnered just a few looks.

At 10:45 that night they were tired, grumpy, and sure of the numbers inside the shop.

Davidson held the binoculars tight against his eyes. *Yes, the big man returned with the tray. Dishes. That meant food for someone downstairs. Syd. She's alive!*

Another wave as his emotions ran back high. The rollercoaster was clouding his judgment.

Near as they could figure it, three men remained in the pawn shop. Slutskaya himself had left around 9:00 pm. It took everything Davidson had to not run the man over with the car.

Cold. He needed to be cold.

"Last bathroom break," Ira theorized watching the men shuffle around inside.

Sydney was tucked in for the night.

The pair watched the men arrange themselves around a small TV mounted on the display case. One actual Lazy Boy chair was dragged out from Feydor's office and two small folding chairs allowed a reasonable comfort level for the watchers. These three looked like Feydor's 'cousins', who always seemed to be hanging around. Michael didn't even know their names. They appeared to be engrossed in the game. College basketball on the tube, he noted.

"Let's go."

The men exited the Camry and Ira removed his gear from the trunk. Davidson also removed his duffel and slung it over his shoulder. The street was deserted; with no pedestrians hanging out and only the occasional car going down a cross street. Since the avenue was lined with businesses and not homes, no one was watching out any windows as the men crossed and went to the alley behind the establishment.

The small man immediately went to the phone junction box which sat near the building. Picking open the lock, Ira began attaching probes to lines and looking at readings.

Michael's paranoia about Feydor, and his reason for taking Ira along when they'd briefed the extra muscle, became real at this moment. Davidson had engaged Ira in a special project at Feydor's on their recruitment visit. That project being to familiarize himself with the pawn shop's alarm system.

Originally, Michael thought that they might have to break in to plant evidence on the fence, but now...

"Simple three line system, tapped into the phone right here," Ira muttered as he worked. Leads went into his box which fed the laptop.

Some tapping on the keyboard and...

"Okay. We own the place."

It was his turn. The back alley door led to Feydor's office. Reaching in the duffel Michael pulled out his lock pick set. *Silently!* Any loud noise and the goons would come to investigate and the bullets would start flying. He wanted that to be a last resort.

Seven minutes of work and the lock yielded with a 'snick'.

A motion to Levinson to remain outside and he crept into the office in the dark. Another reach in the duffel and he pulled out a small cylinder connected to a clear tube. Davidson went to the door to the main shop floor area where the watchers sat, too involved with basketball to care.

The tube was pushed under the crack of the door about two inches. Davidson retreated to the duffel and put on a gas mask and drew a gun from his pocket. He was ready. The small valve on the cylinder turned easily and the hiss of the gas escaping was not very loud.

Medicinal grade ether flooded the room.

Davidson gave them the full dose. He wasn't sure about the amount. Neither was Ira. During the planning session back in Dubai, Gretchen told him it depended on the weight of the men, if they'd eaten.
Plus a bunch of other factors.

"You could kill them, if you give them too much."

That wasn't the biggest concern, but it was a factor. He was certain Sydney was in here, and the dishes clinched it, but he wasn't an indiscriminate killer. Normally.

But this might be different. He waited ten full minutes to allow the gas to do what it wanted with the men outside. Michael pulled the tube and restored the gas canister. After a deep breath through the mask, he gripped the gun tightly and eased open the door.

The three men were out cold. A shake tested their response, but they were unresponsive. Excellent.

Ira scared the living shit out of him when he said, standing right next to him, "Nice work." His voice was muffled by the mask, but Davidson still tried to jump out of his skin.

"Jesus, Ira! Stay here. I'll be back with Sydney in five minutes."

Michael crept down the stairs. No light on now, he did not want to alert anyone who might be down here.

Pausing a moment for his eyes to adjust in the blackness, he wished for night vision goggles.

The dim shape of the large basement room took hold in his mind and vision.

Crossing to the right, he went into the smaller room where he knew the desk sat. The same room where they'd interviewed the Russian muscle. Two doors led further into the bowels of this basement. Eenie, meenie, miney, moe.

Another grip on the gun and he tried the left side door. The deadbolt sounded very loud to his ears as he worked it.

Michael opened the door quickly to reveal a small room containing a cot and a night table which held a tiny lamp throwing the room into harsh shadows.

Sydney lay awake on the cot chained to a pipe. She leaned up on her arm and took in the scene.

"No! Oh, God, No!"

Michael realized his mistake and whipped off the gasmask. He lowered the gun to assure her it was all right.

She still struggled and screamed, a look of confusion on her face.

What? Oh! The beard and the dye job. "Syd, it's me! It's Michael!," he said going over to the cot.

She recognized the voice through her pain and confusion and stopped shouting. "Michael?"

"Yeah, give me a second and I will have you out of here." He bent to work the handcuffs.

He looked her over while he worked. Hair a mess and dirty, Sydney had a bruise on her jaw. The scrapes on her wrists and elbows looked painful. Every time she breathed she seemed to wince a little. Ribs- he knew.

They'd hit her. *Hurt her.*

A low growl worked its way out of his chest and into his throat. The restraints gave way and Sydney gasped and gave him a brief hug.

"Can you walk?" he asked, voice rough, wanting to growl again.

"Yes, but Michael!" She rose painfully to look at him. "They have someone else down here."

Someone else? He frowned. And adjusted to the contingency.

Syd indicated the opposite door through the interview room.

"Okay, get behind me," he ordered as he crept out and to the new door. As they left the room, Davidson reached into his pocket and threw a large paper clip on the floor. As a handcuff pick, he knew it would take the average person a week to get out of the restraints, but he was betting Demetry did not have a huge forensics background. Give the man an obvious trail...

The pair got to the new room and this time Davidson went in boldly. Half expecting to see Jimmy Hoffa, he was shocked to see another cot and Nicholas Roybokov chained like Syd.

If Sydney had been roughed up, Nicholas had been beaten. Face a bloody mess, the man was barely conscious.

Mike gave Sydney the gun. "Shoot anyone who comes through that door," he told her.

No back talk as he went to work on Nicky and the cuffs.

This might be my fault as well, he thought.

Another few minutes of work got the man free and roused to at least some level of awareness.

"Mike?" The man said through bloody lips as Davidson worked to bring him around.

"Yeah, kid. I got ya."

An arm slung over his shoulder and Michael half-walked, half-dragged Nick across the basement and up the stairs following Sydney.

"Syd! Wait!" He gasped as she went from the dark of the stairs out to the light.

Too late! She was onto the main shop floor. *Shit, she could shoot Ira!*

But Sydney Devereaux was focused on another target. Feydor's men.

She stood a step behind the counter, looking over the top at the sleeping figures. The gun wavered as she pointed it at them.

"Sydney, wait please!" Michael pleaded.

The gun wobbled more, but did not lower. "Honey, I guarantee you these men will be dead very soon!" He never knew if it was the 'honey', or the fact that vengeance would come for her tormentors, as to why she put the gun down.

Ira crept cautiously out of the back office and towards the group. "Mike?" he asked in a low voice, eyeing the woman with the gun and the wobbly man holding onto his friend. *Thank God the gas has dissipated enough to take off our masks.*

"Mike, the basic plan still works," he reminded Davidson. "Just have the two of them do it."

Good idea! Michael took a few seconds and told Sydney what he had in mind. Another minute saw him transfer Nicky to the woman and retrieve his gun. She gave it back with a look that said, 'I still might use this on you.'

The pair retreated back downstairs and Mike shut the door behind them while getting his gear and Ira into the back office.

Ira worked the pawn shop's video surveillance system. The man had been busy while Mike was downstairs.

"Okay! Come on out!" Ira yelled to the former prisoners.

Syd and Nick lurched out of the basement stairwell, paused a moment to watch the sleeping guards, and then swept on to the back office.

"Perfect," he told Mike. "Get them to the car while I clean up."

Give them something obvious, Davidson knew. When Feydor returned in the morning, the tape would show the guards sleeping and the prisoners walking out right past them. He also knew that Feydor would *never* give that tape to Demetry. Much too incriminating for him. But...

Ira knew the system inside and out. It was why the small man was here.

Ira spent five precious minutes copying the video file to his laptop. He and Michael had a plan for Feydor!

Grabbing gear and his toys, Ira carefully relocked the door and scampered back to the car. After stowing his gear in the trunk, he got into the driver's seat.

"Drive!" Michael commanded. He was in the back getting a few ibuprofens into Nicholas Roybokov and coaxing some water down his throat. Syd was in the passenger seat holding a water bottle, but not drinking. She stared straight ahead. Dazed. Ira knew that look well.

Levinson drove steadily down Atlantic, back to the storage unit. Syd slowly came back to herself and gingerly sipped her water.

"It's the only way," Michael said, restarting an earlier conversation he had been having with the woman.

"It was Temescal and his partner that grabbed you, yes? The same cops who killed Mary. I told you they are dirty and are working for both Demetry and the FBI." Mike reminded her what was going on. "All O'Rourke can do is put you in protective custody. The Bratva can get to you there."

He said it sadly to the woman. Mike noticed Ira risk a glance at her. They both knew her world was shaken right now. Davidson sealed the deal with this: "The only way I can protect you is to have you near. I can't help if there is an ocean in between us."

Chapter Nineteen

Unspoken in that thought was the fact that Davidson had put her in the danger in the first place. Michael figured she would come around to that point eventually. And then she would rip him a new one. But they didn't have time for that right now! Time was the enemy.

"Where are we going, then?" she asked, as Ira drove to the storage unit.

"Dubai," Mike told her getting Nicholas more comfortable.

Sydney choked. "What? I can't go there! I don't have a passport." She twisted to glare at Davidson.

Mike held up a hand. "I have one for you. My team made up one for you before we left."

God bless Gretchen and God bless their San Francisco passport agency contact.

The problem was Nicholas Roybokov. He was not in the original plan. A contingency that would have to be dealt with.

The cab was waiting on them as they pulled into the storage place. Ira spoke to the cabbie, and then the four of them went into the garage door to the unit to take stock. Nicholas sat on a small folding chair and swayed, still out on his feet like a punch-drunk fighter.

Michael noticed Sydney gawk at the items in the storage unit as the thieves worked. Guns went into boxes, money came out of safes, and Mike and Ira talked and sorted through IDs. No doubt she recognized this version of Michael even through the disguise. Calm. Cool and decisive. His personality fitting the situation again. It was the jar of the beard

and hair color that had thrown her a bit. But at the same time, she was no doubt coming to realize that she really did not know this man.

"This one," Michael said decisively, shoving the ID at Ira. "Syd, trim his hair," he showed her where the disguise kit was located. Scissors and clippers, along with dye and cosmetics.

Just like that.

Envelopes got stuffed with money: Euros, pounds, and dollars. Suit cases got clothes put in them. Michael found a pair of flip flops to at least give her something to protect her feet.

"That's great," he told her, looking at her styling when she finished with Nick. The man was coming around.

Davidson did not know the extent of his injuries. He hoped nothing seriously internal. Ribs and a general beating seemed to be the worst. "Mike?" the man said again through swollen lips.

"It's me, Nick. How you feelin'?"

"Bad, Mike. My dad..."

He cut him off. "Yeah, man, we know. Quiet now. We got to move fast."

The four jammed into the cab.

Michael turned to the other two in the large back seat while Ira rode in the passenger seat.

He went through customs and passport control at the JFK private terminal. Both were experienced travelers, so it was just the differences. That, and the fact that both would be moving around under fake names and addresses. Money was passed out.

"I thought we could only bring in ten thousand to a foreign country," Syd said, looking at the cash.

"Ten thousand of each type of money," Mike told her. "Just tell them we intend to do a lot of traveling around Europe, so we need the different currencies. If someone asks you about your injuries just tell them to shut the fuck up."

While he briefed the former prisoners, Ira was on the phone with Gold Jets. He was informing them that a change of plans was in the offing. A stop in London was now on the schedule. Neither the plane people nor Ira was happy about that.

Davidson did not think he could hide Nicky in Dubai. The gang was only ready for Sydney. He did not think the young man could be quiet in a Muslim country. Just his...*biological leanings*, would be trouble.

Demetry would be looking all over for them, but he would start in The States. Eventually, he would get over to Europe and the Middle East.

Hiding Nicky in the same city where Demetry had found him once before? Well, Michael knew Nick hadn't exactly been hiding from his old man. Different trick if the person was actually trying not to be captured. That was the best he could come up with on the fly.

They were taking an awful chance just by grabbing the man and stopping in London.

Time. They had very little.

Torkleson and O'Connell breezed the former prisoners through customs and JFK. Passport control was a nonevent. The rich don't get hassled about little things like money and cuts and bruises. The flight attendants on the private jet had seen things that would shock the normal flying public.

The Lear jet streaked back east.

Now the time zones sucked away the advantage and exposed them all to danger.

Michael figured eleven, or maybe twelve hours before Feydor finds his captives gone. He hoped an hour or two while the fence searched. Then the inevitable call to Demetry.

That is where things got dicey. No way Feydor gives the tape to the mob head. He might suggest the guards were at fault, but he, himself, was blameless. There was a strong possibility that Feydor delayed telling Demetry for a long time, but the thief could not count on that. Michael was stacking the deck against the man in exchange for the reality that

Demetry would know sooner and be able to suspect Davidson and his gang all that much sooner.

Ira's copy of the tape was going to drop to Demetry in an email from his pet cops.

It was an awful risk.

Demetry was going to suspect Michael, but the tape and his body double phone call during dinner was going to tell him something else. Sure as shit the only recourse for the Bratva man was to have Sergei or one of the other Lieutenants go over to the villa and check on everything.

Five and three-quarters of an hour to London. About an hour to transfer Nicky to his boy toy. (Have to remind Nick to dump that guy.) Then they disappear. *If they can.*

Nick used the plane phone to arrange for the man to pick him up at the airport.

"We will all clear customs and accompany you to your friend," Mike told him.

Ira writhed. "Mike, we can't afford the delay!"

"Only way we can give Nick the money we are carrying. He gets the pounds."

"Oh!" said Syd. "That's very clever. That way he has just under forty thousand pounds to hide with. That should be enough for a while."

Mike gave Nick another phone. "Go to the opposite of where ever you were before," he advised the man.

Nick's eyes shone with pain and gratitude and a little...love?

Mike caught the look that flashed across Sydney's face, as she'd noticed Nick's gaze, too. She realized that Nick loved him. But then she

Thief in Law

glanced to Ira, and the respectful expression on his face, and that seemed to give her pause.

Mike came down the aisle a few rows to where she sat, eating a gourmet meal complete with wine. He squatted next to her seat to keep their conversation private. "How are you holding up?

"Pretty shaky," she admitted.

He bowed his head. "I'm sorry about all this..." he gestured and looked into her eyes.

That was the same mistake he'd been making for a while with Sydney Devereaux. A look at those blue eyes and he got lost. Or maybe found. It was definitely one of those two options.

"I tried to stay away, Syd. Should have stayed away... I guess I'm not as smart as I think."

She was plenty pissed at him, Michael could tell, but since he had just rescued her, she seemed willing to defer the fight. The dispassionate doctor part of her probably said: *get out of danger, then kill him*. But what she did say was, "What now?"

"After we get Nicky to London we need to hustle to Dubai. We've got a place all setup for you. I will take you over on the shuttle."

When she had no response to that, Mike went on. "It is a nice place- it'll be just like Kauai." The joke sounded forced, even to his ears, and she was giving nothing away, so he went on.

"Anyway you just need to stay put. Order room service or stick to the restaurants at the hotel. Lay on the beach or take a spa day or two." He waited a beat. "Just don't go into the city." He tried to put the best face on the whole package.

"So it is a prettier prison," she stabbed at him with that.

337

A mental wince. "Yeah, kinda. But only for a week or so."

He reached into his suit jacket and took out a burner phone. Holding it out to her, he said, "This is blocked. When we land take a minute to call O'Rourke, your parents, and work. Tell them that you are okay and just working through some things and need a little time."

Sydney eyed the phone like it was a reptile.

Mike just held it out and waited. She would get there eventually.

A full minute passed while he was certain her heart said to punch him, but eventually her head convinced her hand to grab the phone. "O'Rourke won't be happy," she predicted.

"Tell him from me to watch the mail. He'll get my present soon enough." Michael told her.

A flitter of worry ran over her face. *Worry for him?* A flare went through his heart and he tapped it down.

He gave her another envelope with a fake driver's license and real corporate card. "Gretchen kept things simple. Your

address is just reversed- 481 Washington Park. Social is the same with the last four reversed- okay? See?"

JFK had been easy. Michael just dropped the mess of paper on the counter and the agents took care of everything. They dealt with rich people all the time. Heathrow and Dubai would be different.

"You have to get thru London on your own. You need to be ready. Just tell them the truth: Flying to Dubai and dropping off Elias," he hooked a thumb forward at Nick.

"What if they ask why I'm getting off the plane?"

Good question. She was so sharp and saw deeply into things... Focus!

"Uhhh, stick close to the truth. Stiff and sore after the flight and you want to stretch your legs."

"Michael, I'm only wearing flip flops!"

That was all the storage unit could provide her. Davidson shrugged. "The rich don't get cold," he said, making no sense. "By the way, that corporate card is real. Sort of. You can buy whatever you need. Clothes, shoes, suitcases, whatever." He stopped embarrassed. "Uhh." Unsure now of how to go on now. "You can't buy a Lamborghini, or anything, there is an upper limit. On any one purchase..."

"But I can make a million smaller purchases, though," she said shrewdly.

"Well, yeah. But... uhh... don't..."

A flick of her hand dismissed him. A knee cracked as he rose from his crouch to retreat back up to the front of the plane. He'd lost that round. Handily.

Hours later, at passport control, Sydney had a moment of panic. Michael watched the exchange from behind.

"How long will you be in London, Miss?"

"Under an hour," she told him.

The agent frowned. "What flight did you come in on?"

The panic hit. "No clue. It was a private flight out of JFK." She gave her haughtiest tone to the man.

The passport agent tapped his screen. "Here you are. We don't like it when through passengers exit the plane," he told her.

"Any law against it?" Sydney was in enough pain to be bitchy to Michael's ears.

"No, Miss, not exactly."

"Then let me go walk around a little before I have to get back on that damned plane."

He stamped her passport.

She joined Ira with Nick at the exit to the baggage carousel and the waiting area, with Michael bringing up the rear.

A young, black man came up to the group and embraced the wobbly scion.

Davidson collected the envelopes from everyone and gave them to Roybokov.

"Stay hidden. I'll text you when we come in around the 30th."

Hugs all around and the two men disappeared into the swirl at the airport.

Ira checked his watch.

"Okay, man. We are going," Michael replied to the unvoiced urging.

Getting back on the plane was pretty easy. The civil side embarkation desks were on the same level, just a different side of the terminal.

The Gold jet reps were only too happy to assist the Americans. IDs and passports were dutifully checked.

"Our luggage is still on the plane," Michael told the trim, pretty, young woman with his best smile.

It had an effect. She beamed back a smile and went out of her way to help them. "Thank you, Mr. O'Connell. Should you require any further assistance on any other London travel, please don't hesitate to call." She handed Davidson a card. "My home number is on the back."

The look on Sydney's face told Michael she'd seen the whole exchange with the Gold Jets agents. And she looked pissed. Somehow he was certain it was his fault the lady decided that today of all days it was fine to flirt with him. In the end he just hustled them out of the terminal.

The three re-boarded the plane and settled in for the flight.

Ira had not missed the byplay with Sydney. "She upset?" he asked.

"Yeah. I'm not her favorite person right now."

"She has had a rough few days. A certain amount of anger is to be expected," Ira told him sagely.

A grunt was Davidson's only reply.

The captain came over the intercom to tell them they were number fourteen for takeoff. Heathrow was always busy.

Michael and Ira both kept checking their phones. Time was killing them. The plan called for them to be in the air right now. Take off happened at 12:11 pm.

Three hours, fifty-three minutes to Dubai. Plus the time zones they had to gain back.

That put them into the UAE at 8 pm. Conversely 8 am in New York. Just about the time the ether should wear off.

They thought.

Again, it depended on many factors. The size of the men. How quickly the gas had dissipated. The amount of food eaten by the victims. Hell, even what time Feydor came in to work. Best guess was twelve hours.

That put them landing right about when the men would wake up. What then? Eating the antacid only put a disgusting cherry flavor in his mouth, it did nothing for his stomach. There just was not any way to predict the response. Even the part where they'd setup Feydor- No way to know when Demetry would react. Or how. The planes ahead of them took off one by one from Heathrow.

It made for a nervous flight. He would normally try to work or even sleep, but he kept bouncing up to check on Sydney. His mind would not let him rest. Davidson felt he needed a long run to clear out the cobwebs.

During one of his up periods, Michael attempted to go through Dubai customs procedures with Syd, but she was madder than before, so he let it ride.

Ira snickered when he came back to sit next to him.

"Fuck you," Mike told him, leaning back, trying to relax.

The angst must have helped with the physics because the plane did make up nineteen minutes in flight. They landed at 7:39 pm in the dark at Dubai International Airport.

He stood behind Sydney in the passport line willing her to get the questions right.

"Where will you be staying in Dubai, Miss?" the man behind the bulletproof glass asked her.

"Uhhh,"

He heard her search her tired brain for the answer.

"The Anantara Resort," she said.

Thank God, he breathed out silently.

"Excellent!" The man stamped her passport and swished her

through. Ira was already waiting, hunched over his phone texting.

Ira made ready to leave as they joined him. He was taking a taxi back to the villa. Well, to a spot nine houses down from the villa. He did not want to attract attention.

"Ms. Devereaux, I will probably see you in a couple days. I will look a little different though," he laughed.

She reached out an arm and stopped Levinson from departing. "Ira, I'm so sorry. I haven't even thanked you for getting me out of there!"

Ira grinned at her. "No problem at all, Miss! It was fun! See ya." And he wheeled his bag out the terminal to the waiting line of taxis.

Michael led Sydney further along the transportation options for the weary traveler to the hotel shuttle busses.

The red Anantara bus was waiting. Thankfully they were alone on the van as it pulled out to crawl along the Al Zakar. Davidson kept checking his phone as the ride went along.

"Graeme says no issues yet," he reported.

She just nodded, as if not really caring. Exhausted. "I've just flown all night, been kidnapped and beaten, no big deal!" He winced, but Michael knew she had to be feeling the effects of five days in that basement.

It couldn't wait any longer. Wanting to hold her, but dreading her reaction to it, Mike asked her quietly about the kidnapping.

"It happened four days after we spoke... that night on the phone... at the house?"

He closed his eyes and nodded. Guilt washed through him. *They had my house under surveillance. A tap on my phone... stupid, stupid, stupid.*

"I answered a knock at the door and a huge guy clamped a rag over my mouth and it was lights out!"

She kept one arm locked tight under her ribs while the other clung to the bus pole, reliving the moment. Davidson recognized it for a fear reaction.

Guilt changed to rage in him as she described days and nights, chained to the cot. "They just kept asking about what you were planning and what you were doing."

The long sleeve blouse hid the wrist chaffing and the makeup hid the worst of the bruises but it did nothing to protect her psyche.

The van lurched along as she watched him out of the corner of her eye.

"Syd, I can't tell you how sorry I am about this," he started for the millionth time.

He could see she was fully coming to grips with what had happened to her. And more importantly who and why it had happened. He could see her focus on his beard and dyed hair. What it represented. What it stood for. The lies. The deceit, the asshole-ness.

She trembled as she stood, clutching the pole the van used to assist passengers when moving.

Both were standing after the flights, even though they were the only people aboard the van. Michael saw the tremble and reached a hand to touch her back.

Sydney flinched away from his touch.

Ahh God, that hurt anew.

"We'll be there in a few minutes," he said to cover.

The gang had selected the Anantara Resort for a number of

reasons. The first being it was very close physically to their villa. Located on the barrier strip that protected and ringed Palm Jumeirah Island, the hotel was situated on the lower south east quadrant of the ring.

The resort itself was a series of three-story wood and stone buildings, all surrounding an artificial lagoon on an artificial island. A private beach on the wilder gulf side allowed for water sports. The more sedate inner side was given over to the lagoon and the shops, restaurants, and spa that made the place a destination for tourists. The rooms were nice and secluded and very expensive which meant she would have few fellow guests.

A week's stay plus reservation at 2,000 USD a night meant an easy check in process.

"Right this way, Ms. Laurent." Charlotte Laurent was a fellow doctor at the hospital where she worked. So she would recognize the fake name, Gretchen tried to keep things simple and familiar.

Once in the room, Michael checked his phone- nothing.

He showed her pictures of Sergei and the other stooges. "If you see these guys, just run. Get to the American Consulate and tell them I kidnapped you."

"You did," she said flatly. "So this is the prison?" Acid came with the comment.

"It's better than the basement and I won't beat you," he said softly.

Sydney turned to look out the window rather than debate. The moonlight sparkling off the water was magical. The place really was gorgeous, but he could tell the view was lost on her.

"Look- tomorrow we can't have any contact. Demetry's men will be all over us. But I will be over the next day to check on you. We can go over... things." He was not looking forward to that conversation.

"Text me if there are any problems."

Lacking a response, he left her staring out the window.

Leaving the room, Michael hurried down the stairs and out to the inner side shops. His destination was the other main reason they'd picked this place: The water taxi.

The resort kept a fleet of small boats to ferry its guests to other parts of the island. So if a guest wanted to check out the huge water park that was on the top of the barrier strip all they had to do was ask. Same went for the shops or restaurants on the trunk. The whole place was accessible by water.

Mike checked with the ship's crew and, "Of course, Sir, we are at your service. Over to Frond E. Just the tip? No particular spot?"

"No, no particular spot. The tip would do nicely." He wanted to attract as little attention as possible.

He boarded with his bag and his weariness.

The phone buzzed incessantly in his pocket as the boat touched the tip of Frond E. Uh oh.

"Sergei just pulled up," read Graeme's text.

Michael flipped the bill at the boat and jumped off onto the sand. He hurled his suitcase further up the beach staggering and trying to remove his jacket and shoes. He took twelve seconds to type- "I'm in the pool," back to Graeme and he was sprinting down the beach.

It was only half a mile.

Legs churning, he yanked the beard off with one hand. Shirt and pants followed as he sucked great breaths trying to will himself to more speed. His underwear went off with the pants, but he could not stop.

The lights of the villa were on and beckoning as he sprinted the last two hundred yards.

Tossing the phone onto a lounge chair, Mike dove into the pool as he spied people moving towards the lanai area. He could only make out shapes as he swam towards the house end of the pool.

A flip turn and he continued back to the far end away from the bodies he could sense above the water.

He emerged dripping and breathing heavily.

"Here he is! Working out in the pool!" Graeme exclaimed.

Graeme, Gretchen, and Sergei were standing at the sliding glass entrance to the patio and watching the gang leader.

Mike blinked water and tried to breathe normally. "What's wrong?" he asked Sergei right away. A good offense being the best defense. "Did one of those idiots fuck up again?"

The trio moved towards the thief- in-law, with Gretchen snatching up a towel as she came over.

Sergei stopped to look at Davidson.

The thief could read the confusion on the capo's face.

But the three gang members were all now looking at the capo- putting him on the defensive. He had to explain himself.

"Sorry, Mike- Demetry called. He said there was a problem back home and I was supposed to make sure everyone was accounted for."

"Problem?" Michael asked, catching the towel as Gretchen threw it. "What kind of problem?"

Sergei watched as the man dried off and kept the towel around his head. More confusion over Michael's nakedness was plain for him to see.

"Sergei! What kind of problem?" Michael asked sharply.

The lieutenant backed off. "I'm not sure. Demetry just said to make sure everyone here was okay. Accounted for," he repeated.

Out of the corner of his eye, Michael saw Rick and Ira emerge from the house. Levinson looked perfectly normal.

"We are fine man," he told the Russian. "If there is something that is affecting our jobs, I need to know about it!" he said, hammering at the man, not letting him get a foot set.

Mike started out of the pool, still wearing the towel on his head, ignoring everything else. "Let me call Demetry and..."

"No, no, no...that's okay Mike," Sergei backed tracked. "Demetry said he was going to be busy with... something," he finished lamely.

The rest of the gang breathed for the first time in a bit.

Davidson spent a full minute berating the capo...

"Jesus Christ, we have cell phones...!"

"Not supposed to have contact...!"

"Dangerous and stupid...!"

The Bratva man left the patio in a hurry.

A huge sigh of relief went through them as Graeme walked the man back to his SUV.

"Fuck, that was close!" Rick marveled.

Michael noted the dark stain on the cloth as he finished drying his hair. "Ira could you go collect my shit?" To the rest of them, he went on, "It worked."

"Yeah, but it looks like 'Little Mike' got a bit scared!" Gretchen flashed at him.

Michael walked into the house wrapping the towel around him with as much dignity as he could salvage.

Chapter Twenty

"No! No! No! No!"

Michael could not be any more emphatic than that. Not without more yelling and screaming.

He faced Sydney across the living room in the villa. How had she gotten here exactly? Davidson recalled that a bit too well.

Charlotte Laurent sashayed around the couch, wearing a bikini and an evil grin on her face. That was the same couch that Gretchen had recently occupied, and had had the nerve to say as she got up from it, "You know Mike, that might not be such a bad idea." She walked from the room without a backward glance at his negative tirade.

"Gretchen thinks it will be okay," the now-dark-haired, brown eyed woman told him, standing with her arms crossed under her breasts. Her breasts which were round and full and peaked with pink nipples...

Dammit!

This was supposed to be their downtime! The time when they played cards and ate junk food before the job. Now? In no way did his plan call for Sydney to participate.

It was Thursday, the 28th of March 2013, at the villa. Two full days before the eight -- and only the fucking eight of them-- were due to fly to London to pay their last respects to the utility tunnel under Hatton Garden and Greville Streets. That visit should clear the alarm system out of the way the next day and allow them to rob the place blind.

But the gang floated the idea of using Sydney as the tester in London versus one of them. And he rebelled. Loudly.

Oh, all of the gang loved Sydney Devereaux very quickly after they started interacting with her.

***

On the Friday, six days earlier, Michael and Gretchen called up the water taxi to come get them to check in on their guest.

A courtesy text to Sydney told her they were on their way. It was 12:45 in the afternoon, not a particularly busy time, and it had taken that long to ensure the stooges were nowhere around.

Gretchen had her makeup and ID kits with her. Ostensibly, she was there to perfect the quick passport and IDs they'd done up from before.

In reality, she was there to prevent Sydney from killing Mike. Davidson checked his phone on the boat. "She says, 'K'." He showed Gretchen the phone so she could read the one letter response. Like he was proving that the woman was allowing them to visit.

Gretchen watched him closely. He knew it'd been a LONG time since she'd seen him this nervous.

Suite 307, Building E- he pointed her towards the lush plant-lined path from the dock to the suites.

The pair knocked on the door and a terrycloth robe wearing, and obviously drunk, Sydney Marie Devereaux opened it.

As Michael entered the room he noticed quite a few things: Syd had been busy with the room charges. The remains of several meals seemed to be scattered around the room. Two empty Champaign bottles, lobster shells, and fresh flowers littered the table and the TV stand. Some new clothes adorned the back of the couch and the two opposite chairs. The mini bar looked to have been wiped out. Tiny liquor bottles dotted available flat surfaces.

How much had she fucking charged? He turned towards Sydney who screamed at him, "You broke my heart, you bastard!" And then she slapped him before storming off into the bedroom.

Gretchen grinned, white teeth gleaming out of her thin face, at him as she sat her cases down. "I like her already." She went into the bedroom after Syd.

Michael sighed and started cleaning up the living room. *Was she having lobster and champagne delivered every hour?* he wondered. He cringed at the mini bar macadamia nuts. The twenty-two dollar package was opened and it looked to have six nuts eaten.

Twenty minutes later, his teammate came out of the bedroom.

"How is she?"

"Drunk."

Jesus! Sydney was a sorority girl. How much liquor would it take to get her drunk? "Did you get her corporate card?" he asked, trying to sound innocent.

"She loves you so much, Mikey."

That hurt anew. "Yeah, well... not anymore," he said, sounding miserable. His friend was silent to that.

An hour later, after vomiting and showering, a reasonably sober and calm Sydney emerged.

Gretchen's suggestion of, "Let's go back to the villa," was practical and casual. No doubt she knew Syd needed people around her to make her feel better.

But, of course, Michael hated the idea. "She is supposed to be incognito."

"Who's gonna cognito her on the water taxi?" Gretchen asked.

The sigh from Michael was long suffering and signaled defeat.

Despite all his misgivings, he had fun over the next few days. The risk of Sergei dropping by was fairly small and he could at least keep an eye on her here. And Sydney was buoyed by being around the gang. Meeting Rick and Graeme, and giving a welcome hug to Ira, seemed to bring her back to life.

Having another woman around sparked some fun for Gretchen as well. She gave Syd one of her smaller bikinis and the two took a swim before the blonde woman got her dye job.

"I will put a bullet in your brain," Michael told Rick as the two men watched the woman splash around the pool and the blond young man drooled. Gretchen was pretty, but Sydney was curvy and toned and...

"How much money do you have, shammer?" Graeme asked, coming to stand next to the pair watching the show. "I've seen your willie, it's not all that," the Irishman asked eyes twinkling.

And how she fit right in! Burgers on the grill that night and Ira taught her how to pick locks. She fleeced the lot of them at gin rummy and Gretchen taught her how to make fake passports.

Rick followed her around like a house boy, fletching drinks and laughing at her jokes.

The whole time she flared whenever Michael suggested toning down the fun.

The last straw was when Graeme suggested getting her "checked out on the guns," calling across the pool to her. She stuck her tongue out at him as she scooted out to the garage, following the man.

Davidson had had enough. It was already too much when she double- crossed him and took his bedroom in the villa. It was enough when he was relegated to the couch. It was enough when he tried to reason with her. He wanted peace, he wanted quiet, he wanted things as normal as possible. In truth he wanted Sydney, but he settled for a fight in the living room in the villa.

***

Separated by the couch physically, and the cold hard truth emotionally, he took a different tact once his yelling, "No!" seemed not to work.

"Sydney, stop this. You are a doctor, not a thief." Michael started again in a very soft tone.

Maybe it was the change of tone, but she stopped smiling and got sad. An inner struggle showed on her face when she finally admitted. "I'm scared Michael. Those men took me and there was nothing I could do about it. I don't feel safe."

"I know that... but let me extract the revenge. Let me take care of this. Your best bet is to lay low and let me finish what I have to do and you can go back to your old life."

The silence built as she struggled. "I want to believe that but... Can, I Michael? I'm not sure about anything. I'm not safe. Not alone. Can I go back and just resume my life? I need some protection."

The sad, quiet, hurt tone in her voice ran up his nerves and filleted his emotions. *His fault. This was all his fault.*

He moved around the couch slowly, like he was approaching a fawn. "It'll be okay. It's okay. I promise to keep you safe." He cautiously wrapped his arms around her. She resisted, and then slowly hugged him back.

Every fiber screamed to kiss her, but he just held her carefully. The bruised ribs being the smallest reason to hold her gently, he knew.

They broke apart without words. The smiles between the two were small and tentative, but he would take any thaw in their relationship.

And later that evening, over more gin rummy and Graeme's famous Irish stew, Sydney worked Michael's 'it's okay' line into a ninja invitation to accompany the gang to London.

Defeated again, Davidson just incorporated her into the plan. The world's greatest thief worked his way around contingencies.

The 29th was nothing but planning and review for the thieves. For

Sydney. it was a fascinating peek into the world of high end stealing.

It helped that she had been to the city several times and was familiar with the tube, and the airports, and the Hatton Garden District. "I've gone shopping on that street!"

"Well, now you are going to rob the place, luv!" Graeme told her.

Basic logistics was still okay for the gang. The five, plus the three stooges, would fly in on Gold Jets, landing at 7 pm. All of the papers were ready for the trip. At 1 am they went into the tunnel with the gear and goodies. A little over an hour should see it done. Syd would follow on a commercial flight arriving at 8 pm. Since the Russians were occupied they would not be staking out the airport.

"Syd makes the test the next day while we fly back to the desert," Ira finished up.

Not bad, Michael thought. Plan B would be installed as well while they were in there. *Always a plan B.*

"Tell me again what I have to do?" Sydney asked as the bloom came off the

rose.

"It's easy," Gretchen jumped in. She pointed to the detailed schematic on the villa table. "This phone box is down the block and in the alley near the safety deposit building. It's relatively hidden from the street. You pick the lock and hook up the monitoring gear right here."

She showed Sydney the phone line test points. Ira demonstrated the probe clips.

"Once it is installed, all you have to do is break a window on the back of one of the diamond shops."

"Wig and makeup, please," Michael reminded her.

"The monitoring gear will record the values. We just need you to note the time it takes the cops to get to the place and how long it takes them," Ira finished.

"Oh, and tell us which shop they go to." he added as Sydney nodded.

"And I do this at 9:30 the next morning, right?"

"April fools!" Rick said.

Michael got serious. "Syd, make sure you look for this guy." He held out the picture Gretchen had taken of the Flying Squad investigator they had tried to set up.

He wasn't too happy about that whole deal. The Yard's investigators had cleared both the agent and the boss very quickly. A small item in the paper had informed them of the fact. Michael figured the guy would be pissed and looking for any of them at any time. He said nothing to Sydney about that other than to look for him. In truth, she was more anonymous than any of them. It made sense, but it felt wrong.

Wrong as it might feel, the gang was tight and this was what they did.

The flight into London was uneventful. The capos watched Michael and his team like vultures, but there was nothing wrong they could detect. Everything was going exactly like it had gone before. Sergei might suspect, but... *Fuck 'em*, Davidson thought. They can suspect all they want. Now was not the time he knew for them to take out the loose thread that was the gang of thieves.

The white van was still in its storage place and dusty. The light mist was griming up the sides, but London had been, and would be, very dry for the English spring. That was very helpful to the gang. No one liked going into a flooded tunnel.

Michael got a buzz on his phone and checked it. Syd texting- she was in the Rosewood Hotel. "Super nice hotel." No problems getting out of Dubai then. Good.

It was becoming routine for the crew. The Russians rode the tube while the gang drove the van. Hard hats, vests, cones, and checklists. Anton and Viktor took up positions with the signs while Sergei dealt with the metro police. Not Robert this time.

A 12-inch wide ventilation duct ran from the van down through the manhole cover that allowed the workers entry into the tunnel. The ventilation was 'required' this time, as Mike briefed the cop topside before they'd gone underground. What were really required were the twenty-five small packages that were dropped into the tunnel, and down the vent duct while the briefing was going on.

Ira led the rest of them down the metal ladder into the darkness. The lights showed that nothing had changed except the foot of water was gone and a wide trickle of a stream stood in its place. Levinson had his gear, and the rest had lights and toolboxes, but those were fake. The bottoms held the plan B packages and equipment. The other portion of plan B was in the yellow vent tube.

The gang set to work. Ira walked to his access point and set up the gear while Rick and the rest grabbed the small packages from the vent line.

The small 18 by 1 by 6 inch packages expanded enormously when the tight plastic wrapping was removed. The compressed cellulose fiber pieces- ten to a package- now were 18 by 12 by 6. The other four scurried about, wedging the material in between the pipes. The alarm line got packed all along its length. The weather, and the huge amount of trash in the tunnel, would help if plan A did not work.

"Pick up the bags!" The boss warned as they finished.

No need to worry. An hour and twenty-seven minutes in the tunnel was all it took.

"Wrap it up!" Michael called to keep the Russians happy.

"Not too bad officer," he told the cop, who'd swung back to check on them, as the rest stored tools and vests. "We may have to go back one more time in a few days," he told the man who shrugged. He didn't care one way or the other.

The crew held strictly to the plan.

Russians by tube to Paddington, and then Heathrow Express to Heathrow Civil Terminal. The five would follow once the van was returned to its spot.

That gave them just enough time for one stop at the Rosewood. Michael held his breath when Sydney opened the door. He knew her fondness for ordering room service.

She'd at least had the grace to look chagrined when he and Gretchen had checked her out of the Anantara.

Michael was sorely tempted to stay when Ira handed Sydney the monitor unit and the leads. He lingered and said, "Make sure you don't run after breaking the window, just walk." Sydney nodded accepting the tip. "Also make sure the leads are clipped tight..." More words just to hang around a bit longer. A weak smile from Sydney told him she was grateful. That made him grateful until the sigh came from Graeme. The thieves' left after everyone wished her luck.

***

Turned out, to Sydney's surprise, she was a natural. The simple padlock on the phone box took twenty seconds for her to pop. The cover door opened wide and she clipped on the leads, just like Ira had shown her. The box matched the detail in the drawing very closely. Easy. *Not like biopsy on a tumor*, she thought. A flick of the switch to turn the unit on and she closed the cover part.

"Step one accomplished-easy as pie," she texted at 8:35 am on the morning of April first.

Sydney continued down Greville Street, away from the safety deposit company and the phone box where she'd just been.

She went into the Oasis to get a cup of coffee and sat next to a nice young man about her age who did not acknowledge her and whom she did not recognize at all. Although she should have, as the squad man was back on the case. He had no reason to recognize her though.

At 9:20, like clockwork, she went outside and picked a small shop on Greville Street as her target.

The back area was hidden from the street, but the security camera would clearly show a woman chucking a broken brick at the back window of the shop.

Sydney hustled out to the front, across the street, and down a ways.

She needed to hustle. About forty- five seconds after she was in position a car pulled up outside her target with the two toned 'wa wa' European siren waling.

Wow! She was impressed. Two more cars sped to the scene.

She did not wait around. After calmly walking back to the phone area she snatched the gear from the box and closed the cover. With the monitor in her bag, and the bag over shoulder, she threw the wig, glasses, and frumpy coat into a Dumpster on Hatton Garden's alleyway. The cops put it down to crazy woman vandalism.

***

His phone chirped at 1:00 pm local time, just as they'd rehearsed.

The five of them were back in the villa, with the Russians back at Deira, chilling out.

"Michael, it went perfectly," she said, her voice breathless and rushed. He knew that feeling.

"Easy, kid. Talk to Ira." He handed off the phone to Levinson who took Sydney through the monitor readings. Three times.

"You're sure? Ninety seconds? And the shop where you broke the glass?" Uh oh.

Graeme took Michael's arm, interrupting his intent watching while Ira talked to Sydney.

"Shammer-" he showed his friend his tablet.

Michael read the proffered news story. *Shit!* His stomach sank. Mind working furiously, he took the phone back and locked eyes with Ira. "Plan B?"

"Yeah, no. It didn't work. B is the only way," he confirmed.

"I'll do it on the fourth," Michael told them all as he put the phone back to his face.

"Syd? Lay low until I get there in two days, okay?"

He clicked off and looked over at his friends. "It's starting."

Chapter Twenty-one

Phone calls, phone calls, phone calls. Even with all hell breaking loose, the thief had to deal with shit. His lawyers, his mother, even Nicky in London. He had to arrange things with people. The gang did that while watching the news, trying to get information. Michael even called Sergei to tell him the change in plans.

"Don't worry, my next call is to Demetry to inform him," Michael told the capo, absolving him of responsibility. Sergei was grateful as the boss was 'busy' right now.

The burner phone was hot to touch- living up to its name as Mike pushed buttons for the Brooklyn area code.

"Da!"

"Mr. Roybokov, it's Michael, Sir."

"Yes, Michael. I am very busy. What do you want?" The boss sounded irritable on the phone.

"I understand that, Sir, but I can't seem to get a hold of Feydor and I need to go over some logistics with him about the proceeds."

"Feydor is dead, boy." Roybokov said quietly and with ice in his voice. "He betrayed me."

Michael feigned ignorance. "I didn't know that, Sir. I never liked the guy anyway, so..." he plowed ahead establishing what he needed to get done.

A grunt sounded from Demetry. That could be taken a lot of ways.

"Sir, we have a slight change of plans, in that I am going to London in a day to deal with the alarm, but I need to know how you want me to get the package to you. I can't ship to the pawn shop now, obviously."

That was both items dropped on the man. Michael waited him out.

"Da. Send them to the tea house," the Bratva head decided.

How should I respond? If I was playing this straight no way would I agree to that. Davidson decided on a mild protest after a pause to think it through.

"Sir, that doesn't make a lot of sense. Geological samples coming to a teahouse? A warehouse or office would be much better."

"Michael."

The quiet tone again sent shivers down his spine. This was Demetry's killing voice.

"Yes, Sir. Look for them about three to four weeks after the job. At the teahouse," he confirmed.

"Da."

Mike knew that Sergei was going to be following up his call with one of his own. He would do nothing, but tell Roybokov that the jobs were on track and the gang was proceeding normally, with slight modifications. Good.

The next call was fun of a different sort. "Detective O'Rourke? How are you today? This is Michael Davidson."

"Is it? Who the hell *are you*?" And that was clearly implying that Davidson was anything but the man he'd presented himself to be. "Where is Sydney Devereaux? Where are you? What the hell is going on?"

Davidson let the cop get out some of his frustrations. "Listen, Detective." Michael sketched out a highly edited version of what was going on.

"Are you admitting to being a part of the Russian Mafia?"

"Brotherhood, Detective. They call it 'the Brotherhood'. And I'm not a part of it, just the thief-in-law."

James O'Rourke let that part slide.

"Demetry Roybokov is responsible for the four floaters you just pulled out of the east river. Talk to the FBI."

"Where is Ms. Devereaux?" The cop repeated in a more normal voice.

Michael sketched out Mary's killing and Sydney's kidnapping without adding in minor details like what he was doing and why.

"Sydney is not involved with this. She is just a victim. Demetry killed those guys after I busted her out."

"How in the hell did you do that?"

"I'm a thief, Detective. No one steals from me."

"Davidson, I have to report you to Interpol, you know?"

"I realize that, man. The Flying Squad can't catch me."

But they could. He knew that and took precautions. The full costume took him hours to put on at the villa. The bald cap was the sweatiest thing he'd worn in a while. The glasses and the mod clothes allowed him to walk right by Vladimir, one of the Russian muscle at the Dubai airport, without a second look by the man. Sergei was probably under strict orders: "Track them at all times." Roybokov need to know where they all were in order to kill them.

He knew the disguise was good when Sydney gasped as she opened the door to the Rosewood Hotel room, where she was staying.

"Syd, it's me."

"Michael?" She grabbed an arm. "What is going on?"

"Let's sit."

The Rosewood was an old-style hotel in London. Smaller rooms, but very tastefully decorated. The suite had a small couch with a coffee table and desk. The bedroom was off the small door in the corner of the room. The heavy curtains blocked out the puffy white clouds and actual sunshine from outside. Spring had finally come to the British capitol.

Davidson sat on the couch next to her and showed Sydney the news story from the Post: "Four bodies pulled from the river!"

She read the iPad in horror and guilt and fascination with a frozen look on her face.

"Syd, honey? You okay?" He asked, after a while. Just like the first time, that 'honey' just kind of slipped out.

"What does this mean?" she asked the air in general.

"It means that Demetry has punished the people responsible for losing you. Detective O'Rourke says 'hi', by the way. He's going after the two cops who killed Mary." He told her all this, to get her to stop dwelling on the murders. Syd was silent a while, and then got up to look out the window. Michael gave her a moment to adjust. No more tears, he saw. She was done crying over this situation. *Tough woman.*

Michael came up beside her and watched the clouds drift by. "I know you did not want those men to die, Syd," he started.

She shook her head, starting to protest, when he continued, "You may have thought you wanted them dead, but the reality is far different. You are not responsible for their deaths, Sydney."

She seemed grateful for that statement so he went on, "Let me finish my work and let the FBI take care of Demetry. Then you can go home."

She absorbed that and seemed to agree. The woman went back and sat on the couch. "I was beginning to enjoy my time as an international jewel thief. Fancy hotels, first class flights, excitement." She risked a smile at him.

He sat and grinned right back at her. "Yeah, my gang would be happy to have you on board."

"Those people really do love you, don't they?" she asked, watching him while she spoke.

"I guess so. We've been together for so long now we are like a family."

"They are. They *are* your family," she agreed.

Michael found himself sitting next to her regaling her with tales from his jobs. How he met Graeme. Fortezza. The Harry Winston job. KLM.

"I've read about those!"

He nodded. "We found Rick in '08, kind of hanging around the neighborhood, and..."

"That young man thinks the world of you, Michael."

Davidson nodded and was silent until he said, "I'm probably not the role model he needed."

"Michael..." she started, and then stopped as a confused look bloomed on her face.

"Its messed up, huh? You want to say, 'No, Mike- You are a fine role model for that boy.' But..."

She did not have any response to that. because he knew that was exactly what she was thinking. That he was a fine role model, and he was a thief.

He was trustworthy, but he was a thief. He didn't lie, but he was a thief.

It had to be hard for her to wrap her head around the contradiction. *This happens all the time*, he thought to himself, while he let her come around mentally.

It seemed to work. A slow smile grew on her face and she relaxed.

"Why did you get involved with me in the first place?" she asked.

"Have you seen yourself naked?" That thought came out out loud slipping through his mental guard, and her defenses, which made both of them laugh.

"I couldn't help it, Syd. I can't stop thinking about you and I'm miserable when you aren't around. Course, I've been miserable when you yell at me lately."

"I was mad at first, and then scared, and then miserable, too."

He held his breath and looked at her. Michael Davidson said the only three words he could think of. Just three little words that embodied the trust and love he felt for her.

She smiled and tentatively reached a hand to his face. They kissed, and it turned passionate as she clutched at him.

"Are you sure? Syd, I'm s..."

"Shut the fuck up. And stop saying that word."

Davidson started undressing.

She ran a hand down his flat chest and stomach as the shirt came off, the abs standing out and the V muscles in his groin rippling as he moved.

"What the hell have you been doing?"

He laughed and picked her up to take her to the bedroom. She only weighed little over a billet box.

His last clear thought for a long while was: *She still might kill me at the end of this. Well, that's okay.*

***

Wednesday, the 4th of April, was a hot, windy mess in Dubai. Graeme and the rest of the team chaffed at the villa and tried to keep the stooges from going over to London.

Sergei complained, "We are going over in two days anyway."

"The squad is on to us. If they see us hanging about the place..." Graeme left the rest unsaid.

Sergei growled and left. He was plenty pissed Michael had given them the slip, but could not openly vent, lest the gang know they were being watched. Which they did anyway.

"I should be the one doing this," Ira complained. "I'm the alarm expert."

"Sydney and Mike can clip the fucking gear onto the lines just fine, shammer."

"It was more fun when Sydney was here," Rick chipped in.

"Jesus, you need to get laid!"

Gretchen had nothing to add, thank God.

***

Meanwhile in London, the other two members of the group slept in late, ate room service, and made love. The perfect, sunny weather held true as they prepared for the work.

It was the most relaxed Michael had ever been to start a job. It was more like a date than an op.

The evening crowds on Greville and Hatton Gardens Street were taking advantage of the weather to swarm around and shop. After the full work day, and the pre-Easter rush, the pubs and restaurants filled up quickly. The smartly- dressed couple was obviously fresh from work, as briefcase and messenger bag occupied a third chair of their table at the pub, which just happened to sit diagonally across the street from the Hatton Gardens Safety Deposit Box Company.

The bald dude looked like Professor Xavier from X-Men and the woman like a brown-haired Reese Witherspoon.

Two leisurely drinks and some bar snacks allowed the crowds to thin and no one took notice as they walked the blocks to the back of the alleyway. The junction box still stood next to the shop buildings, away from the eyes of shoppers.

As he worked the padlock he could tell Syd resisted the urge to give advice. It took him forty-five seconds to unlock the device.

"What?" he asked to her secretive expression. She stayed silent.

The cover flipped open and the leads clipped on just as easily. The door closed back with a bang.

"Okay, let's do this."

The pair moved back to the front of the street and Sydney reached into her briefcase and activated the remote.

She stared at the street, waiting for the explosion.

Nothing.

"It didn't work," she complained out the side of her mouth.

"Hang on a moment. Give it time."

Michael was concentrating on the manhole cover at the intersection of Greville and Hatton Garden. The round metal lid was less than thirty yards from the entrance to their target.

A puff of black smoke seemed to burp up from the manhole.

Thirty seconds later, a larger belch of smoke went up as the heavy cover lifted off its seat before settling back down.

They noticed that all along the street now covers were bouncing up and issuing Indian smoke signals into the darkened sky.

"Here we go!" Mike's eyes were alight with fascination.

The pair watched as traffic was affected now on both streets. First one, then another cover was permanently blown off its foundation to make the cars swerve around the smoke and a small shot of flames.

"Why is it doing that?" Syd asked.

"Heat, smoke, and gas from the fire," Michael said. "It's going to get going now. So should we." They made their way back to the junction box, unnoticed as the crowds started watching the fire.

The 'it' he mentioned was the fire and he was right. The tunnel system acted as a sideways chimney as the gas and flames had exit points. This caused air to rush into the void from other ends of the tunnel system.

The fire roared to full life as fresh air fed the flames. Within minutes the fire achieved flashover as temps hit 1800 degrees Fahrenheit.

Everything in the utility tunnel burned. Trash, insulation, newly placed wood fiber material, pipes. Everything. Most importantly for the thieves, the alarm lines for the whole system along the diamond district melted into a slag pile.

Ira's equipment was also burned into lumps of electronic waste.

Crowds watched as the firemen poured water down the tunnels trying to extinguish the flames.

Hundreds of people were on their cell phones taking pictures, so Mike being on the phone with Ira in Dubai was perfectly normal.

He read off the monitor values to Levinson.

"You sure, Mike?"

"Line one is set high. Line two is ground. Three is open, and four is blinking. How did you know?"

"Wrap it up, Mikey! We are golden! Or should I say, diamond certified." Ira crowed.

The couple detached the gear and closed the box and picked their way carefully down the street. The Rosewood was only a few short blocks.

Turned out to be one of the worst fires in London in a long time. The late BBC news program detailed the damage to the utilities tunnel.

"The Diamond District shopping centers will be closed on Thursday. Officials are hopeful to reopen on Friday, which coincidentally is the date of the last diamond site for the venerable De Beers Company in London..." The BBC late news program gave the particulars on the consortium's move.

Davidson clicked off the TV in the room. "Jesus, sometimes we are too smart for our own good."

"What's wrong? It's not a coincidence that site thing is Friday-right?"

"No, it is not," he told her. "We set the fire to defeat the alarm system, but if the safety deposit company cannot open then the whole thing is moot."

"Pretend for a second I'm a doctor not an international jewel thief, and only vaguely aware of what a site holding is and why it's important."

"International jewel thief?"

That got the look from her, so he went into detail about the way De Beers operated. The whole story of the convergence of diamond distribution and moving to Africa along with Easter weekend and the deposit company came out.

Sydney was incredulous.

"Yeah, it's kind of messed up." Like so many things he thought. "So Hatton Gardens has to open up in order for the job to work."

A series of tense emails and phone calls crisscrossed the world all day on Thursday. Demetry, Sergei, Graeme, Trevor, Lloyds, and even Nicholas Roybokov were all informed or updated as required.

The early news at 5:00 pm confirmed the competence of the British working class, and the can-do attitude that won the Empire.

"The district will be open Friday with little impact to shoppers. Other businesses along the streets will be open as well."

"Thank you, Nigel, that is excellent news," the female presenter said.

Sweetness you have no idea, Mike agreed in his head, clicking off the program.

The follow-up texts to his contacts all said one word: *Go*.

Chapter Twenty-Two

The white panel van, marked with a Hastings Elevator Works sign on the side, pulled into the rear loading area of 28 Hatton Garden Lane at 5:35 pm on Friday, the 6th of April 2013. The security camera recorded the van disgorging four workers in coveralls and sweatshirts. The tall man wore a "Michigan" shirt and seemed to be in charge.

Three other workers entered the picture from the street side on foot and they wore hard hats, vests, and normal work clothes.

After a brief discussion, the Michigan man entered the building while checking his clipboard. He searched the first and second floors of the back area of the building looking for the renovation supervisor on day shift. He had trouble locating anyone, let alone the supervisor. Finally, he spied a thin, black worker sweeping up the remains of some sheet rock in the second floor hallway.

"Mr. Pattinson?" Michael Davidson asked the kid who was clearly not in charge of anything.

"No, mate, he's gone."

"Oh. What about David, uh Ludgate. Yeah, Ludgate?" he asked, checking his clipboard.

"The swing shift guy?" The sheet rock worker said. "He's not coming in- It's Good Friday, yeah?"

Davidson suspected the man was Muslim, which would be why he was willing to work today, but it did not matter to him. "Believe me, I know," he acknowledged. "We got the order to work this. I had to come in from The States..."

"Oh yeah?" the man said, interested.

"Yeah, but we got two to three days of work. We got to align the tracks and grind..."

The sheet rock guy had heard enough. "Have at it as far as we are concerned. I'm finished." The guy threw one comment over his shoulder as he placed the broom in the corner and started down the stairwell. "I think you'll have the place to yourself the whole weekend."

Thanks, kid! Davidson thought as he followed down to direct his people. A clipped motion to Rick, and the others got the ball rolling. The van disgorged the metal tube tripod and the tools the gang would use.

The capos and the gang shuttled the gear towards the building and the door which was propped open. The hallway was deserted and dusty as the men hauled the lifter to the dark maw that was the elevator shaft. The car itself was all the way at the third floor and the flimsy tape did nothing to keep the thieves out as they staged what they needed.

Papers, cups, dirt, and trash revealed themselves as Rick shone his flashlight down the hole. The renovations workers had obviously been using the shaft as a convenient trash disposal spot while they worked.

"Going in," was the word on the radio that Michael relayed to the remote stations. An answering click from Ira at his spot at their favorite telephone junction box a few blocks away. Michael supposed they were going to have to provide British telephone with a new lock for the box, theirs being picked so many times.

Sydney's response came from a mile away, across from the nearest metro police station. Davidson wanted her far away from the stooges and the action as he could get. Rick and Anton were slowly descending into the hole attached to the standoff bar on the tripod lifter. The motorized winch was capable of several hundred pounds, so it was a simple drop.

"Send it down," came Rick's voice after clearing and picking his spot.

Graeme, Sergei, and Viktor manhandled the drill next to the shaft and hooked it up.

The industrial drill was from the DeMater Company and was the UK's finest drill. The XBS1 was both a beauty and a beast. 24,000 rpm, with a twelve-inch diameter core width, the water cooled and lubricated drill could bore through a full twenty-four inches of granite. Or, sixty-five centimeters of hardened concrete. A vault wall that could withstand a missile blast stood no chance against the carbide-tipped bits. The heavy motor and base unit brushed up against the wall on its trip down.

"Easy!"

This was Rick's baby, as he was doing the drilling tonight. He was the one who'd gone to school and knew all about the thing. When you spent $8,000 and another $2,800 on accessories, the company treated you to a full-day class and demo checkout, not just a cheesy video.

The string of lights, water tank, extra blades, and a shop vac all followed the drill. Water cooler jug after jug went down and back after filling the tank.

Davidson was topside, pacing, and freaking as the forty-six minutes it took Rick to align and setup the drill dragged by.

"What's the hold up?" He couldn't help but ask after he could take no more.

"Just a minute. it's not like adjusting your jock," Sanderson shot back.

Graeme and Michael exchanged looks. Fuckin' kid.

Another few anxious minutes and the quiet, "Ready here," call drifted up.

"Hold!"

A click on the radio and he spoke briskly, "Test run, thirty-second trial, green set ready."

Ira and Syd just clicked back acknowledgements. The Russians were under the impression that Trevor was the second remote spotter.

Rick powered up the drill, the noise abysmally loud to those in the hole and in the hallway.

Outside, Davidson thought it wasn't as bad as he feared in his nightmares. The screech and whine was tolerable, and given that they could shut the outside doors to quiet it down even further, he was pleased.

"Go, Rick." The call was followed by flashes on the string of lights. The sound turned higher pitched and the drill chattered as the guide bit dug into the wall. The water spray splattered off and then the teeth bit deep, grinding through the concrete. The drain unit ran clear, and then chalky, thick and grey as the drill did its job. Anton hopped to with the shop vac to stay ahead of the debris.

Michael eyed the phone timer and kept the radio up to his ear for any alarm. He was outside the building and the cameras would catch him anxiously pacing around the courtyard.

More lights flashing let Rick know to cut off the drill.

"Status?" The key call to Ira.

Levinson was monitoring the hastily installed phone line, backup alarm system the diamond shops had rigged up. They and the safety deposit company were relying on an old system which piggy backed on the phone signal to alert the police of any problems.

Trouble was the system was terrible. The second the drill started up the pressure and vibration alarms went off for the vault.

Unfortunately for the Safety Deposit Box Company, their depositors, the insurance people, and everyone who was not a gang of thieves, the alarm was bundled up along a similar line as every other alarm that was plaguing the district since the fire. The alarm went to police headquarters and was logged as a 'low level residual problem from the fire. No response necessary.'

"Green." Ira's voice was calm, professional.

"Movement?" That call was to Sydney. He risked it, with no Russians near.

"Nothing," she said. Excited and breathless, Michael knew she was high as a kite and bored to tears all at the same time. He knew that feeling well. Welcome to high-end burglary.

"Roger, two-hour run commencing."

Starting back he gave Graeme the signal and the drill roared back to screeching life.

The excitement quickly became boring drudgery. Two hours later, Rick came back up splattered and wearing a cocky grin. Gretchen, Sergei, and Graeme scrambled down to clean up.

"All most through! Another two and a half inches," he proclaimed to the

boss.

"How's the machine?" Mike asked. "I need to swap out the drill bit," he said. "We are chewing through them pretty fast."

"We only have eight of those mother fuckers. Stretch it." Michael instructed. The gang had more holes to drill. And a problem. When the drill changed pitch again a short while after Rick's short break, it signified the first actual hole into the vault, and Graeme took a moment while it was being repositioned to grab Mike for a consultation.

"Time, shammer. Too much time!"

"I can't make it go any faster, man." Davidson was out of options here. The plan called for six hours of drilling and three hours of work in the vault. It was taking them four hours for this first hole. True, the next three would not be full cores, just half moons as the drill ground out overlapping circles and would take much less time. But it took *some* time, and they were swiftly running out.

What did it mean?

The two men discussed options while Rick worked away. The solution was scary.

"Really? You'd do that Mike?" Graeme asked his best friend in the world.

"No choice, man. Give me a better option?" He shot back.

But the Irishman had none. And neither did Gretchen, or Ira, or Rick for that matter.

The rough opening in the vault was going to be about 36 by 12, if the drill worked properly. The weight loss plan, Michael had insisted on, would pay dividends here- If...

If the twelve-hour break in the robbery didn't totally fuck them.

"Are you shitting me?" Sergei was livid upon hearing the news. "We leave this thing wide open for twelve hours while we SLEEP?"

It was almost 7 am on Easter Saturday. A rosy dawn was breaking over the buildings of the city. More people were beginning to appear on the street. It might be a holiday weekend, but things would be open. Shops, bars, the tube. The police.

But not the safety deposit box company, thank God. And none of the renovation workers would be coming in, Michael knew. It was a risk, but a reasonably small one.

"Only thing we can do now," he told the Russian. "We need to get some sleep. Time to go," he finished stoutly.

But Sergei was still adjusting to the change. "What about..."

"We can't do this during the day," Michael told him emphatically.

It has got to look deserted. The paper permits I got specify night work only. Anything else will draw eyes. Especially the Squad."

Silence stretched. *What if...* the capo seemed to be sending that telepathically.

"Then we are fucked," Michael said out loud. He cut off anything else. "We are beat. Go back to the Thistle. Get some rest. 6 pm tonight, right back here."

He was taking an awful risk. The vault was gaping open like a... well, he knew what it was gaping like.

"Green. Come help with cleanup." He radioed Ira.

The click from Sydney signifying she was headed back to the Rosewood was gratifying. He would text her once he got to the Thistle Hotel himself.

The exhausted, dirty crew assembled by the van just out of sight of the cameras.

"We have the slop in the schedule. Gretchen, change the flight, please. We are still mailing everything, just tomorrow morning." The men and woman nodded. "Back in at 6 tonight. Let's haul up that drill," he told them and they wearily returned to work to finish up.

It took them another two hours to stow everything and lock it away in the storage facility. The tube ride back to the hotel was hot and crowded, despite the holiday, and the mood was down. Tough thing to maybe give up the shot at the huge payday.

Mike texted Syd during a small meal break. She was good to go. "Same position as yesterday- 6 pm tonight." the text was brief.

The "K" answer back was heartening.

The alarm that blared him awake was unwelcome. What was

welcome was the absence of news in the early evening. No BBC talking head screaming about a 'daring robbery thwarted.'

"Stop the lights!" Graeme exclaimed as the van pulled up to an apparently undisturbed vault area and building that evening.

"The fuck does that mean," Viktor asked, in his thick way.

"It means, 'Really!?!'" Michael told him. "Graeme is surprised my plan worked."

He could tell Sergei wanted to say something very badly, but wisely held up.

The cameras recorded the thieves going back into the building on Saturday night. This time the Michigan sweatshirt was replaced by a Montana one.

Gretchen was the first gang member to set foot in the vault. The lithe, thin woman snaked into Rick's handiwork and finished kicking in the wood paneling that was clad onto the interior of the vault wall. Lights, tools, and bags followed her in.

By the time Mike squirmed through and joined Graeme, Rick, and Viktor alongside the woman, the men had completed cutting away the protective steel cover on the bank of deposit boxes along the back wall next to their hole.

Rick was taking a saw's all- diamond blade cutter to the thin gap between the door to the box and the hinges. The long thin blade of the tool slipped in easily. A solid twelve minutes of cutting finished off the hinges and the door was pried open.

The box, and its contents, were rifled through under the headlamps of the men. Stock certificates, wills, legal papers, a bit of cash and a three carat ring.

Cash and ring went into a bag and the box was piled up on the opposite wall. All this was done while Michael, Graeme, and Gretchen huddled.

"Too long again, shammer."

Michael agreed. The process was killing them. Even with four of them cutting through hinges it would take too long.

"We ain't gettin' a third bite at this apple," Gretchen told the air.

Contingencies. This was what they planned for.

"Try the slide hammers."

Rick did as directed, and picked up a specialized tool. About twenty inches long, the slide hammer had a heavy iron sleeve that travelled along a bar. On the butt end a flared portion kept the sleeve in place. The other end contained a retracted pair of steel brackets.

Folded into the hollow 1/2 inch cylinder, the brackets were activated by a trigger button on the shaft. When depressed the brackets snapped out and formed a "T" on the end of the shaft.

Viktor took up a 1/2 horse, cordless drill with a 1/2 inch tungsten bit attached. Five minutes of grunting produced a hole near the key lock. The balding Russian reamed out the hole and stepped back.

Rick inserted the slide hammer bracket end into the hole. Depressing the button produced a muffled click as the brackets slid home. Rick then forcefully hurled the heavy sleeve towards the butt end of the hammer. The flange stopped the sleeve, transferring the force and mass and energy to the brackets and the door of the box with crashing results.

The door to the storage box flew opened and Rick grinned at the assembled people in the lamplight.

Better.

The second box was inventoried. A ruby signet ring along with a gold coin and a small bar of gold.

"Okay- here it is. Viktor, Graeme, Rick and I will drill holes. Gretchen pops 'em. Sergei, Ira, and Anton will spell anyone who gets tired." Michael paused.

"We got sixteen target boxes. They should be in the one meter cube slots, but not necessarily. Systematically, and as soon as we find number sixteen we are gone. Got it? Go."

As with yesterday, the work quickly sucked the big one. The eighth box opened was a jackpot. The beige container that came out had latches, but no other markings. Since no one had ever seen one no one was prepared.

"Jesus!" Graeme breathed when he flipped open the lid. The compartmented velvet lined 18 by 12 inch box glittered in the headlamp glow.

Diamonds. White gems sparkling in the light, throwing off colors. 250 to 300 half or three quarter carat stones were bunched in a large compartment on one end. The stones graded up in size until Mike plucked a five carat stunner from the small spot on the other end. The pea sized gem was worth a $150,000 easy. The whole box- was worth $15 to $16 million.

Viktor watched the stone flash and breathed out. "Holy God!"

"Yep. Fifteen more. Let's move." Michael got them focused back.

The beige box went into the special loot bags and the work continued.

Bags filled with scrap and diamonds and other interesting things as the fever gripped them. Four boxes down twelve to go and the gang was working systematically top to bottom on the larger bank of cubes.

Gretchen squirmed her way out of the vault as the air got stale and Michael soon followed. The replacements did not complain as they went in this time. Graeme joined his mates topside and he dearly wanted a cigarette while he sucked in lungs full of air.

"Four more hours," he told Michael between breaths.

"Then the real work starts," Gretchen added, mirthlessly.

"Yep."

The police car pulled into the loading area while the three took their ease. Michael wasn't alone in nearly jumping out of his skin. The car stopped near the van.

Gretchen and Graeme seemed frozen between running and trying to get loved ones and friends out of danger.

"Stay here," Michael commanded, his voice steady. He pulled a weary face, which in truth was not much of a stretch. As he got to the van he grabbed the clipboard off the front seat and went to the side of the car.

"What can I do for Scotland Yard's finest?" he asked, purposely misidentifying the metro cops.

The bored cop just took him in and the other two with the van and the building. "Yank?" he said.

"Yes, Sir. We're over here working on the elevator." He offered the paperwork he'd obtained to detail the renovation work. All fake, of course. If the officer did an even cursory check they were fucked.

But the London Works Agency stamp looked very, very good.

"Holiday weekend?"

"Yeah- can't be helped. We gotta align the tracks and grind down the..."

The man waived at him to stop. "How long then?"

"Another five hours," Michael told the man with every bit of sincerity and truth he could muster.

"All right, then. Crack on." And with that the policeman drove off.

Fucking A!

Davidson was very proud his knees did not buckle on the walk back to his stunned colleagues. "No problem."

Irish curses, mixed with Portuguese and Spanish epithets, filled the air.

"Don't say anything to the others. Let's go."

Full bags of scrap money and byproduct loot started coming out of the vault. Gretchen took charge topside with Anton watching her closely. In reality, Anton watched Gretchen's ass much more than he did what money went where.

Davidson and the rest were surprised at how much US currency was stored in the boxes. At least a million came out in those duffel bags.

Gretchen took the pre-labeled, prepackaged boxes and hundreds of envelopes and started shoving money and rings and even gold into them. Anton was kept hopping counting out bills in stacks containing $8800 to $9500. Just under the $10,000 limit for shipping overseas. The Cayman Islands would accept numerous deposits by mail. You just needed to have slips. The outside envelopes had been written out by the gang over the preceding weeks and days. There was nothing the authorities could do. Dropped in different mailboxes and slots, the envelopes would route through different handling facilities and all arrive in the Bahamas without incident.

In addition, special boxes were stuffed for the gang's numerous contacts around the world. Lawyers, shipping agents, insurance adjustors, and others all would get retirement boosters. Rings, watches, coins, necklaces, all got put into mailing envelopes. Declared value- $50.00 US. Costume jewelry. Trevor got himself a nice bonus, as did their California passport lady.

Two hours after the cop left, a full bag of special beige boxes came up to the van. Gretchen packed this bag very carefully topside. The huge crate, marked 'Sutton Geology (Samples)' was already layered on top with round cylinders of rock. Packages of fake crystals would conceal the diamonds. Gretchen took special care to show Anton the felt bags the stones were going into, as she poured them from the De Beers box into the bag in which they would ride to America. Anton nodded along as she worked. And watched her ass.

Rick came up to help with Sergei for the packing. Davidson knew Demetry would insist on having his men watch the proceedings to make sure the gang stayed straight. No problem with that.

Back in the vault, Michael popped open a half meter cube on the top row of the side wall and... There it was.

The beige box they'd come to know so well sat nestled in its temporary home. The last site holder's box. That they knew of anyway.

"Got it."

Graeme, and Viktor threw down their drills in disgust. "Thank God!" The men were exhausted.

Davidson popped open the last three deposit boxes with holes in them and shifted the goodies. "Tools, lights, and loot, guys. Move."

As the last man in the vault, Michael took a second to survey the place by his headlamp. Empty safety deposit boxes lined the front wall to the vault, blocking the door. He could just imagine the look on the Ms Buxton's face when she opened the door at 8:30 am Monday morning. *Missile blast my ass!*

Spent cordless drill battery packs littered the floor. *There must be fifty of them*, he thought. Fingerprints? Not from his people. The latex gloves he was wearing were still on under his leather work gloves. You can't be too careful.

A last look for anything stray left behind and he saw nothing. Good.

"Mikey!"

He wormed his way out of the hole with Graeme and Ira hauling on his arms. Grabbing the canvas cloth that had lined the hole he rode the rope harness up the elevator shaft. While the others broke down the tripod, he replaced the security tape on the open elevator shaft. *Can't have someone getting hurt on the job.*

Especially can't have anyone get shot by the Russians on Demetry's orders.

Davidson approached the van. The original plan had called for three of his people to drop the bounty off for shipping. Now?

"Sergei, I want you and Viktor to go with Gretchen and Ricky to drop everything off."

The hard man eyed Michael for some kind of trick. It was just what he was going to demand and now the man was telling him to do it. Was this some kind of reverse psychology?

"Dammit, listen to me. These diamonds aren't money. They are rocks. Valueless. I can't eat them. I can't trade them and I can't spend them. They are nothing to me! I...we, don't get paid, until the stones are fenced and the wholesalers pay Demetry and us together. That's how this works." He finished up leaning tiredly against the van.

Sergei searched for the trick, looked for the hidden agenda, and could not find it. Something of the speech must have penetrated because he said, "Yes," and shot Viktor a look that sent the two men into the van.

"Stick to the plan," Davidson told everyone else. "Plane leaves at 2:00 pm. That's over six hours from now."

The cameras recorded the van pulling away and the other group of men walking from the scene on foot to the tube stop. The CCTV coverage was limited in the area and the men were soon lost to electronic eyes.

Michael sending Sergei and Viktor with them actually helped Gretchen and Rick. They got the shit detail from this job. The van made drops all over the royal mail route and package drop boxes throughout the greater London area. Rick split the driving as a handful of envelopes and mailers went in each distinctive black and red post box.

Cargo shipping offices were open, even on Easter Sunday. Rick and the woman did not think the Cargill agent, a man of Indian descent, gave a shit one way or another.

The two largest crates were being man handled into position by Viktor and Sergei while Gretchen filled out endless forms. Sergei watched like a hawk as the box was palletized and plastic wrapped.

"Three weeks at the earliest, but it looks like May 1st. Depends on the ship, and the port, and the weather," the man told her.

"Just the cheapest option- time doesn't matter," she replied back. Bored.

'Just a job to do, no reason to note anything here,' her whole demeanor told the man.

Rick and Viktor got to deal with the Pakistani man over the van. The other two were at the storage unit stowing the vests and hard hats and little things they'd used for the robbery.

"Twelve thousand pounds for the van and all those tools, plus the drill," Rick lamented to the capo.

The thief and the Russian cracked up, chuckling at the absurdity while they split up the money. Rick hauled his backpack with him on the tube back to the hotel. The one Gretchen had so carefully packed.

Chapter Twenty-Three

The world woke up Monday to the news of a stunning robbery in London. Breathless headlines screamed out the take- "$150 million in gems!"

Not even close.

The perpetrators of that robbery woke in Dubai; tired, sore, and jetlagged. It was a subdued group of six, with Sydney included, who ate lunch at the villa. The mood was very confused.

Quiet, with bursts of talking and emotions. Despite the euphoria at getting the job done, there was only tempered retelling of funny instances during the robbery. Fear about the upcoming job tamped down everyone's emotions. After they'd landed, the phone call to Demetry reporting success was quick and perfunctory, and got no real response anyway. Now the gang had too much on its collective mind to really celebrate.

"Shouldn't we be celebrating?" the confused newcomer asked Michael in a quiet moment.

Davidson shrugged. "Too many things can still go wrong. We do have another job..."

So they all waited, laying low in the villa while quietly stewing. These few days were devoted to final prep and clean up. Ninety-nine percent of the work was done, just the last minute adjustments that were a standard part of any job still remained to be accomplished.

Even though Graeme was in charge of Dubai, it was Michael who kept harping on things:

"Make sure you've checked the...."

"Did you remember to..." "Have you..."

"Enough!" Graeme snapped at him at Tuesday's dinner. "One thing I won't miss is your anal nagging." He took leave from the table and went out to the pool area.

Michael let him go. The looks from the rest of the team told him that they were done with his attention to detail routine, too.

He apologized to the Irishman that night. "Sorry, Graeme. I'm just worried."

"Easy, shammer. We are ready for whatever."

Yeah, maybe, he thought. *Hope, is more like it.*

Wednesday, the 9th of April, dawned hot and windy. Mike intended to write the Dubai tourism commission about the weather. Holy shit, it was going to be hot. Over ninety degrees Fahrenheit today.

The gang packed carefully for their trip into the desert. The two jet-black Hummers were loaded to the top with gear, and clothes, and guns. The huge SUVs had an enormous cargo capacity, a high wheel base, and lots of power. It was like the vehicles were designed for military operations. Which, of course, they were and it also made them perfect for the gang's needs.

Several changes of clothes for each person were included: Standard oil field garb, with the full Xi Services uniforms, and then some regular clothes for afterwards, hopefully. Everyone needed some duplicate sets. The Desert Camp Resort had laundry facilities so the men could wash up sweaty polo shirts and cammo pants, but that attracted attention.

Graeme and Michael went over to the Deira buildings to check on the Russians. Michael found them ready and did not bother to sweep the rooms for telltale left behind items. He knew they would fuck that thing up, but that was fine with him. By noon on the 9th, Vulcan Geology was checked into Desert Camp for their third set of corporate team-building exercises and meetings.

Graeme Donniger got everyone situated and reviewed the plan. The 10th being the last full rehearsal day, with the 11th being the staging period.

The 12th would be go time, if everything cooperated.

Mike spent the session with the full team, daydreaming, not really listening. He was thinking about his future. He should be on a boat on the 12th- free to restart his life. Well, truth be told, he had more work to do, and then some loose ends to tie up, but he would be free.

And one of those loose ends was bouncing around the last bungalow in Desert Camp. Sydney Devereaux had arrived in Desert Camp late that night after the gang and the Russians. Darkness hid her from the watchers that Michael figured were out there, keeping tabs on the gang.

Michael felt the risk was low, as the now short-haired brunette was better at being Charlotte Laurent, as she grew accustomed to evading notice.

She was bouncing off the walls of the nicely air-conditioned room when he managed to sneak over very late that evening.

"I'm not going to spend this robbery watching a police station or waiting for you in my hotel room like London!"

"Are you asking to be allowed to break the law and participate in a robbery?" he asked, a little facetiously, but trying to calm her down.

"Don't fucking give me that bullshit!"

Okay, Ms. Devereaux was a little wired. It took him thirty minutes to talk

her down, and another ninety to go through scenarios and what he wanted her to do. "Just be dressed, ready, and drive to the rendezvous point okay?"

She agreed, with a grudging amount of belief. Clearly, she did not like to be kept in the dark.

Michael convinced her to go to bed with him in short order after the robbery was detailed. Both knew it might very well be the last night they'd spend together. "We can't see each other tomorrow. We have to be careful," he told her. *Can't mess up like the house in Brooklyn*, he thought.

Those kinds of thoughts lent a desperate urgency to their lovemaking.

As he slipped back to his bungalow very early the next morning, Michael had some regrets. Chief among them was his potential last words to Sydney: Not "I love you," but "Stick to the plan!"

Last thing I may say to her. Jesus! I am a piece of work sometimes.

"Why should today be any different than any other day we have been here?" Mike asked Rick when he complained about the hot, windy day on Friday morning.

The whole group was up before dawn to prepare for the job. Packing, loading, and breakfast all took time and they were on a schedule.

Graeme had been busy. Early morning phone calls and texts confirmed a UAE C5 Galaxy transport plane was fueled and being loaded at the airport in Zurich. Their contact had texted a picture of the plain grey billet boxes being loaded aboard the cargo plane. Security was off the charts at the load out with police, military, and private guards all watching each other. The Irishman gleefully showed the Russians. "Three hours, friends. Game Time!" Sutton Geo was already checked

out of Desert Camp that morning courtesy of Rosario Dawson. The company would hold its last training event and leave that afternoon.

"Is madam aware that the airport and several roads in the area were scheduled to be closed around noon?" The check out agent tried to be helpful.

Oh yes, all of Vulcan was aware of the closures and had planned for them she assured the staff.

Ira and Rick returned from ferrying the first group of haulers out to the remote airstrip site around 9:30 am.

Two Hummer SUVs remained along with one Mercedes to take the last eleven people out to the airbase. Michael hoped Sydney was getting to sleep in today. He missed her already.

An exchange of looks with Graeme to say, *your show*, and then...

"Move out," Graeme spoke confidently into the radio.

The convoy rolled into the desert. Ira was driving with Mike in the backseat and Graeme in the third row. Both of those men were changing clothes from their -resort wear look' for the Desert Camp people into their robbery gear.

Michael felt weighed down by the clothes and the equipment as he dressed. Sunglasses and keffiyeh were on top with the polo shirt over the cammo pants. The tactical vest held sidearm, radio, and ammo as he adjusted the straps. A fanny pack held his IDs, money, and passports, which went to the rear for safekeeping. The heavy combat boots pinned his feet to the floorboards as they drove on. Two new items adorned his dress this time. Gold oak leaf collar devices identifying him as a Major in the XI Services hierarchy and a small plastic armband ID holder covered with a flap on his shirt sleeve. His holder contained a copy of a mercenary ID badge. The gang had them, but the Russians did not. Graeme's plan hinged on the Russians not noticing that the thieves all had on subtly different uniforms from their rehearsal times.

Plus, some other 'minor' differences that Mike fervently hoped they missed as well. Lots of variables with this job.

In the scramble to get out to the site, Mike knew that Sergei and the other four Russians were trying to keep track of things, but it was difficult when you are dressing and bouncing on the road.

The convoy reached the airstrip and came on through the gate and up to the series of low buildings adjacent to the runway.

The all-too-recently re-cleared runway on the rehearsal day had held a shock to Graeme's plan: The wind had mounded up foot-high miniature sand dunes in ripples across the cracked tarmac. The gang didn't have shovels. Rick saved the day when he went into an outbuilding and pulled out a scraper blade that attached to the front of a Hummer. "Thought we might need this," he said, moving to attach it.

Fuckin' kid is an excellent thief, Michael marveled.

Graeme was out of the Hummer and screaming at the group of Russians standing around the three vehicles that had brought them out first. "What the fuck are you doing? You are supposed to be dressed and have these trucks decaled and painted! Move!" He badgered them when they did not hop-to quickly enough.

The man rounded on Anton and Viktor while the others ran around like chickens. "You are supposed to be in charge."

Forty-five minutes of activity saw things sorted. The first four Hummer SUVs were now decked out with the yellow decals covering the top, sides, and hoods. Red accent paint and special Arabic lettering designated these trucks as command vehicles in the Dubai Fire Department.

Michael gawked at the expense. A $95,000 SUV as a city vehicle. He knew that kind of thing would never pass in The States, but here? The fucking police department drove Lamborghinis for Christ's sake!

During his inspection round, Graeme was happy to see the Russians wearing the uniforms that they'd worked so hard to obtain. Gretchen went around handing out the guns and ammo clips. "Safeties on!" she kept yelling. She personally outfitted everyone just as she'd done in every rehearsal, shoving clips into vests. Practice makes perfect. Ira and his charges unpacked and setup their goodies near the berm. The lee side blocked the wind which was the newest obstacle to the plan. They needed the wind to die down a bit.

The pattern that had held for weeks now was for the winds to blow hard in the early morning, and then drop around noon. A fresh blow sometimes accompanied the sunsets, but usually it was calm. Right now, that morning wind was howling at 22 knots, sand stinging as it impacted everyone and everything. *Can't do anything now*, Michael thought as Graeme fretted. *Under 20 was the key.*

Sergei, Graeme, and Michael held a war council near the cars.

"The plane took off an hour and twenty minutes ago. Another two hours until it reaches us," Graeme told Sergei.

The man nodded. "Let's feed them, give them plenty of water, and then a piss break. We should be fully ready by noon." The Irish gave out his statements like a general taking his troops into battle. Which he was.

The activity level increased again as Rick and Joey handed out MRE packs to the assembled crowd.

It was a quiet group that ate beef stroganoff from the brown self heating packets. Michael kept shoveling food into his mouth and watching Graeme. *This had better work or we are all dead.* The Irishman had nothing to say to that look he knew all too well.

Chapter Twenty-Four

At noon straight up Donniger ordered Ira, "Get 'em up!"

Levinson and his charges were ready. Vladimir and Constantino joined him on the other side of the berm where the other two drones sat on the black cases. The two new craft were identical in most ways to Ira's camera unit: four blades and the 10,000-foot ceiling. The gyro stabilized machines would be steady in the now 15 knot winds. Where Ira's drone held a camera slung underneath, the two new units had black tubes mounted on the top about six inches long. The XQC-700 Hyashi drones were specialized per the client's unique needs and the gang had some big requests. Extended lift and range being the biggest two.

The RF signal booster was the first thing laid out that morning by the gang. Situated four miles east of them, the device had a large battery pack and would be vital to the success of this mission. The booster would allow them to talk to the drones for a very wide range while they went about their business.

The men went through the preflight checks carefully, but quickly. With a lurch, the drones came off their perches with a dizzying visual as the ground fell away on Ira's monitor. The scene on the ground showed the SUV's and the men alongside the runway as the craft gained altitude. The buildings and the men dwindled as the max height was reached. Desert Camp was just visible on the western edge of view as was the E44 road bordering the east. Miles of empty dominated the rest of the scene in any direction.

"All clear, team lead." Ira's voice came over the radio. "Units in position." The three drones were steady at 9,700 feet along a line three miles east and south of the runway. Breaths exhaled all around. Step one completed. The most basic step. Now, all they needed was a plane.

***

At 12:27 pm the huge four engine plane completed its long, sweeping left hand turn over Oman to line up on final approach to Dubai International Airport. The routine flight was just boring enough as the pilot leveled out at 9,985 feet and slowed the bird to 210 knots of airspeed, positioned just south of the city of Kalba on the Omani peninsula. The "J" shaped route the plane took to get here was necessitated by two things: The wars raging in Iraq and Syria and the wind. That wind being right off the nose on this 280 degree course. The heavy transport plane needed all the lift the wind could give it.

The pilot, in constant contact with the tower, eased speed down to 180 knots and put flaps at full. The plane was responsive as she was able to haul whole battle tanks to the front, so this minor load was nothing. He casually told the copilot that he always felt the giant cargo plane was crawling along, barely able to maintain its place in the air at this speed.

***

"My God that plane is coming fast!" Ira exclaimed to his helpers. The drones were ready. Vlad and the hulking Constantino had their craft spread about 500 feet on either side of Ira's camera drone. The three formed a gangly triangle with the nose of the plane pointed straight at Ira's baby. Hence his concern.

"Get ready!" Ira's voice cracked over the radio. The other twenty-one men and one woman winced at the sound and fretted checking positions and gear.

They'd only practiced this twice before and never with any degree of realism. Can a drone bring down a military plane?

The gang was about to find out. "Now!" The Russians hit the buttons on their controllers like they were killing aliens in a video game. The RF booster amplified the signal and passed it to the craft who accepted the order with electronic indifference. The top mounted launchers came into play as the two kilos of specialized graphite micro beads were chucked into the air in a burst.

***

The pilot never saw the drones, only the rapidly spreading and disbursing cloud coming at him. The micro beads were swept up by the wind and the forces of aerodynamics as the plane came on.

"What the hell!" the pilot exclaimed.

The micro beads impacted the nose of the plane with little damage or noise. The hardened window glass saw no damage. The slip stream of air caused the beads to run down the fuselage and get sucked up into the two inboard engines in large quantities. The graphite itself was encapsulated in a very thin shell coating which burst on contact with the rapidly spinning turbine blades. The heat of the blades caused the powdered material to fuse to the turbine blades forming a new thin layer. The micro tolerances that made up the complex machine that was a modern jet engine just could not stand that buildup of material.

The graphite clung to the blades which caused the outer blade to stop spinning. In micro seconds the outcome was written: The blade exploded and the engine ate itself. As shrapnel destroyed the engine, it quit in a puff of smoke and a burst of fire. Both inboard engines died within a second of each other.

In the cockpit, all hell was breaking loose, and neither pilot nor copilot saw the drones dive to safety. Alarms and digitalized warning voices blared while the men desperately tried to keep the plane in the air.

"Mayday!" The pilot got out as the two outboard engines flared and died.

The Galaxy transformed from a graceful bird, to a rock within seconds. A crash at this point was inevitable, it was just a question of where.

**

"Come on! See it!" Graeme breathed, his heart racing.

The next critical moment had arrived. The abandoned airstrip was three miles to the east- on the left at 090 degrees. If the pilot saw it... If... The old and cracked runway was their only chance. If...

"Come on!" Ira yelled as the plane staggered and dropped in the air.

The left hand turn took the plane twenty-two agonizing seconds and cost 6,000 feet of altitude.

"Jesus, is he going to make the runway?" Michael sounded the newest concern as the assembled group watched the plane wobble in the air.

"He is," Graeme yelled back, voicing more confidence in the pilots than might be realistic. "Move! Be ready. It might be short!" he advised on the radio to his troops.

The Irish willed the plane to make it. The possibility that the giant plane could crash right on top of them, killing everyone, suddenly dried his mouth. Graeme dry swallowed painfully. Everyone paused in the scramble to adjust position, to watch in abject fascination and outright admiration as the pilots lowered the landing gear and kissed the tires down on the sandy tarmac.

The smoke from the engines was not that bad as the tires screeched and the plane rushed at them. The runway was deliberately short for the C5 and the berm that Rick had spent so much time setting was placed for a reason. The gang wanted the plane stopped at a certain point with the nose up and the cargo section lowered to the ground. Graeme had planned for that but knew there could be other outcomes.

Things continued to change and go out of whack from the basic plan as the plane ran over the small mounds of sand and pits on the runway. The ten Russians on the opposite side of the runway, with Anton in charge, were running down to get lined up when the plane smoked over a pot hole hidden in the softer sand. The tires all blew and the plane rock violently from nose to tail.

The gear collapsed in a shower of sparks and noise. The nose began to yaw to the left towards Michael, Graeme, and the rest of the group as they tried to get their people to be reasonably close to the bird when it finally stopped.

"Fuck! Short! Short!" yelled Graeme, waving to Anton and Sergei.

Contingencies, that's what they did. The plane ground to a hissing, grinding halt, nose into the sand berm, miraculously with wings attached and not on fire.

"Twenty-five minutes!" Graeme bellowed into the radio as the trucks scrambled to reach the plane.

The first two SUVs rolled up on the plane and disgorged twelve men, with Rick included, as the fire suppression foam gushed out of four engines. *The pilots taking actions*, Graeme thought.

Rick approached the fuselage and, per the plan, readied to pump four rounds of Mk 4 tear gas canisters into the cargo area. Graeme felt that would take the sting out of any troops guarding the gold.

Of course, that's not what happened.

Just before he could fire, the plane gave off a loud, sharp 'ping' from the cooling and damaged engines. That sound scared the fuck out of the Russian muscle. One of whom promptly opened up with his HP5 submachine gun.

Within seconds it seemed all twenty Russians were hosing down the plane in a hail of bullets. The rounds

punched through the aluminum skin and went ricocheting around inside the plane.

***

Fuck me, Graeme thought. He exchanged looks with the rest of the thieves and his team merely gripped their guns tighter and waited for the gangsters to run out of ammunition. Which they did in thirty seconds.

"Cease fire! Reload," Graeme shouted into the sudden silence.

Clips dropped as the men reached up to vests and slammed home new ones.

Mike grabbed Sergei by the shoulder and eyed his gun as he growled, "Stop!" to keep the man from shooting again.

The capo wrenched away and glared at Davidson. But he stopped firing and started listening.

Donniger stepped forward and ordered, "Door team, go! Slide teams ready! Load team one ready! Trucks into position! twenty-three minutes left!"

Men scrambled as adrenaline pumped and their training took over.

The cargo door access panel on the C5 was fourteen feet off the ground, and even with no landing gear it was still too high to reach without a ladder. Two men hauled and braced while a third climbed and dropped the cover plate. He threw the handle down not quite knowing what would happen.

The cargo door slid down on residual hydraulic pressure.

Other men stood, waiting for a response from the mercenaries inside, while still others handled the box slide ramps near the plane. Gretchen and Rick drove two of the painted SUVs into position.

The men waiting on the mercs did not have to bother. The fusillade from Demetry's men had wrecked the plane and... Graeme could not count the bodies.

Red was splattered everywhere as he peered into the hold. *At least ten.* His gorge rose. Pilots, too, he supposed asking Michael what he thought in a low voice while the Russians setup in the hold. That the victims were hired killers themselves was a small fig leaf at this point. Killers killing killers.

Fucking Sergei, came back from his partner... That mental image got shoved down into a compartment and would be dealt with later. Graeme hoped they could deal anyway.

"Twenty-one minutes! Go!"

Graeme along with Michael took a good look at the billet boxes while the load team began hauling them out. Neat holes were punched into the thin metal skin by the rounds but the heavy internal metal had prevented the bullets from blowing large exit holes in the boxes. The main damage was to the web strapping which was shredded on both stacked piles of gold.

Within seconds it seemed billet boxes were sliding down the ramps and out of the plane to be transferred to the trucks.

Grunt work. It always seemed to come down to grunt work with them, Graeme had that stray thought.

It took seven minutes to unload and reload sixty boxes into the back section of one of the SUVs. The specialized palleted shipping crates ready to receive the merchandise.

Not even close to their best time and Graeme looked worried.

"Second load team in!" Graeme rotated the haulers to keep them fresh.

"Sergei- A hundred and twenty boxes per car. Too much time to swap them." The Irishman adjusted on the fly.

The Hummers could take the weight. If the men could unload it. Four minutes for the next sixty as the haulers found the rhythm. The second truck moved into position and more haulers grabbed boxes.

"Graeme look at the bodies," Rick gasped as he went by him inside the hold.

"Stick to the plan!" God damn that sounded hollow. "Two trucks, two teams!" Graeme bellowed, as they put maximum effort into the unload.

Every swinging dick in the place was hauling, including Gretchen as the frenzy to steal gold overtook them.

Seven more boxes to go when Ira came on the radio. "Graeme, helo taking off!"

Twenty-six minutes into the crash and the Dubai authorities were taking action. The last billets slid home as Graeme ordered Ira to hustle over to them. The men exited the cargo hold to find Sergei and the Russian's spread out waiting for them.

Here we go, Michael thought as he watched the men grip guns tightly, leveled at him and his friends.

"Just a second everyone. We got about nine minutes before we have company, but I need one last favor," he said in a quiet voice. "I want Sergei to shoot me."

The baffled man stared at Davidson.

"Go ahead. Shoot me please."

An evil grin spread on the man's face as he sighted the submachine gun and ripped off a three round burst at the thief-in-law.

Nothing happened.

Thinking he'd missed, the Russian stepped forward and flipped to full auto. A longer ten second burst produced more nothing. The whole group gaped at Michael. "Yeah. Blanks. You didn't think I was going to give you a chance to kill us did you?"

The gang now leveled their weapons at the muscle boys, as it looked like they wanted to rush in and club them.

"Go ahead! Look at your guns. You all have orange dots on the clips. Blanks! I'll kill every one of you fuckers, if anyone comes for us!"

A small voice from the side said, "I don't have an orange dot."

"Thanks, Vlad," Ira told him, going over to relieve the idiot of his dangerous weapon. "You didn't shoot up the plane like the rest of these morons."

Michael kept his focus on Sergei. The man was seething. Meeting the cold stare with his own hard and emotionless one, Michael stared down Demetry's man.

Looking Sergei in the eye Davidson told him, "I know he told you to kill us, but here's the deal. Those trucks are my 'get out of jail free' card. Take them and go."

"But..."

"I don't give a fuck what you tell him. Tell him we are dead in the sand. You will never see any of us again. Tell him you are his new thief-in-law."

The thief could see the wheels turning in the Russian's head. Time to seal it. "You bring him $700 million in diamonds and gold and he won't give a shit. Your other option is to die right now."

The man went white at the tone in Davidson's voice.

"Mike!" Ira said, "We got to go!"

Sergei gestured and the Russians broke for the trucks. Davidson had one last bit of advice for the men: "Stick to the plan and you will be fine."

The gang broke opposite for the other two unpainted Hummers and fled the scene.

Michael, Ira, and Gretchen were in one truck while Graeme and Rick drove in the other.

The two groups headed out of the airbase in opposite directions: The three stooges and the four SUVs with the gold went west to the port city of Fujairah. The practice runs gave the fleeing Russians an excellent idea of what to do: The cargo shipping offices were next to the Hilton they'd stayed at. All they had to do was seal the billet boxes in the crates, drop them off, and board the freighter. It was due to sail in three hours and Davidson figured they would be out of port by the time the authorities closed off the country. Even an idiot like Anton could do it.

The gang went east, back towards Desert Camp. They did not go into the resort, but continued past for another seven miles, hooking up to the E44 highway, heading south and east towards Oman.

They rotated drivers as everyone changed into fresh Xi Services uniforms. Davidson retained his Major status, but the rest went to grunt mercenary level.

The road was empty as they drove for twenty minutes, seeing and hearing nothing.

A third black Mercedes SUV appeared on the road, parked and waiting on the side of the highway.

Sydney.

She was dressed in desert cammo fatigues and sunglasses. She also had a med kit in her hands as the other two SUVs pulled up.

Ira drove up to her and Mike pushed the button to roll down the window. Grins on everyone's faces told her the story.

"Good, no one hurt then?" she asked.

"I about shat myself when Mike told the idiot to shoot him," Graeme said, coming out of his truck.

A quick game of musical chairs as Mike and Sydney took a car, Graeme and Rick in another, with Ira and Gretchen in the third.

"Let's go."

The convoy headed south and east following the road. There was nothing out here, except a little border town called Al ain. There was not much in Al ain either. Just an oasis for water and a small airport, as the town was situated just on the Omani border. The empty quarter stretched out here. Sand and wind and rocks and pain. That was it.

"Well, what happened?" Sydney demanded.

"Graeme was right," Michael told her. "Turns out we could bring down a C5 Galaxy transport plane using drones and an abandoned airstrip, all the while unloading sixteen thousand pounds of cargo in under twenty-nine minutes." His voice sounded strained, and she could no doubt see he was upset, but was dealing with whatever had happened. Thankfully, she let it slide for now.

Sydney looked in the back of the SUV for the gold boxes to see the loot. There were several back packs in the car, but no containers.

"So where is the gold?"

"Oh, it wasn't on that plane," Davidson said casually. "The Ministry got nervous when we made our weapons purchase and changed things up. There was only scrap metal on the plane we brought down." He paused a second. "The real shipment landed about forty-five minutes ago in Al ain and is being snuck in via a small convoy."

Syd gapped at the switch. She asked what had happened at the airstrip and Michael sketched it out for her.

"And the Russians?"

"They have the fake stuff and are catching a slow boat back to The States."

He paused and spoke into the radio. "Game time, switch to channel 93."

The gang was leveraging some hard won knowledge here. One of the things they knew was what tactical channel the Ministry and the mercenaries were using.

Chaos reigned at the airstrip. At least three helicopter units were in the air as well as numerous official vehicles and military personnel. Fire, police, and security all buzzed around the area. So far they seemed to be concentrating on the airbase and the Desert Camp sites.

Good.

The three trucks drove slowly on the road. Michael had Sydney don a Kevlar helmet with a red cross on the side. "You are medical," he told her. She was very quiet, now.

After what a seemed eternity, but in reality was only a few minutes, the SUVs topped a small rise that allowed them to see down the road a fair ways. The sand dunes mounded up on either side of the ridge forming a saddle. The target convoy was just starting up their side of the rise.

Three clicks on the radio signaled to his team to be ready as the six vehicles, three on each side, converged.

Contact was made cautiously, given the events of the day, and about twenty yards separated the forces when they stopped.

Michael immediately hopped out of his SUV and approached the lead escort Hummer. He could see the truck packed with six men, armed to the teeth.

The Xi mercenary lead officer was in the front passenger seat and Davidson slowly came up to that side. He ripped open the protective flap on his ID badge holder. He didn't proffer the arm or anything, just ripped it to show he was friendly. His HP5 was slung to the rear, in the most unthreatening position an assault rifle could achieve. He barely took in the plain cargo truck with its mercenary driver and the trail Hummer with five more men. *Jesus, that was bad odds.*

The tinted window cranked down and a gun muzzle poked out while he looked at the lead merc.

"I'm Davidson, Intel. Grennock sent me with a sit rep. Are you in charge?"

Brisk, military, and efficient. Michael dropped more knowledge with that statement. Colonel Robert Grennock was Xi Services head of intelligence. He was the Ministry's point man liaison on the gold shipment and most of its operations.

The hard stone sunglasses stare of the Xi Services Lt. Colonel was not encouraging, but he said, "I am. Report!"

Michael took a deep breath and unconsciously stiffened. "Sir, an unknown force has attacked and downed the decoy plane. We suspect a Russian made SAM. The Colonel feared an attack on you. I have medical with me." Michael motioned at Sydney who stood next to the Hummer, white faced. "If you need it."

"No, we've seen nothing."

"Good. Grennock suspects an ambush would be along here..." Davidson reached into his vest and pulled the Google map printout of the lonely stretch of the E44 they'd just driven. He pointed out the area near the turn off to Desert Camp. "The plane was downed here." Again he indicated the spot on the map. The mercenary asked a question about force size and structure.

"I suspect, and Grennock concurs, that it would be about ten to twelve men with small arms."

"IEDs?" The Lt. Colonel asked about Improvised Explosive Devices, which were so bad in Iraq.

"Unknown, but probably not. We think they want the truck intact."

Another critical moment had arrived. So many in the last days!

"Sir, I advise you to retreat to Al ain and await further orders. However, Grennock says to tell you- I and my team are at your disposal. What are your orders, Sir?"

A good con has to be well played but the main element is this: You cannot make someone do something they do not want to do. You have to make them think it was their idea.

And it really was the Xi Service officer's choice. Kind of.

When Graeme and Michael planned this out they were betting on the come, so to speak. They put this man- a hard-charging, military killing machine- on the horns of a dilemma. Retreat- OR - charge ahead and break up that ambush.

It was no choice really.

"Major, can one of your men drive the truck? I want my full team with me." The sunglasses asked Davidson.

"Yes, Sir!"

Michael motioned to, Rick who jumped out of the SUV and ran to the cargo truck. He actually high-fived the merc who ran to the trail Hummer, gleeful.

"You can fire that weapon?" The colonel asked the intel weenie.

"My team is weapons proficient. I made sure of that!" Davidson put a little heat in his voice.

"Stay here, guard the truck. We will be back!"

"Hoorah!"

Vehicles sprang into motion. The trail SUV closed on the lead unit and both navigated around the three gang cars which pulled up near the cargo truck.

The Xi Services trucks roared off north and west towards a battle and destiny.

"Are you fucking kidding me?" Syd asked incredulous.

"Give 'em what they want, what they desperately want, and you will never go wrong," Michael told her with a smile.

"Ira!" Graeme called to the thin thief in the other Hummer.

Ira exited the SUV holding a box and using the last bit of knowledge the gang possessed. He passed the box around the truck and within a minute the tracking unit was beeping softly, buried

an inch below the roadside sand.

"Where to Rick?" Donniger now asked the young man. "About two miles back that way and four miles off road. There is a little track..." He hooked a thumb behind him.

"Got it. We will follow."

The thieves drove off without even looking in the back of the truck.

An hour later Michael was getting ready to close up the cargo truck door when he took a velvet bag from Gretchen's SUV.

"Here, Syd, put this in the van."

"What's this?" she asked, huffing from effort. It was hot scooping sand!

"$200 million in diamonds from London," he told her sweetly astonished face with a grin. "Anton should have watched Gretchen more carefully."

The woman peaked into the bag and freaked just a tiny bit. "Oh my God!"

"Yeah, fuck Demetry. He tried to kidnap you and kill me, not to mention double-crossing us. Nobody steals from me."

Syd carefully placed the bag on the stack of gold billet boxes. The real ones. The thieves had opened one box to make sure this time. The gleam was mesmerizing. One last sweep for trackers and the door was sealed.

The gang kept scooping sand into the trench, the one Rick had dug, just for this purpose. The wind was helping, but it was still hot and dusty work.

"I told you no one could steal and reload six hundred boxes of gold in under thirty minutes," Michael chided the Irishman.

"Yeah, shammer. No one at all!"

"Shovel, you fucking idiots," Gretchen scolded.

Michael figured the Xi mercenary Lieutenant Colonel was just now realizing how badly he was fucked.

The gang finished up and drove to Al ain. Scrubbing and changing clothes yet again. The six of them dumped weapons in the desert, along with any uniforms or clothes. Michael told Rick the locals would strip the Hummers they left abandoned in less than a day.

***

At 4:15 pm a small freighter undocked from the pier at Fujairah. Its cargo was x-rayed again to ensure no contraband or stolen gold, the ship left just a few minutes late. That made no difference to the twenty Russians onboard who were drinking vodka in the galley, trying to get their story straight for Demetry.

At roughly the same time, four Americans, one Irishman, and one Brazilian crossed the border into Oman at Al ain.

Their only luggage was the backpacks they carried. The tall guy was a typical US asshole.

"No, we don't have any drugs, as you can see. No, we don't have any artifacts. Where would we carry them? And what the fuck do we know about gold? Where is the American consulate?"

They drove into the country without a care in the world.

Chapter Twenty-Five

But Michael Davidson was not finished fucking with Demetry Roybokov just yet.

Six days after the robbery in Dubai, three men walked into the offices of the Luxembourg Freeport; valued client and representatives of a valued client, all.

They'd arrived via a series of airplanes, starting in Goa, India and London.

"That is highly unusual," Ms. Stoerman started at Nicholas Roybokov's request.

"Phillipa, confidentially, this is being forced on us by the IRS," he went on smoothly. "I represent my father in this- and this is what we want done."

The formidable woman glared at Helga and Graeme flirting in the back of the office while the adults tried to work.

"I can't seem to get a hold of our contact... your father," she started again.

"I'm still valid as a signatory on the account, yes?" he asked, in the nicest way possible. "If you cannot help us, I would speak to the Director." Still in his politest voice.

Nicely done kid! Sloppy, Demetry, sloppy. Should have taken you off the account a month ago, Davidson thought.

Michael did not doubt Demetry was busy with other things right now. First, he'd had to kill Feydor and his boys. Then, he had to worry about Hattenfeld and Temescal getting arrested four days ago. And just this morning, Nicky told him that Kat was dead.

"Killed by Putin's thugs. A message to my father," the man said sadly.

Michael was very sorry about that, but it also meant that the Bratva head had a lot of plates spinning. Too many to worry about his safety net in Luxembourg.

And Ms. Stoerman plainly wanted to get a hold of Demetry right now. But... These men had all the correct forms. And the son was on the account... and, here was the key point: They were not taking possession of anything. They just wanted the contents of the vault shipped back to The States. Right where it had come from!

"But, Sir, the tax implications are..." she tried one last time.

"Rest assured, madam, we are fully aware of the bite this is going to cause. But you must know how it is to deal with the IRS? They make Al Capone look soft! The deal is -we repatriate and pay this part and they don't seize everything we own."

Nick played it superbly.

Paperwork, paperwork, paperwork, sealed the transaction.

Of course the Freeport can package and ship everything to the US for you. The first of May at the Teahouse for delivery? Strange, but certainly, Sir.

The perfect robbery was completed with the stroke of a pen and some passwords. Nick, Graeme, and Mike walked out of the Freeport offices together quietly debating whether this act counted as a robbery.

"If you have all the passwords and don't keep anything, it's not a robbery," Graeme opined. He had a point.

After a brief goodbye Nicky moved to the back of the terminal line. He was going to try Switzerland for a while. Mike hoped he would be able to avoid the coming storm.

The last two gang members stood and looked at each other for a second.

The friends embraced on the airport sidewalk. It was a beautiful April afternoon.

"Shammer, it was fun!" the Irishman said with his twinkle. He waved and was off.

"Be well!" Michael called to him and got a last wave in return.

No tears, no hysterics, just goodbye. That's it.

The members of the gang had been sloughing off like dead skin for a while now. Davidson was getting good at parting from friends.

Ira and Gretchen started it in Goa. The pair was breaking off for South America after the charter boat dropped them all in India.

After hugs for the others, Gretchen kissed Michael. "Thanks Mikey!"

"I'll get in touch when it goes down," he told Ira. "Take care of each other."

Ira grinned at him and poof! They were gone.

Rick Sanderson took his leave in Paris, two days later. A quick stop at the storage unit and he was good to go.

A steady rain provided the back drop as mentor and protégée hugged. "I never want to read your name in the paper," Michael warned.

"Nah, thieving is too dangerous. I'm going to San Francisco... be a Silicon Valley venture capitalist."

Mike laughed. "Any man with a briefcase..."

"Can steal more than any man with a gun..." Rick finished up the old saying. And he, too, was gone.

As Graeme Donniger walked away at Luxembourg Airport, Mike turned to see Sydney standing there watching him, tears in her eyes. He suspected that she was sad, but happy, from her expression. She asked, "You okay?"

He said, "Yeah, I did right by them. I know they will be okay." Just like they were going to be.

"What's next?" she asked.

***

The sun glinted off the sea outside the window and Mike could see the waves crashing on shore. *I must love that sound because somehow I always end up near the ocean.*

His office was cluttered, which was not like him. Monitors and keyboards, three of each, dominated the desk. Cell phones were lined up, along with paper and notes all over. This was complicated and needed to be right.

He checked texts and messages from several places around the world. It looked like they were ready.

Michael leaned back in his comfy chair. He was cool and comfortably dressed, but as soon as he stepped outside the locals would know him for an outsider. *How did I end up here?*

As he reached for the black burner phone he flashed on the last time he'd used that particular phone. Another time and another place.

Today was June 4th, 2104. His sister's birthday. He'd better call her, too.

Focus!

He could not help but think of the last time he'd held this phone.

Thirteen months ago. May 2nd, 2013. He'd been in Luxembourg and called O'Rourke. That was a great phone call!

***

"Detective, Michael Davidson here. How are you?" He'd asked when he could finally get the cop on the line.

"Exhausted, you son of a bitch!" the man yelled.

"Now, Detective, is that any way to speak to the man who made you famous?"

Michael could hear the rustling in the background and forestalled the work, "O'Rourke, please don't bother with the trace. I'm using VOIP over an internet gang line. By the time you figure out where, I'll be long gone."

The rustling stopped and was replaced by a sigh. Still the cop said nothing. He was a hard man.

"Okay, man. You tell me about yesterday and I will owe you one." Davidson figured the officer was so tired he might bargain. And he knew the man was curious, so...

Another sigh and the cop said, "How in the hell did you manage to sell your house?"

His answering chuckle might have been a bit too smug. "You can do amazing things with powers of attorney and trusts and lawyers," he told the cop.

"Yeah, what the hell is CRAT anyway?"

"It is a Charitable Remainder Annuity Trust," he went on, because he knew the officer would have no idea what he was talking about. "See, basically you can donate a chunk of money to a trust. The chunk can be the proceeds from a house sale, yeah? So the trust then invests the money for a certain period of time and gives a portion to a charity. But here's the thing, the portion can be a small amount and the time period can be for a short time, as little as 3.8 percent for three years."

The cop grunted as that hit home.

"The remainder in the trust, after the time period expires and the proceeds go to charity, go straight to your relatives or heirs." Davidson finished up. "The best part is the money passes on tax free!"

"Holy shit! And who is your beneficiary?" O'Rourke asked bluntly.

"You know Detective the laws in South Dakota shield the trust and the heir from having to come forward. The United Way likes it like that."

"How did you learn all this?"

"Man, I'm small potatoes. I learned all about CRAT's and GRAT's and estate planning from the best. Sam Walton."

"The Wal-Mart guy?"

Mike was impressed the cop knew who Sam Walton was. "Yep. He passed on billions to his children and grandchildren, tax free." He paused, getting antsy, but he added, "Makes me look like a choir boy."

"Uh huh."

"Quit stalling, tell me!" Mike's request came out desperate sounding.

Davidson heard another sigh and a muttered, "Haven't been to sleep in two days," before O'Rourke told him the story.

"Based on an anonymous tip, members of the Brooklyn homicide division, backed by SWAT and the FBI, raided a Tea House on May 1st, owned by Demetry Roybokov, a known Russian mobster."

The man told it like he was speaking to the press at first, but then he dropped his voice down and confided, "Davidson, I tell you we got to the place about 11:00 am. While we are outside, setting up, we hear a gunshot." The on- scene SWAT, guy- Marlin, says 'Go!' and we bust in."

Davidson was fascinated. "Yeah?"

"It was dicey for five or six minutes, lots of guns swinging around. Mobsters will shoot you in the back, but they rarely stand toe to toe with the SWAT boys."

Michael could agree with that, but remained silent, other than an, "Oh yeah?"

"When we broke in we must have interrupted a meet or a deal, because there were forty-eight guys inside that restaurant. Forty-eight living and one dead guy- a Vladimir Alensky."

He was sorry to hear that. Vlad was stupid, but mostly harmless. Maybe. Davidson was not sure how to feel about that, so he kept silent.

O'Rourke paused and took what sounded to Mike like a slurp of liquid before continuing. "Damnedest thing I ever saw. It looked for all the world as if half the Russians in there wanted to kill the other half. But in the back we found a bunch of crates. Two of them marked 'Geological samples' and some marked, 'Scrap metal'."

"And what did those crates contain, Detective?" Mike asked, even though he knew damned well what they contained.

"That's the thing, man. They had rocks and scrap metal inside, no drugs. Or anything else," the cop said in a probing tone.

"Imagine that!" Mike said, trying to keep the glee out of his voice and not succeeding.

"So anyway, we start processing the guys, doing the IDing when this DHL van pulls up."

"Holy crap. More deliveries for a Tea House in Brooklyn? Boy, that's strange!"

"Uh- huh. We gonna get to that in a second," the man said, sounding serious and Davidson knew he'd better tone it down. "When we opened the DHL boxes, the ones from this Freeport thing in Luxembourg. Roybokov about had a heart attack. The guy was spluttering and going crazy!"

Believe that! Davidson thought.

"Best part is that ten minutes after the paintings and statues make their appearance, this woman from the IRS strolls into the place."

Mike shuddered. "I think your stolen art people are going to rate a call, O'Rourke."

"I figured as much," the man said back quietly. "I heard some interesting stories from those mooks. You figured prominently, Davidson."

"You aren't going to believe a bunch of Russian Brotherhood members are you? Those guys are thieves and killers. And noted liars," he added.

"It was the signet ring that caught my eye," the man admitted.

"Detective, you are, without a doubt, the smartest cop, I have ever spoken to," Mike told the guy.

"Sergei Tikanov had on a fancy ruby signet ring and a very expensive watch. Not a Rolex, but a Robert W. Smith." He was puzzled on that point.

"Robert W. Smith is England's finest watchmaker, O'Rourke.

You're gonna want to take pictures of all those watches and rings and send them to the Flying Squad," Davidson said quietly.

"Yeah."

And this was the tough part. Now he had to get out of going to jail.

"Look, Detective. I know you guys have arrested the two bad cops for Mary's killing, right?" A grunt from the cop said he was at least listening. "I guarantee you someone in that Tea House, yesterday, killed Feydor Slutskaya and his men. And they did it on Demetry Roybokov's orders." "Not to mention Vlad."

Mike continued, "You have your killings accounted for. Let the FBI get Demetry and Sergei for their mob stuff, while the IRS twists the knife. Sergei and his friends participated in the two robberies. All of the stolen things eventually will make their way back to the rightful owners and everyone is happy."

"Not all the stolen property, Davidson! There is still a hell of a lot of diamonds and gold missing!"

A sigh came from Davidson. "Detective, I will also guarantee that the diamonds and gold from Sergei's robberies will get back to their rightful owners. Eventually."

"I'm supposed to believe that Sergei pulled off these jobs?" The skepticism was plain.

"All the evidence you have supports that," Mike said, sounding like a lawyer.

The silence stretched on the other end.

"Hey, how's Rodriguez?" he asked, to change the subject.

O'Rourke snorted. "She's been lights out. I think the FBI is going to offer her a job over all this."

"That's fantastic!" He was enthused when good things happened to good people. "Well, Detective, it's been fun..." he tried to break off when the cop broke in.

"Wait! The robbery boys wanted me to ask you a question. They need help on a case."

"I'm a retired oil field man, but sure, what's going on?"

"Armored car job- $1.2 million taken off of I-95 just north of Jersey. Supposed to go down to Florida," he related the particulars.

"I don't need the files or any more info," he told the man. "Come on- They know this. You know this! When a wife gets killed, who did it?"

"The husband," O'Rourke immediately returned.

"Odds are seventy percent, right? In any armored car job it's the guard or the dispatcher telling the thieves where and when." Davidson breathed in. "Either this end or that. Florida side, some redneck will buy a $60,000 boat on an eighteen dollar an hour salary. New York side, the guy will buy a Cadillac."

A groused "thanks," came from O'Rourke. Mike suspected the first question was a test to see if he would really cooperate. Well, he would help as much as he could.

"No worries, Detective. You got a pen? Write this down..." He rattled off a website. "That is a dark web chat site." Knowing his audience, Davidson continued. "Ask your tech guys about the dark web. You need help, just post a message for Davidson and I'll get in touch."

"Thanks." The voice was still gruff, but not outright hostile.

"Get some sleep," Mike touched off.

He walked back to the sleazy hotel in Luxembourg City.

"You can go home now," he told Sydney.

***

Back in his trailer, he remembered and ached for Sydney. He had not seen her in so long. More sunlight reflected as the phone rang, disrupting his memories. He had one more big job to go. More than a year after the robberies, it was time to get paid.

Here we go.

A click on the first computer monitor refreshed the screen as the phone buzzed in his ear. The screen showed an aerial desert scene. He was getting used to watching the world like an eagle from drone camera views.

The bleak, empty quarter of the UAE looked the same. A group of eight men stood around three black cars pulled off the side of the road.

Why always black? he wondered.

Six of the men looked incongruous in suits, while the two Ministry sheikhs looked fine in white robes. The sun glared down on the group and Mike had a little sympathy, given his own experience with the Dubai sun. The phone rang for the third time.

"Ya?" The thick South African accent of Geoff Pederson was the same.

"Geoff, my man. How are you?" he asked.

"Piss off- arsehole!" Geoff screamed back.

"Now, now, Geoff! Is that anyway to speak to an old friend? I'm sorry De Beers fired you after our last exchange, but that's exactly why I asked for you this time. I trust you. I know where you stand." Davidson spoke quickly, typing on the other two keyboards.

He could hear the security man grind his teeth.

"Do me a favor and hand the phone to the insurance guy on your right."

Pederson looked around wildly.

"Yeah, we got eyes on you. Just like you have three helos up looking for me. Hand him the phone!" Mike barked.

Geoff did as he was bid.

"Take your phone out and dial this number," Mike ordered the guy.

The insurance man panicked.

"Fucking do it, or we are out of here and you don't see diamond one."

A brief hesitation and the man reached into his jacket pocket and took out his phone. He worked the buttons.

The next phone in line in front of Mike buzzed. He clicked off one and clicked on the other.

"Hand the phone back to Geoff." The suit complied. "Okay, you guys know the drill. Suits and pants and robes off." Mike waited while the men disrobed.

This was actually his second attempt to get paid. Three months ago he'd gotten to this point and one of the lawyers had an RF tracker device to try to hone in on phone calls or his drone signal. Mike immediately hung up and told Ira to get out. Which he did.

He'd retaliated by placing an internet rumor that the gold from the heist was buried on the beach in Dubai City.

Two months later, travel sites were remarking on how much

tourism was down due to the 'crowds and prospectors, pock-marking the beaches'. The Ministry put a full page ad in the Wall Street Journal.

"Call us- Dubai Gold Exchange," was all it said.

Mike glanced at the framed news sheet on his office wall and smiled.

They'd learned from that last exchange. Ira had ten RF boosters scattered around the site while he was hidden in a small bunker with plenty of water and a fan. Mike felt a bit bad about the amount of radio energy zooming around for Ira.

Stuff gives a guy cancer.

When the eight, fat, pale, men (except for Geoff) stood around in socks, Mike spoke up again.

"Geoff, what have you been doing these last years?" When the man said nothing, he went on. "Me? I've been studying international banking transactions. How money gets moved around. I daresay I am an expert on the systems," he bragged. "Point is, you fuck me and I will know."

"Ya!"

"Say it, Geoff," he went on like before.

Geoff complied, remembering. The man surely knew in his gut they were beaten.

"Get the computer from the other insurance man." The South African did as told and placed the laptop on the car hood by the tire well.

"I'm going to give you an account number and the amount- remember, I can see what you are typing."

Ira zoomed in for him as Mike typed a request to his friend on the middle keyboard.

"A little to your left."

A grudging shift from the Afrikaner.

"Good. You have thirty seconds to complete this part from the second I start speaking. Any fuck ups and I'm gone, right?"

"Ya."

"Ready?" Mike rattled off an account number followed by a routing number and then an amount.

"But..."

"29, 28,..."

The former De Beers man bowed his head and typed. As he hit enter the lawyers and insurance men started gesticulating wildly.

Davidson rattled off a second set of numbers and again the security man typed away. This time the sheikhs had to interfere to keep the lawyers from smashing the laptop.

The third set of numbers and the final amount and Mike was finished speaking. At the four second countdown mark, Geoff hit enter the final time.

"Shall we move on to the gold?" Mike asked in a reasonable tone.

"Fuck you." That came out a trifle bitter.

"Oh, wait. We have to shift phones and computers," he directed.

Davidson did know a thing or two about international banking transfers. That, and the software and laws surrounding those transfers.

While the second laptop was booting, he heard and saw a lawyer move up next to one of the sheikhs. "Monte Carlo," was part of the conversation.

He seized on that. "Yeah, Monte Carlo is nice, Geoff. The sun, the beach, the women. I especially love the banking secrecy laws. If you ever have to illegally transfer money or transfer illegal money- not sure of the difference in that- I recommend Monte Carlo."

The helos were racing to converge over one of the booster packs they'd hidden.

"Don't bother. My drone operator is not even in the same country," he told Geoff.

The man was resigned. He spoke to the Sheikh and the men calmed down, as well as the helos. A gesture and Mike started the second set of three groups of numbers. The whole transfer only took twenty-two seconds this time.

The third monitor on his desk beeped as an update hit his third screen. The screen where he watched money flow around the world.

He could watch because he was behind the firewall. On the split screen, two of the accounts went to a red/locked status. Another two soon followed.

Millions lost as those two accounts were now frozen and would be tied up in the court systems for decades. $2 million gone on the electronic wind. Sacrificed...

While $48.95 million in another account flowed on and divided and went merrily on a worldwide odyssey of destinations: The Caymans. Dubrovnik. Rio. And San Francisco. The screen also showed the next $98 million from the

UAE divide and flow. The problem with the monitoring software for international transfers? It was limited to a primary and an alternate for a single transaction.

Oh, you could watch millions of transactions flow from one bank to another. But, if you wanted to track a single account as it went zipping over the wires, you had to attach to the account. *And you could only watch two.* The third and largest amount of the transfers went into an account to be divided up amongst his friends' banks.

Theoretically, you could blanket stop every bit of money flowing from Monaco to the Caymans. But, not without pissing off a bunch of people.

You could also wait and watch the money as it sat in an account, waiting for the banks to do their reconcile on a periodic basis.

In the same way, when you deposited a big check from someone, only a small percentage of the funds were available to use right away.

Authorities used that to watch where the money went on an internal basis while it waited to clear.

But...

If you put up a 'bond amount' you could have instant access to the money.

Davidson had shifted a ton of money in the Caymans to be held as collateral while he got quick access to the money the targets shifted to him as his $150 million finder's fee for returning their stolen items.

The key part was that the authorities were not watching his bond money. And neither he nor his bank was required to tell anyone about that part.

The monitor showed the $30 million split the gang had agreed to as it went out. His hostage money would have to wait four days, but it would soon be back home. Minus a nice fee for the bank, of course.

Geoff Pederson was through being nice. "Okay you miserable prick. Where are the diamonds? Where is the gold?"

"You got a pen?"

Davidson shot off a latitude and longitude point about fifty miles from where the men stood.

A strangled "wait!" did not stop him and Davidson clicked off the phone. Fuck him.

"Wrap it up!" He typed to Ira, sitting in his bunker. Mike knew he would have to wait several hours for the coast to clear before he could make his way back to Gretchen.

"See ya!" Levinson typed back.

That guy could steal a virgin's...

An hour later the front door to the trailer banged open.

"Mike? Hello!"

Mike sauntered out of his office to meet Sydney Devereaux. The hot, humid air from South Padre Island in Texas battled with the doublewide's air conditioner for supremacy. Davidson was not sure which side was winning.

"Hey!"

"Hey, yourself."

"How was the flight?" he asked her.

"Ughh. I hate coach. And commercial," she exclaimed, giving him a quick kiss. "Worst part was, it took me an hour to lose O'Rourke."

Michael grinned and grabbed her.

"Stop!"

"I've missed you."

"Behave," she said slapping his roaming hands.

"How'd it go?"

"Fine. We're rich. Er."

She smiled at him. "Did you speak to Ira?" she asked about the important part.

"Just a bit. He's fine and so is Gretchen. They send their love."

The suitcases were dragged in and they sat on the tiny couch, getting comfy. "Did you tell them about Rick?" she went on.

"You mean, Mr. Palm Jumeirah investments out in California?" He said it with multiple syllables. Like Mary. "Yeah."

She laughed at that. Mike had shown her the web chat site where he'd gotten an announcement stating the firm had reached its goal of $25 million raised for venture funding.

Knock 'em dead kid.

"Any word on Graeme?" she asked, turning serious.

"Nope. None needed- he's fine," Mike assured her.

She was doubtful, but seemed okay with his faith. "Tell me about the construction...?"

The pair went outside. The secluded and heavily treed lot went right to the water's edge with a strip of beach. Very expensive and very private, the area catered to people who wanted to be lost for a while.

"See? It's going great. The stilts raise it above the flood plain..."

Syd made the appropriate noises at the house, but marveled at him, here.

"A confirmed Denver fan in Texas?" She was still teasing him about the Super Bowl shellacking.

But still, he loved her. He was sure of that, now. Had been since England. It wasn't the physical, although that was fine. It wasn't the money or the brains. Those were add-ons for him.

It was the trust. That was what was missing from before.

A year ago in a nice room at the Rosewood Hotel in London, Michael Davidson said the only three words in the world that he knew would make her sleep with him again. Make her love him again. Trust him fully.

He'd finally looked at her that night and said, "Michael Stephen Davis."

His real name.

The End

Thank you so much for taking the time to read **Thief-in-Law**! We enjoyed sharing the adventure with you!

The excitement doesn't have to end here! If you haven't had the chance to join the mailing list yet, now is the perfect time. You'll get the bonus story for **FREE**, all you have to do is tell us where to send it.

If you enjoyed this novel, we hope you'll take a minute to leave a review.

Other Works by Michael Dirubio:

Unity - 2013

System 112 - 2014

T*he Journal of Daniel Alfredson* - 2014

Empire Man - 2015

Quinru, California - * * forthcoming

Thief in Law

This is a work of fiction. Names, characters, places, and incidents are either the product of the author's imagination or are used fictitiously. Any

_____ _____

resemblance to actual events, places, organizations, or persons, living or dead, is entirely coincidental.

www.ingramcontent.com/pod-product-compliance
Lightning Source LLC
Chambersburg PA
CBHW060339260626
47160CB00006B/2144